Elizabeth Villars is ... include *Wars Of The Heart* and *Lipstick On His Collar*. The late Helen Van Slyke called her 'a spellbinding storyteller'. She lives in New York City.

One Golden Night

Elizabeth Villars

HEADLINE

First published in Great Britain in 1991
by HEADLINE BOOK PUBLISHING PLC

10 9 8 7 6 5 4 3 2

ISBN 0 7472 3637 2

Typeset by Medcalf Type Ltd, Bicester, Oxon

Printed and bound by
Collins Manufacturing, Glasgow

HEADLINE BOOK PUBLISHING PLC
Headline House
79 Great Titchfield Street
London W1P 7FN

For Judith and JoAnn

From the July 25, 1912, issue of *Town Topics*:

Le tout Newport is buzzing about Mrs Hermann Oelrichs' gala ball scheduled for Saturday the twenty-seventh. Of the many dinners planned for the evening, the most glittering will surely be Mrs Elias Leighton's party at Belle Isle. Since Mrs Oelrichs and Mrs Leighton are the dearest of friends there can be no question of rivalry in their attempts to entertain the summer colony, although it must be admitted that speculation at Bailey's Beach and the Casino runs high as to the nature of Mrs Oelrichs' surprise entertainment and the value of Mrs Leighton's party favors that are being designed specially for the occasion by Tiffany.

Mrs Stuyvesant Fish has postponed until Monday, August 19, the ball in honor of her niece Helena that she had planned to give on Saturday evening. Mrs Fish has let it be known that her change in plans has nothing to do with Mrs Oelrichs' ball, but rather with her recent decision not to entertain on Saturday nights. She does not think it seemly for early

1

churchgoers to be shocked by troops of unsteady revelers streaming home from their merrymaking. One must applaud Mrs Fish's scruples, but can only wonder how she will fill the ballroom of Crossways with a sufficient number of gentlemen on a Monday evening.

Many long-absent guests have returned to Newport this season. Foremost among them is the Duchess of Duringham, Mrs Leighton's daughter, who is staying at Belle Isle. The duke has elected to remain in London for the season, but since Her Grace's behavior thus far has been above reproach, I see no reason to give credence to the rumors that surround the couple.

Another welcome visitor here is the celebrated artist, Mr Douglas Kimball. Since Mr Kimball is not in the process of capturing on canvas any of Newport's belles, I can only speculate that he is here to recover from his brush with death last April. Mr Kimball was one of the fortunate passengers who was rescued from the *Titanic*, but many other Newport gentlemen perished with the ship, and their passing casts a pall over the festivities here this season. Beechwood is closed and the revels expected of the late Colonel Astor are sorely missed. Unfortunately, the same cannot be said of the entertainments scheduled by the late Mr Stilson Hutchins. His widow has displayed a vivacity thus far this season that clearly shows she does not intend to waste any time in enjoying the millions she fought so long and hard to acquire. I can only wonder if Mrs Hutchins' premature emergence from mourning is the reason for the expected arrival this weekend of her old friend Mr Samuel Van Nest. Formerly one of Newport's most popular young sportsmen, Mr Van Nest has not graced the summer colony with his presence since the tragic automobile accident that killed his beautiful young wife, Georgina, four years ago.

On the more serious social side – or is it the more laughable side – Mrs Oliver H. P. Belmont, formerly, as readers of these pages will remember, Mrs William K. Vanderbilt, and her suffragists have invaded Newport and are taking over . . .

Belle Isle, Newport, 7 a.m., Saturday, July 27, 1912

BUTLER'S PANTRY: seven footmen are polishing 185 gold plates, 259 silver plates, 67 silver and gold serving platters, 370 pieces of silver and gold flatwear, and 222 crystal goblets.

WINE CELLAR: under the supervision of Hatfield, the majordomo, ten footmen hired specially for the day are transporting to the pantry 53 bottles of *Moet & Chandon*, 1893; 37 bottles each of *Château-Latour*, 1878, *Clos-Vougeot*, 1893, and Rhine wine, 1893; 19 bottles of cognac, 1805; and 15 bottles of Amontillado sherry.

KITCHEN: two regular kitchen maids and three hired specially for the day are peeling 17 bushels of vegetables, two maids are opening 444 clams, two cooks with the help of two maids are preparing 19 terrapins, 37 partridges, and fileting 53 pounds of fish and 74 pounds of beef. Five pounds each of camembert, *pont l'evêque*, and stilton are ripening under cloths. The chef, having prepared two stocks for fourteen sauces and transformed five dozen eggs into *oeufs à la neiges*, is enjoying a cup of coffee. One maid is shucking 11 quarts of raspberries.

LAUNDRY: four laundresses are ironing a cloth 51 feet by 9 feet, 37 matching napkins, and assorted personal items for the ladies of the house.

SERVANTS' DINING HALL: three regular ladies' maids, two guests' ladies' maids, one regular valet, and one guest's valet, waited on by one footman, are finishing breakfast.

POTTING ROOM: 13 bowls for centerpieces, 53 vases, 74 cachepots, and 37 miniature enamel flowerpots are awaiting 15 dozen orchids, roses, and calla lilies, 74 flowering plants, 37 bonsai plants, and 32 pounds of greens to be delivered by special boat from the gardens and greenhouses of Raleigh on Long Island.

GREAT HALL: two men are replacing the 172 bulbs in the two crystal chandeliers and twelve wall sconces, two men are waxing and buffing 3,200 square feet of parquet flooring, and behind the Aubusson Chinoiserie tapestry an organ tuner, not a regular employee, is tuning one of the largest private organs in the world.

ENTRANCE HALL: two maids on the ground floor and four men on ladders are cleaning the twelve panels of the three-story-high stained glass window, and a clockmaker, not a regular employee, is setting the thirteen-foot-high French clock to which the thirty-two others in the house will be synchronized.

SMALL RECEPTION ROOM USED AS A MEN'S DRESSING ROOM: one footman is arranging in an ebony stand 20 miniature crystal vases to hold 20 *boutonnière*.

FOURTH-FLOOR STORAGE ROOM: one lady's maid and three maids are bringing 84 dresses – one week's supply for four women at three changes a day – down to the bedrooms on the second floor.

THIRD-FLOOR SECRETARY'S ROOM: one social secretary is moving cards for 37 guests around a cardboard chart and one calligrapher is printing 37 menus.

GARAGE: three chauffeurs and four helpers are cleaning and polishing one Dusenberg, one Royal Standard Cudell, and one Marquette, while a fourth chauffeur is backing out a Brewster town car in which he will meet the early ferry carrying an envoy from Tiffany.

STABLE: two drivers and four grooms are attending eight carriage horses, five hunters, and four carriages. Ten horse stalls and two carriage stalls remain empty.

GROUNDS: seventeen gardeners are clipping and manicuring 87 acres of lawns, topiary shrubbery, and formal gardens.

DELIVERY GATE: one gatekeeper is admitting a truck with two men and a cargo of 400 candles, 300 scented and 100 unscented.

FRONT GATE: one gatekeeper stands guard.

Mrs Elias Leighton, the mistress of Belle Isle, is entertaining thirty-seven for dinner.

I

Eight o'clock of a July morning was one of the finest hours at Belle Isle. The sun, still low over Rhode Island Sound, danced off the white stone and marble of the mansion and cast oblique shadows that turned the sea blue-black and the lawns a rich, glistening green. When the wind was up, as it frequently was, there was no mist, and the air felt as if it had just been laundered. There was no doubt about it. Eight o'clock was one of the finest hours at Belle Isle. It was a shame so few people noticed. Edith Leighton, mistress of Belle Isle, was too preoccupied. Elias Leighton, her husband, was rarely there. The three Leighton girls and the assorted houseguests were, more likely than not, still asleep behind the heavy draperies of their bedrooms. And the servants were far too busy.

Two hours later, when the morning had begun to wilt and the sun had invaded the second- and even third-floor bedrooms, Amelia Leighton Pugh felt it hot and unwelcome against her face. She opened her eyes to find her maid drawing back the draperies and two sets of curtains from the wide french windows. Turning away, she

9

murmured something in protest. She'd been having such a nice dream, not one of those intense dreams of Michael she had so often these days, but a pleasant, lighthearted dream, a dream of freedom. She was eighteen again, eighteen and unmarried and riding her chestnut mare, Clio, like lightning along the shore of Long Island Sound. The dream was so vivid she was sure it was happening, but now her mind was stumbling into wakefulness and she felt disappointment and annoyance at the maid for taking her from it. Amelia was sure she hadn't left orders to be awakened. Then she remembered where she was. Belle Isle, not Thynnleigh or Ardsley House. The sun rarely entered the high narrow windows of her bedroom at Thynnleigh Castle and never intruded into the eighteenth-century London town house, but she was at Belle Isle now and that meant sun. It also meant there was no need to leave orders to be awakened or anything else. At Belle Isle orders were her mother's purview.

'Good morning, milady.' The maid was advancing on her with the breakfast tray, according to her mother's instructions. There would be no returning to sleep.

Amelia squinted across the room at the marble and gilt clock on the mantel. Ten o'clock. Of course. In Newport coffee arrived an hour earlier than in New York to allow time for Bailey's Beach before lunch. It was all a carefully choreographed ballet. Amelia could envision it without even glancing at the schedule Miss Wilkens, her mother's secretary, would have placed on the Sheraton desk across the room. Luncheon at Mrs So-and-So's at two, bridge afterward, driving out on Bellevue Avenue, a reception to benefit this or that charity from five to seven, someone's dinner at eight, a ball afterward if it were a formal night, cards or music if it were not. The names of the hostesses varied from day to day, but not the schedule. Bailey's was always the start, and Amelia was required to attend whether she liked it or not.

'I wish,' her mother had announced when she'd arrived two weeks earlier, 'that you'd learn to think a little less of yourself and a little more of others, Amelia. There are times when I'd like to do exactly as I please, but I've always realized that duty comes first, duty not only to you and your sisters, but to society. That's one thing you've never understood. If everyone began sulking in her room or flouting convention, there would be no more society as we know it.'

'There's an argument to be made for that.'

'It's just as I said, Amelia. You've never understood your duty. To your position, to society, and in this case to your sister. This is a delicate time for Elizabeth.'

'A delicate time? You mean there's another scandal in the family?'

'I am not amused, Amelia.' It was one of her mother's favorite expressions, and Amelia was always surprised it didn't come out as the regal *we are not amused*. 'That sort of talk may go well at your country house parties – I've heard all about those weekend parties – but it doesn't at Belle Isle.'

11

Her mother had heard all about those country house parties, and yet she'd been the one who'd sent Amelia off to a life of them. Amelia remembered that weekend at Wentonhurst, the sound of Charles' laughter in the adjoining bedroom, and his brother later that night. A small warning flag appeared in her mind, like the sign in the servants' call box on the pantry wall, but instead of summoning, it banished. She'd sworn she wasn't going to think of any of that.

'What I meant,' her mother continued, 'is that Elizabeth's engagement has not yet been announced.'

'Or even arranged. But you'll bring it off, Mother. I have confidence in you.'

'All the same, I don't want to give Mrs Hallenbeck any reason for opposition.'

'Do you really think my absence at Bailey's would make a difference?'

'I think, Amelia, an older sister who has left her husband and gone into hiding is enough to give Beatrice Hallenbeck pause. That's why we must be careful to make it clear that you have not left Duringham . . .'

'But I have.'

' . . . and that you are not in hiding. You'll appear at Bailey's and everywhere else and behave appropriately.'

'Give Sydney some credit, Mother. Maybe he's really in love with Lizzy, enough to marry her in spite of me or his mother or anyone.'

'You've always talked so much of love, Amelia. As if it were your personal discovery.'

'It was never that.'

'In my day,' Edith continued as if Amelia had not spoken, 'one married for sensible reasons. One did not marry for love. As a result, one did not have to divorce for the lack of it – or the pursuit of it in other places.'

'In my day, Mother, if you can remember back ten years, one did not marry for love either. Which is why divorce is becoming so fashionable.'

'Fashionable? I thought you despised fashion.'

Amelia did not answer. Even when her mother was wrong, she managed to sound right.

'It's a lovely morning, milady.' The maid had put the tray on Amelia's lap and was taking things from the *semainier* in the corner. She stooped to the bottom drawer. That meant today was Saturday.

'It's always lovely in Newport, Ellen. Except when it rains.'

'Even when it rains, milady. Newport rain isn't like that English rain.'

'You're glad to be home, aren't you?' It was a rhetorical question. Amelia knew Ellen was glad to be home. It hadn't been easy for the girl at Thynnleigh Castle. Never mind that it was her mistress's dowry that had bought the new plumbing, never mind that the new plumbing made the other servants' lives easier. Ellen was still an outsider, like a new boy, the maid had once told her, and by that time Amelia hadn't been surprised that the public school expression should have filtered down to the servants' quarters.

'It's nice to be home,' Ellen answered.

13

'What about Bobby?' Bobby was one of the gardeners at Thynnleigh, and Amelia knew that he'd broken Charles' rules regularly to take flowers to Ellen.

'Why he's only a gardener, milady.'

'A perfectly honorable position, Ellen. And a nice one. What could be nicer than making things grow?'

Ellen had finished laying out her things now and stood at the end of the bed with her hands folded in front of her. The stance said a great deal. Ladies' maids did not marry apprentice gardeners. 'Salt water or fresh this morning, milady?' Ellen's tone completed the message. Her Grace knew very well that ladies' maids did not marry apprentice gardeners, and Ellen would appreciate not being teased about it.

'I don't care, Ellen. Why don't you run both together and I'll have a mixed bath.'

'Oh, I couldn't do that,' she said. 'Madame told us never to do that. An ocean bath is good for the health and a fresh bath is good for cleaning, but both together aren't good for nothing at all. That's what Madame says.'

'All right, I'll have fresh water then. We'll save the salt bath for Bailey's.'

The hot water of the bath kept her from lingering there, but she took her time dressing. The July sunlight that flooded the room seemed to reveal every flaw. Amelia watched her reflection in the mirror as Ellen fastened the coils of hair. Ten years ago, when she'd lived in this room, her hair had been shades lighter. Like white gold, someone had said. Who was it? Not Charles, she was certain of that. Charles had his eye on another kind of gold.

The maid finished arranging her hair and Amelia stood. At least she hadn't got thick and matronly. Her waist was barely half an inch wider than it had been before she'd had the baby. The baby, indeed. Anthony was almost nine now and less like a baby than a small edition of Charles.

Amelia was still facing the mirror as Ellen fastened the long line of buttons that ran down the back of her dress. Silly to pride herself on not growing thick and matronly when everyone had always told her she was too thin and boyish looking. Caroline was the beauty. That's what people always said about the Leighton sisters. They were all lovely, but Caroline, the oldest, was the beauty. Caroline whose hair was still like white gold though she was three years older than Amelia and whose huge violet eyes, made her look like something out of a Byzantine painting. Caroline, who was voluptuous and rosy and absolutely secure in her own beauty. Caroline should have been the one to become the tenth Duchess of Duringham. Everyone had said so. Amelia had even thought so at the time, but that was before she'd come to know her husband. The duke's tastes did not run to voluptuous rosy beauties. Tugging on the long white gloves, Amelia took a last look at her reflection. Strange to think that if she were more conventional looking, more suitable looking, if she were, like Caroline, the very incarnation of soft feminine beauty, she would not be in her present predicament.

On her way out of the room she stopped at one of the two tall windows facing the ocean and pushed it open. The day had that fresh feeling to it still and the sea looked very blue in the morning sunshine. She could hear the waves breaking on the beach below and the steady, monotonous sound of the gardeners' shears working at the hedges. The irony of the two sounds struck her. The waves might keep lapping at Belle Isle, eating away at it inch by inch, year after year, but the gardeners would keep clipping, keep shaping nature into manageable forms. Her mother would see to that. Her mother, Amelia supposed, would even see to the ocean. Silly to worry about erosion when Edith Leighton could so easily build a sea wall. And silly to keep harping on her mother this way. Whatever she'd done, she'd done a long time ago. And whatever had to be done now, Amelia had to do herself – with her father's help.

From the window she could see a long sleek steam yacht making its way toward the harbor. Its wake was a thin white ribbon in the sapphire sea. It wouldn't be her father's boat *Nereids*, not from that direction.

The breeze felt soft against her face, but her clothes were already sticking to her. It was too warm for the tightly fitted bodice and the long narrow sleeves and skirt. And the corset was the worst of all. The stays were hot and sticky against her skin. The corset, come to think of it, was the most foolish of all too, since she didn't need it for posture or weight, only for propriety. Someday, she swore, she'd put on her bathing suit first thing in the morning and drive to Bailey's in it. And be banned forever, she supposed, like Mrs Thorndike who had dared to emerge from her cabana a few years ago without her black silk stockings. The incident had caused enough of a scandal for Caroline to devote an entire letter to it.

'I've been sent to get you,' her sister Elizabeth said from the doorway. Standing there straight and willowy with her dark hair pulled back from the smooth heat-flushed cheeks and her eyes bright as cornflowers, she looked like a vivid bouquet fresh from the garden. No, not the garden; the fields. Despite the stiff white dress, despite the wide-brimmed hat anchored securely to the heavy coils of hair, she gave an impression of something wilder than a well-manicured garden. Her coloring was high, her mouth mobile, and her eyes lively. Elizabeth didn't look exactly untamed, but she did look vibrant. 'Mama,' she continued, her voice accenting the second syllable as a series of French governesses had taught it to, 'is furious. She says this is the third day in a row you've made us late.'

'I was thinking, Lizzy, of all the time I'd save – to say nothing of effort – if I went to Bailey's in my bathing suit. Of course, it would cause something of a scandal. Mrs Hallenbeck would never forgive us. And then poor Sydney couldn't marry you.'

'At the moment, Amelia, I'm more worried about Mama than I am about Sydney. Will you

17

please hurry? I can't stand the idea of another row.'

'No, you never could. Stand rows, I mean. Even as a little girl.' Amelia had been teasing her, but she noticed that Elizabeth looked more distressed than she should have. 'All right, I'll hurry, Lizzy. We don't want to miss Sydney.'

'Sydney won't be at the beach this morning. At least I don't think he will. He's coming up on someone's boat.' Elizabeth began smoothing her gloves over each finger the way the shopgirls did when you tried them on, and when she spoke again her voice was elaborately casual. 'So is Sam Van Nest. He's coming to dinner.'

'Mother invited Sam Van Nest to dinner? I *have* been away a long time.'

'Not that long.' Elizabeth laughed. 'Papa insisted she invite him. It was his price for coming.'

'Why does Father want Sam here?'

'Do we ever know why Papa wants anything? All I know is he told Mama he wouldn't come tonight unless Samuel Van Nest were invited. She was livid.'

'But she gave in?'

'If Papa had stayed in New York or been in Europe or somewhere, she wouldn't have missed him, but she couldn't very well have *Nereids* sitting out there in the bay and Papa not sitting at the head of the table. Not tonight. Not for her most important dinner of the season.'

'So Mother gets Father for the evening and Father gets Sam Van Nest.'

like Morgan, to watch the scenery, and waiting to be called.

'Tell Mr Van Nest I want to see him in the library.'

The secretary started off at a brisk clip, but Morgan called him back 'If he's not in his stateroom, try Mrs Hall's.' It was one of the problems, Morgan thought, of surrounding himself with beautiful women and handsome young men. He'd heard the Wall Street quip more than once. 'When the angels of God,' it went, 'took unto themselves wives among the daughters of men, the result was the Morgan partners.' It was true only up to a point. The older members of the firm had nothing special in the way of looks to recommend them, but several of the younger men, and Samuel Van Nest was foremost among them, were as blessed physically as intellectually. In fact, Van Nest's appearance was a definite financial asset. He had regular, even classical features with a straight nose and large gray eyes set far apart. He wore his dark hair parted a little to one side, and it was always perfectly trimmed. Van Nest was the kind of man who could walk off a polo field looking impeccable, the kind of man who could wear rumpled clothes without looking rumpled himself, and the fact that his manners were good but his manner casual only intensified the impression he gave. Other men tended not to take Van Nest seriously in business. Other men, Morgan knew, were wrong.

Morgan also knew that people thought it strange that an ugly old man like him enjoyed the

21

company of handsome young men, but for Morgan there was no question of comparison between them and himself. He stood alone and above. Therefore, why not enjoy the beauty?

That was what he'd chosen to do years ago when he'd hired Bacon and more recently Van Nest. And it hadn't hurt that they'd both been gentlemen as well. Morgan preferred to deal with gentlemen though he'd done business with his share of rogues and thieves. The only difficulty was that on a cruise like this one, the handsome gentlemen and beautiful young women tended to discover each other. He suspected King would find Van Nest in Mrs Hall's cabin. Well, why not, Morgan reasoned as he started for the library. That's where he'd be if he weren't seventy-five and ailing.

'Good morning, Mr Morgan,' Samuel Van Nest said as he entered the smaller of the ship's two libraries, the one Morgan used as an office. Van Nest could not bring himself to call the old man 'Commodore' as the other partners did, though he knew Morgan preferred the term from those he considered his intimates. The problem was that Sam didn't feel like Morgan's intimate. His equal certainly, his successor perhaps, but not his intimate.

Sam knew from the manner of the summons and the look on the broad fleshy face that Morgan had something on his mind. The bulbous nose was more inflamed than ever. At least it was serious. Sam hadn't liked the idea of leaving Dolly Hall for something trivial.

'Sit down, Van Nest.' Morgan nodded toward one of the two throne chairs that stood before the massive desk. Behind his head the wall of books formed a muted tapestry of brown and burgundy and gold. The smooth leather bindings shone in the sunlight that streamed in the porthole across the cabin, and Sam guessed the books had been oiled very recently. It couldn't be easy to keep books in that condition at sea.

'I understand you're dining at Mrs Leighton's tonight before the ball at Rosecliff,' Morgan began.

Understood he was dining there! The old man had ordered him to. Until he was twenty, Sam had spent every summer of his life in Newport. Since he was twenty-five he'd returned only twice, except for race week, and race week didn't count since Sam confined himself to the regatta and avoided the social functions. The first time his mother had fallen ill; the second, and longer, he'd come because Georgina had asked him to. They'd been married less than a year then, and he'd found it hard to say no to anything Georgina asked. Since that summer four years ago, he hadn't returned, but now Morgan had insisted he sail up on *Corsaire* and attend both Mrs Leighton's dinner and Mrs Oelrichs' ball. Sam was dreading both. He could get along very well without Edith Leighton and her three daughters.

'I'm sure it comes as no surprise to you that I have my reasons for asking you to attend both the dinner and the ball, Van Nest. I'm well aware of your feelings about Newport and its ladies.' Morgan hesitated for a moment as if waiting for

23

a sign, but Sam gave none. His expression indicated that his private life as well as predilections were his own. Morgan did not agree. Gossip bored him, but anyone who didn't know as much as possible about the men he did business with was a fool. He knew all about Van Nest's personal life, both past and present. Sam considered himself a cynic about women, a knowledgeable, worldly cynic, and to be sure he'd had some bad times. The Leighton girl had taught him his first lesson. That woman he'd married had completed his education, only it wasn't much of an education, despite what Van Nest thought. Sam was sure he'd learned about women, but in Morgan's opinion all he'd done was pick up a few prejudices.

'It may interest you to know,' Morgan continued, 'that your sentiments are reciprocated in certain quarters. It was no easy task wrangling you an invitation to Mrs Leighton's. Nevertheless, neither your social scruples nor Mrs Leighton's interest me at the moment. Do you know Jason Walsh?'

'I've never met him.'

'Neither have I, I'm happy to say. He makes Mr Gould and Mr Harriman look like gentlemen.'

'Don't tell me Walsh is going to be at Mrs Leighton's?'

'Not Walsh, but certain of his friends, or shall we say certain of our friends whose friendship Walsh is cultivating. That's why you're dining with Mrs Leighton tonight. To prevent Walsh from making too many friends.'

Sam wished Morgan would get on with it, but knew there was no rushing the old man. He loved to play – and win – cat-and-mouse games. He'd tell the story in his own time and his own way. Still, Sam could guess at some of it. He thought of the rumors he'd heard about Walsh in the last weeks. They hadn't been the usual ones of heavily watered stock and manipulations that ruined men and companies simultaneously. They'd been much vaguer than that, and therefore more intriguing.

Sam had got his first inkling that something was up two weeks before when he'd dropped in at the Knickerbocker for a drink late one afternoon. Jason Walsh, one of the members was telling another, had cornered the market on shares of the First Midwest Bank and Trust. A typical Walsh coup, the man had said, but Sam didn't think it typical. Walsh had always used his own banking house to take over industries or transportation lines or great land tracts rich in one mineral or another. He'd never played with other banks before, but now he'd begun to, and he'd begun with one of the most powerful in the country.

A few days later Sam had dined at his mother's house on Thirty-third Street. Lavinia Van Nest entertained rarely and almost never went out, but she'd had several old friends in to dine that Wednesday night. One of the guests was an elderly and only moderately successful banker who'd grown up with Sam's late father. He was very cheerful that night. After the ladies had left the table and Sam had passed around the brandy and cigars, the man told Sam why. He'd just sold his bank to Jason Walsh. Walsh, the man reported, had given him two shares in Walsh and Company for every one of the small private bank. It wasn't a fluke anymore. It was a trend, Sam had thought that night as he looked up at the portrait of his great-grandfather who presided over the dining room impassively. Well, the old man, long dead and secure in the legend that surrounded him, could afford to be impassive to the name Jason Walsh. The old man could also ignore the darned table linen Sam noticed as he passed the brandy decanter. But if Sam were going to worry about things like darned table linen, and his sisters had convinced him years ago that he must, then he had to worry about Jason Walsh. Walsh was up to something.

Sam wondered if it were the trend he'd spotted that night that Morgan had in mind now. He leaned across the wide desk and handed Sam a sheaf of papers. 'I want you to look at these, Van Nest. You'll find they're arranged by personalities. One file for each man in question. When you've gone through them, I'd like to talk to you again. Shall we say three o'clock?' It was not, of course, a question.

Sam took the fat folder from him. Personalities. What in hell did that mean? He was accustomed to reports on companies or on a man's holdings, but Morgan and Company didn't deal in personalities – at least not openly.

Morgan knew that Van Nest was annoyed, though the clean-shaven face with the sharply defined features showed no anger. Only the intelligent gray eyes gave him away. They looked as if they'd like to tell Morgan to take his papers and his dinner party and go straight to hell.

Van Nest stood and started for the door. He was tall, taller even than Morgan's six feet, and moved with the ease and confidence of a sportsman. And a sportsman, Morgan suspected, was all he would have been if the senior Samuel Van Nest hadn't died leaving only a house in New York, another in Newport, and two still unmarried daughters.

Nothing in Sam Van Nest's youth, Morgan thought, had indicated his present success. Van Nest had been the sort of young man people predicted would never amount to anything. He was an iconoclast, they said, irreverent about the things they revered and serious about the things they did not. To put it more plainly, he had shown no interest in financial or social success. As a young man Van Nest had lived entirely for his own pleasures, though to be sure the pleasures he chose were not the easy ones. In a single year he'd broken his arm in a polo match, his ankle in a football game (though he was not a varsity player), and lost a tooth when he capsized in a regatta. It wasn't that he was clumsy or even accident prone, only that he was hell-bent on winning and would drive himself mercilessly to that end. He'd done badly at Yale except for the year his father had bribed him with the promise of a new polo pony if he did well, yet Morgan had discovered that when it came to history Van Nest was one of the most knowledgeable men he'd ever known, and as a collector Morgan had known some of the most renowned professional historians.

Van Nest had a good mind and a hard spirit, but he was erratic, or perhaps, Morgan thought, merely willful. He'd been with the House of Morgan for twelve years and had proved himself reliable again and again, yet Morgan knew he could not rely on Van Nest in the same sense he could the other partners. He always had the feeling that one day Van Nest would decide he had enough money and simply stop. There wasn't another man at 23 Wall Street you could say that about. Still, Van Nest hadn't reached that point yet, and Morgan knew he was the right man – indeed the only man – for the job at hand.

'Elizabeth!' Edith Leighton's voice stopped her daughter at the door of the cabana. It scraped like the rusty hinges of the old changing cabins. 'You forgot your parasol. Your complexion is dark enough without exposing it to the sun.' Edith snapped open her own parasol and started across the beach. Her daughters fell in step behind her as they were expected to.

Through the soles of her bathing slippers Amelia could feel the heat of the sand, and her black bathing dress seemed to absorb every ray of the sun. The beach was parched and white, and the glare on the water was blinding.

'I think Lizzy's complexion is just fine,' Amelia said. 'And I don't see how a little sun could hurt it. We had a woman at the castle one weekend – a Russian princess, but she didn't use her title –

who never carried a parasol or even wore a hat or veil. She got dark as a nut, and she was absolutely striking. Like an exotic flower. All the men were in love with her.'

'I don't want to criticize any of the duke's guests, Amelia – I know how careful Charles is about whom he receives – but it has been my experience that people who choose not to use their titles are people whose titles are not very impressive to begin with.'

'Not anymore, Mother.' She was thinking of Michael again, though she'd sworn she wasn't going to think of him. He'd been disdainful of titles and had told her once that he couldn't understand marrying for one. It was only later that she learned he couldn't understand marrying at all. 'These days titles . . .'

'Amelia.' Her mother's voice cut her off. She'd been away too long. She'd forgotten that her mother didn't discuss; she pronounced. Edith turned away from her daughters to a man in a black woolen bathing suit with a black-and-white striped top. 'Good morning, Mr Kimball.' Edith's voice was clear now, a crystal bell rather than a rusty hinge. She looked up at the slim, wiry man with the neat moustache and goatee standing at the water's edge and smiled. Edith never forgot that she had been the most beautiful Leighton of all, and she was especially aware of the fact in the presence of men whom she regarded, in one capacity or another, as eligible. Douglas Kimball's portraits hung in the best houses here and the greatest palaces and castles abroad. He would be a magnificent addition to her entourage. The only trouble was that Kimball had shown no inclination to be attached to her entourage or anyone else's. He'd shown, in fact, little taste for society, but rumor had it he'd changed. That awful incident last spring had changed him. It had made him, people said, more human.

If anyone had bothered to ask him, Kimball would have said the incident had made him not more human, simply more aware of his own mortality, although he supposed that was one definition of being human. Half an hour in the icy Atlantic, his half-frozen hands clutching desperately to the lifeboat full of screaming women and children had made him aware of his own mortality. The sight of the greatest ship in the world, the unsinkable ship, sliding into the black sea, the sounds of things crashing and breaking up, of the thousands for whom there had been no lifeboats, some screaming, some praying, some merely singing, had made him acutely aware of his own mortality.

Face to face with the Leighton women, however, he was not thinking of any of that. They went through the customary greetings. Mrs Leighton commented on the clearness of the day, Kimball remarked on the temperature of the water, Caroline called their attention to the warmth of the sun.

'We were just talking about the sun and Lizzy,' Amelia said. 'How it would turn her into an exotic flower.'

Elizabeth looked embarrassed, but Kimball

merely turned his artist's eye on her. 'That's one image I hadn't thought of, but it only makes me more eager to paint her. I haven't given up hope.'

Elizabeth brushed a wisp of dark hair back from her forehead and looked more uncomfortable than ever.

'Perhaps some day,' Edith said. 'After Elizabeth has married. I've had all my girls painted, Mr Kimball. Or rather Mr Leighton had Boldini do us all. Just before Caroline's wedding. Now it's up to their husbands. Though I must say, there isn't an artist I'd rather see paint Elizabeth. I've never liked what Mr Sargent did to Amelia. He made her neck look exactly like a giraffe's. And they say Boldini's extreme. Of course, her neck is too long, but I would expect Mr Sargent to remedy the fact rather than accentuate it. No, I've never liked that portrait.'

'Then isn't it lucky, Mother,' Amelia said as they moved off from Kimball, 'that you won't have to see it anymore.' But the words hurt her more than they did Edith. Charles had commissioned Sargent to paint all three of them, Charles, their son Tony, and her. After all, the tenth Duke of Duringham and the future eleventh duke must be properly commemorated and the duchess ought to be recorded for posterity, too, even if she were an American. Amelia had liked the portrait of herself, despite the neck. It wasn't the picture of her that hurt, but the one of Tony. He didn't look like the Marquess of Thurston, only a four-year-old boy whose impatience Sargent had managed to convey beneath the veneer of good manners and better breeding, and whose affection for his mother was obvious in the way he leaned against her chair, his small hands pale against the dark folds of her gown. It was hard to believe now that they had ever posed that way. It was hard to believe that the picture had ever approximated reality.

'I'm quite sure,' Edith answered, 'that I will see not only the unflattering portrait again, but all of its subjects reunited.

'Schuyler,' Edith turned without missing a beat from her daughter to the man who had joined them. 'How nice to find you here. I can't remember how long it's been since you turned up at Bailey's.'

'Last Tuesday, *Belle mere*.'

'Now I know you're in a good mood. When you're not, it's Mrs Leighton.' Edith's thin lips turned up in a wicked smile. 'Caroline is fortunate to have a husband who's so easy to read.'

Schuyler Niebold smoothed his neat dark moustache with thumb and forefinger. It was an uncharacteristic gesture. He was not a man given to nervous mannerisms, but his mother-in-law's comment made him uncomfortable, as it was intended to.

'Oh, no, Mama,' Caroline said. 'Schuyler's simply full of surprises. Why, I never know what to expect next. Like turning up here to collect me. I won't be a moment, Sky. We were just going to change.'

'I'll keep Sky company while you do,' Amelia said. She saw her mother begin to speak. 'I have plenty of time, Mother. I'm not lunching with you, remember? Mrs Hallenbeck didn't invite me. And it's much too crowded with four of us in the cabana.'

After the other women had left, Sky dropped down beside his sister-in-law on the sand. He'd grown portly in the years she'd been away, but he carried his weight well. Now instead of a handsome boy he was a substantial-looking and rather appealing man, especially this morning, in his white linen suit and straw hat with the club band. His face was deeply tanned and didn't assume that hot red look so many of his colleagues wore at the beach on days like this.

'No swimming for you today, Sky?'

'Swimming, my dear Amelia. You shock me. No one swims at Bailey's. Mr Oelrichs floats around with his cigar, whiskey, and his book. A menace to navigation, the naval station called him last week. Mrs Belmont wades. My wife, my lovely wife, dips a well formed foot in the surf. Harry Lehr down there at the other end of the beach gossips. But no one swims. They couldn't even if they wanted to. Not with that impenetrable wall of seaweed.'

'Careful, Sky, you sound cynical. That's supposed to be my role.'

They had both been gazing at the sea as they spoke, and now Schuyler turned and looked at her profile. The straight nose and delicately shaped chin were handsome in profile. He'd never paid much attention to her before she'd married and gone off to England – in those days he'd never paid attention to anyone but Caroline – but in the last few years he'd come to feel a peculiar affection for Amelia. It had started, he remembered, that summer they'd spent in London with her and Duringham. He'd begun to realize then that he would have been better off – they all would have – if he'd married a different Leighton sister.

'Is it that bad?' he said. 'Being home, I mean.'

'Let's just say it has its difficult moments.'

'Difficult enough to drive you back.'

She turned to him abruptly and her eyes were wide with alarm. 'Good Lord, no.'

'Was it that bad then?' he asked though he was fairly sure he knew the answer.

She was still looking at him and she tried to force a smile. 'Yes, it was that bad. And I'll never go back. Even if I can't get a divorce, I won't go back.'

'Well, for what it's worth – which, in case you haven't noticed, is nothing – I'm on your side. But your mother is going to put up a battle.'

'*Belle mere*, you mean?' Amelia laughed. 'I'm sorry, Sky. I shouldn't tease you. Mother always preferred being a French mother or mother-in-law, and you've always had beautiful manners.'

'That's me. Beautiful manners. Schuyler Niebold never offends anyone.'

'Oh, I don't know. I remember the summer you were engaged to Caroline. That afternoon you came to the house and found her with Elliott Norton. She said she was just sending him away. "Finally and forever." But you weren't having any of it. You certainly offended Elliott then.

34

Threatened to "beat his brains out" – I believe
that was the expression you used – if he didn't
stay away from Carrie. It seems to me you
offended Elliott considerably, and I know it took
Mother weeks to get over it. If you hadn't been
a Schuyler as well as a Niebold, I swear she would
have called off the wedding then and there.'

He leaned back on his elbows and laughed and
the fine lines at the sides of his eyes crinkled as
he did. 'Poor Norton. I was such a damn fool.' He
turned from Amelia back to the sea. 'But I didn't
know Caroline then.'

'I didn't think you were a fool at all. I thought
you were the bravest, the most dashing, the most
romantic man in the world.'

It was true. She had thought all those things and
infuriated Sam Van Nest by saying them, and he
had ended up infuriating her in return.

'He's a fool,' Sam had said, foreshadowing Sky's
own judgment of himself.

'For being jealous of Carrie and another man?'

'He ought to know Caroline better.'

'Well, if I were in Carrie's place, I'd want my
fiancé to behave just as Sky has.'

They were sitting side by side on the low wall
that separated the Cliff Walk, that long winding
path that ran along the water and was open to all
Newport, from the privacy of Belle Isle, and Sam
looked at her in the gathering dusk and laughed.
'Now that's different. In your case, I imagine
there'd be cause for duels and all sorts of lurid
scenes.'

'You're no gentleman, Sam Van Nest.'

He laughed again. 'Because I kissed you this afternoon or because I reminded you of it now?'

The sun had dropped low on the horizon and the darkness was growing thicker around them. Amelia was glad. It meant he couldn't see her face when he mentioned that afternoon. It was strange to remember now how much a kiss meant when you were young.

They'd gone for a sail in the Buzzard's Bay fifteen-footer that Sam spent half his summer on. He hadn't paid much attention to her – he never did when he took her sailing – and as she'd watched him at the tiller, his eyes riveted on the sails, she thought he'd forgotten she was there, but suddenly he'd leaned over and kissed her. She'd been surprised and a little embarrassed, but mostly glad because his mouth had felt soft on hers and very nice, and to be perfectly honest about it – to herself if no one else – she'd been thinking about kissing Sam for a long time. And from the way he'd looked at her afterward she knew he'd been thinking of it for a long time too – longer than just the few minutes he'd been quiet and seemingly preoccupied with the sails. He'd begun trimming them furiously then, though there'd been no change in the wind. She'd pretended to look at the water, but out of the corner of her eyes she'd watched him at the lines. She liked the way his shoulders pulled against the soft white shirt as he'd tugged at the sheets and his hands moved swiftly to make a cleat. She loved his hands. They were large and strong, with long slender fingers that made them look graceful despite their size.

Now as he sat beside her on the wall the hands were toying with a shell he'd picked up on his walk over. They were always moving, practicing knots, exploring surfaces, unconsciously molding and shaping and rearranging.

'Sky would never do anything like that.'

'Kiss you or tease you about it?'

She ducked her head a little, as if the darkness were not enough. 'You know what I mean. Sky worships Carrie.'

'Absolutely. But then Carrie's so worthy of worship. She's above reproach.'

'I suppose that means I'm not.'

He turned to face her and even in the gathering dusk she could see the wicked light in his eyes. 'The real question is whether you want to be above reproach or only want me to think you are.'

'You're impossible.'

'I concede the point, but then so are you. Everyone says so. Except Mrs Goelet. She used the word scandalous. Dashing around on your bicycle in that divided skirt with your hair flying out behind you. At your age. You're far too old for that sort of thing, you know. Then those novels your governess found in your room. *Anna Karenina*. And you haven't even come out yet, which means you're far too young for that sort of thing. Mrs Goelet's right. You are scandalous. If you keep up this way, they'll never marry you off. Unless, of course, you're clever enough to hold on to me.'

'You're not only impossible, you're insufferably conceited.'

'At least I'm smart enough to have found the only interesting girl in Newport.'

Interesting. She was interesting, but Caroline was beautiful and above reproach. Caroline was the kind of girl men fought over.

That had been true then, and it seemed to Amelia it was still true today. Everything that had happened in the intervening years had proved it true. She turned back to Schuyler. 'I don't care what anyone, including you, thought that day. As far as I was concerned, you were a hero.'

He tipped his hat to her. 'I'm honored, Your Grace.'

'Please don't call me that. Mother's always doing it in front of other people, and she has the servants miladying their heads off.'

'Well she went to a lot of trouble for that title.'

'To say nothing of expense.'

'To say nothing of expense,' Sky agreed. 'She's not going to give it up easily.'

He rolled over on one elbow to face her. 'But tell me, Amelia, weren't you just the least little bit impressed by it yourself? Weren't you just a little thrilled about marrying the tenth Duke of Duringham? Weren't you just a little proud of having made the marriage of the year – correction, the marriage of the decade, maybe even the century?'

'Not that, Sky. Remember Consuelo Vanderbilt's wedding? Everyone knows a Marlborough takes precedence over a Duringham.'

'Still, didn't you enjoy all the attention and the

fuss and the envy? Just a little? Now tell the truth, Amelia.'

'About what?' Caroline's shadow fell between them. They both looked up quickly, but the sun was behind her and it was impossible to read the expression on her face. 'What do you want Amelia to tell the truth about, Sky?'

Schuyler stood and brushed the sand off his trousers. 'Nothing. We were only joking.'

'What were you joking about?' Caroline asked when they'd left the small enclosure of sand that was Bailey's Beach and had reached the Auburn Sky had parked at the side of the road. Would he really go that far, she wondered. Her own sister. And if he would, what did that say about Vanessa Hunter? Before Sky had taken up with Vanessa, his tastes had been eclectic, to say the least. She thought of the maid she'd had to dismiss years ago and flushed. But for some time now – Caroline wasn't sure exactly how long – there'd been no one except Vanessa. Perhaps Sky was getting restless. Perhaps he was thinking of expanding his interests again.

Schuyler saw the color rise in the smooth pale cheeks. She was still pretty. Damn it, she was still beautiful. 'We were talking about that time when we were first engaged and I got into a row with Elliott Norton.' He reached over and straightened the collar of her duster. 'I wanted to kill him.'

'To kill Elliott Norton?'

'Don't you remember? Amelia said I threatened to "beat his brains out." '

'Oh, now I remember,' she said adjusting the veil

39

so it would leave no mark on her cheeks. 'That was the night you gave me my ring.'

The Auburn had one of those new self-starters. When Sky pressed it, it made a violent sound, and Caroline jumped. He was glad.

A dark green cabriolet had pulled up on the wide brick drive before Belle Isle. Edith saw it as soon as the chauffeur turned the Dusenberg off Bellevue Avenue and passed through the tall wrought-iron gates. She recognized the Van Rensaleer crest on the side, and knew what the visit meant. No one would be leaving a card at this hour. Mr Van Rensaleer was canceling. If someone had to drop out, why couldn't it be the Corcorans or Samuel Van Nest?

The innocuous looking envelope lay on the Buhl table in the entrance hall. Edith tore it open. 'A broken leg. It's unforgivable. Especially at this hour.'

'I'm sure Mr Van Rensaleer didn't break his leg on purpose, Mama.'

'His intentions have nothing to do with it, Elizabeth. He's ruined my dinner.'

'He's ruined his leg,' Amelia said.

'His leg will heal. Even at his age. But where am I to find an extra man at this hour? Especially on a Saturday night in July. There are at least two dozen dinners before Tessie's ball. And I'm going to have the only one without enough men.'

'Call the naval station,' Amelia said. 'Or isn't that done anymore?' She remembered the custom from her debutante days. Her mother and every other Newport matron would simply send a note to the Admiral asking him to deliver a dozen or two presentable officers to a certain house at a certain hour.

'It's done for balls and occasionally for a reception, but not for a dinner.'

'Surely they've learned to handle a knife and fork in the officers' mess, Mother.'

'If you can't be serious about this, Amelia, I wish you wouldn't say anything at all.'

'What about that Lieutenant Atherton who was at Mrs Norton's last Wednesday?' Elizabeth asked. 'He was my partner at bridge and he seemed perfectly nice. I've met him at at least half a dozen places this summer, so people must keep inviting him.'

'Atherton? I don't remember a Lieutenant Atherton.'

'Tall. Very fair. He's got a perfectly lovely voice.'

'Did he sing at Mrs Norton's?' Amelia asked.

'No silly. He has a nice speaking voice. Kind of low and soft, but very musical. Lieutenant Timothy Atherton. You remember him, Mama. You asked him if he were related to Admiral Atherton.'

'He wasn't,' Edith said. 'Pity. Still, he'll have to do. Go dress for lunch, Elizabeth. I don't want to be late for Mrs Hallenbeck. And I'll telephone the lieutenant.'

'Tall. Very fair. A soft musical voice.' Amelia followed her sister up the stairs, mimicking her voice. 'And all that after a single evening of bridge.'

41

'I told you, I've met Lieutenant Atherton more than once.'

'Apparently.' Amelia stopped on the broad landing and turned to her sister. 'Are you very fond of him?'

'Of Lieutenant Atherton? Don't be silly. I barely know him.'

If she were lying, Amelia thought, she was good at it. The large blue eyes were as clear as the sea that glistened beyond the second-floor piazza and her voice was light; as light, Amelia imagined, as the musical Lieutenant Atherton's.

'In other words, you don't want to talk about it.'

Elizabeth started down the hall toward her room. 'There's nothing to talk about. Mama needed an extra man, and I found her one. And now I'd better hurry and dress or Mama and Mrs Hallenbeck will have my head on a silver platter for lunch.' She started to open the door to her room, but Amelia caught her hand.

'If you don't want to marry Sydney, you don't have to, Lizzy. You know that, don't you?'

Elizabeth hesitated for a moment before she spoke, but there was no telling what she was thinking. There rarely was with Lizzy. 'Of course, I know that.' She took her hand from her sister's. 'But I do have to lunch at his mother's,' she added, 'and I'm late for that.'

'And where are you lunching today?' Caroline asked as she entered her husband's room. He'd gone there as soon as they'd arrived home and hadn't bothered to open the door to the sitting room that connected his bedroom with her larger one.

'I haven't made any plans.'

'You mean you don't want to tell me.'

'I mean I haven't made any plans. Maybe I'll lunch at home.'

'It won't do any good, Sky. Amelia isn't lunching at home. She's going to Mrs Pembroke Jones's.'

He looked up from the stud book he'd been pretending to read and smiled at her. 'Lucky girl. One of the few houses in Newport where you can get a cocktail before lunch. I'll still probably lunch at home, Carrie. I told Lee I'd take him sailing this afternoon.'

'Leighton is going to Reggie Wilcox's birthday party this afternoon.'

'I think he'd prefer to go sailing. At least that's what he said.'

'Nevertheless, he's expected at the Wilcox birthday party.'

Schuyler closed the book on his lap and placed it on the table beside him. He didn't want to fight about the children. There were enough things to argue about without bringing the children into it, though God knows the children were going to come into it soon enough. He'd be damned if he'd let her keep the children from him. He had rights. These weren't the dark ages, and divorce was no longer a shocking matter, though somewhere in the back of his mind Schuyler was still profoundly shocked that it was going to happen to him.

'Perhaps he can do both. If I lunch at home with

the children, I can take Lee for a sail and have him back in time for the party.'

'I can't imagine why you want to go rushing about like that' – her voice took on what Sky had come to think of as her languid tone, and she looked bored – 'but I won't object so long as you have him back before four. And I won't have any excuses about dying winds or being becalmed.'

'Carrie, my dear,' he said as he stood and crossed the room to her, 'the elements wouldn't dare fly in the face of your wishes.' He took her hand and raised it to his lips, and she didn't pull away. Caroline had always liked having her hand kissed. The only thing she'd prefer, Sky suspected, was a similar homage to her ring or the hem of her dress.

'Well, Van Nest, did you enjoy your morning reading?' Morgan asked. They were in the small library again, but this time Morgan had chosen a large Queen Anne wing chair before the fireplace rather than the one behind his desk. The hearth was filled with fresh flowers, but the smell of Morgan's cigar overpowered the more delicate fragrance.

'It was enlightening, sir, to say the least.'

'You don't seem much surprised. I have to admit I was looking forward to surprising you.'

'I won't say I expected all of it – especially the business about Wainwright's holdings and the rest about Kirkland Selby . . .'

'Nasty business, that.'

' . . . but I like to think I'm no longer easily surprised by human nature, sir.'

44

Morgan raised his eyebrows, but said nothing.
'And after all,' Sam went on, 'even Kirkland
Selby is human.'

'I daresay. Well, you're probably curious why
I've gone to such lengths to provide information
about your fellow guests for the evening. It all
goes back to Jason Walsh. As I said this morning,
he's watered more stock than Gould and Harriman
put together, and in his younger days he had a
tendency to buy companies only to ruin them. I
hate to see that, Sam. I've never objected to
takeovers – provided it isn't my company being
taken over – but I've never liked the idea of
buying a company only to ruin it in a fast killing.
I've always liked to build things, not destroy them.
At any rate, I'm sure I don't have to tell you about
Walsh's past. His manipulations were spectacular
enough and successful enough to become common
gossip.' Morgan stopped to relight his cigar. He
took a long puff and looked at Sam carefully. 'And
he's about to undertake the most spectacular and
the most daring of all. Walsh is setting up a
combination that will make the steel trust look like
child's play. Or at least he's trying to.'

Sam could read the rage in the black eyes. The
old man doesn't like being outstripped, he
thought. Morgan had put together the steel trust,
the greatest combination in the world, and now
it's going to be relegated to second place. And him
with it. 'What sort of combination?'

Morgan smiled as if he'd been waiting for the
question. 'A banking combination. A financial
combination. To put it as simply as possible, Walsh

will control all the investment capital in this country, and a goodly amount in England and France as well.'

Sam stood and walked to the porthole. He was overwhelmed, just as Morgan had expected him to be. He looked out at the handful of yachts anchored nearby and the great houses on the slopes beyond. Those houses and those boats represented a great deal of wealth, but it was nothing compared to what Morgan was talking about. Walsh was planning to corner all the investment capital in the country. Anyone who wanted to build or enlarge or even keep afloat in lean times would have to come to him. Sam had just said that little about human nature surprised him, but the breadth and daring of Walsh's plan did.

'Needless to say,' Morgan went on, 'we can't let him do it.'

Sam turned back to him. 'You mean we're going to do it first?'

This time Morgan permitted himself a smile. 'Twenty years ago I would have tried, and I'll be damned if I wouldn't have succeeded. Walsh is a smart operator, but old Andrew Carnegie was nobody's fool either. He didn't exactly hand over the steel interests. But the Steel Trust is beside the point, or rather very much to the point. No, Van Nest, we're not going to beat Walsh to the mark, but we are going to keep him off it.

'Times are changing. You know that as well as I do. Though perhaps we don't agree on how they're changing. I trust you aren't still brooding about that airplane thing.' Morgan smiled again, and Sam knew it was meant to be an avuncular smile, but he couldn't help feeling it was more patronizing than anything else.

'The days when the public and the government would stand by while we set up a combination like this are gone,' Morgan went on in a more businesslike tone. 'This is 1912 and no matter who wins the election – the Colonel, that man Wilson, or Taft – they're going to fight this banking trust. They broke up Standard Oil and the Tobacco Trust last year, and they're after the Steel Trust right now. I hope to God they won't win, but we can't be sure of that. We can't be sure of anything except that they'll put up a fight. People think it's only Roosevelt, especially since he managed to blame that *Titanic* disaster on Taft. The Colonel had a heyday with that. ''Tool of the corporations'' he called Taft. Would that he were. Let me tell you, Van Nest, the President is no better than Roosevelt. No better and no worse. They all want to be known as the big trust busters. They all want to be known as the people's champion. The people's champion! I've done more good for my investors than any one of them has ever done for ''the people.''

'All the same, times are changing. The government is changing them. We both know it's only a matter of time before enough states ratify this amendment and we have an income tax. Damn socialist notion! What a man makes is his property – and business. Still, the government is fighting that notion and it will fight this Walsh scheme, fight it with every weapon at hand. And

47

you know what will happen then, Van Nest? Imagine what will happen when the government decides to bring suit against the single combination that controls all the investment capital in the country. A panic. A panic that will make 1907 seem like a ripple in the stream rather than the tidal wave it was.'

'Or would have been, if you hadn't stepped in.' Sam was not flattering the old man. There were a lot of things he didn't admire about Morgan, but there was no denying he'd headed off one of the worst panics in Wall Street history. His enemies said Morgan had done little, but taken the lion's share of the credit. Sam knew that wasn't the case. He'd just been made a partner that year and he'd been in on some of the negotiations. Morgan's shrewdness as well as his reputation had saved the day.

'Which brings me to my second point, Van Nest. As I said, the government will bring suit, and that will start a panic. And who will be the only person with the power to head off the panic? Jason Walsh. Good Lord, man, that's like setting a fox to guard the chicken house. But even if Walsh chose to act with honor and try to head off disaster rather than take his profits and head for the hills, do you think he could? Does his word carry any weight? It's a threat, perhaps, but not a promise of good intentions, not a bond. I'm sure you remember, Samuel, that back in '07 I managed to get eight million in gold from London in a single day on the basis of my word. And the cotton bills. Tell me, how much do you think Walsh's word would bring from England? Not a shilling. Not a single shilling.'

Morgan was, of course, right. Walsh's scheme was grandiose and their colleagues might allow him to carry it off, but the government would not, and the result would be disastrous.

'So you see, Samuel, you must stop Walsh.'

Sam crossed the cabin again and sat facing Morgan. '*I'm* going to stop Walsh?'

'I'm too old to.'

'There are, if I may say so, several partners in the firm who rank between you and me; that is to say, between the top and the bottom. Including your own son.'

'That's quite true, but you're uniquely suited to this task, Samuel, and I feel certain you'll carry it off. You'll be able to take care of everything this evening. I don't imagine your work will give you much time to enjoy the festivities, but then business before pleasure.

'This morning I gave you files on five men,' Morgan continued. 'Those men will all be present at Mrs Leighton's tonight and at Mrs Oelrichs' ball. It's those men who stand between Walsh and his success or to put it another way, between us and Walsh's failure.

'I'm sure, Van Nest, during your visits to Washington you've heard that unpleasant term "the money trust." It seems they've got it into their heads down there that a handful of us – fifteen, they say – control the economy of the country. More accurately, I'd put the number at eighteen. Between them those eighteen men hold a hundred and eighteen directorships in thirty-four bank and trust companies, a hundred and five directorships in thirty-two transportation companies, sixty-three directorships in twenty-four producing and trading corporations, and twenty-five directorships in twelve public utility corporations. All in all we hold three hundred and forty-one directorships in one hundred and twelve corporations, and those corporations can be capitalized at more than twenty-two billion dollars. Incidentally, there's no water in that figure. At this very moment the government is setting up a commission to investigate the facts behind the numbers I've just given you. As if a Senate committee could ever get at the facts behind anything.

'You could probably list those eighteen men without being told who they are, Van Nest. As a junior partner you've probably thought about joining the group, and after tonight . . . after your success tonight . . . I think we'll be able to say that you have.'

Morgan reached out and touched a large silver tankard on the table beside him. Some people said he was deeply moved by anything of beauty; others, that he was a wily old man who simply liked the idea of collecting. Sam had never been sure of the truth, but the old hand with the swollen joints moved over the silver tankard lovingly. 'Handsome piece, isn't it, Van Nest? Queen Mary gave it to a Dutch master named Simon Janszen. It was a token of gratitude for conveying her husband, William III, across to The

Hague in 1691. There are many ways to show gratitude materially, Sam, and I don't think I have to tell you that I personally and the House of Morgan will be very grateful to you for your aid in this matter. You will be second in line to my son.' Morgan saw the startled look on his face. 'Yes, even above Davison. So you see, tonight will mean a good deal to you, Sam, as well as to me and to the country at large.

'Now that we've discussed the magnitude of the reward, let's get down to the specifics of the work. As I said, there are eighteen men in what the government insists on calling the money trust. Walsh, of course, is one of them. A few others are behind him in this scheme. Several more have allied themselves with us. Elias Leighton, your host for this evening, at least your nominal host is squarely in our corner. His son-in-law Schuyler Niebold is not, but I'm not worried about him. The Niebold name still carries some weight in banking circles, but the Niebold holdings aren't big enough to make a difference one way or another. The five men you spent your morning reading about, however, can make a difference. All of them are seriously considering throwing in their lot with Walsh. More than seriously considering it, I'd say. My guess is two, perhaps three of them, have already made up their minds.'

'And my job is to change it.'

'You have a rare trait for a banker, Samuel. You're persuasive. Most of us are simply smart or shrewd or ruthless, but you're persuasive.'

'I doubt I'm persuasive enough to convince men

51

like Selby and Wainwright and the rest of them to turn their backs on Jason Walsh. At least I doubt I can do it in one night.'

'It must be done this way, Van Nest. If we start paying visits or calling meetings, Walsh is bound to get wind of things, and we'll have open warfare. I don't want that. I can't afford that. So you'll have to work quickly and you'll have to work behind the marble walls of Belle Isle and Rosecliff. Come now, it oughtn't to be that hard. Wainwright and Selby are virtually taken care of. As for the other three men, Maxwell Fingerhut has controlling interest in the three largest insurance companies in the nation. That means a great deal of capital to invest. Those papers you read this morning made all that clear, but perhaps they did not reveal his character as fully. Fingerhut inherited his fortune from his late father, and with the aid of his father's lieutenants he's managed to hold on to it, but Fingerhut is touchy. He's the small son of a big man, big physically and financially. While old man Fingerhut was alive, he never let the boy do a thing. Rather like Victoria and the late king, I like to think. Oh, Max would go to the office every day and sit in on the directors' meetings, but let him just try to open his mouth and the old man would slap him down quicker than a wink. I know. I was present at the humiliation more than once. You saw in his file that the first few deals Fingerhut *fils* tried to pull off after his father's death were somewhat less than successful. Fortunately, the lieutenants were on hand to snatch the coals from the fire, and fortunately Fingerhut has had the sense to listen to their advice since then. He's not a stupid man, only a bumbling one. And he's sensitive about it. There's only one way to win over Fingerhut. Flatter him.'

'You think he can be flattered into turning against Walsh?' Sam asked. Morgan made it sound easy, but Sam had a feeling it wouldn't be.

'I thought you told me that you understood human nature.'

'I said I was rarely surprised by it.'

'Then you ought to know that greater men than Maxwell Fingerhut have been won over by flattery. Good Lord, how do you think women get on, Van Nest.'

'With all due respect, when it comes to flattering a man they have advantages I don't.'

'Of course they do, but Fingerhut wants what no woman can give him. He wants to be looked up to by other men. He's tired of being the runt of the money-trust litter, if I may use a barnyard analogy for such an illustrious group. He wants us to respect him and the public to idolize him. It's up to you to show him how he can obtain those ends.

'Now for Sturgis and Corcoran. I don't think you'll have any trouble with Tom Sturgis. He and I go back a long way together. I made Tom his first million. Unfortunately, I made it for him too late. By the time he had the money to win the girl, he'd already lost her to someone else. Elias Leighton to be specific. Don't look so surprised, Sam. We were all young once. Even Edith Leighton. She was Edith Kimberly then and a real beauty. Had a great deal of charm too. She was ambitious though. Even then. You couldn't miss the ambition, though Sturgis somehow managed to. Well, Sturgis and Edith Leighton are beside the point. What matters is that Sturgis and I go back a long way together. He'd never be considering joining Walsh's camp now if I hadn't spent so much time the last few years traveling. Tom and I have lost touch, but you're going to reestablish the old bonds. You're also going to talk sense to him. Tom's smart and quick on his feet, but sometimes he lacks judgment; foresight perhaps. The way he did with Edith Leighton. Any fool could have seen the kind of woman she'd turn into, the kind of girl she was, but Tom didn't. Neither did Leighton, but that's another story. The point about Tom Sturgis is that sometimes he misses the long view. You'll have to show it to him. It shouldn't be difficult. I feel certain Sturgis will listen to reason. Especially from a partner in Morgan and Company.

'As for Corcoran . . .' Morgan pulled himself out of the chair and walked to his desk. He took a fresh cigar from the humidor, struck a match to it, and stood puffing thoughtfully. Then he turned back to Sam. 'I honestly don't know what to tell you about Corcoran.'

Sam was startled for a moment, then he put it all together – the walk to the desk, the measured speech, the way Morgan was watching him. The wily old bastard! He didn't know what to tell him. He'd done all the work up to this point, now he was going to make Sam earn his keep.

'I don't have to go over the material in the file,' Morgan went on as he lowered himself into the wing chair again. Sam couldn't help thinking he moved like an old man. He might be having a good time flexing his mind and exercising Sam's, but his body no longer gave him pleasure.

'James Corcoran is no gentleman,' Morgan went on. 'Of course, he's no Walsh either, but he came up too quickly to be polite about it. His father was a cook in a miners' camp. Poor devil was sitting right on the Comstock Lode and never made a penny out of it. Corcoran started with a grocery store. Now he owns half the municipal gas and electric companies in the country, and I don't have to tell you how many city councils and small-time politicians he bought to get them. They used to call him "Cross Their Palms" Corcoran. Of course, he's in good enough company there. The point is Corcoran wants to be in good company everywhere. He's eager to make people forget who his father was and who he was for that matter. He wants to be respectable. Mix with the right people. I imagine Mrs Corcoran and his daughter have some ideas in that area too. The point is, Corcoran is ambitious. Of course, I'm only speaking in generalities. You'll have to find out exactly what it is Corcoran wants and how we can help him get it.

'I think that about covers it, Van Nest. The launch will be ready to take you in at seven-thirty. One of Mrs Leighton's automobiles will be waiting at the dock. I imagine you'll be driving over to

Belle Isle with Elias Leighton. I noticed *Nereids* as we came in this morning. In the meantime, you might as well enjoy the afternoon. I doubt you'll have much time to enjoy yourself tonight.'

Up on deck Sam was pleased to find that Mrs Hall was nowhere in sight. Something was bothering him, something he had to work out, and he found it impossible to work out anything with Dolly Hall beside him. Of course, that was one of the things he liked about Mrs Hall. She kept all thought of business at bay. But right now, Sam wanted to think about business.

Morgan had said he was uniquely equipped for the task ahead of him. He was persuasive. He had a natural entrée onto the stage Morgan had set. There'd been a time when he was a regular visitor at Belle Isle as well as the Leighton House on Fifth Avenue, but that had been long ago. How many years now, ten, eleven? He could still remember the last time he'd been to Belle Isle, or to be accurate, the last time he'd been turned away from Belle Isle.

He wondered if Hatfield were still the Leighton major-domo. He'd liked Hatfield with his great bald dome of a head and the mint-scented breath that never quite camouflaged the smell of gin. There were times when he'd thought of Hatfield rather than Elias Leighton as the master of the house. Hatfield, at least was always on hand, and he looked the role more than Mr Leighton did. The major-domo changed three times daily until at dinner only his black vest distinguished his costume from Mr Leighton's — when Mr Leighton was at dinner.

Hatfield never answered the telephone and almost never opened the front door, but he'd opened the front door that day, and Sam suspected he'd done so under special orders. A no from Hatfield was more final than a no from one of the footmen.

'I'm sorry Mr Van Nest,' Hatfield had announced in that resonant tone and clipped accent that half the actors on Broadway would give their wax moustaches for, 'Miss Leighton is receiving no one today.'

'Did you give her my letter, Hatfield?' Sam heard the note of desperation in his voice and hated it. And himself. Had he no dignity?

'She's receiving no one, sir,' Hatfield repeated, as though it were the single line he'd been given, and he'd learned it well. He'd stood there not wanting to close the door in Sam's face, but wishing Sam would have the sense not to force him to. And Sam had stood there knowing he should leave, but unable to tear himself away. Then over Hatfield's shoulder he caught a glimpse of his own reflection in the huge gilt-framed mirror that, like the marble foyer, had been torn from a Venetian palace. He was standing with his shoulders hunched forward and his head half down. Sam straightened and put on what he hoped was a careless smile. He'd said something jaunty and careless too, though he couldn't remember what it was now. Then he'd turned and walked quickly down the long curving drive and past the gates that the gatekeeper hadn't bothered to close after he'd entered.

He hadn't gone back to Belle Isle after that. There'd been no reason to. Amelia didn't want to see him. Of course, he hadn't received an invitation to the garden party in her honor three weeks later. Amelia and her mother weren't taking any chances. They'd worked too hard to have things ruined at the last minute. It was just as well. He wouldn't have gone if he'd been invited. The afternoon of the party he'd stayed at the Reading Room and got roaring drunk. He'd ended up making a scene anyway, but not as bad a scene as he would have at Amelia's party. And at least the particular scene he'd made hadn't had any repercussions for Amelia or her engagement. Sam supposed he ought to be proud of himself for that, but he wasn't.

He turned from the railing and started down the deck at a brisk pace, his hands jammed into the pockets of his white flannel trousers. He'd come on deck to work out something about Morgan and his plan, not to think about Amelia Leighton, Lady Amelia now.

Who is Amelia? He heard the words again and saw the pretty girl with the round baby-doll eyes and the luxuriant body requisite to a chorus line. 'Who is Amelia?' The girl had asked afterward, and the words had come out with a harsh nasal twang because someone had taught her to enunciate the lyrics of a song properly but hadn't bothered to teach her to speak properly. Sam didn't suppose it mattered much how she spoke. Certainly that was the last thing he'd cared about when he'd gone backstage with two friends after

against tonight – in the case of Wainwright and Kirkland Selby implacable enemies – and of Walsh. The man who had done that would have no place in the banking firm of J. P. Morgan and Company. Certainly Morgan would not risk his son or any of the more important partners in such a dangerous game. Certainly Elias Leighton would not risk his own reputation. But they'd both risk Samuel Van Nest. He could picture Morgan calculating the odds. Such a minor risk in the long run. Who, after all, was Van Nest? Only a small cog in the great wheel Morgan kept so well oiled. The old bastard. The wily old bastard.

Sam had had little taste for the task Morgan had set him, but now he was just angry enough to carry it off. He'd carry it off, all right – for a price, and it wasn't the one Morgan had named. Sam started back to the library.

Morgan hadn't moved since Sam had left him, and Sam had the feeling from the way the old man shifted his weight in the large chair that he'd dozed off. The skin condition that was always hard to ignore looked more inflamed than ever. Morgan could keep saying he felt fine, but Sam didn't believe him.

'Did I forget something, Sam?' Morgan asked and rubbed his eyes slowly with his thumb and forefinger.

Morgan hadn't forgot anything, merely miscalculated. 'You said before that if I brought this off, when I brought this off, I'd move up in Morgan and Company.'

'Right to the top. Second in command to Jack.'

'But still second.'

'Blood is thicker than gratitude, Sam.'

'Exactly my point. And I don't want to have to rely on gratitude. Yours or Jack's. I'll head off Walsh for you.' Sam stopped for a moment. He'd decided what he wanted, but not how much he wanted. The figure came to him quickly. 'For thirty-five million.'

'That's a lot of money,' Morgan said, but he didn't sound as if he thought it was a lot of money.

'You have a reputation for generosity.'

'You mean a lot of people from old Andrew Carnegie down to all those art dealers say they've taken me because I won't bargain.'

Sam smiled and said nothing.

'Very well, Sam. Thirty-five million. Incidentally,' he went on when Sam reached the door, 'you probably could have got a little more out of me.'

Sam smiled again. 'Maybe, but you couldn't have got me to do it for any less. Thirty-five is my price, so thirty-five is the figure I mentioned. You see, I don't like to bargain either.'

II

'On afternoons like this,' Edith said, handing Harry Lehr a cup of tea, 'I always envision our little group here on the piazza as done by John Constable. Only he could have captured the Palladian perfection of the house and the peace and beauty of the grounds.'

'To say nothing of the charm and beauty of its mistress, my pet,' Harry said, setting the cup and saucer down on the glass-topped table beside him. He had taught Edith Leighton to serve a good dinner, but he could not teach her to pour a good cup of tea. It was always too weak or too strong.

'I see it as something by Sargent,' Caroline said. 'Mama in gray silk, Amelia in white, and Harry's violet vest a spark of color among the light and shadows of the piazza.'

'And we mustn't forget you, Caro,' Lehr said, tugging at the satin vest that pulled against his considerable expanse of abdomen. 'A brilliant golden rose in the gardens of Belle Isle.'

Constable and Sargent. Next would come Corot and Millet. Amelia felt as if she could recite the litany from memory. They'd been saying the same things for the past twenty years and would probably go on saying them for the next twenty. Nothing had changed while she was away, not the elaborate orchestration of time or the awful boredom it was meant to alleviate; not the stilted conversation or the spiteful gossip. They changed clothes at least three times a day and never wore the same costume twice, but they saw the same people, went through the same motions, murmured the same inanities day after day, season after season. Amelia wondered how she'd put up with it for so many years. She wondered how she'd be able to put up with it again.

'I see us all by Fragonard,' Harry went on. How had she forgotten Fragonard? The walls of her mother's bedroom were covered with magnificent examples of Fragonard's work that had decorated a château in the Loire Valley for a century until Edith had found a more suitable use for them. 'Only he,' Harry pronounced, 'could have captured the sense of imminent love – perhaps I should say *amour* – the romantic readiness of three such beautiful women.'

'Why Harry,' Amelia said, 'what a wicked thing to say to three old married ladies.'

Edith smiled at Lehr. European women always had a courtier or two in attendance, and Harry made the perfect courtier. Witty, amusing, and absolutely safe. He'd said more than once that love had wrecked more social careers than lack of money and breeding combined. 'Harry is always just a little naughty, Amelia. You know that.'

'Yes,' Amelia said. 'Just a little.'

His faded blue eyes, heavy lidded and porcine,

caught hers. 'You know I won't argue with you,
Amelia my pet. I never argue. There are three
ways of taking an insult. You can resent it and
walk out of the room, in which case you have
committed yourself to a quarrel you may later
regret. You can pretend not to hear. Discreet but
not very original. Or you can laugh and turn it into
a joke. I always choose the last. I find it the most
disarming. No one can be angry at a man who
laughs his way out of everything. And as for being
naughty, I've just done a very good turn for Mrs
Schuyler. Sky's Aunt Lydia. You know, of course,
that Kirkland Selby is staying with her. She'd
planned to give him the green room. She couldn't
give him the ocean suite because the Arch Duke
rated that, but the rose and gold rooms were too
small for Selby. And, of course, the blue room gets
no breeze at all, so she's stuck poor Vanessa
Hunter in there. Must be devilishly unpleasant for
the girl' – he noticed that Edith and Caroline were
no longer smiling and decided he'd gone far
enough – 'but what can a penniless spinster
expect. At any rate, Mrs Schuyler went into the
green room to make sure that everything was
ready for Selby, and suddenly she realized that the
painting over the bed simply wouldn't do. She'd
completely forgot about the painting. Lydia
inherited one of the best collections in Newport
from her late husband, and she doesn't see any
of them, you know. An absolute peasant when it
comes to pictures. She may have managed to
marry a Schuyler, but she didn't manage to
acquire his taste.'

'Which picture is it?' Amelia asked.

'I don't know. Just something Mr Schuyler picked up in France years ago. Not one of his more valuable acquisitions.'

'What a shame Mrs Schuyler doesn't share your taste as well as her husband's,' Amelia said.

'I told you I won't argue, sweet pet. The point is not the quality of the picture but its subject. A young girl being chased by a satyr. A particularly nasty satyr, if you ask me. And the young lady would make *September Morn* blush.'

'I warn you, Harry,' Edith said 'not one more word about *September Morn*. You know I'm not a prude, but I'm sick to death of hearing of that picture. Ever since it was shown last spring, people can talk of nothing else.'

'Only a passing reference, pet,' Harry said taking a *petit four* from the silver tray one of the footmen held out to him. 'I was merely trying to describe the picture for you without actually describing it, if you get my point. Well, you can imagine putting Kirkland Selby to sleep under something like that. The man who's built more churches than anyone in the country. Impossible. Simply impossible. Lydia sent for me immediately.'

'How we all rely on you, Harry dear,' Edith said, but she was thinking that she didn't like the idea of Lydia Schuyler's summoning Harry, and she especially didn't like the idea of Harry going so quickly. If he were not to be her exclusive property, she'd have to begin annexing someone else. She thought of Douglas Kimball again. Maybe she'd let him paint Elizabeth after all. Or better

66

still, she'd say that Elias wanted to have her
painted again. She hadn't been in years. All those
sittings would give her time to work on Kimball.
Her only fear was that he might not prove as safe
as Harry, or safe, at all, for that matter. Artists
so often had a bohemian streak, though she'd
never heard any rumors that Kimball did. He
might look it with that jet-black goatee and those
wide tartar eyes, but there'd been no talk about
him in that respect. Edith tried to remember how
old Kimball was. Harry said fifty, but when it came
to available men who might steal the limelight as
well as a few invitations from him, Harry was not
a reliable judge of age or anything else. Edith
suspected Kimball was closer to forty-five, and he
looked a good deal younger than that. He was
boyishly slim with a wiry strength that Edith
imagined many women found attractive, which
only brought her back to the question of Kimball's
safety. He'd never married, but there'd been no
scandals about women either. Not like that
dreadful business with Stanford White. She was
glad now she'd commissioned Mr Hunt rather than
White to do Belle Isle. But Kimball, she decided,
was nothing like White. She was certain he'd be
safe. She'd see to it that he was safe.

'Obviously,' Harry said, taking a second *petit
four* from the silver tray on the table, 'the picture
couldn't be replaced. It's simply huge, and we
couldn't find another that wasn't in one of the
main rooms large enough to cover the marks on
the damask wall. I never did like damask at the
seashore. Marble is so much more practical. I

suggested that Lydia simply turn the picture around for the weekend. Selby would be unlikely to turn it back, but if he did, he'd simply realize that his scruples were being respected. Lydia was horrified. "And have Kirkland Selby and everyone else say that Lydia Schuyler has to turn her pictures to the wall when guests come! I should say not." Then it came to me. We'd dress the picture. Clothe the young lady being pursued and turn her pursuer into a docile pony. The last was no easy trick. The artists were still working when I left. I only hope they finish before Selby arrives.'

'Harry, my dear,' Edith said, 'you're inspired. Tell me, whom did Lydia find to repaint her picture on Saturday afternoon?'

'She telephoned Douglas Kimball. He's staying with the Goelets, you know. Yes, of course you know. He's dining with us tonight, isn't he? But Kimball refused. She offered him five thousand dollars, ten, finally fifteen. After all, it isn't as if it will be one of his pictures and worth anything when he's finished. But he still refused. I gather from the way Lydia looked when she came back from the telephone closet that he wasn't very polite in his refusal either. I thought we were back at square one until I remembered that awful woman Mrs Corcoran . . .'

Edith shot him a look. 'Oh, sweet pet, how could I? I simply forgot she was dining with us too.'

'Simply as a favor to Mr Leighton.'

'So you explained.' Harry seemed to have forgot his anecdote for the moment. 'I wonder what Elias and that man Corcoran are cooking up. Something shamefully lucrative, I'm sure. Now you mustn't forget your old friends, Edith dear. Bessie's money is all in the most dreadfully conservative family investments. I'd love to get it into something that's absolutely filthy with profit. Keep that in mind when you find out what your husband and Corcoran are up to, won't you, pet? Now where was I? Oh, yes, I remembered that Mrs Corcoran had a whole stable of Italian artists here painting murals on every wall in sight. I can't imagine, or rather I can imagine, what horrors she's perpetrating on that perfectly lovely cottage she bought. Needless to say, Mrs Corcoran was overjoyed to be able to help. She had the artists sent over immediately in her Peerless. And said she wouldn't think of letting Mrs Schuyler pay them. She'd take care of that. "What are friends for?" was the ingenuous way she phrased it. Lydia's going to have to be careful after this. That Corcoran woman got her foot – or rather her painters' feet – in the door this afternoon, and she's going to be pushing to open it wider and wider. I told Lydia she'll be calling all the time, dressed up like . . . well, we all know like what sort of woman, my pets. Did you see her at the Casino yesterday? I almost fell out of the second-floor window laughing. Taffeta with feathers, yes feathers, on the skirt. And her daughter decked out in jewels elaborate enough for an eighty-year-old dowager – when everyone knows a young girl should never wear more than pearls. Well, what can one say except breeding will out.'

'Every woman can't have the advantage of your expert advice, Harry,' Amelia said.

'More's the pity,' he sighed, and took another cake. There was something obscene about the way he savored it behind thick closed lips.

'I think it's wonderful,' Caroline said, 'the interest you take in Bessie's clothes.' She was thinking that Schuyler was always more interested in what she wasn't wearing than what she was.

'Worth says I have the best taste he's ever seen in a man,' Harry answered. 'I might add, my dear Amelia' – the pale eyes darted to her – 'that Duringham runs me a close second. Remember that delightful afternoon we spent at Worth's?'

She remembered it all right. It was the first time Charles had taken her to Paris, and they'd gone straight to Worth's where they'd run into Harry and his wife, Bessie. At first Amelia hadn't paid much attention to the Lehrs. She was too angry at Charles. For two hours he vetoed every gown she liked and kept insisting on his own choices. They were always the most opulent gowns, but not, Amelia was convinced, the most flattering. When she and Charles had emerged from the private show room, the Lehrs were still there, and Amelia could tell from their conversation with Worth that Harry, like Charles, was the one who'd done the choosing. The two men had decided they needed an aperitif and gone off together, arm in arm, discussing the costumes they'd chosen.

Bessie had taken her back to the Ritz in her carriage and asked on the way if she'd like to stop for tea at the house she and Harry had taken. But Amelia had wanted to escape and she'd suspected from the way Bessie's eyes never met hers that the invitation had been more formal than sincere.

'The thing about dressing well,' Harry was saying, 'is that it has nothing to do with money. That's what someone like Mrs Corcoran will never understand. Didn't I dress just as well before I married Bessie, and I was poor as a church mouse then.' Harry had not forgotten that in those days Wetzel had made his clothes for nothing and Black, Starr and Frost had loaned him watches and studs and the like just for the honor – and profit – of having Harry drop their names when his new suit or stick pin was admired. Nor had he forgotten the cellar full of George Kessler's champagne that Edith had bought as a result of Mr Kessler's yearly six-thousand-dollar gift to Harry. But he saw no need to mention any of that. 'No, my pet, it isn't money that counts, it's style. Though too often the lack of the first is used as an excuse for the absence of the second. I saw Vanessa Hunter at Lydia's. She looked worse than ever. No matter how much Vanessa makes them over, Lydia's hand-me-downs don't do a thing for her.' There, he thought. I've served the dish up. Now they can do the carving.

'She was no great beauty to begin with,' Edith observed.

'I always thought she was rather pretty,' Amelia said. 'That thick dark hair and those broad cheekbones. She looks like a gypsy.'

'Another of your exotic flowers, no doubt.'

71

There was no mistaking the distaste in Edith's voice.

'I've always thought she looked more like a peasant,' Caroline said lifting her face a little as she might lift her skirts crossing a mud puddle.

'She's no peasant,' Harry said. 'She's a Livingston on her mother's side and a Penrose as well as a Hunter on her father's. It's just a shame old Penrose Hunter had such bad luck with women and with horses. Spent his entire fortune on them and they never seemed to come in for him. Not even Vanessa's mother. Ran off with an actor when Vanessa was only a year old.'

'Exactly my point,' Edith said. 'I don't care if she is a Livingston and a Penrose and a Hunter. There's bad blood there. On both sides, as you've just pointed out. And Vanessa's no better. I'm not taken in by that air of quiet humility she wears to keep Lydia Schuyler inviting her back every summer and everyone in New York asking her where she has no right to be. I'm not taken in at all.'

'She's no better than her mother or her father,' Caroline said.

'Carrie, you don't mean that,' Amelia said.

Caroline turned to her sister, and Amelia noticed the two circles of red on her cheeks. She would have looked like a clown if she hadn't been so angry. 'You don't know anything about her,' Caroline said sharply. 'You've been away for so long you don't know the first thing about what's going on.'

So that was it, Amelia thought. Caroline was

right. She'd been away for too long. She only wondered if her mother and Carrie were right about Sky and Vanessa Hunter or if the whole thing were merely a figment of their fevered imaginations. After all, they had to do something to pass the interminable hours.

'I'm sorry,' Amelia said.

No one, not even Harry, asked what she was sorry for. She'd been leaning against the wall of the piazza, and now she turned to the view of the ocean. Behind her she heard them discussing the evening ahead.

'Have you heard who it's to be?' Harry asked.

'What do you mean?' Edith looked off across the garden as if she were just a little bored by Harry. She knew he was referring to the entertainer Mrs Oelrichs had engaged for the ball tonight, and she was fairly sure Harry knew who it was, but she would not give him the satisfaction of being curious.

'Tessie's performer, of course. Everyone's guessing.'

'Everyone except you, Harry.'

'I do have my suspicions.'

'Actually, I don't much care who Tessie has. Whatever entertainment she's planned can't possibly compare with my ball last December. Engelbert Humperdinck and Giacomo Puccini in one night.'

'I admit Tessie will have to go some distance to rival you there, sweet pet,' Harry said, but he was still smiling, and Edith wondered how far Tessie Oelrichs had succeeded in going. Thank heavens

Diaghilev and his Ballet Russe had returned to Europe:

'What about the favors?' Harry asked, holding his tea cup out for the footman. Harry was especially interested in the favors Edith had chosen for her dinner. At first she'd planned to place a black pearl in one of the dozen oysters served to each guest until he reminded her there were no r's in July. The oysters had been changed to soft clams *à l'anncienne*, and Harry had suggested a small bonsai plant before each place from which would hang various pins and charms for the women and jeweled stick pins for the men. When the jewels arrived, however, Edith insisted they were not the ones she'd chosen. She had wired Tiffany immediately, and the store had wired back that one of their men would arrive with a new selection of jewels by Saturday morning.

'I trust your man from Tiffany arrived,' Harry said.

'Wickert brought the jewels,' Edith said. 'I think these are quite satisfactory, although one of the . . .'

Amelia had stopped listening. She'd been hearing about the favors for days now. In the distance she could see a figure coming up the Cliff Walk. She could tell from the long-legged, athletic stride – like her own, people used to say when they were younger – that it was Elizabeth.

When Lizzy reached the gate she turned back and waved with the large straw hat she'd been carrying. Then, as if remembering that she was in full view of the house, she dropped her hand suddenly and started toward the house. She was walking slowly, reluctantly, Amelia thought, and turned her attention back to Harry and her mother, who had worked their way from the favors to the guest list. Harry was as unsympathetic as her mother about Mr Van Rensaleer's broken leg.

'But who will you find, my pet. True it's Saturday and there are plenty of men in town – the harbor is absolutely full up with boats – but I'm sure everyone acceptable is already engaged to dine.'

'We've already solved the problem,' Edith said calmly. It did not hurt to remind Harry that, unlike Lydia Schuyler she could get along without him. 'Elizabeth remembered an officer she'd played bridge with at Mrs Norton's. Admiral Atherton's nephew, I believe.'

Elizabeth reached the stairs of the piazza just in time to hear the last. She smiled but did not comment on her mother's vetting of Lieutenant Atherton.

'Ah, our little savior herself,' Harry said. 'You're looking blissful, pet.'

Amelia had been thinking the same thing. Elizabeth's color was even higher than usual, and there was a remarkable freshness about her. Lizzy looked like Venus rising from the sea or, at the very least, emerging from her bath. Amelia wondered if she'd ever looked that fresh or that young.

'I take it you've just left Sydney,' Harry said.

'No, I haven't seen Sydney. I was out on the Cliff Walk.'

'Alone?' Edith asked.

'Quite alone.'

Amelia watched as her sister's eyes held her mother's. Perhaps Elizabeth wasn't as young as she'd thought. At least she had the sense to avoid a confrontation. Amelia had never been that clever. It seemed now that she'd always been provoking arguments about one thing or another though sometimes she'd known they were hopeless. She remembered that afternoon she'd come home from the Brearley and announced she wanted to go to college. Edith would not hear of it. She reminded Amelia that she had a single task in life, to marry early and well. Four years at some dangerously liberal school where she might pick up all kinds of ideas and, worse still, meet all kinds of people could only deflect her from that purpose. During her last year at the Brearley, Amelia had tried a variety of arguments and ploys, but Edith had remained firm. College was no place for a girl like Amelia.

Then the winter she'd come out, the winter she'd attended ninety-seven dinners and dances, there'd been all the bickering over Sam Van Nest. It had got worse the following summer when she'd returned from the cruise on her father's boat and found herself trapped in Edith's plans for her marriage to Duringham.

Of her own friends only those who could be relied upon to take the proper attitude were admitted to the house. When Amelia remained intransigent, one of Edith's contemporaries would remind her of the delicate state of her mother's health. At those moments everyone seemed to forget that Edith prided herself on never having been sick a day in her life. She had as little patience with physical infirmity as with moral.

Elias might have helped that summer, but he'd chosen instead to deposit her in New York and go off again on *Nereids* for an around-the-world cruise. Edith did not meddle in his business or personal affairs, and he did not interfere with her management of the girls' lives. As for her sisters, Elizabeth was only ten at the time, and Caroline, her most logical ally, had been almost as excited about the match as Edith.

'Think of it, Amelia that great castle and the grounds. Just imagine all those peasants tugging their forelocks and murmuring "Your Grace" as you walk by. You'll be presented at court and painted and cast in bronze and sculpted in marble and immortalized as the tenth Duchess of Duringham.

'You will have,' Edith added, 'enormous power.'

'I don't want enormous power. I want to marry someone I love, someone who loves me. You know he doesn't care about me. All he wants is Father's money.'

'It is up to you to make him care,' her mother said.

'That won't be difficult,' Caroline added, certain that given the chance she could make Duringham care for her, though when she'd had the opportunity before her own marriage, he'd remained remarkably unimpressed. 'And it certainly won't be unpleasant. The duke's terribly handsome. It isn't as if he were that dreadful Marlborough. Poor Consuelo Vanderbilt. He barely comes up to her nose. What an absurd couple they make, but you'll look splendid with Duringham. He's inches taller and terribly robust. Powerful really. I'd look like a frail flower beside him, but you've got that nice racy look that will complement him perfectly. You'll look smashing in all the wedding pictures and portraits.'

'I won't look smashing at all because I have no intention of marrying him.'

They'd been sitting in Edith's bedroom while the maid dressed her hair. 'That's all for now, Sarah,' Edith said, without looking at any of them. When the girl had left the room she turned to Amelia. Her face was a mask of perfect disdain. 'And what do you plan to do? Live out your years with me as an old maid?'

'Are you saying I'm not welcome to stay with you?'

'I'm saying the idea of having as a guest in my house a girl so foolish she'd rather be an anonymous old maid than the Duchess of Duringham fills me with distaste.'

'At least I know where I stand,' Amelia said, with more bravado than she felt. 'Still, if I don't marry Duringham, it doesn't mean I won't marry at all.'

'Have you had any other offers?' The narrow lips turned up in a superior smile. 'Serious offers, I mean. I don't consider proposals from a dancing master in Vienna or that dreary minister's son serious offers.'

'But, Mama, your own grandfather was a minister,' Amelia protested.

'That's an entirely different matter. In those days it was a respectable calling.'

'Isn't it respectable anymore?'

'Don't be impertinent, Amelia. It's still respectable, it's simply no longer sufficiently successful. My father was a judge, but what is even a judge to a duke? If you have a better offer than the duke's, I'd like to hear about it.' Edith's eyes held hers in challenge.

'When you say better you mean in terms of Burke's Peerage, but perhaps better means something else to me.'

'Or someone else,' Edith said. 'You're thinking of the Van Nest boy, of course.'

'I didn't say that.'

Edith turned back to the mirror. 'You didn't have to. I suppose you think he's not after your money. I suppose you think he loves you for yourself.'

'Is that so impossible?'

'You're a pretty girl, Amelia – not as pretty as Caroline, but pretty – but do you really think your rather limited beauty overshadows the Leighton fortune. Especially for a young man from one of those old Knickerbocker families with more quarters than dollars.'

'He's not a horse, Mama.'

'No, but he has a taste for horses. Expensive hunters and polo ponies as I understand it. And for large yachts. I expect he'll want more than that small skiff he takes you sailing in now. At least

he will if he thinks your father's money will
provide it.'

'Sam is doing perfectly well on his own.'

'Perfectly well? He has a job – not a position,
Amelia, a job – with Mr Morgan. I don't call that
doing well. And I don't expect Samuel Van Nest
to do well. He has drive, I'll give you that. Why,
I imagine nothing can stop him from walking off
with some hunt cup or sailing trophy once he's set
his mind to it, but that's the sort of drive only a
very rich man can afford, and unfortunately your
Mr Van Nest has the income if not the tastes of
a poor man. He'll have to marry well. Someone
with a fortune. And you have a fortune, child.
What else do you imagine is your attraction in Mr
Van Nest's eyes?'

'It's my only attraction in Duringham's eyes. We
know that.'

'Perhaps, but at least Duringham has something
to offer in return. What does Mr Van Nest have
except an old New York name that's growing
dreadfully threadbare?' Edith caught her
daughter's eyes in the mirror. 'And don't tell me
love, Amelia. I trust I've already made myself
clear on that point. You'll see. Once Samuel Van
Nest finds out that I'll cut you off without a penny
if he marries you – your father will back me up
on that – his ardor will cool considerably. In fact,
I'd be surprised if he even called again.'

Amelia had no answer for her mother then, but
she knew that with time, Sam would prove he
cared for her rather than her money. She'd been
sure of that, but she'd been wrong. Sam had never

called on her again. He hadn't even answered the letter she'd bribed one of the footmen to take to him. And then within two weeks she'd found herself engaged to Duringham.

The duke had been in Newport for a month when she and Edith had argued about Sam, a month of hours spent in the duke's company. Everything he said to her was perfectly polite, but beneath the words Amelia sensed a coldness and, worse still, a condescension. It had not taken long for her to decipher the unspoken message. I am heir to one of England's oldest and greatest titles and the castle, always the castle Amelia was to learn, that accompanies it; you are an unimportant American girl whose father was fortunate enough to make a great deal of money. On one side stood England, its history, its law, its greatness; on the other an accident of fate accomplished by means to which no English gentleman would ever stoop. When he accompanied her to Bailey's Beach, when he gave her his arm to go into dinner, when he handed her into a carriage for one of the coaching parties, Duringham always managed to make his importance and her unworthiness clear.

It was only a few days after her argument with Edith that Duringham proposed. He arrived early that day, a little before eleven, and Amelia was not yet down. Edith had come to her room herself rather than sending a maid, and the minute Amelia saw her mother's face, mobile in its excitement rather than composed in its customary mask, she'd known what was about to happen. She supposed she should have known ever since she'd come home from South America, but she'd kept telling herself it wasn't possible. She'd told herself Duringham was too cool to her; she'd told herself her mother wasn't that cruel; she'd told herself something so terrible simply couldn't happen to her. But now she knew it was going to. Duringham was going to propose, and she was supposed to accept.

'You know what I expect of you,' Edith said arranging the folds of her daughter's white silk morning dress as if it were a bridal train. Then she'd taken a step back, looked Amelia up and down slowly, and pushed her from the room.

Amelia had walked down the great staircase slowly, as if Duringham might tire of waiting for her and leave. She could still feel her mother's eyes on her. Foolish to worry how she looked. Charles wouldn't care how she looked. She doubted he even knew the color of her eyes. Sam Van Nest knew the color of her eyes. 'Brown when you're serious,' he'd said once. 'But when you're excited the green lights go on. Like fireworks.' Amelia turned the wide landing and started down the last flight of wide marble steps that led to the main floor. She wasn't going to think of Sam. Not when it was so obvious Sam wasn't thinking of her.

Behind her was the huge stained-glass window depicting great moments in the history of European royalty. The window reached all the way to the third floor and had a lot of yellow in it. On sunny mornings like this it flooded the marble entrance hall with color so that the whole area appeared to be washed with gold. It usually made her feel warm, but this morning she felt a definite chill, though there was none in the air.

In the music room she found Duringham standing at the piano looking over the music on the rack. For a moment before he looked up she saw his face in profile. Did he find Brahms wanting too, or only the fact that Brahms had sunk so low as to enter Belle Isle? Perhaps he imagined the composer and himself brothers in decline.

He crossed the room to her quickly and took her hand in his two large ones. It would have been a gesture of affection if only he'd been looking at her rather than an inch or two above her head.

'I came early purposely.' His voice was strong; commanding she supposed. 'I wanted a chance to speak to you alone.' He led her to one of the red satin chairs before the fireplace and without word or gesture managed to indicate that she was to sit.

He took a few steps back until he was standing before the hearth facing her. The pearl-gray suit echoed the marble of the mantel, and the yellow rose in his lapel was as bright as the gilt trim. Had he dressed with the setting in mind?

'Amelia,' he began, his hands clasped behind him, his eyes still focused somewhere above her own, 'surely you know why I'm here.' The words sounded as if he were somehow shy of broaching the subject, but there was no fear in his voice. It resounded with confidence. The voice went on, but Amelia had stopped paying attention to what it was saying. Something about Thynnleigh, something about Duringham's position, something about the obligations attendant to that position. He had that British habit of speaking without opening his mouth, and the full lips barely moved beneath the sandy moustache. He was perfect, she thought, exactly right, every inch the dashing duke that *Town Topics* called him, tall, strapping, with a strong neck and powerful shoulders that could support the weight of the realm. The face was too broad, the nose not quite sharp enough to be what was generally called aristocratic, but somehow Charles managed to look patrician despite his features. Perhaps it was his arrogance.

Charles was winding down now. He'd finished with his obligations, run through those of his prospective wife, and enumerated her requisite traits. Now he'd reached the personal part, as if there were anything personal in this exchange. No, not exchange. She hadn't said a word.

The full lips closed. The sandy moustache ceased moving. Amelia realized he was finished. He had the honor of asking her to be his wife, and now he was finished.

She tried to remember what he'd said. He hadn't mentioned love. She was sure of that. She seemed to recall the words *affection* and *respect*, but he hadn't said love.

Well, what of it? Sam Van Nest had mentioned love. Twice. The first time had been the night after she'd come home from the cruise on *Nereids*, and he'd come to the house in town. He'd spoken with an urgency then as if he'd been thinking of it all the time she'd been away. The second time had been only two weeks ago. Amelia caught herself. There was no point in thinking about Sam. He obviously hadn't meant it either time. She supposed she ought to be grateful to Duringham for sparing her the hypocrisy. Well, she might be grateful, but she wouldn't be acquiescent. She wouldn't marry him.

'I'm flattered,' she began, 'and honored.' Oh, they were both so full of honor this morning. 'But . . .' Did she say she simply didn't love him?

The 'but' must have gone off in his head like an alarm. He was looking at her now, not above her head or beyond it, but right at her, and the ice-blue eyes were incredulous.

Was the girl half-witted? Didn't she know everything had been arranged? Didn't she know the agreements had been drawn up? His own attorney and Elias Leighton's had settled the matter during a week of meetings in New York.

She was apologizing now. Did she think she'd actually offended him? 'All I ask,' he cut her off in mid sentence, 'is that you consider my proposal, Amelia. You needn't say yes now. I ask only that you don't say no.'

He left the room abruptly, with anger, Amelia thought, and he must have run into her mother on his way out of the house because Edith came bursting into the music room like a northeaster howling down on the island.

'Did I understand the duke correctly? Is it possible you're a bigger fool than I thought?'

'I've told you over and over, Mama. I won't marry him.'

'*You've* told me over and over. As if you had anything to say about it. Do you understand the lengths I've gone to, the diplomatic maneuverings, the delicate negotiations? I've worked myself to distraction to make you the Duchess of Duringham, and now you fling it all back in my face.'

'I never wanted . . .'

'Be quiet!' Edith screamed. 'I don't want to hear your voice. I don't want to see your face. I can't stand the sight of you, you stupid, stupid child. But you'll learn. You'll learn if you have to spend the rest of the season locked in your room.'

'But Mama,' Amelia began, finally frightened in the face of her mother's rage.

'I told you not to speak,' Edith shouted grabbing Amelia by the wrist, 'and I meant it. I don't want to hear another word from you.' Edith dragged her from the room, across the front hall, and up the wide staircase. Amelia had always thought of her mother as physically delicate, but she was dragging her along, pulling with a force from which there was no escape, and all the time she kept shouting, hurling threats at Amelia, barking orders at the servants. One minute there was the noise of her mother's screams and Hatfield's answers, of Lizzy running into the hall crying only to be pulled back into her room by *mademoiselle*, and servants running back and forth in terror. The next minute there was only the ominous silence of her room. She heard the key turn in the lock and her mother telling the footman to remain outside Miss Amelia's door for the rest of the day.

Her mother had actually locked her in her room and stationed a guard outside it. It was all too ludicrous to believe, but it was happening.

No one came to her for the rest of that day. Amelia had expected a maid with a tray first at lunch time then in the evening, but apparently her mother intended to starve her into submission. And she'd been foolish enough to contemplate a hunger strike like the suffragists.

It was after midnight when she heard the key turning in the lock again. Caroline looked pale and beautiful in a blue silk dressing gown. 'Mama's been crying all night,' she said in a hushed voice.

'*Mama*'s been crying all night!' Weren't her red eyes even visible, Amelia wondered.

'I'm afraid she's going to make herself ill.'

Sitting up in bed, Amelia hugged her knees to her and said nothing.

'Why won't you marry him' Caroline demanded in a louder voice. 'It would solve everything if you'd marry him.'

Amelia looked up at her sister still standing beside the bed. 'I don't love him, Carrie.'

'He's a duke.'

'Would you have married him? Instead of Sky? Would you have married Duringham if you hadn't loved him and had loved Sky?'

'But Mama wanted me to marry Sky. It was the right thing for me to do.'

'Is that why you did it?'

Caroline turned from the bed and began pacing the room. 'What I did or why has nothing to do with it. Mama wants you to marry Duringham.

87

She's arranged everything. And now you're upsetting everything. Mama's been crying all night. Sky and I had to cancel our plans. Hatfield's turning everyone away. You've set the whole house upside down. And for nothing. You'll have to marry him in the end, you know.'

'I won't,' Amelia said. She was still hugging her knees to her and she could feel her nails digging into the flesh of her thighs. 'I don't care how long she keeps me locked up here, I won't.'

Caroline moved to the door. 'You will, Amelia. And if you have any sense you'll do it before you get all pale and skinny and pathetic looking locked away here. The minute you say yes there are going to be a million parties, and if I were you, I'd want to look my best for them.'

It was close to dawn by the time Amelia fell asleep, but even then Duringham tramped through her dreams irreverently. He kept telling her how happy they'd be, but all the time he seemed to be laughing at her.

At ten o'clock the next morning the door to her room was opened again. Her maid, Ellen, said Mr Lehr was waiting downstairs to see her. Amelia said she had no intention of seeing him. Ellen simply held her dressing gown for her and said Madame had ordered her to show Mr Lehr up.

Harry entered the room like a mourner approaching the gravesite. His step was deliberate and the pale piglike eyes were serious under half-closed lids. Clearly he appreciated the solemnity of the drama and his role in it.

'Good morning, Amelia. You're not looking well

this morning, but you're looking better than your dear mother. She's prostrate with grief.'

'But not too prostrate to give orders that you're to see me.' She hadn't meant to sound cruel, but Harry always brought out the worst in her. Of all the emissaries her mother might have sent, he was the one most likely to drive her to intransigence.

Harry shook his head sadly. 'She only wants what's best for you, and she was hoping I might make you see what that is.'

'I can't imagine how.'

Harry sat in one of the chairs before the windows open to the morning breeze and crossed his legs. The fabric of his trousers pulled against his thick thighs, and Amelia turned her eyes away. 'Because, my dear Amelia, I'm a man of the world. Not a romantic child like you or an ambitious boy like your friend Mr Van Nest . . .'

'Sam has nothing to do with this.'

'. . . but a man of the world who understands its realities, and one of those realities is the marriage of convenience. I ought to know. I made a most successful one.'

'That's a terrible thing to say.'

'Terrible? I can't imagine why. Bessie and I are quite happy together. I'm very good to her. I've certainly made her life more pleasant. Do you think she'd be accepted in the houses here or the courts in Europe she has been without me? Not for a minute. She had an old name and money, but not enough of either to get on without my style. It's I who have made her welcome in those places. And she, in turn, has enabled me to live well. I can't abide not living well. So you see, we've each done the other a good turn, and we're both quite happy.'

'I'd like to hear Bessie say that.'

'You can take my word for it, pet.'

Amelia did not answer that she would take Harry's word for nothing. There was no point in arguing with him. The more she talked, the longer he'd go on, and all she wanted was to get rid of him. It was bad enough being held prisoner without having to share her cell with Harry Lehr.

Harry was only the first of a long line of visitors. All of them had, of course, been selected by Edith. And all of them came armed with the same double-barreled argument. She was making her mother ill. She was a foolish child throwing away a chance most girls would sell their souls for.

'Perhaps those girls don't have souls,' Amelia snapped at her Aunt Gertrude, her father's sister who had more in common with her mother.

'You always did take yourself too seriously, Amelia. Do you think you're the only girl with sensibilities or scruples? Do you think other girls – many of them prettier and brighter than you – haven't hesitated to accept the husband chosen for them? But they have accepted because, in the long run, they've recognized the wisdom of their elders' choices. Even I,' Gertrude said, 'was such a girl once. And I'm glad I finally listened to my mother. The man I'd chosen to marry, a penniless fellow who wanted to write, drank himself to death years ago. Your Uncle Daniel, as you know, left me a considerable fortune.'

It went on that way for three days. Amelia was getting trays now to keep up her strength and receiving visitors to wear down her resistance. Never was still never, but she no longer managed to put as much force in the word. Reports of her mother's health grew worse. There were hints that the strain would prove too great for her heart. Amelia was afraid to believe them and afraid not to. There was no discovering the truth. She had no contact with the outside world. This time the servants could not even be bribed to carry a message, though Amelia wasn't sure to whom she'd send one if she had the chance. Perhaps her father, but she doubted he could or would help. Elias must have been beaten down before she'd been. Hadn't he agreed to part with the millions that would bring her mother the title?

The last and most surprising visitor was Elizabeth. Caroline had been in and out of the room regularly during Amelia's imprisonment, sometimes sympathetic, occasionally annoyed, often impatient, but Lizzy had not been permitted near the pariah until the morning of her capitulation. She came hurtling into the room like a small white organdie whirlwind. 'Amelia, Amelia, are you all right?'

Amelia looked down at the awkward girl clinging to her waist. 'I'm fine,' she lied. After all, what else could she say to a ten-year-old child.

'It's so scary,' Elizabeth went on, releasing her waist, but still holding her hand. 'They wouldn't let me see you at all, and mean old *mademoiselle* said Mama was going to keep you locked up until you came to your senses – whatever that meant – and there've been all sorts of people in and out of the house, but not the way they usually are. Nobody comes to lunch or tea or anything like that. They simply come one by one and go into Mama's room and then after a while they come out shaking their heads and looking just awful.'

'Have you seen Mama?'

'Aunt Gertrude took me in last night. It was just terrible. Mama's face was all white, and she didn't even open her eyes while I was there. She just lay there on the bed. Not sitting up with all her lace pillows the way she does in the morning when Miss Wilkens takes letters and things from her, but lying back as if she were going to sleep – only it seemed much worse than that. She lifted her hand a little and said I was to take it. It was awful, Amelia. So cold. And then she said no matter what happened I should be a good girl and listen to Caroline. And she said it in a funny voice. Not like she was angry or even telling me to do something, but as if she were asking a favor. And then Aunt Gertrude said she mustn't upset herself and sent me away.

'I wanted to come see you right after that, but they wouldn't let me. And no one else will explain anything. Carrie's always off somewhere whispering with Aunt Gertrude and Mr Lehr and the others. Except when she and Sky are fighting. I heard them screaming the other night. About you and the duke. Sky said it was inhuman, whatever that means. Oh, Amelia, I don't understand it. What's going to happen?'

'I don't know, Lizzy.'

'Is Mama going to die?'

'What?'

'Aunt Gertrude said she might. She said it right after Dr Quarrels left. Just a little while ago. She was talking to Carrie, and I don't think she knew I was in the room, but when I started to cry, she told me not to pay any attention to what she'd said and that's when she told me I could come see you. Carrie said I shouldn't repeat anything I'd heard, but I had to tell you, Amelia. There's no one else I can tell, and I'm so afraid.'

'Carrie really said you shouldn't repeat anything to me?' Amelia asked.

Lizzy nodded her head. 'She said you were upset enough without knowing what you were doing to Mama. Oh, Amelia, what's going to happen? Please tell me what's going to happen.'

Amelia was still holding Elizabeth's hand, and now she drew her close and stroked the thick dark hair. 'Nothing's going to happen, Lizzy. Except Mama's going to let me out of here, and then everything will go back to normal.'

Things went back to normal for everyone at Belle Isle except Amelia. Things would never be normal for her again. She'd suspected that the day she'd told Edith she'd marry Duringham after all, and the intervening years had proved her right.'

III

Kimball reached the end of the Cliff Walk and stood staring out at the ocean while he debated his options. He had no inclination for the formal afternoon drive on Bellevue Avenue or the reception on the lawn of Beaulieu. He'd lived among the rich for a good many years now and he'd spent a great deal of time in Newport, but he still didn't understand how they did it, how they went on day after day, battling the tedium and seeming to enjoy the battle. He'd always considered himself a tolerant man, except when it came to bad art, and he told himself there was no reason why the hosts who'd thought up the costume picnic, a definite improvement over the everyday picnic they all agreed, or the servants' ball where the guests came as their own butlers and maids, should not be proud of themselves. He'd lived off, as well as among, the rich for too long to criticize, Kimball told himself, and for a long time he'd regarded Newport as merely childish. It was a nursery filled with toys and free of nannies. But lately he'd come to see that its inhabitants, like children in an unsupervised nursery, could do a great deal of damage.

It was not something he wanted to think about at the moment, and he debated dropping in at the Reading Room. He could get a good stiff whiskey there, and though he wasn't a member, he knew he'd be a welcome guest. The Reading Room was a necessary retreat from female Newport, but like so many exclusive men's clubs that served as retreats it wasn't a very stimulating one. The same old walrus-faced millionaires and aging dandies sat around telling the same old stories and tying on the same old mild drunks day after day, summer after summer. Occasionally someone got drunker or more restless than usual and managed to tear the fabric of respectability that hung over the yellow wooden building as limply as the lace curtains in the windows. There was the time old James Gordon Bennett convinced that English polo player to ride his horse up the stairs and into the front drawing room, but Bennett had resigned from the club after that and gone to live in Europe. Kimball had been too young and too obscure to be present at that bit of hellraising, but he remembered another, about ten years ago. That one had to do with Sam Van Nest and in view of his own position now, Kimball found the incident ominous.

He'd been staying with the Townleys while he painted Mrs Townley and her two daughters. One looked like a Pekingese, the other was merely dyspeptic. Even now Kimball could remember how her stomach had growled and raged throughout the sittings. It had been the summer everyone had stopped comparing him to Sargent and begun listing their differences, as if suddenly Douglas Kimball could stand on his own merit. But Kimball knew the most important difference was that Sargent had announced he would no longer paint the wives and daughters of the rich. Lucky man.

Mr Townley had told him to feel free to visit the Reading Room whenever the rest of Newport became too much for him. By the rest of Newport he meant, and Douglas understood, the Townley women. That afternoon they'd been too much indeed. The fuss of getting them off to the garden reception at Belle Isle in honor of Amelia Leighton and the English duke she'd snared was more than enough to drive Douglas to the Reading Room. It had been empty except for the Van Nest boy. Kimball had met him once or twice in the past and rather liked him if for no reason other than, unlike most of his contemporaries, he seemed to have noticed what was hanging on the walls of the castles and châteaux and museums of Europe and even the houses here and in New York. It was not, however, art Van Nest had on his mind that afternoon. Kimball found him alone on the lower piazza with a half-empty bottle of whiskey beside him and a glassy look in his eyes.

'Care to join me?' Van Nest took his long legs from the white wicker chair opposite his own and reached for the bottle on the table beside him. He poured a glass for the artist and refilled his own. 'Glad you're here, Kimball.'

'Honored.' Douglas lifted his glass toward Sam.

'Wanted to toast and can't propose a toast alone.'

'All right,' Douglas said. 'What are we toasting?'

'Women. The fair sex.' Sam took a long swallow. 'Their fine sensibilities.' Another swallow. 'Their delicate natures.' A third. 'Their essential honesty.' He finished off the drink, and refilled his glass.

'I believe I detect a note of irony in your toast.'

Sam lifted his glass again. 'And now to "nice girls." Not to women in general, but to that special class, branch, subdivision known as "nice girls." They're the worst of the lot. To "nice girls" and their boundless hypocrisy.'

'They can't all be bad.'

Sam looked across the tree-shaded lawn toward Bellevue Avenue and something at the lower corner of his mouth moved, almost like a tic. 'Can't they though? Listen to me, Kimball. Don't be taken in by any of them. Oh, sure, some of them pretend they're different. Special. "Nice." But they're all the same. You find some chorus girl and she wants a fur cape or a diamond bracelet. But the "nice girl," the nice girl shoots higher. She won't settle for the fur or the bracelet. She wants the whole fortune. And if she's already got that, then how about a title? How about an English dukedom?' Sam had been leaning back so the chair was balanced on two legs and as he came forward, the front legs hit the wooden floor with a sharp sound. 'Or a French or German or Russian one,' he added lamely.

'I knew a girl in New Haven, Kimball.' Actually Sam hadn't really known her, only of her. His experience with women had been considerably more limited than that of the roommate who'd regaled him with stories of the pretty and acquiescent girl he'd found on a train returning from spring vacation their sophomore year, but whether the story was his or his roommate's, it seemed applicable at the moment. 'Beautiful brunette. Just like something out of one of your friend Gibson's pictures.' If Kimball the artist was offended at being linked with Charles Dana Gibson, Kimball the gentleman was not about to say so. 'She liked nice things. Oh, not the fur cape or diamond bracelet kind of things. She knew she wasn't going to get that from an undergraduate. But a gold locket or a new dress or just a good dinner with champagne and all the works. She made no bones about it. She liked nice things and she was willing to do what was necessary to get them. You see, she wasn't a hypocrite. But you take our "nice girls" . . .'

'Since when did they become ours?' Kimball laughed. He knew Van Nest was feeling rotten and now he knew why, but he knew too that it was important he pretend he didn't. It was important they both pretend the conversation was hypothetical and the 'nice girl' generic rather than specific.

'What I want to know is why don't they just come out and say what it is they want. Like that little girl in New Haven. Why don't they just come out and say "I'd like to be a duchess or a marquise or a princess and be presented to the King of England or the Czar of Russia or any of those old blue beards . . ."'

99

'You're mixing your metaphors, Van Nest. They have blue blood and gray beards.'

Sam stood and walked to the railing of the piazza. Kimball watched the play of sunlight on Van Nest's face as he lifted it to down the last of his drink. He saw it all as it would look on canvas, a mosaic of lines and planes, light and shadow. He had an interesting face, an unusual face despite the regular features, more unusual certainly than his monologue which Kimball had heard in a variety of forms over the years. He wondered idly if he fell prey to these lectures so often because other men thought him naive about women, or knowledgeable. In truth, he was only matter-of-fact about them. He liked women well enough, enjoyed painting them when they were beautiful or interesting, enjoyed making love to them when they were beautiful or generous-natured, but in the long run they didn't matter very much to him. The women on his canvases always held him more powerfully than the women in his life.

'Point is,' Sam went on, 'if they'd just admit that's what they want and they're willing to do whatever's necessary to get it, I wouldn't care. Hell, why should I care if some silly debutante wants to be Lady Something-or-Other. But it's the hypocrisy I hate. They're all so busy pretending to be better than that, pretending they'd never dream of selling themselves to the first title that comes along – or rather having their fathers buy it for them. Until they get the chance. Then they forget those fine sensibilities. It makes my head spin to think how fast they forget them.'

Van Nest had gone on that way for the better part of an hour and Douglas had let him. Finally he'd had to leave to dress for dinner, but Sam had refused to part with the fresh bottle of whiskey he'd secured, and Douglas had left him alone on the piazza scowling off into the middle distance while he drank. He looked less mean than miserable.

Kimball could only piece together the rest of the story. Apparently Van Nest had not remained alone for long. Some of the men who'd been at the Belle Isle reception had turned up as well as another group from a party at the Clambake Club. None of them was very sober, though by that time Van Nest must have been the worst of the lot. He must have returned to the old monologue, but his new audience did not receive it with the same good grace Kimball had. Amelia Leighton's cousin Graham called out Sam for mentioning a lady's name in a club. Sam replied that he'd mentioned no lady by name. The result was a scuffle that broke the railing of the piazza in two places and left Graham without one of his front teeth.

The board met the following morning. Several older men were in favor of asking for Van Nest's resignation. Only the memory of Sam's late father and the position of his mother convinced them that leniency was in order. They agreed to ask Sam to refrain from visiting the Reading Room for the rest of the season. Next summer, when he could be expected to have learned his lesson, he would be welcome again. Van Nest had flung their leniency in their faces. He'd never returned to the Reading Room.

Strange that he should be thinking of that day now, Kimball thought, yet he knew there was nothing in the least strange about his suddenly remembering Sam Van Nest and that business with Amelia Leighton. It was strange only that he hadn't remembered it before. He should have thought of it that first day Elizabeth Leighton had come to his studio, or if not then, certainly afterward when she'd returned with her mother.

Kimball had never liked the idea of the artist's studio as a salon. In his younger days he'd put up with it because, as his colleagues had told him again and again, it was good for business. The people who came to watch you work and to see and be seen by others were likely to buy your paintings and commission portraits. By the time Kimball had ceased to need those patrons he'd grown accustomed to their presence. It would have taken a concerted effort at rudeness to banish them, and Kimball had never been good at rudeness, even rudeness disguised as artistic temperament. So he'd continued to permit visitors to his studio and after last April he'd become more of a drawing card than ever. Drawing card, hell, he was a curiosity, an oddity, a freak. And a coward, Kimball knew they thought. Only a coward would escape with his life when hundreds of women and children had gone to their deaths. He knew that was what people thought and the reason they flocked to his studio in such numbers. He wouldn't stop them, anymore than he'd try to explain how he'd reached safety when so many had not.

He knew his visitors were eager to hear his story just as they were eager for him to paint the disaster. When he'd returned to New York, Kimball had been besieged by demands for pictures of that terrible night in the north Atlantic. The newspapers had offered considerable sums for sketches from a survivor who just happened to be one of America's leading artists. Acquaintances had suggested it was a subject just waiting for his brush. The son of one of the millionaires who'd perished with the ship had offered a vast sum for a final memorial to the father whose body had been retrieved from the wreckage days later, water-logged and unidentifiable except by the sapphire-and-diamond ring on his finger and the six thousand dollars in cash in his evening suit pocket. Kimball, the son said, was to paint the *Titanic* sliding into the sea while his father stood on the deck, undaunted in the face of death, listening bravely to the final strains of 'Nearer My God to Thee.' Kimball did not tell the son that the band had not been playing that particular hymn, nor did he add that though some died bravely, very few died undaunted. He did not even mention that his hands trembled so violently these days that he could barely attempt the most superficial portrait, let alone recreate the scene that haunted his unsettled sleep night after night.

Kimball had told no one of the dreams. Whom could he tell? What could he tell? Could he describe the feeling of panic that returned each night with such immediacy? He'd be standing on the boat deck, wearing the awkward life jacket, watching the women and children being lowered in the collapsibles, and he'd feel the same terrible fear he'd known that night. The officers and stewards were insisting there was no real danger – the lifeboats were only a precaution – and most of the passengers were believing them because after all wasn't the ship practically unsinkable, but he'd feel the list of the deck, feel the angle from bow to stern getting steeper, and know the unsinkable ship was in serious trouble. Then the bow would take a sharp, sudden lurch downward, just as it had that night, and he'd know the unsinkable ship was going down. He'd start to run to the stern with the other passengers as he had that night, fear at his back like the rising waters that lapped at the decks, the same fear that would finally, mercifully wake him. Some nights his own screams awakened him, others his physical exertions as he fought his way up the deck of the ship that rose in the dark night like a perfectly curved mountain, but behind the screams and the physical struggle was always the same panic.

He'd get up then and pace his room smoking cigarette after cigarette in a desperate attempt to shake the dream, to believe the reality of this night rather than that one. Finally, he'd go back to sleep. Sometimes the dream returned, sometimes there was another. In the second dream he was in the lifeboat and the sun was rising, brilliantly, amazingly, illuminating the ice floating all around him like glistening shrouds in the calm seascape, and he'd see the rescue ship *Carpathia*, taking on survivors and there'd be not the feeling of fear, but one of shocked, shamed relief. He had survived.

They were not dreams he could relate to anyone, so he kept his silence, about the dreams, about the story of his survival, and concentrated on willing his hand to hold brush to canvas without trembling and his mind to forget the horror. And this man, Kimball thought, this fearful, guilt-riddled man, fleeing from memory, barely in command of his body or mind, was the artist whose studio Elizabeth Leighton had visited that afternoon early last May.

He'd seen her enter out of the corner of his eye, and even before he'd turned to look at her, something about her appearance had struck him. When he did look, he noticed a certain diffidence as if, unlike the other visitors, she sensed she might be intruding. Still, she'd been curious, her small well-shaped head turning this way and that on the long neck, as if she didn't want to miss anything. She'd been wearing an absurd hat laden with ostrich feathers that drooped over the wide brim, and she kept pushing them back impatiently. She'd make, Kimball had thought immediately, an excellent subject. He'd been working on a portrait of one of Elizabeth's friends – traditional society portraits were all he dared attempt since his rescue – and struggling to control his hand, but suddenly he forgot his subject and his trembling hand and all he could think of was how much he'd like to paint this girl with the overpowering hat and the lively eyes. It would be hard to capture the vitality of those eyes, but he was eager to try.

He'd told her as much when they were

introduced, making it clear that it would not be a traditional society painting, and he would expect no payment. 'You'll be doing me a favor, Miss Leighton.'

'Does that mean it won't be a flattering picture?' she'd asked.

'Will you care?'

Elizabeth had smiled, the quick easy smile of a girl who has never had any need for guile. 'Of course, I'll care, Mr Kimball.'

'In that case, I'll let you be the judge. If you're not satisfied, I'll never show the picture. If you're not satisfied,' Kimball heard himself saying and was horrified, 'I'll destroy it.' He had many paintings he'd never shown, but he'd never been able to destroy one.

She looked horrified herself. 'I'd never ask you to do that. I might not like it, but I'd never ask you to destroy it.'

'Does that mean you will sit for me.'

Elizabeth had said she'd have to think about it. He'd learned later that meant she had to ask her mother's permission. A week later Elizabeth returned to his studio with Mrs Leighton. She seemed different that day, more subdued, but he still wanted to paint her.

'Of course, it's quite a compliment,' Edith had said. She pretended to be considering Kimball's offer, but she'd already weighed the possibilities and decided. To have Kimball ask to paint Elizabeth singled her out as a reigning beauty, but the girl had already been acclaimed that. On the other hand, there was something *déclassé* about

modeling for an artist, even an artist of Kimball's
stature. To commission a portrait was one thing,
to sit for an artist something else, something a
courtesan or actress might do. It was not the sort
of thing Beatrice Hallenbeck would approve, and
Edith was after Beatrice Hallenbeck's approval –
and her son. 'But I'm afraid it's out of the
question. There simply isn't time. We'll be leaving
for Newport soon.'

There had been, Kimball discovered as the
month passed and Elizabeth continued to visit his
studio, ample time. He'd asked her again to sit for
him. That time she'd simply said it would displease
her mother.

'It would displease her to have you sit for me,
but it doesn't displease her to have you visit my
studio?'

'Would you prefer I didn't come?' she asked.
There was no guile behind the question, not even
an implied threat. It was as if she realized for the
first time that her refusal to pose had offended
him.

He'd assured her she was always welcome in his
studio and gone back to trying to paint her from
memory, but it was an impossible task. It wasn't
only the eyes that eluded him. There was
something about the contour of the cheek,
something delicate, yet sensual that escaped him.
Only the Italians could have captured the line of
that cheek, he told himself, and put the canvas
aside.

But he'd gone back to painting after that, even
painting seascapes which were ostensibly his

reason for being in Newport. He'd discovered a fascination with the sea, with its peace as well as its violence, its life-giving force as well as its destructiveness. He'd been trying to capture that and thought he had. In the last weeks he'd done some of his best work, but he was in Newport to capture more than the spirit of the sea, and his life wasn't going as well as his art. In fact, his life, and these days Elizabeth was life to him, wasn't going well at all. He wanted only Lizzy, but Lizzy seemed to elude him in reality as well as on canvas. He told himself it was her age, or rather the difference between their ages. His love was like a vintage wine, full-bodied and heady. How could he expect her, at twenty, to summon more than a watery *vin ordinaire*? And yet if he couldn't expect passion from her, he couldn't stop hoping for it. He swore he wouldn't go on this way, but knew he was lying to himself. He knew he'd go on this way just as long as she let him.

It turned out to be much easier than Amelia had expected. All week she'd known that her mother had suspected her intentions and planned to thwart them, but now with the dinner only hours away Edith was too preoccupied with the evening's favors and the evening's seating arrangement and the evening's success to pay much attention to her daughter. Edith was usually like a vaudeville juggler, able to keep any number of objects in the air simultaneously, but today she'd dropped one, thanks to Mr Van Rensaleer's broken leg, and she couldn't seem to get the rest back in the air. Amelia announced that she was going to the afternoon reception at Beaulieu, and it did not occur to Edith that her daughter had refused to attend half a dozen similar receptions since she'd arrived in Newport. It was not Beaulieu Amelia was headed for, it was her father's yacht, and on any other day her mother would have known as much.

As the Dusenberg passed through the driveway's tall iron gates, Amelia noticed the green autobus with its group of sightseers pulling up in front of the property. A man with a megaphone was retelling the Leighton family saga. He'd just got to the part about her marriage.

'The second daughter, Miss Amelia Leighton, married the tenth Duke of Duringham. On the occasion of their wedding the duke presented Miss Leighton with a dog collar of diamonds and pigeon's blood rubies. The collar had been presented to Marie Antoinette by Louis XVI only a month before the storming of the Bastille. It is valued at one million dollars. The duchess now lives in England . . .'

As the automobile passed the sightseeing bus, Amelia felt the curious eyes upon her and turned her face away. The man had got it all wrong, just as the papers always did. The collar, which had been bought by Edith to be presented to her by Charles, wasn't worth anywhere close to a million dollars.

She leaned forward, picked up the speaking tube, and told the driver to take her to the yacht club. If he thought there was anything peculiar about starting out for Beaulieu and ending up at the yacht club, he didn't say as much.

The steward at the boarding gate didn't recognize her, but then how could he? She hadn't been aboard *Nereids* in years. She gave him her card and asked if her father was aboard. Elias might be anywhere at this time of the afternoon, the Reading Room, the Clambake Club, someone else's yacht. The steward said Mr Leighton was aboard and if she'd wait here, he'd take her card to him.

In a few minutes Elias came hurrying along the deck toward her. He was not a tall man – fortunately none of the girls had inherited his short legs – but he was solidly built with strong shoulders and arms. His features were strong too and not unkind, but in the clear afternoon light his face looked unnaturally rosy. Amelia didn't know if the color were the result of embarrassment, whiskey, or the sun. A little of each, she suspected, as he took her arm and kissed her lightly, almost diffidently on the cheek.

'My dear,' he said, 'what a nice surprise. You should have told me you were coming and I would have sent the launch for you.'

Amelia could hear the sound of voices from the afterdeck. She was sorry she'd taken him from his party and wanted to tell him as much. She even wanted to reassure him that he needn't be embarrassed about it, but she knew the words would only embarrass him more. 'That's all right,' she said instead. 'The club launch brought me out. I hope you don't mind, Father, but I had to talk to you.'

'Of course, I don't mind, Amelia. You know I'm always glad to see you.' In fact, she knew nothing of the sort, but this was scarcely the time to say as much.

'Is there some place we can talk? Just for a moment.'

He led her away from the afterdeck and held open a door, and she stepped into the main saloon. She would have preferred a more intimate room for their talk − the vast space with its glistening parquet floor covered with Indian carpets, formal furniture, and elaborate murals of seafaring myths was anything but intimate − but she had little choice. Both the solarium and the library were aft, and her father clearly wanted to keep her away from the afterdeck and the people who were gathered on it.

Still, she had some pleasant memories of this room. On that cruise so many years ago whenever they'd taken time off from collecting flora and fauna and dropped anchor in some outpost of civilization, and they'd done that often, her father had always invited the local governor aboard and made sure he'd brought some of his younger diplomatic or naval officers along, and often there'd be a few of the local ruling families as well and native bands that played strange music on peculiar instruments. Her father knew how to give a good party, though not by her mother's standards, and she'd had some good times in this room.

'Can I get you some tea?' Elias walked to a bell cord in the corner of the saloon.

She hesitated for a minute. 'Actually, I'd prefer a cocktail.'

He looked at her curiously as he pulled the cord.

'It's good to see you, Amelia,' he said again when they were seated in one corner of the saloon. The portholes were open and the curtains rippled in the breeze while the sunlight flooding in the starboard side danced off the polished surfaces. 'And I won't pretend I don't know why you're here. I take it this has to do with your husband?'

'I want to divorce him.'

'You don't beat around the bush, but then you never have. You've always been outspoken. I guess that comes from being more intelligent. It's hard to put up with all the sham when you can see through it so clearly. That's why your sisters have got on better than you, Amelia. Let's face it, Carrie is not exactly the most brilliant woman who ever walked the earth, but fortunately with her beauty, intelligence is beside the point. And Lizzy, well, Lizzy's so good natured no one could fault her. Besides, Lizzy is curious. Her mind isn't as sharp as yours, but it is lively. But yours has always been more than that, hasn't it, and that's what's got you in trouble. I guess it's also what's made you my favorite. Whenever I think about having a son – and I used to think about it a good deal – I picture you in the role.'

'I never knew I was your favorite.'

'No, I don't suppose you did. I wasn't around enough to play favorites. But why did you think I took you to South America that winter. I'd never done that with Carrie, and I haven't with Lizzy.'

The steward entered then with a tray and two glasses, and she waited until he'd served them both and left before she answered.

'I thought you did it to rile Mother.'

Elias had been sipping his whiskey reflectively, and now he looked up at her sharply. 'Children always know more than you think they do. Still, it wasn't only to rile your mother. You're good company. It's a shame your husband doesn't seem to recognize the fact, though I'm not surprised he doesn't. Perhaps it's indiscreet of me to say so, but I never liked Duringham.'

'Then why didn't you stop Mother from forcing me to marry him?'

Elias looked into his glass. At first Amelia thought he was considering the answer, then she realized he simply couldn't meet her eyes. 'It was too late for me to stop your mother, Amelia. I'd relinquished those prerogatives or that power – call it what you want – long before she married you off to Duringham.'

'You could have tried. You could have come back and tried.' Her voice was a childish whine in her ears. 'I'm sorry. I keep telling myself there's no point in blaming anyone, yet that's all I seem to be able to do.' She was quiet for a moment, trying to control her anger, trying to remember the various openings she'd worked out, but her mind was blank. 'I need five million dollars,' she blurted out.

This time he was not afraid to meet her eyes. 'To live without Charles?'

'To get away from Charles. That's his price for giving me a divorce.'

Elias was quiet for what seemed to Amelia an ominously long time. 'Your duke is no gentleman,' he said finally.

'Did you ever think he was?'

'I guess I hoped he was.'

'I'm sorry to disappoint you.'

Elias heard the sarcasm in her voice. 'Don't become hard, Amelia. It's one thing to be clever, another to be hard.'

'Then give me the money for a divorce.'

'Can't you get one without it? Do you need his cooperation?'

'There are only two grounds for divorce in England, Father. Failure to consummate the marriage and adultery.'

Elias took a sip of his whiskey. He'd stopped looking at her again. 'I imagine if the marriage turned out as badly as you say it has, he's given you grounds. Ten years is a long time. There must have been other women.'

Amelia looked down at her hands spread open in her lap. She was wearing the emerald ring Elias had bought her when Tony was born. The sun streaming in the portholes glittered off the stone, and it looked as if it were winking at her. 'It isn't that simple. I can't just accuse Charles of something like that. Even if it's true,' she added lamely. 'I can't simply go into court and say I think he was having an affair with this one or that one. I'd need proof, and surely you don't think any of our friends – his friends, really – are going to testify on my behalf against him.'

'I don't see why not, if it's the truth.'

'We're talking about England, Father, not America. The king doesn't approve of divorce. Didn't you see the headline in the *Times* just the other day? The king and queen are opposed to the Marlboroughs' divorce. Poor Consuelo. All she wants is her freedom and it becomes front page news.'

'You will be too, my dear.'

'I suppose so, but that's beside the point. What I'm saying is that as long as the king and queen are opposed to divorce, no one's going to testify against Charles. It would be as good as testifying against the royal family. That was what the article was all about. King George and Queen Mary express displeasure at the idea of Consuelo and Sunny divorcing and society closes ranks to hold them together.'

'Then I don't see how you're going to get your divorce even with my five million.'

'Charles has decided to be reckless. For a price. Apparently he's as eager to be rid of me as I am of him. He's sure he can convince the king it's all for the best. Charles can be quite winning when he chooses to, you know, and he always chooses to be with the king and queen. At any rate, he's willing to chance it – for five million. There's nothing Charles won't do for money – except work. He's quite the gentleman in that respect. He says he'll arrange it all properly. Go away with two detectives and a woman hired by them. It's the way these things are done when they must be done. Apparently they all use the same detectives. I guess you could say the right detectives. There's probably even a right woman.'

Elias swirled the whiskey around in his glass as if it were brandy, then with a sudden motion drained it. 'What if we decided not to play by the rules, Amelia? What if we decided not to go along with Duringham and his friends and their damnable notions of right and wrong? What if we decided to get you a divorce in our own vulgar, pushy, honest, if you can call anything about divorce honest, way? What if we hired our own detectives, not the right detectives, of course, but efficient detectives and get our own proof of what's going on? In other words, what if I keep my five million and cause one hell of a scandal in the bargain?'

Amelia looked down at her hands again. The ring wasn't winking at her now. She could imagine her answer, or rather the impossibility of it. *Well, you see, Father . . . I don't think that would be a very good idea because the scandal might just backfire. You see, Father, there was a man. Michael was his name.* No, it was not an explanation she could make to her father, but neither was it a chance she could take. She didn't know if Charles had ever found out, but he must have suspected something, and if she started to make a row, he'd be sure to retaliate.

'I don't think we can do that to Tony,' she said, and hated her own hypocrisy. 'It isn't only that the scandal will reflect on him. Charles has sworn that if I don't do things his way, he'll never let me see Tony again. And he can do it, you know. No court in England would turn the future Duke of Duringham over to some obscure American woman, even if she happens to be his mother.

'There's no way out, Father. Either you give Charles the five million, or I stay married to him.'

'Then I'm afraid you'll have to stay married to him.'

'You can't mean it!'

'Contrary to your mother's opinion, and yours I see now, I am not made of money, Amelia. Good Lord, she made me give the man twelve million to marry you.' He saw her wince, and the reaction hurt him. 'I didn't mean that the way it sounded, my dear. I didn't mean that I had to pay him to marry you.'

'It's exactly what you did mean. It's exactly what happened. Charles never would have married me if you hadn't given him the money. What I don't understand is if you gave him twelve million to marry me, why you won't give him another five to divorce me.'

'Seventeen million dollars, Amelia. You speak about seventeen million dollars as if it were nothing.'

'I know it's a great deal of money.'

'A great deal! It's more than most people – even people we know, Amelia – dream of. And it's more than I'm willing to give that damn Englishman. Whether you believe it or not, it's more than I can afford to give him. Oh, I don't mean it would ruin me, but it would make a difference. Your mother isn't exactly frugal.

Neither are you girls, for that matter. And I like to live well.'

Elias stood and walked to the tray the steward had left. He did not offer to refill her glass though it was empty. 'You say you realize that five million is a great deal of money, Amelia. I don't think you do. I don't think you have the least inkling of how much money it is. Do you have any idea how much it costs to run Belle Isle or the house in town or Raleigh? What does a private railroad car cost or this boat?' He stopped as if expecting an answer, but when she said nothing he went on. 'I'm going to tell you, Amelia, because I think it's time you had a lesson in finance. I suppose it's my fault you never had one before. Belle Isle costs me seventy thousand a year just for taxes and repairs. Add another twenty-five thousand to that for fuel, electricity, and servants' wages. There's eighteen thousand for the automobiles and chauffeurs, and remember we're only talking about the summer season now. Your mother insists on a minimum of thirty-five thousand for mistakes in clothes for herself and you girls. The mistakes you don't wear, Amelia, not the clothes you wear. And we mustn't forget the jewels. Then there's entertaining. In the last four years she hasn't given a ball that cost less than seventy-five thousand, and every summer she sets aside three hundred thousand for "extra entertainment." I'll be damned if I'll ever understand what she means by "extra entertainment." Those are the ongoing expenses, Amelia. I'm not talking about the original three million for Belle Isle or the two million for the house in New York. Fourteen million in furnishings between them. Another five for Raleigh inside and out, and that doesn't count keeping the streams and fields stocked. We had some trouble with the pheasants this year, to say nothing of the gamekeeper. Then there's the stock farm in Kentucky. I've got ninety brood mares and eight stallions, each worth seventy-five thousand. Add a mere hundred thousand for the railroad car we all use, another half million for this boat. I won't even mention the upkeep on either of them. This year there will have to be money for Lizzy. You don't think that dragon Beatrice Hallenbeck is going to let her one and only boy marry a girl without money. You don't think I'd let Lizzy marry without money. Surely you don't expect it all to go to Duringham and the upkeep of that damn castle.' Elias stopped and looked into his glass thoughtfully. Then he took a long swallow. 'Besides,' he went on finally, 'I don't like highway robbery, Amelia, and that's what your husband is up to. I've never allowed myself to be bested in a business deal, and I'm not going to start now. Not even for you.' He stopped abruptly as if he regretted the last words, and when he spoke again his voice was kinder.

'Take my advice. Let things ride for a while. I'm willing to bet that in a year or two Duringham's price will drop considerably. When it does, you come to me again. I'm sure we'll be able to work out something eventually.'

'Eventually!'

'You always were impatient.'

'I'm not impatient. I simply don't have the time. What if Charles changes his mind. He could at any moment. He could decide he doesn't want to risk offending the king or being ostracized at court. He could decide he wants the appearance of marriage after all and come after me.'

'I'm afraid that's a chance we'll have to take.'

'No, Father, it's a chance *I'll* have to take.'

Elias had told her not to run off after their discussion, but she'd known he hadn't meant it. On her way to the boarding gate she'd caught a glimpse of a woman, a very young woman, in a bathing dress and bare legs, and she knew her father hadn't really wanted her to stay. Besides, they'd said everything there was to say.

Still, that wasn't the end of it, she realized back in the Dusenberg. In a way it was only the beginning. In a few weeks or months Charles would realize he wasn't going to get the five million that would alleviate the weight of the king's displeasure and his own disgrace, and if he couldn't have that, he'd want the appearance of marriage if not the fact of it. That meant a wife on the same continent. Charles would either come after her, or Edith would send her back. Between them they controlled the money that her father had referred to as hers. And without money of her own there was no freedom and no chance of escape. She fingered the single strand of pearls around her neck. She knew how to get money, not enough for Charles but enough to get away from him and her mother.

They were on Bellevue Avenue now and she told the driver to keep going past Belle Isle to the shops. She wouldn't sell anything at the Newport shops – she'd go to New York for that – but suddenly she was impatient to hear the figures, to know how much she'd have and how she'd manage.

Amelia looked out the window at the people strolling along the avenue. She noticed a man in a brown suit with a stiff collar and recognized the pale face with the sparse blond whiskers. At first she couldn't place him, then it came to her. He was the man Tiffany sent when her mother summoned. She picked up the speaking tube and told the driver to stop. When she rolled down the window, the man looked startled but attentive. There was no doubt he knew her. Amelia asked him to get in the automobile, and the look turned to discomfort, but he stepped quickly into the back seat.

'This is most kind of you, Your Grace,' he said. His eyes darted nervously as he spoke, taking in the wood paneling and soft upholstery of the Dusenberg. 'I've just come from Belle Isle. Lovely favors Mrs Leighton has got for the dinner. Exquisite workmanship.' He knew he was talking too much, but couldn't stop himself. It was one thing dealing with these people at the store or even in their drawing rooms when he was summoned, but he'd never been alone with a woman like this in an automobile like this. It was more than a little unnerving.

'Perhaps you could do me a favor, Mr . . .'

121

Amelia hesitated, wishing she could remember his name.

'Wickert.'

'Mr Wickert. I have a few things I'd like to sell.' Amelia pulled the glove off her right hand. 'This ring. And these pearls.' She touched the strand around her throat. 'Perhaps a few other things as well.' She was speaking quickly, as if now that she'd started, she couldn't stop. 'Can you tell me how much they're worth?'

Martin Wickert knew little about the world, but he knew a great deal about two things – gems and loyalty to the people he served. If Miss Leighton had been a girl, he would have gone straight to her mother and reported their conversation, but Miss Leighton was a grown woman – and the Duchess of Duringham. She was also, obviously, in difficulty, and it was Wickert's task, as he saw it, to help her.

Amelia was tugging at the emerald ring. 'There's no need for that, Your Grace. I remember what your father paid for the ring and your mother for the pearls. Magnificent pearls. They were for your debut, weren't they?'

Amelia was not so sentimental. 'What do you think they'll bring?'

'Perhaps fifty thousand. Prices fluctuate with the times, of course.' Wickert did not mention that the sum she'd get would be less than that her parents had paid. In the hierarchy of Martin Wickert's loyalties, Tiffany stood high.

Amelia was wondering how long she could live on fifty thousand dollars. Not very long according

122

to the figures her father had just given her, but then her father's figures didn't apply because she was no longer going to live according to her mother's lights.

'If I bring it all to the store this week, Mr Wickert, the ring, the pearls, a pair of sapphire and diamond ear clips . . .' Her mind was racing over the jewels Charles had allowed her to take because appearances must be maintained and a duchess without jewels could not maintain them very well. 'If I were to bring certain things to town this week, how quickly could you get me some money for them?'

'Immediately, milady, but . . .' Wickert stroked his whiskers nervously. He was debating where aid stopped and impertinence began.

'But?'

'Well, if you're looking to realize a large sum, Your Grace . . .'

'Yes?' Amelia was eager now. This was going to be easier than she'd thought.

'Then I'd advise selling the Marie Antoinette collar. That would clearly bring the highest price. Unless, of course, the sentimental value to you is too great.'

He was right, of course, not about the sentimental but about the monetary value. It wasn't worth a million, but it was worth a great deal. She'd discovered that months ago in London when she'd first decided to leave Charles. 'Not the collar,' Amelia said.

'Of course, milady. I didn't mean . . .'

'I'll bring the other things down this week, Mr

Wickert. And I would appreciate it if you didn't mention this to my mother.'

His small mouth pursed a little, as if he were offended that she felt the need for such a warning. 'Of course, milady.'

Amelia told the driver to head back to the Casino where they'd picked up Wickert, but when they pulled up in front of the long half-timbered building Wickert sank back into the upholstery as if he were trying to make himself smaller.

'Perhaps we'd better keep going, Your Grace. You can let me off farther down the road, and I'll walk back. That's Mr Louis Feeny standing there in front of the Casino. The reporter for *Town Topics*. If he saw me getting out of your automobile, it wouldn't be much of a secret from Mrs Leighton or anyone else.'

'Thank you, Mr Wickert. Thank you very much.'

Wickert got out a few blocks past the Casino and when the Dusenberg headed back up Bellevue Avenue toward Belle Isle, Amelia saw the man called Feeny was still standing there, his hands in his waistcoat pockets, his eyes missing nothing.

She wondered if it had been Feeny who had bribed the maid so many years ago. She doubted it. Feeny looked too young. It must have been his predecessor, one of his many predecessors. At the time stories about the Leightons had begun appearing in *Town Topics* with annoying regularity, and Edith had been furious, though Amelia had wondered how her mother had known about them since she, like all the women, denied ever seeing the rag let alone reading it. The stories

had been innocuous for the most part because
with Edith in charge there was little enough that
could be blown up into scandal, but all the same
they had to stop. Edith had suspected that
someone in the house was selling information, and
had questioned Hatfield. A week later the major-
domo discovered one of the upstairs maids going
through the wastepaper basket next to Sky's desk.
Hatfield had fired the girl on the spot without
references. Perhaps it had been the lack of them
that led to that story in *Town Topics* the following
week about Sky and the Contessa de Costellani.
After that Amelia had found a new hiding place
for her letters from Sam. The spot must have
remained a secret, or the other maids must have
been properly frightened because the stories about
all of them had stopped. Perhaps it would have
been better if they hadn't. Perhaps if her
reputation had been sufficiently sullied by *Town
Topics*, Charles never would have consented to
marry her.

Sam sat alone on the afterdeck of *Corsaire*. The
late afternoon sun hung like a garish orange ball
over Conanicut Island and he pulled the brim of
his straw hat lower over his eyes. Then he turned
his deck chair toward the town. It looked
deceptively peaceful from this distance, like a
small New England village huddled respectfully
around the spire of Trinity Church. It was a
peaceful view of Newport if not an accurate one,
although it had been accurate at one time. In the
years after the British had destroyed the town as

a commercial center, in those early years of America's independence, Newport had been so peaceful it had almost died. But then people from Boston and from the South had discovered that the breezes off Rhode Island Sound were as cooling during the summer months as the rocky coastline was exhilarating, that the quiet of the sleepy town was as pleasing as the play of sunlight on the brilliant blue bay was inspiring. The intellectual and artistic families like his mother's had come from Boston and the more sociable families had come from the South and they'd made Newport pleasant again. It was only when the families from New York had arrived, the four hundred, that it had become more than that – or less.

Still, from where he sat on the deck of *Corsaire* he could ignore what it had become. From here the town still looked simple and tranquil gathered around the spire of Trinity Church, and there was no evidence of the elaborate rituals and riotous extravagance that went on beneath the occasional roof that stood out against the green patchwork quilt of the island. From here Newport appeared peaceful and quiet. The only sounds were the waves slapping monotonously against *Corsaire*'s hull and the occasional shriek of a seagull. Gradually he heard an engine, at first barely audible in the distance, then growing louder until it drowned out the sound of the waves. The launch would be returning from town with Mrs Hall and the rest of the party that had gone ashore that afternoon. Sam knew if he walked to the gangway to greet them, Dolly Hall would be pleased to see him. He knew that she'd hold back a little while the rest of the party greeted him, then she'd put her arm in his, seemingly shyly, though she was not shy, and draw him aside and tell him quietly that she wished he'd been along that afternoon. He knew too that he had plenty of time before he had to dress for dinner, and if he wanted, he could go down to Dolly's cabin and pass a perfectly pleasant hour, but he was not in the mood for Dolly Hall or her pleasantries.

Sam went back to thinking of the job before him. He'd worked out a loose strategy that began with Wainwright. Wainwright would be the easiest, and he'd get him out of the way first. Hell, there was nothing to do there but tell the man where he stood, where Morgan had put him. Sam didn't want to think about Wainwright. The man was a bungler and a fool, but that didn't mean Sam would enjoy telling him as much.

He'd decided to take care of Kirkland Selby next. Selby was another sure thing – and an even more unpleasant task than Wainwright. Not that Sam liked Selby any more than he did Wainwright. If anything, he supposed he despised Selby most of all, but that didn't mean he was going to enjoy what he had to do. Some men would, he knew. Some men would see themselves as agents of vengeance, defenders of justice and goodness, but Sam saw himself only as a doer of Morgan's dirty work.

Sam thought of his father. He'd been the most honorable man Sam had ever known – and a financial failure. It was his father's contention that honor and business success were, by definition, mutually exclusive. 'These days,' he used to say in that bitter, defensive tone, 'no man can make money without losing his self-respect.' There'd been a time when Sam had hated the complaint and the self-pitying voice that expressed it. When he'd first gone off to Groton, he'd listened to the other boys' talk of their fathers and sensed there was something inappropriate about his own. Those fathers made money with ease and were proud of the fact. Jim Weston's father was extreme, yet typical of those men who seemed to rule the world that was destroying his father. 'Go to bed every night,' Jim's father counseled, 'richer than you got up that morning.' Sam could imagine where his father would stand in Mr Weston's estimation and that of the other fathers and their sons, and he was ashamed for him and of him, but as he began to see more of the world than the bucolic campus of Groton or even the more urban and urbane environs of Yale, Sam had learned that if Jim Weston's father were not entirely right, his own was not entirely wrong, and he'd come to admire his father and in some respects to emulate him. Even as a financial success – and he was that at least until tomorrow morning – Sam liked to think he had not left honor entirely behind, although it was not his father's particular brand of black-and-white honor.

Then what, a faint voice within him demanded, *are you doing blackmailing two men for the greater glory of J. P. Morgan and Company?*

Fighting the greater evil, he answered promptly, of Jason Walsh. *Ah*, the voice returned, *the means justify the ends?* You're damn right they do, Sam answered himself.

And what of the means? What of the idea of returning to Belle Isle? It seemed to Sam that the house was more than just another of Newport's white elephants. It was the incarnation of everything he hated about Newport, just as Edith Leighton and her daughters were the kind of women who made the colony what it was. Mrs Leighton and her daughters! Why in hell hadn't he thought of it before? Why in hell didn't he read the social pages? He'd been thinking of Amelia Leighton as someone in his past, as dead and finished as his late wife, but Amelia Leighton was very much alive. It was entirely possible, more than possible, that she was in Newport for the season, showing off her title and her son, the marquess. It seemed to Sam he'd read somewhere about a son. And showing off the duke too. Mustn't forget the moving force behind the whole show. Well, what if she were in Newport? It made no difference to him. *Who is Amelia?* The girl's voice came back to him. No one. At least no one important. If he could blackmail two men to get the job done, surely he could dine with Amelia Leighton and her noble husband. Hell, he could dine with the devil if it meant getting the job done.

And he could survive Newport too. He'd had plenty of experience surviving Newport, first that season Amelia had become Lady Amelia, then that summer Georgina had taken the house. He hadn't wanted the house, but Georgina had had her heart set on it. They'd married the previous fall and at the time it had seemed that Georgina ought to have whatever she'd set her heart on. Of course, at the time he hadn't had any idea of what Georgina had really set her heart on.

He kept wondering, though he tried not to remember any of it, how he'd been so blind. 'She reminds me,' his mother had said the first time she'd met Georgina, 'of Amelia.'

'She's nothing like Amelia,' he'd said, and he'd known even at the time that he'd said it too quickly.

'I didn't mean she was like Amelia. I meant she looked like Amelia.' And she had, though there were no green lights going off in her eyes and her hair was darker. She had Amelia's high forehead and Amelia's cheekbones and Amelia's habit of holding her head a little to one side when she was looking at a picture or some sight he'd pointed out. She had Amelia's height and Amelia's long narrow waist and Amelia's way of swinging her body when she walked. There was something about the movement that made him think neither of them was wearing a corset though he knew for a fact, since he'd seen Georgina's and been able to feel Amelia's, that they both did wear corsets. Even her voice sometimes reminded him of Amelia's when Amelia's had sounded low and husky like wind through the trees on a summer night. There had been several similarities and one more that he hadn't seen at the time. Both Amelia and Georgina had wanted to marry well. For Amelia that meant a title and a castle in England. Georgina had been satisfied with the title of Mrs Samuel Tyler Van Nest and a house in Newport. He could still remember that night Georgina had come to ask him to take the house.

He'd been sitting at his desk in the library of the house he'd rented in New York while Georgina decided what she wanted to build, writing the letter that accompanied the monthly check to Hussey, and he hadn't heard her come up behind him. 'What are you doing, darling?' She'd put her hand on his shoulder and leaned over, and he remembered he'd wanted to do two things at the time – put an arm around her waist to draw her close because she'd looked very pretty with her pale skin glowing that way above the lamp, and cover the letter. He had not covered it but he had put an arm around her waist as she'd bent closer to look at the letter. It would never have occurred to him to read one of her letters without asking.

'Who is Hussey?'

'Just a man.'

'Just a man with a child. A sick child who . . .' She picked up the letter. '. . . you're pleased is coming along well after the operation.' There was a chair beside his desk, but she sat in another in front of the window. She was still holding his letter.

'Hussey's a man I knew in New Haven. An engineer. He designs airplanes. Or rather he wants to, but no one else seems to want him to, so I help him out occasionally.'

She was smiling at him now as if he'd just said

131

something amusing – no, not amusing, silly – and he was sorry he hadn't taken care of the letter and the check at his office. He didn't like to do that because he didn't want anyone at Morgan and Company to find out about the arrangement with Hussey. It wasn't that there was anything wrong with it, only that he didn't want anyone to think he was a rank sentimentalist. He wasn't doing this out of sentiment, though he supposed that was what Georgina thought and that was why she was smiling at him in that funny way.

'In other words,' she said, 'you pay him to design airplanes.'

'More or less.' He couldn't understand why she sounded so peculiar about it. She'd never seemed to care about money before. With her father's fortune and his own fledgling one she hadn't had to.

'In other words, you and this man Hussey have a business arrangement.'

'More or less.'

'Yet you write about his sick child and' – she looked from him to the letter again – 'and Mrs Hussey.'

'I told you, I knew him at New Haven. There's . . . well, I guess you might call it a kind of friendship between us. He sent you his best wishes, if you're interested. I told him in one of my letters that I'd married, and he sent you his best wishes.'

'And you inquire about Mrs Hussey. And the child.'

'Those are only the beginning formalities. Mostly

we write about his work. That's what the letter will be about – if I ever get to finish it.'

'I never knew you were interested in airplanes, Sam.'

'You never knew I was interested in cotton bills either.'

'What do cotton bills have to do with it?'

'Nothing. That's the point. You don't know about most of the things I spend my days on. Why should you?'

'But those are things you do at your office. This' – she was still holding the letter in one hand – 'is something you do at home, something a little more personal.'

'Look, Georgina, Hussey's a good engineer. A brilliant engineer. Someday he's going to do something really important. And make someone a lot of money in the bargain. I'm just helping him get on with the work.'

'By supporting him and his family.'

'If you think about it, it isn't even a favor. More like a long-term investment.'

'I'm sure that's the way you made Mr Hussey see it. Or perhaps it was Mrs Hussey who made him see it that way.'

'What does she have to do with it?'

Georgina was smiling again. It was a very superior smile. 'I don't know, Sam. Why don't you tell me what Mrs Hussey has to do with it. And the child.' But she didn't wait for him to tell her anything. 'Really, Sam, I'm not a fool. And I'm not even particularly shocked. After all, you weren't exactly a child when you married me. And you would do the decent thing.' She had a way of saying the decent thing that made it sound like the indecent thing. 'Though I do find it somewhat bizarre that you keep up a correspondence with the woman's husband. Isn't this sort of thing usually done through lawyers?'

And he'd been afraid she'd think he was a rank sentimentalist. '*That* sort of thing usually is, but this isn't *that* sort of thing.' He wished he hadn't sounded quite so holier than thou because, of course, it could have been that sort of thing. He supposed that was what made him sound the way he did. He explained the whole thing to her again, and she said if he said it was simply a business arrangement then it was simply a business arrangement, but she hadn't believed him and he'd known it. It had bothered Sam that she hadn't believed him, but something else had bothered him more. She hadn't been troubled by what she'd gone on believing. He couldn't help wishing that she had been troubled by it, if only a little.

When she'd given him back the letter she'd still been smiling in that peculiar way, and then she'd told him about the house she wanted to take in Newport that summer. There was something demanding in her voice when she'd asked him to take it, but she hadn't been unpleasant about it. If anything, she'd been very pleasant that night and for several nights afterward. Georgina had always put on a good act, though at the time he hadn't known it was an act, but he had the feeling, even now, even after everything that had happened, that for a little while after that night she hadn't been acting. It was the damnedest thing, but he couldn't get over the feeling that the idea another woman wanted him or had wanted him at some time suddenly made Georgina want him.

The change in her feelings had been temporary though, and by the time they'd taken the house in Newport that summer Georgina had forgot all about that other woman and her child. At least she'd never mentioned them again. He supposed she was too busy. Georgina had a lot on her mind that summer. First she'd been busy fixing up the house he'd neither wanted nor enjoyed, then she'd been busy filling it with people he either didn't know or didn't like. 'Old friends,' she used to say when Sam had complained he might like to be alone with her occasionally – he wished now he hadn't said that – but with the exception of her cousin Franklin who, it seemed to Sam, was always visiting them, they weren't old friends at all but new conquests she'd made as Mrs Samuel Van Nest. Georgina was no longer an outsider, and when Franklin drove the Packard off the road that night breaking Georgina's neck and his own skull on the cliff below, all of Newport had gone down to New York for the funeral. Georgina would have liked that. Her only disappointment would have been that Franklin's body had been shipped home to Chicago rather than buried beside hers in the Van Nest family plot.

Sam heard the sound of footsteps on the deck behind him, not the soft sound of a steward's rubber-soled shoes but the click of high heels. He remembered watching Dolly Hall put on a pair of red high-heeled shoes that morning and closed his eyes. He could sense her standing over him and felt the way he had as a child when he'd stayed up beyond his bedtime reading and had been forced to feign sleep at the sound of his mother's approach. He'd always been afraid he was going to smile, and he felt the same way now, but he didn't smile or even blink, and soon he heard the sound of the high-heeled shoes moving away from him down the deck. Tomorrow, Sam swore, he'd be especially nice to her. Tomorrow, after he'd got tonight out of the way, he'd spend the whole day with Dolly. And Monday, when they were back in New York, he'd go to Tiffany and get her something nice. If tonight went as planned, he'd get her something very nice.

IV

Amelia was sitting on the satin chaise before the leaded windows open to the sea. The breeze had died as it often did in the late afternoon, but the room was still comfortable. Marble and stone did tend to keep out the heat; she had to give Harry Lehr that. A copy of the new Dreiser book, *The Financier*, lay on her lap unopened. In England she'd read constantly. In England there had been times when the fictional world had seemed more real than her own, but since she'd returned home, she hadn't been able to concentrate on anything. Every time she opened a book she found herself returning to the life she'd fled.

There was a knock at the door and Caroline entered without waiting for an answer. She'd taken down her hair, obviously in preparation for having the maid put it up again for the evening, and it fell down her back in soft blonde waves. She looked very beautiful, Amelia thought, and wondered what it was like to be so beautiful and so loved. Whatever their quarrels, Sky was still in love with his wife. Amelia was sure of that.

'Mama wants you to wear your black lace with

the pearl-and-jet embroidery tonight. She told Ellen to bring it down.'

'I told Ellen to bring down my white Poiret,' Amelia said, but she was feeling more sorry for her maid than herself. There had already been one argument in that area. On her second day at Belle Isle Amelia had told Ellen which dresses she wanted brought down from the storage rooms for that week. There wasn't room in the armoires of the bedrooms for more than a week's wardrobe of course. Edith had given her own orders, and poor Ellen had come to Amelia with the problem. Amelia had stood her ground, but since then Ellen had come to her less and less often with the problem of conflicting orders. She was becoming Edith's servant again just as Amelia would become her mother's creature if she stayed. But she wouldn't stay. She'd known that ever since she'd spoken to Wickert this afternoon.

'You can't wear the white,' Caroline said. 'Lizzy's to wear white. Mama has it all arranged. And it won't be fair to Lizzy if you wear white.'

Amelia shrugged her shoulders. 'Then it's the black lace.'

'And the Marie Antoinette choker. Mama said to be sure to wear the choker.'

Amelia had expected that. She hated the collar, and not merely because it symbolized her marriage. It made moving her head and swallowing almost impossible, and tomorrow she'd be sure to have an ugly red rash from it.

'You needn't look as if it's a great sacrifice to

wear the collar, Amelia. You might at least try to get along.'

'I am trying, Carrie.'

'It would be so much simpler for everyone if you'd agree to go back to Charles. I don't mean you have to go back now. Just give up the idea of a divorce and then you can spend a perfectly pleasant summer.'

'It wouldn't be simpler for everyone, Carrie. It wouldn't be simpler for me.'

The short upper lip turned up impatiently. 'You always did dramatize yourself, Amelia. Even when we were little, Amelia's tragedies were so much more important than everyone else's. I remember when that old sheep dog at Raleigh had to be put to sleep. You carried on for days. Anyone would have thought it was the end of the world.'

'I suppose I thought it was at the time. After all, I was only seven.'

'Which means I was only ten, and I didn't carry on for days.'

'Maybe you weren't as fond of Queenie.'

'I loved Queenie. As much as you did. But I didn't go to pieces when they put her to sleep. I suppose that makes me callous in your eyes, but people have to be a little callous to get along in this world. You can't go around falling apart over every little thing. That's simply self-indulgence. Like this business about a divorce. Do you think you're the only one whose husband is difficult? No one's marriage is easy.'

'Easy! It was impossible.'

'That's exactly what I mean, Amelia. You're

always exaggerating, always dramatizing yourself. Impossible. What could be more impossible than my position?'

'Sky adores you.'

'Of course. When he can spare time from Vanessa Hunter.'

'Perhaps you're imagining that.' Amelia had guessed from the way Sky talked that he'd had his affairs, but she couldn't believe he really preferred someone else to Carrie. Amelia, if no one else, still remembered their courtship.

'You're not only one of the most selfish people in the world, you've got to be one of the blindest.' Caroline had been standing behind a Louis Quinze chair, her delicately shaped hands resting on the blue satin upholstery, and now she moved around it and sat across from her sister. 'Let me tell you about Schuyler. Let me tell you about my husband and how much he adores me. Let me tell you about the maid I had to dismiss – we'd been married four years then – because of my husband and his adoration. And don't tell me I was imagining that. Not in my own house. Think of it, Amelia. In my own house. In Sky's bedroom right next to mine. Can you imagine what it felt like?'

'I can imagine,' Amelia said quietly.

They were both silent for a moment listening to the sound of Caroline's short, shallow breathing. She'd never been able to erase that image from her mind. Even now she could re-create every detail, the girl's skirt hiked up awkwardly about her waist, the thin girlish legs in black woolen stockings locked around Sky, and Sky absurd in morning coat and no trousers. Neither of them had noticed her and she'd stood there horrified, disgusted, fascinated, watching her husband and the girl thrashing around on his bed, watching him as she'd seen him so often, but it was different now because she could see him from a distance and the girl too, see herself as she must look, only her legs, better shaped, Caroline thought, would not be encased in woolen stockings and they certainly wouldn't be clasping Sky to her, and her body would not be pumping and thrusting like some animal in heat.

They'd been disgusting, but then Caroline often found Sky with his naked desires and urgent needs disgusting. For years she'd tried to reform him by the example of her own fine sensibilities, but Sky did not want to reform. He seemed to think his behavior was perfectly acceptable. He seemed to think there was nothing wrong with naked bodies and sticky perspiration and acrid odors. 'It's all part of nature,' he'd said early in their marriage when she'd complained. Perhaps it was, but she preferred nature on a canvas by Corot, just as she preferred skin freshly bathed, odors camouflaged by *eau de cologne*, and bodies fully clothed, just as she preferred being admired as a work of art to being touched as a woman.

'I dismissed the maid, of course,' Caroline continued, 'but Schuyler is a very resourceful man. He had the tact to stay away from the maids and governesses after that, but the following winter he spent a good deal of time comforting Sally Reddington while Harry Reddington was abroad. Then he found Vanessa Hunter, and that's been going on ever since. Right under my nose. She's invited everywhere we are, and she and Sky make no bones about their *friendship*. So don't tell me about impossible marriages, Amelia.' Caroline stood. 'I'm an expert on them.'

'But have you ever spoken to Sky about it. If what you say about Vanessa is true, have you ever asked him to give her up?'

'Beg him to, you mean? Never. I'll never give him the satisfaction.'

'You mean you'd rather have your pride than Sky?'

'I have Sky – and the dignity to live with the situation.' Sometimes it amazed Amelia how much like her mother her sister could sound.

'Well, I don't want Charles. And I find no dignity in my situation.'

'You're not going to tell me Charles' behavior is worse than Sky's.'

Amelia was silent for a moment, imagining Caroline's reaction if she told her about Charles. She could picture the violet eyes growing wide with shock. It would be pleasant to shock Caroline.

'At least Sky loved you when he married you,' she said finally. 'If you ask me, he still loves you. Charles never cared for me. Not when he proposed, not when we were first married, not since. He told me that on our wedding night. There we were in Father's private railroad car, all refitted in honor of our wedding trip, and Charles sat there in the main saloon, absolutely poised as only Charles can be, and told me he didn't love me and would never love me. He told me he loved someone else, but marriage to me was his duty. That's how he put it. His duty.'

'But you knew that when you married him, Amelia. As Mama said then, it was your duty to make him care for you.'

'The way you made Sky care for you? Good Lord, Carrie, you didn't even have to try. If things haven't turned out any better with that kind of a beginning, how do you expect me to make a go of it with someone who didn't even like me?'

'I'm sure he must have liked you, Amelia. He wouldn't have chosen you, if he hadn't liked you. Even if he was in love with another woman. And as far as that sort of thing goes, the best thing to do is simply ignore it. Let him have his affair with her, whoever she is, and ignore the whole thing. That's what I've done with Sky.'

'But you're not ignoring it at all, Carrie. You're absolutely consumed with hate for Sky – and for Vanessa Hunter.'

Caroline smiled a slow, superior smile as if she'd scored a point. 'Are you saying you don't hate Charles and his woman?' Caroline remembered the summer they'd spent in London. 'It's his cousin Prudence, isn't it? He's absolutely devoted to Prudence. I could see it that summer, and of course they'd never be able to marry. Even if he hadn't needed the money.'

'I thought it was at first.'

'Are you saying it isn't Prudence?'

Amelia stood and walked to the window. She

loved the way the water looked at this hour, a mosaic of shimmering muted colors. 'What does it matter who it is? Or what, for that matter? I married Charles as directed. I produced an heir as directed. And now I just want to be free of him.'

'Well, if you won't talk about it . . .' Caroline turned abruptly and started for the door. She was sorry she'd told Amelia about Sky and the maid and Sally Reddington and Vanessa Hunter. She'd been trying to make Amelia understand the way things were, and to warn her off, just in case. But Amelia didn't want to understand. She wanted to withdraw behind that mask of suffering and leave Caroline feeling foolish and exposed. 'I'm going down to see if Mama needs help. You'd better start to dress. Mama said she wanted you there to receive with her.' Caroline left the room quickly. Never, she swore. She'd never say a word to her sister about Sky again.

Amelia went back to the chaise, but this time she didn't even bother to pick up the book. Prudence. She had thought it was Prudence at first. He loved someone else, Charles had said that night in the private railroad car going out to Raleigh, the Leighton estate on the North Shore of Long Island where they were to spend their first week of marriage. He loved someone else and would go on loving someone else, he'd said, but it would not affect their marriage. He was prepared to be a dutiful and affectionate husband. Amelia wondered if he'd believed that at the time. Perhaps his ideas of duty and affection were different from hers. Certainly he'd been dutiful that night, and she supposed he'd tried to be affectionate. The attempt had been less than successful. It had been about as bad as those things can be.

She'd been terrified. She knew now that Charles had been too, though she never would have guessed it at the time. He'd never been with a woman before. Her own experience had been limited to several rather chaste kisses with Sam Van Nest. Nothing had prepared her for that night. He'd taken a long time, not out of deference to her, she realized now, but out of distaste for her. Still, he'd done nothing to prepare her, and when he entered her abruptly, mechanically, she'd cried out in pain. He seemed not to notice. She supposed he was too preoccupied to notice. She couldn't see his features in the darkness, but she could hear the sound of his labors. Even after all these years she could still hear that sound. There was no passion to it and certainly no pleasure. It was not an animal sound. It was the sound of a determined human being struggling to complete some unpleasant physical labor. And he had completed it, to his satisfaction if not to hers.

She supposed he'd tried to be dutiful and affectionate that night, despite the abruptness and the pain and the awful grunting sounds in the darkness. She supposed it wasn't his fault that he cared for neither her nor the task at hand.

Things had not improved during the week at Raleigh. Charles seemed determined to get started on an heir as soon as possible. Each night after an interminable dinner spent discussing her duties and a quiet brandy in the library while Charles picked over her father's books, they'd retire to their separate rooms. Ten minutes later Charles would knock at her door and they'd repeat the travesty of that first night. On the last night, the night before they were to return to New York, he'd begun more slowly, more tenderly, and she'd thought that perhaps he might be starting to care for her. He'd strayed from the pattern then, kissed her a second time, and even touched her breast. Amelia was surprised and pathetically grateful and something else as well, and she'd clung to him, her arms around his neck, her body pressed to his. She felt herself moving against him though she was not aware of willing herself to and felt fear of him draining away and the dislike. It would be all right. She'd make it all right. 'Charles,' she whispered, her mouth against his ear. He pulled away then and she saw the look on his face. The bold features were a mask of disgust.

'Control yourself, Amelia.' His voice was sharp, as if he were telling a dog to heel.

She turned away quickly and pulled the skirt of her nightdress down, but it was no good. She had exposed herself.

When they arrived in England and she met his cousin Prudence, Amelia thought she understood Charles' coolness to her. It was a shame. Under other circumstances, she was sure she and Prudence would have become friends, but if Amelia did not love Charles, she could not bring herself to befriend the woman he loved. She supposed if she were a 'good woman' full of human kindness and Christian forgiveness she would, but she had always known she was not a 'good woman' in that sense.

Prudence, for her part, had gone out of her way to be kind to Amelia, but then, Amelia reasoned, Prudence could afford to. She was the loved one, by her own husband Simon, and by Charles. When the four of them were together, and they seemed to be so much of the time that first year, both during the season in London and at country house parties, Amelia felt more than ever the outsider. The three of them had grown up together, Prudence and Charles as first cousins, Simon and Charles as childhood friends. The two men had gone through Eton together and Oxford. They were even in the same regiment. The only thing that surprised Amelia now was that it had taken her so long to understand. Had she really been that naive? What was it Charles always said about her? She was educated, but she was stupid, too stupid to understand that Simon rather than Prudence was her rival, too stupid to see that the four of them were always together not because Charles wanted to be with Prudence, but because he couldn't bear to be without Simon. He loved another, Charles had said that first night, but it was his duty to marry her. She was his duty, but Simon was his passion, and once she'd produced Anthony he'd given full rein to that passion.

That weekend at Wentonhurst returned, the sound of Charles' laughter in the next room, then Simon's voice in a half-whisper and more laughter from both of them. She'd told herself there was nothing peculiar. They were probably having a nightcap together. She'd sat in her own cold room, too large to be warmed by the fire in the hearth, too formal to be comfortable because nothing in it had been changed since Queen Victoria's visit in 1853, and wondered what they were laughing about. Hunting stories? Women? Her? Anthony had given her the answer, not Anthony her son, but Anthony, Charles' younger brother. She'd been surprised when he'd knocked at her door late that night, but glad, too, because she'd been lonely sitting there listening to her husband enjoying himself in the next room. She didn't want Charles, she told herself, and she dreaded the times he still came to her because in order to be safe he really ought to have another son, a backup model, a spare, but she didn't like being ignored either, or ridiculed. Some of that laughter must be directed at her. Why else the long silent periods between?

Anthony was wearing a dressing gown and carrying a bottle of brandy and two glasses. Looking back on it now, she realized he'd been anything but subtle. And still she'd been too naive to believe what was happening. 'But Charles . . . your brother,' she'd said when Anthony had pulled her to him and tried to kiss her. What a clever response! What an original response! Charles was right, she was stupid.

'What about Charlie?' Anthony had laughed without letting go of her waist. She could smell the brandy on his breath.

'He's my husband,' she said. It was hard to sound dignified when you were struggling to pull away from a man twice your weight and strength. Anthony resembled his brother in appearance, if nothing else. 'Your brother.'

'Which means we're simply keeping things in the family.' He'd bent to her again, but she'd turned her face from his mouth.

'He'd never forgive you.'

Anthony dropped his hand from her waist, and she stepped back quickly. 'Do you mean you really don't know? Is it possible you've been married to Charlie for a year and a half and don't know?' Anthony sat in one of the bristly horsehair chairs before the fire and poured himself another brandy. 'Charlie's right about you American girls. You're not very bright.' He laughed again. 'Your husband, my dear Amelia, doesn't like girls. He likes boys. Simon to be specific, though there have been a few others over the years. Your husband, my dear, is homosexual.' He filled the other brandy glass and crossed the room to give it to her. 'So I doubt very much he'd be in the least furious with me or you. I doubt very much he'd even mind a little help in producing the spare. After all, it's not quite Charlie's line, and the blood's the same. Your spare will still be a Pugh, still a rightful heir to the Duringham title.' He'd pulled her to him again, spilling the brandy down the front of her dressing gown, but he'd seemed not to notice. His mouth was wet on hers and devouring, and his hands were hot against her skin as he fumbled beneath her dressing gown, but the mouth and the hands, blind, rough, uncaring as they were, were not as bad as the words. 'Stop acting, Amelia. You want this as much as I do. You're in heat. Like one of Charlie's bitches.' And he'd begun working at the trousers beneath his robe as he spoke, tearing them open, pressing himself against her, forcing himself on her, and taunting her all the while with her obvious embarrassing need.

Amelia stood suddenly. She wasn't going to keep going over that night. She wasn't going to keep remembering the absurd scuffle with Anthony's hands on her body and his own exposed in his desire, her inane protests and again the burst of laughter from the next room. He'd left finally, leaving her robe torn and her pride shredded because he'd left laughing at her. Damn all of them and their laughter. Damn her memories of that night and all the others, the nights she'd had to put up with Charles and his cold, superior invasion of her privacy and her body, the nights she'd lain awake thinking of Charles and Simon, horrified by the thought of them together, fascinated by it, pained by it and the rejection it implied, though she'd admit to none of those emotions.

But she'd sworn she wasn't going to think of any of that now. She left the room quickly and started for the Cliff Walk. It was a good hour for the Cliff Walk. The sunset would be perfect and the Walk deserted.

When she reached a small glade several estates down, she sat on the grass and looked out toward the ocean. She'd been right about both things. The Walk was deserted and the sinking sun spectacular. Amelia loved the sea at this hour. The glistening reflections of blues and greens and twilight pink always reminded her of an Impressionist painting. She remembered the first time she'd seen that and had mentioned it to Sam Van Nest. 'But it really is the way they paint it,' she'd cried looking out across the water.

'You're learning, Amelia. Improving,' he'd added, but there'd been nothing unkind or even patronizing in his voice.

She wondered about Sam and how he'd turned out. He'd married, of course, the daughter of a Midwestern oil baron. No name but plenty of money, though by that time she imagined Sam hadn't needed the money quite so badly. From what she'd heard by that time he'd made quite a bit of his own. She wondered what Sam's marriage had been like. Even if Amelia had known his wife, it would have been hard to tell. You could only guess about other people's marriages, and then more often than not you were wrong. Still, it must have been happy because people said he'd turned bitter after the accident. For once public opinion was on Sam's side. Losing a wife after less than a year of marriage, they agreed, would make any man bitter. At least he'd had that, Amelia thought, pulling up a few blades of grass and rolling them between her hands. She'd rather have less than a year of a good marriage than ten of a bad one. Still, she'd hung on for the ten years, through the birth of Anthony and the awful delivery and immediate death of the spare – Charles' spare, not his brother's. She'd stuck it out until Anthony was off to school, and she probably would have

151

continued to stick it out if it hadn't been for the humiliation. She could live with the rest of it, with Charles' passion for Simon, with his lack of feeling for her. Certainly she could live without sex. Wasn't that exactly what she was going to do now? But she couldn't live with constant humiliation, with being criticized in public and ridiculed in private. She walked badly, he said, like an American baseball player, and spoke even worse. She read too much and laughed too little. She was without grace at the tea table, without wit at the dinner table, without attraction in the bedroom.

Charles had a heyday the year her father's colt ran in the Derby. 'We know about the horse's bloodlines,' he'd told friends one evening in Amelia's presence, 'but we can't be so sure of my esteemed father-in-law.' Amelia left the room then, but Charles had simply come to her later and told her she'd made a bloody fool of herself.

Then there was her social conscience, her damnable social conscience, Charles called it. When he discovered that she'd instructed the kitchen maids to sort the scraps destined for the needy rather than dump them all into a single pail, he told her not to waste the maids' time.

'But it's disgusting,' she'd protested. 'Beef and fish and cheese and pudding all mixed up that way.'

'It's not disgusting to them. They're grateful for the scraps. You see' – the superior smile twitched beneath the sandy moustache – 'they don't have your delicate palate, my dear Amelia.'

As the years passed he'd managed to instill his

prejudices in Tony. It hadn't been a difficult task. The society they inhabited conspired to reinforce Charles' view and undermine hers. Finally, a few months before she'd left she overheard the boy telling a friend that Amelia wasn't his real mother at all. His real mother, an English noblewoman, had died giving birth to him. Amelia was his stepmother. She'd never mentioned the incident to Charles – she wouldn't give him the satisfaction – but she'd never forgiven him for it either.

When they'd married, Charles had promised to treat her with affection and respect, but there had been little of either in his conduct to her. He was unable, it seemed to Amelia, to forgive her for two things: for being a common American and his wife.

In the end it had been the humiliation that had driven her away, the humiliation and Michael, her conscience added. Michael had done more damage to her marriage in six months than Charles had in ten years.

She'd been a fool about Michael too, taken him more seriously than he wanted to be taken, mistaken his desire for a stronger emotion. Had he laughed at her when she'd talked of leaving Charles and going off with him, or had he been too alarmed to laugh?

'In England, Your Grace . . .' he'd begun trying to make light of it that afternoon in his rooms in Croydon.

'Don't call me that,' she'd said and moved closer to him in the big bed. The first time they'd made love she'd been shocked by his leanness. Now she loved the wiry strength of his body.

'In England, Amelia,' he went on and his voice was gentle, though he was not a gentle man, 'duchesses do not leave their castles – or their dukes – to go off with penniless younger sons.'

'They do if they love them.'

He got out of bed and crossed the room to a small table where he'd left a package of cigarettes. He moved confidently, even without his clothes, and she loved watching him. He took a cigarette from the pack and lit it. They were Turkish cigarettes, she remembered, Helmars. 'You don't love me, Amelia, you love making love. I'm grateful to you for that, as I imagine you are to me, but gratitude isn't love. And love isn't what I'm looking for. I thought you knew that.'

She knew now he'd been right. She hadn't loved him, but she hadn't been able to resist him. From the first time she'd seen him, an irreverent fox among all those social chickens at Lady Millicent Townsen's *soirée*, she'd felt some physical cord in her tighten. His face was thin and pale, but the lips beneath a thick moustache were full and sensual. She found her eyes drawn from the mouth to the bright animal eyes. They looked at her openly, curiously.

She asked Prudence who he was. 'Michael Broughton,' Pru said. 'The Duke of Bensington's youngest boy. And quite the renegade. Wouldn't go into the army. Couldn't go into the Church, if half the stories one hears about him are true. Be careful, Amelia. He fancies himself a poet, and though I've never seen his verses, I hear his life is more than a little Byronic.'

She hadn't been careful. From the moment Pru had introduced them she'd been anything but careful. He'd asked her to come to tea the next day and she'd pretended to hesitate, but he must have known she was pretending because he'd merely smiled and given her his address.

It was odd how easy it had been. No, not easy, simply unavoidable. She'd pretended to debate the decision. All the next day till tea time she'd let her conscience do battle with her desires, but when the time came to leave for Croydon, nothing short of Anthony's falling ill or a national disaster could have stopped her, and the latter, she supposed, would only have given her more reason to grasp at whatever momentary pleasure she could find. That was her mood on that afternoon last autumn when she'd gone to Michael's room. That was her state of mind after ten years of marriage to Charles. And that was why she hadn't hesitated. She'd been leading up to Michael for longer than she knew.

She'd gone that afternoon and continued to go until one day six months later when she'd spoken of running off with him. She'd stopped going then, but she hadn't regretted the six months. They'd been a shock to her, a revelation that had turned everything in her life inside out.

Amelia closed her eyes against the sun, low now on the distant horizon, but the gesture only intensified the images. She could see Michael's room as vividly as if she were there. It was a bleak room without sunlight or view, furnished meagerly with a few good pieces that looked out of place – a massive armoire, a Renaissance library table, and a deep four-poster bed. The room was simpler than any she'd inhabited, yet she'd been happier in that room than ever in her life. No, not happier, simply alive.

Just as she hadn't known what to expect with Charles, so she was unprepared for Michael, and at first she was shocked by the force, almost the anger of his desire. But the shock passed quickly and the fierceness of his passion fired her own. She was no longer shy or embarrassed or surprised at anything, and the things that had disgusted her with Charles, the nakedness of spirit as well as body, the intimacy and the vulnerability that sprang from it held her in a kind of thrall. He wasn't abandoned. He was too deliberate for abandon, but he made her abandoned. Even when she was not with him, she found herself moving in a state of heightened physical sensitivity. She was suddenly aware of the way things felt, the breeze against her face, the chafe and caress of her clothing, the warmth of someone's hand taking hers in greeting. And she began to see things differently. She began to look at men. Wherever she went, to tea or dinner, to the theater or a ball, she found herself noticing men as she never had before. They were no longer remote personages, Sir So-and-So or Mr Somebody, but men made of flesh and blood, tendon and muscle, strength and desire. She noticed their eyes and mouths, the clothes they wore and the way they wore them. She imagined their bodies beneath the clothing, watched them move and pictured them making love. She felt one's beard against her shoulder, another's hands on her breasts, a third's thighs gripping hers. She told herself to stop, but she couldn't stop, and she moved through her familiar world numb to the old concerns, unaware of what people said to her or how she answered, living only for her new awareness and the hours she spent in Michael's room.

He'd been right. She hadn't loved him, any more than he'd loved her, yet she couldn't stop thinking of him. She'd stopped seeing him, but she hadn't stopped wanting him. Night after night she'd lie in bed, unable to sleep, unable to stop remembering the way his body felt against hers. And when she did sleep and dream of him, as she often did, it was even worse. It would be so real and she'd awake hot and trembling, hating herself, hating him, hating her loneliness most of all.

She found she was shivering and stood abruptly. The sun was almost gone and though the wind had not come up again, there was a chill. Behind her she heard the sound of a gardener's shears keeping time to a ragtime beat. The voice was off-key but cheerful.

> At the devil's ball, in the devil's hall
> I caught a glimpse of my mother-in-law
> Dancing at the devil's ball

She started back along the Cliff Walk. This had to stop. She had to stop brooding, about the husband who hadn't wanted her and the lover who hadn't loved her. She had to stop brooding about sex. It was something no nice woman did.

When she returned to Belle Isle, she found her mother and Caroline in the dining room with Hatfield and Miss Wilkens, the secretary. The table, set with gold, silver, and crystal for thirty-seven, was more blinding than the setting sun. Edith stood at one end directing the major-domo to move one enamel place marker here and another there.

'We can't put the lieutenant in Mr Van Rensaleer's place,' Edith said, and there was a faint echo in the huge room despite the heavy velvet draperies and the huge tapestry that covered one wall. The dining room was meant for more than five people. 'Grace Vanderbilt would never forgive me for giving her some obscure lieutenant as a dinner partner. Perhaps next to Bessie Lehr. Bessie never complains.' Hatfield carried one plaque down the table and another up.

'I'm afraid that won't work, Mrs Leighton,' Miss Wilkens said. Miss Wilkens was even better than Edith at the nuances of social relations. She had to be. With family connections, a little luck, or a great deal of beauty Miss Wilkens might have lived as Vanessa Hunter did, but unfortunately she had none of those attributes, so she kept up on other people's lives and sustained her own as a social secretary. 'Now the lieutenant is between Mrs Lehr and the baroness. If we put Mr Kimball next to Mrs Vanderbilt, the lieutenant can sit next to Miss Elizabeth.'

Edith looked thoughtful for a minute. 'I suppose it will have to do. Elizabeth has Sydney on her other side so that's all right, and we'll leave Mr Sturgis between Bessie Lehr and the baroness.'

Amelia walked down the long table until she found her own place. She was to sit between Kirkland Selby and Sky. Well, Sky would help. She smiled when she noticed the sapphire pendant hanging from the small plant next to her name plaque. Her mother had given it to her years ago. Edith might not know the value of money, but she understood the importance of its visibility.

Amelia wondered where Sam Van Nest was to sit. She began to make her way around the table reading the plaques. 'Amelia!' Her mother's voice and its faint echo called her to a halt. 'Why aren't you dressing?'

'I was just going to dress, Mother. I stopped to see if I could help you and Carrie,' she lied.

'You're a little late for that. You'd better dress. And do something about your hair. I can tell you've been out walking. It looks dreadful. I only hope Ellen can fix it.'

She left the room quickly but couldn't help noticing the look Hatfield gave her as she did. She'd never been able to figure Hatfield out. Years ago she never had been sure whether he'd been proud of her for marrying the duke or disappointed in her for giving in. She'd never known what Hatfield thought of her. The answer was probably, nothing. She was, as her mother and Carrie said, simply dramatizing herself. Hatfield had enough to do keeping the other servants in place, the silver polished, and the guests' names straight. There wasn't much time, or inclination she imagined, to think of her.

She was wrong, of course. Hatfield, like all servants, thought a good deal about the people who employed him. He also knew a good deal about them. He knew something about Edith Leighton, for example, that he was sure no one else knew, except perhaps Elias Leighton. Mrs Leighton was what would be called below stairs a tease. It was hard to believe, but Hatfield knew it was true. Occasionally in the morning when she'd finished with Miss Wilkens, she'd call him in for some special instructions, and frequently on those occasions her bed jacket or peignoir would be open in the most disconcerting ways. The first time it had happened, years ago now, he'd thought it was an accident and struggled to keep his eyes directed at some innocuous area like the canopy over the bed or the Fragonard mural behind it. But as these incidents continued, he'd come to realize they were not accidental. He'd also stopped playing the gentleman's gentleman, or to be more accurate in this case, the lady's gentleman, and let his eyes linger where they naturally would and where he knew Mrs Leighton wanted them to.

There were always secrets like that in a house like this, but if you wanted to hold your position, you kept the secrets and your opinions to yourself. He hadn't mentioned to anyone that Miss Elizabeth was up to something, though he was sure she was. He didn't know what it was, but he was willing to bet it had to do with a man and the man wasn't Mr Hallenbeck. He didn't mention the telephone calls he sometimes heard Mr Niebold making. He'd never talked about that incident years ago when poor Miss Amelia – Her Grace, Mrs Leighton insisted these days – had been locked in her room, though heaven knew enough people had asked him about it. And he'd never told Her Grace that she'd get along a lot better in this world if she had some of Miss Elizabeth's reticence and her mother's guile. She'd be a lot better off if she'd learn to hide that light of hers under a bushel now and then. He'd never said any of those things, though he thought about them often. The important thing was never to talk about them and never to look as if you were thinking about them, and his face now was a perfect mask of ignorance as he closed the door behind Her Grace and told Mrs Leighton in answer to her question that no, Mr Niebold had not yet returned.

Edith had been expecting the answer. She told Hatfield and Miss Wilkens that would be all for now. 'Do you know where he is, Caroline?'

'I can guess where he is.' Caroline's small mouth pulled down at the corners, and she looked as if she were going to cry.

'Pull yourself together,' Edith snapped. 'Crying isn't going to do any good. He's with that Hunter woman, isn't he?'

'I imagine so. He took Leighton sailing this afternoon, but Lee returned hours ago.'

Edith moved around the table in silence,

adjusting an orchid here, moving a menu there. 'He's becoming more careless. Either that or more obvious.' Her eyes moved from the table to her daughter. 'He's going to ask for a divorce.'

Caroline's large eyes grew wider. She'd told Amelia she didn't believe in divorce, but it went beyond that. She couldn't conceive of divorce. It was a prerogative she'd dismissed. It had never occurred to her that Sky might not have done the same.

'You won't give it to him, of course. I don't believe in divorce, Caroline. I never have and I never will, despite Mrs William K. Vanderbilt.'

'Everyone calls her Mrs Belmont now, Mama.'

'*Everyone* may follow Mrs Vanderbilt in her folly, but I needn't. Like that absurd office she set up on Bellevue Avenue for those suffrage people and the way she opened her house to them. Mrs Vanderbilt may make a spectacle of herself marching up Fifth Avenue demanding the vote for women, but that doesn't mean I have to. And she may divorce her husband and go right out and marry one of his friends, but I'm not going to let my daughters make the same mistake. That goes for you as well as Amelia. It doesn't matter that Duringham's a duke and Schuyler isn't. It doesn't matter that Amelia has no reason except her own willfulness and you have to bear the burden of that Hunter woman. Leightons do not divorce.'

'How can I help it if Sky's determined to?'

'You'll simply refuse. He can't divorce you. I doubt Sky would even if he could – he's still a gentleman – but the point is he can't. And you're not going to divorce him. No matter what grounds he gives you. Nevertheless, we can't have him flaunting this affair in our faces. You'll have to make that clear to him. I'm sure we can work out a perfectly reasonable accord. Your father and I have. Sky can have as much time away as he likes, but when he is with us, he must behave as a devoted husband.'

'But I don't want Sky spending all his time away. I don't like being without a husband.'

'You don't like being without an admirer, my dear, and we'll find you plenty of those. There's Harry Lehr and Mr Kimball and a great many others. You can count on them to serve as needed.' Edith looked across the table at her daughter. It was a long, serious look as if she were considering a painting she'd bought. 'I'm sure you'll find the arrangement satisfactory. Perhaps more satisfactory than Schuyler's presence.'

Sydney Hallenbeck arrived at Belle Isle at seven-thirty. The invitations called for eight o'clock, but he did not worry that he would be unwelcome. Mrs Leighton was always pleased to see him, and tonight, he knew, she would be especially happy. Though neither of them had spoken of the matter, he knew Edith Leighton wanted him to marry Elizabeth as much as he wanted to marry her. Sydney wasn't vain, merely realistic. He understood his position in society perfectly. Only five families in America rivaled the Hallenbeck combination of money and lineage, and one of them had no eligible sons while another was

163

notorious for producing alcoholics and wife-beaters. There was worthy competition for Elizabeth, but not a great deal of it. And now that his mother had given her permission, he'd banish what little there was. She'd done more than give her permission. She'd said she was pleased about the match. He could hardly wait to tell Elizabeth, and he'd arrived half an hour early with that in mind.

When the maid came to announce that Mr Hallenbeck was waiting for her on the lower piazza, Lizzy was dressed but still struggling to fasten the orchids he'd sent. She wished he'd stop sending orchids. She hated orchids, though to be fair to Sydney, she couldn't expect him to know that. Ever since his first orchid had arrived – how many years ago now, three? four? – the same game had been going on. As long as she thanked him for the beautiful flowers, he went on sending them, and as long as he went on sending them, she had to thank him for the beautiful flowers.

He was standing with his back to the house looking out over the ocean. The view, Elizabeth knew, was identical to that from the terrace of his mother's house only two properties away.

'Thank you for the flowers, Sydney,' she said. 'They're lovely,' she added.

He turned at the sound of her voice and covered the space between them in a few steps. 'Not nearly as lovely as you.' It was what he always said, and she supposed he meant it, but somehow she never really believed him. There was something curiously unconvincing about Sydney.

'Did you have a good trip up?' she asked.

'Calm and uneventful. Mother said you lunched with her.'

'Calm and uneventful.' She saw him reach up and smooth the reddish-brown hair in a familiar gesture and knew he'd found the comment irreverent.

'Mother's very fond of you, Lizzy.'

'I'm very fond of her,' she lied. She neither liked nor disliked Beatrice Hallenbeck. Sydney's mother was simply another of those women who governed her life from a distance as surely as her own mother did immediately. Some of them were more kind, others more vicious, some more demanding, others more inclined to criticize, but beneath the superficial differences they were alike. There were a few exceptions, of course. She couldn't say she liked Mrs Belmont, but she admired her for opening Marble House to all those suffragists. She didn't know Mrs Van Nest very well, because the old lady never went out in society anymore, but Elizabeth loved to see her moving along the Cliff Walk at a sprightly clip, and when she stopped to talk, she always had something amusing to say, but Mrs Van Nest was an exception and Sydney's mother was very much the rule. Sydney's mother was a fact of life to be accommodated rather than liked or disliked.

'It was you who convinced her, Lizzy. I might have known it would be. I've been arguing with her for more than a year, and she just kept insisting I was too young to marry, but when I got here today, she said she'd changed her mind or at least she was willing to give us her blessing.'

Elizabeth had known it was coming, but she'd relied on Mrs Hallenbeck to keep it from coming quite so soon. Beatrice Hallenbeck had announced more than once, and especially pointedly when Elizabeth or her mother was within hearing, that she did not believe in early marriage for men in general and for her own Sydney in particular. 'I know Sydney better than most mothers know their sons,' she'd add. 'After all, it's been only the two of us for so long now, since Mr Hallenbeck's death. And I know that Sydney is not ready for marriage. I doubt that he will be before he's thirty.' But now something had changed her mind.

'Mother said,' Sydney went on, 'she still thought we ought to wait, but she isn't insisting that we wait. In fact' – Sydney laughed as if he'd finally managed to outsmart his mother – 'she's even begun making plans. She wants to buy the other half of the Fifth Avenue block and build something for us. That way we'll be right next door. She'll have the Fifty-fourth Street side and we'll have the Fifty-fifth. Of course, we'll have separate entrances, but there will be some passage between. And she wants us to stay with her while we're building. Mother said she wouldn't ask us if I were marrying just anyone, but she knows she couldn't ask for a better daughter-in-law. She said she only has to watch you with your own mother to know that.'

Elizabeth cursed the laziness and the dread of confrontation that made her seem such a dutiful daughter. She cursed the manner she wore like a costume, the act that had convinced Beatrice Hallenbeck she'd make no trouble or even change in her life. And she cursed herself for letting things drag on this way with Sydney. Elizabeth had known what Sydney wanted and her mother was working for, but she'd counted on time to take care of everything. And now because of her cowardice she stood here on the piazza with Sydney looking earnest and charting the rest of their lives like a navigator who has taken into account every possible shift in wind and current, but has forgot the set of the sails.

'Slow down, Sydney.' Elizabeth tried to force a laugh, but she could hear the hollowness of the sound. 'You're going much too fast for me. Properties and houses. Next thing I know you'll be planning our fiftieth wedding anniversary.' She wished she hadn't said that. It sounded as if she expected to have one.

He took her hand. His hands were almost as soft as her own. 'I guess I'm doing this badly, but I assumed all the rest. I assumed the important part.' He smiled as if proud of his own felicity. 'I thought you knew I loved you and wanted to marry you, Lizzy. I thought you knew all that.'

She had, of course, which only made things worse.

'I thought the only opposition was Mother.' He was still smiling down at her, a half-shy smile. He'd lost weight in the last year, but his face still retained a boyish roundness. There was something soft and unfinished about the cheeks. 'I never dreamed, not after all this time, that you'd be opposed too.' It was clear, from the way he looked and spoke, that he still didn't dream as much. What did he think, that it was a girlish ploy? 'I can understand your wanting time to think about it, or at least I can try to,' he said and his voice was calm. He did think it was a girlish ploy. 'Only don't take too long, Lizzy. I don't think I can stand waiting much longer. Especially now that Mother's given her approval.'

Elizabeth told herself she couldn't possibly end things now, not with the most important dinner and ball of the season beginning all around them, not with the sound of automobiles and carriages pulling up on the long curving drive before the house, not with the crush of guests in the foyer and the swell of voices as people met and men and women divided to go off to their respective dressing rooms. The windows of the men's dressing room opened onto the piazza and she could hear a dozen deep voices laughing and talking as they collected the flowers for their lapels and opened the envelopes that told them whom they were to take in to dinner. How could she tell Sydney she had no intention of marrying him when the card inside his envelope said *Miss Elizabeth Leighton* and bound them together for the hours ahead? How could she tell him anything amid the growing excitement of the voices and the mounting aroma of perfume and flowers and the shimmering light that glowed from every window. The answer, Lizzy thought gratefully, was that she could not, and she simply took the arm Sydney offered her and let him lead her inside.

* * *

Lieutenant Atherton had been prompt, as befitted an officer and a gentleman, too prompt he felt since he knew none of the people milling around beneath the high vaulted ceiling decorated with paintings of the Muses and so much gold leaf it looked as if Midas himself had done the work. As often as he was invited to these Newport 'cottages,' he never grew accustomed to them. They made him tired. There were too many pictures and murals, too much gold and silver, too much carving and *tromp l'oeil*. There was, simply, too much of everything. It wasn't enough to have a perfectly symmetrical room accented by huge, perfectly matched crystal chandeliers. There had to be a mirrored wall, better yet two of them, that made the room go on into infinity. It wasn't enough to have a huge library full of leather-bound, gold-tooled volumes. The whole library had to look like a rare binding with its coffered ceiling of leather and gilt and its elaborately tooled walls. It wasn't enough to have an authentic Moorish smoking room, there also had to be a medieval hall and a Roman atrium and a Chinese teahouse, all clustered under the same roof. He'd seen how people entertained in these houses, but he still couldn't imagine how they lived in them. He especially didn't understand how Elizabeth Leighton lived in this one. *Very comfortably*, he reminded himself. *And don't you forget it*. And just to make sure he wouldn't, he forced himself to watch her crossing the room to him now. She looked very comfortable with her hand tucked into the arm of one of those smooth-faced polo-playing types who rarely bothered to talk to Atherton unless it was to tell him how the Navy ought to be run. *Miss Elizabeth Leighton looks perfectly comfortable and damn happy as well, and don't you forget it*, Atherton told himself again.

The boy threw the engine into reverse and the launch came to a halt beside the yacht club dock. Sam was out of the small boat before the boy had a chance to cleat the lines. His evening shoes slipped a little on the wooden float but he caught his balance quickly.

It always felt strange being back at the yacht club. Maybe that was because it was one of the few places in Newport that still held pleasant memories for him. As a boy he'd learned to sail here. He remembered one of the first races he'd ever won. His father had been on the dock watching him come in afterward, and Sam, in his euphoria, had started to horse around with a boy in one of the other boats. They'd got rambunctious and had come close to capsizing both boats. It wouldn't have been a terrible thing if they had. Those boats were pretty light and easy enough to right, but his father had been furious. There were rules to sailing, he said when Sam reached the dock, and one of the rules was that you took it seriously. Not just when you were racing, not just when you were on a big boat, but always. His father had taken away his sailing privileges for three days.

Sam started down the long dock. A Royal Standard Cudell was pulled up at the end of it. Just like Mrs Leighton to import her automobiles as well as her sons-in-law. Elias Leighton stood beside the car smoking a cigar and watching Sam thoughtfully.

'I was just thinking of your father,' Leighton said as he held out his hand to Sam.

'So was I.'

'He was quite a sailor.'

Sam's eyes darted to Elias' face, searching for the implication. Quite a sailor, but not much of a businessman?

'I hear you're almost as good as he was,' Elias continued. 'Though I don't imagine you have as much time for it. The word is that Morgan partners never stop working.'

'Like tonight, you mean?'

The chauffeur had opened the door of the Cudell and Elias stepped into it. 'Tonight?' he asked. 'I didn't know tonight was business. I thought it was pure pleasure, the pleasure of my wife's hospitality.'

Sam followed him into the car. The cagey old bastard. He's almost as bad as Morgan. Leighton knew about the five men and the job he had to do. Sam was sure of it. But he was going to let him do it alone.

171

V

Three Peerlesses, a Brewster, a Mercedes, and two carriages were pulled up in the circular drive before Belle Isle.

'That's James Corcoran getting out of the second Peerless,' Elias said. Sam saw a tall, almost gaunt man spring from the automobile as if he were in a hurry. Under a full head of hair that had not even begun to gray his face was long and thin with a prominent nose and a narrow, canny chin. He turned to help a woman out of the car. She came only to Corcoran's shoulder and was too plump for the great jeweled stomacher that flashed beneath her evening cape, but her face, Sam suspected, had once been pretty. Beneath the folds of flesh, the nose was well shaped and the eyes lively. The eyes were in constant motion, taking in the other guests, how they arrived, what they were wearing, whom they greeted first. The eyes were very excited.

'Apparently, my wife is becoming democratic,' Leighton went on. 'Or Mr and Mrs Corcoran are becoming more acceptable. Of course, a hundred million can buy a great deal of acceptability.'

'Not as I hear it,' Sam said. 'I was under the

impression that Mr Corcoran still had a long way to go.'

'Well, of course, these things take time. And effort. Corcoran's daughter, who, I see, has not been invited, has plenty of the former and I'm sure Corcoran is willing to expend a good deal of the latter. Let me introduce you,' Leighton said, taking Sam's arm and leading him across the terrace.

The name Van Nest did something extraordinary to Mrs Corcoran. Suddenly the eyes stopped moving and fastened on Sam. Mr Corcoran shook his hand warmly. 'Been wanting to meet you, Van Nest. In fact, a mutual friend of ours, De Peyster, set up a lunch. At the Knickerbocker,' he added in a tone that for all its gruffness was close to reverential, 'but you were called out of town. We'll have to do it some other time.' Sam agreed they would.

Inside the massive oak doors and the second set of grille ones, Hatfield stood sentry. 'Good evening, Mr Van Nest.' Sam wondered if Hatfield remembered their last meeting. Nothing in his demeanor indicated that he did, but then Hatfield never gave out anything – except the scent of gin.

'How are you, Hatfield?' Sam asked. 'You're looking well.'

'Thank you, sir.' The tone was still resonant. Nothing ever changed, Sam thought, moving with the other guests through the large marble foyer to the great hall. Nothing changed, but he did.

And Amelia, he saw as soon as he entered the room. She was standing between her mother and her older sister in a receiving line. Her head above a wide jeweled dog collar was inclined stiffly toward the man she was greeting. Then she saw him and straightened. Every inch the duchess, he thought. Amelia had changed, all right.

Moving down the receiving line, he would rather, he thought, have run the gauntlet.

'How nice to see you, Samuel,' Edith said. 'And how kind of you to bring my husband. He's always so tardy.' Smoothly, like a conductor bringing an orchestra into harmony, Edith gestured Elias to his place beside her on the receiving line. As she did so, she dropped Sam's hand and there was nothing for him to do but move on to Amelia.

'Your Grace,' he said and bowed over the slim hand that felt like ice in his. She looked annoyed, as if she'd caught the irony in his voice. Well, what did she expect? What in hell did she expect?

'Mr Van Nest,' she said and the tone was no warmer than his own.

Who is Amelia?

She'd changed all right, he thought as he straightened and looked into her face. It was a mask of composure. Even the eyes, the eyes he'd once found so open and a little wild, were haughty. He moved on to Caroline. To think he'd ever believed there was a difference between them. To think he'd ever supposed that Amelia was different. There was only one Leighton woman. She just happened to wear four different faces.

Sam reached the end of the receiving line and looked around the room quickly. None of the men resembled the pictures he'd seen of the duke, but of course those had been wedding pictures that had appeared in the newspapers ten years ago. Perhaps marriage to Amelia had changed him. Or perhaps he wasn't here. Well, it made no difference whether he was or not. There were only five men present tonight who mattered. Sam moved off to the area in front of the Aubusson Chinoiserie tapestry that half hid the organ where Corcoran stood with Sturgis and Wainwright. Wainwright was talking about his breeding farm in Kentucky. He was, Sam knew, passionate about his farm, and foolish about it, too. He'd spent a fortune trying to breed winners, but without much luck. It wasn't merely that he was an inferior judge of horses. He was too hungry to win. Even when he had a colt that looked like a winner, he tended to bring it along too quickly, and pity the trainer who said as much. Wainwright had fired so many of them that few reputable men would work for him.

Sam looked at the long lean face with the cold eyes. One eyelid drooped more than the other, and it gave him a mean look, but there was no strength to the meanness, no discipline. John Wainwright was the son of a rich man, but not the grandson. He'd had all the indulgence and none of the training. He'd been given everything and taught nothing. Sam remembered a story he'd heard about Wainwright several years ago, something about a row at an illegal gambling house in New York. Someone had accused Wainwright of cheating. Sam never knew whether Wainwright had cheated or not, but he knew one thing –

Wainwright was capable of cheating. It wasn't merely his determination to win. Sam could understand that. It was his inability to lose. Wainwright was a bad loser and would do anything to avoid it.

Corcoran inquired about Sam's stables. 'I'd scarcely call it a stable,' Sam said. 'Only a few hunters and polo ponies. I'm not in Wainwright's class.' Wainwright looked pleased about the fact and began talking about a two-year-old he was going to race in New York this fall. As Sam listened half-heartedly, he found himself looking around the familiar room.

He remembered an afternoon when he'd come over to Belle Isle and found Amelia alone here. She was wearing a middy blouse and sailing skirt and looked absurd and a little lost at the huge organ beneath the soaring cathedral ceiling. She'd been playing . . . Damn it, what did it matter what she'd been playing.

He looked across the room at her now. She didn't look ludicrous or lost now. She looked as if she fitted in perfectly. She was standing with her father, leaning over him a little because she was the taller of the two.

'I'm sorry,' Elias said in an undertone to his daughter, 'about our conversation this afternoon. But take my word for it, Amelia, Duringham's price will come down.'

Amelia knew it wouldn't, but she'd gone beyond argument. Now that she'd spoken to Wickert, she'd gone beyond all the conventional solutions. The knowledge made her feel more than a little reckless, but she wasn't going to explain that to her father.

Edith saw her husband move to her daughter's side and noticed the way he leaned to her confidentially. He needn't have bothered to be so secretive. She knew what Amelia was after, and she wasn't going to take the chance of having Amelia convince Elias to meet Charles' demands. Not when she'd finally convinced Charles to meet her own.

'I scarcely think,' she said joining her husband and daughter, 'that this is the time for conspiracy. Amelia, go talk to Bessie Lehr. She seems to be quite alone over there. You might at least,' Edith continued to her husband when Amelia was gone, 'have arrived a little early. The least you can do is maintain the pretense that you're the host. Especially,' she went on smiling as if she were telling him an amusing story, 'since I was good enough to invite Van Nest and those Corcorans.'

'You always were a good woman,' Elias said, and turned away from her as one might from an unpleasant and slightly embarrassing sight.

They were beginning to go into dinner and Sky joined Amelia in a far corner of the room. 'I'm to take you in,' he said giving her his arm. 'I think your mother is trying to tell us something. The pariahs have been assigned to each other.'

'I fit the role, Sky, but not you.'

He looked down at her. 'Hasn't Carrie told you?'

Amelia thought of the stories Caroline had told her that afternoon. 'All my life Carrie's told me things. I haven't always believed them though.'

His face was grave. 'You can this time, Amelia,' he said quietly. 'You can believe what Carrie's told you. And one more thing. I'm leaving her.'

'Leaving Carrie? But you adore Carrie.'

He smiled down at her again, a strange amused smile. 'You know, it's funny, Amelia. Sometimes you seem so worldly, and sometimes you sound like the naive little girl I knew years ago. I'm only sorry about one thing. I'm sorry it's happening now because I think you're going to need a friend.' The words seemed to make him self-conscious. 'Though I doubt I'd be much help. I certainly wasn't when they forced you to marry him.'

'Oh, I don't know. I seem to remember that once or twice you came to my defense.'

'For all the good it did.'

'You're only human, Sky.'

'Correction, I'm only a man. And in Newport, in matters like this, men don't count.'

They passed into the dining room through the massive carved doors, manned on each side by a footman in satin knee breeches. In the darkness that hung from the high-vaulted ceiling two huge crystal chandeliers glowed like twin galaxies and the dozens of candles that ran the length of the table flickered in the soft gusts of air as the guests moved to their places. The candlelight danced off the gold and silver and shot the clear crystal glasses through with a spectrum of colors. At every second place a footman in maroon and gold, the Leighton colors, stood ready to move the solid mahogany chairs that were as huge as thrones and too heavy for the guests to lift. From behind a carved Chinese screen in one corner of the room came the sound of several very restrained violins.

Before she'd even reached her place, Amelia noticed that she was to sit directly across from Sam Van Nest. Her mother must have been upset when she'd rearranged the table this afternoon, or had her mother, like everyone else, like Sam himself, simply forgot? He didn't even look at her as he took his seat between Mrs Corcoran and Mrs Wainwright. In the soft shadowy light the planes of his face looked suddenly dramatic.

Amelia turned quickly to her right. Kirkland Selby was studying the menu. He was a dry husk of a man with a thin mouth that looked stern beneath the sharp beak of a nose and its corola of fine white hairs. Perhaps he was distressed by the prospect of eleven courses and six wines. Selby, Amelia thought as she removed the long gloves, did not look like a man given to overindulgence in food or anything else.

He turned to her and asked if she planned to stay for the season. His voice was thin and raspy.

'Longer than that, I think.' She waited for the question that always followed. When would the duke be joining her?

Sam was trying to listen to Mrs Corcoran, but he heard Kirkland Selby ask when the duke would be arriving and couldn't help straining for the answer.

'I believe my daughter knows your sister,' Mrs Corcoran was saying. Sam smiled at her absently and wished she'd be silent for a moment.

'That's hard to say.' Sam was certain those were

Amelia's words. Trouble in paradise, he thought.

'Mrs Endicott,' Mrs Corcoran went on. 'She's been awfully kind to Agnes.'

Sam forced himself to listen to Mrs Corcoran, or, more to the point, to stop listening to Amelia. 'Nina's a very kind girl,' he said.

'She and Agnes have become such friends.'

Sam had no reason to doubt Mrs Corcoran. Nina was a good-natured girl who delighted in taking up protégés. Still, he didn't think she'd taken up Agnes Corcoran. He would have remembered the girl if she had. Nina had a habit of thrusting her protégés at him, at least until she married them off.

The good thing about Mrs Corcoran, Sam thought as she chattered on about Agnes and her various attributes, was that she was perfectly capable of carrying the conversation alone. He supposed it came from years of being snubbed. If you were going to storm the social citadel, you'd better get accustomed to going where you were not wanted and talking to people who had no desire to talk to you.

From two places down the table Harry Lehr's maniacal, biting laugh erupted through the subdued surface of murmured conversations and the quiet clinking of precious metal against precious metal. 'Mr Lehr is so witty,' Mrs Corcoran said. 'It's easy to see why he's called King Lehr.'

'Is it?' Sam asked. He'd always found the title, whether used in admiration or deprecation, as repugnant as the man.

'Well, yes. It isn't just a matter of style. It's a

matter of style and wit. So few men, or women for that matter,' Mrs Corcoran went on as if she were confiding something, 'combine the two. Mr Lehr's always up to something, but it's always something clever and original. Like his dog dinner. Imagine having a garden party for a hundred dogs. Or the monkey dinner. I've heard that was the best. As I understand it even Mrs Lehr wasn't in on the joke. Harry simply came home one afternoon and said Joseph Leiter had the Prince del Drago on his yacht, and wanted to know if he could bring him along to dinner. Corsican nobility, Mr Lehr said. That was clever of him. And then to have Mr Leiter turn up with a monkey in evening dress! Now, who but King Lehr could think up a prank like that.'

'Who but Harry Lehr would choose to dine with a chimp?'

'As I understand it, the monkey was delightful. Mrs Lehr even said his manners were better than most princes she'd met.'

'Until the third glass of champagne. I believe it was the third that did it. He climbed to the chandelier and began pelting the guests with food.'

'You sound as if you disapprove, Mr Van Nest.' Lila Corcoran was not arguing, merely probing. She'd been led to believe that Harry Lehr, unrivaled social arbiter and irrepressible wit, could do no wrong. The few he scandalized were said to be stuffy. Mrs Corcoran had been careful to take the sophisticated view of Lehr and his practical jokes, but if Samuel Van Nest, of all people, was not amused, could it be the sophisticated view? She was clearly at sea.

'I don't disapprove, Mrs Corcoran. I hope the guests were amused. I'm only glad I wasn't one of them.'

'And what about the dog party?' she pursued. Lila Corcoran had an open mind. If there were two schools of opinion, she wanted to hear them both. She was even willing to espouse them both — depending on the circumstances.

'Now, that I disapprove of,' Sam said.

'You find it decadent to dress pets up in costume and serve them an elaborate luncheon?'

'I find it unkind. I'm sure the humans enjoyed the party immensely, but I doubt the dogs had as much fun. As I heard it, Mrs Dyer's poor dachshund passed out at its plate and had to be carried home. Now I don't approve of that, Mrs Corcoran. You see, I'm fond of dogs.'

'Well, of course, aren't we all,' she said quickly. She was glad that the footmen were removing the consommé and serving the *hors-d'oeuvres varies*. It was time to talk to the naval lieutenant who sat on her other side. The naval lieutenant was unimportant. Conversation with him would give her time to digest the one she'd just had with Samuel Van Nest, and she needed time to digest it. She needed time to make sense of Van Nest with his impeccable connections and unconventional attitudes and of the legitimacy of King Lehr's title. Samuel Van Nest was obviously something of a rebel, and she'd have to talk to Agnes about that. As for Lehr, perhaps he was the fool she'd secretly suspected him to be, and perhaps the time was coming to say as much. It would be wonderful to be in the forefront of fashion for once, rather than bringing up the tail end.

Sam turned from Mrs Corcoran to Mrs Wainwright, but the conversation in her area had already grown general, or rather Lehr had made it general. He was telling a story about old Archie Harris and his daughter Cecily. The story, concerning Mr Harris' chance meeting with an unknown woman on a train and his subsequent invitation to visit him in Newport, was too risqué, but Harry was an expert at walking the tightrope of conversational propriety.

'After a week,' Harry was saying, 'old Archie was desperate. The woman showed no sign of leaving, and his social life was dwindling rapidly. No lady who mattered would accept his invitations or even talk to him, and of course they wouldn't permit their husbands to either. The poor fellow was on the verge of closing up the house and bolting for the rest of the season. Then he hit upon the idea of asking his daughter Cecily to help. He thought if Cecily would receive his visitor, the other women would follow. At first Cecily absolutely refused. Think of her dignity, her reputation, her children. Think of an old widower's plight, Archie pleaded. Apparently Cecily has a daughter's heart after all. She agreed to receive the woman – for ten thousand dollars.' Harry looked directly at Amelia and his eyes glinted maliciously. 'Now there's a lesson in filial duty for you, Amelia my pet.'

'I should have thought,' Amelia said drily, 'she'd put a higher price on filial duty.'

'Is that what you would have done, Your Grace?' Sam's voice was perfectly even, perfectly polite, as if he were asking a serious question, and even in the soft flickering candle-light his eyes looked hard. She was furious. He must have known she was being ironic.

'We had been speaking,' Kirkland Selby said, 'before your anecdote, Mr Lehr, of another sort of duty. I was asking the duchess about her good works in England. I'm sure she must have found a great deal of room for improvement.'

'I'm afraid,' Harry said, 'that few of us can hope to keep up with you in that regard, Mr Selby. Your good works are so extensive, it makes anything the rest of us do look like a mere drop in the divine bucket. I've heard about the orphanage downtown and the new parish house for your own Christ Church, and now I understand you're planning to build a school for a church on Mott Street.'

'St Joseph's,' Selby said. 'The Cardinal assures me they're in need of a grammar school.'

'What I find especially admirable,' Harry went on, 'is that your generosity knows no denomination. A Baptist orphanage, a Catholic school, your own Episcopal Church.'

'It's all God's work,' Selby said waving away the footman holding the turbot in cream sauce with new potatoes.

The old hypocrite, Sam thought, but when it came to religion weren't most of his colleagues?

The more ruthless they were during the week, the harder they prayed on Sunday. Morgan took up the collection at St Bartholomew's, the Vanderbilts filled the front pews at St Thomas's Fifth Avenue, and Kirkland Selby roused himself from the pleasures of Saturday night to renew his faith every Sunday morning at Christ Church. Or didn't he pursue his pleasures on Saturday night? Were those hours too public and popular for him?

'And who,' Lehr asked gleefully, 'would have a better knowledge of the comparative merits of the various sects than you, Mr Selby? Wasn't your allegiance to the Baptist Church at one time?'

Selby lifted the sharp beak of a nose and stared at Harry. 'My father was a Baptist, Mr Lehr. I, as you mentioned, belong to the Episcopal Church. I feel more comfortable there.'

'I never knew a millionaire who didn't. None of those unpleasant democratic tendencies.'

'Certainly you of all people, Harry, ought to appreciate that,' Amelia said. She felt Sam looking at her, but he said nothing.

'You're quite right, my pet. Undoubtedly we will all be equal on Judgment Day, but I'm in no hurry to achieve either that ultimate day or that blessed state.'

'I'm afraid I can't speak of these things with the levity you do, Mr Lehr. Nevertheless,' Selby said, 'I am convinced that this world and its inequities, if you choose to call them that, are all part of the Lord's plan. He cares for His flock in many ways. If He were to bestow a fortune on some poor beggar in one of my mines, for example, the man would only go out and squander it. On drink most likely, or useless frivolities. Surely, if you and I can see that, the Lord in His infinite wisdom understands as much. He has given me not only a fortune, but the conscience that tells me how to spend it. It is all part of His plan.'

'You sound, my dear Selby,' Lehr said, as he motioned to the footman for another helping of turbot, 'as if you are in direct communication.'

'I told you, Mr Lehr, I do not treat these matters as lightly as you seem to.'

'What I don't understand,' Mrs Wainwright, who sat between Sam and Harry, broke in, 'if you'll forgive me for saying so, Mr Selby, is your support of the Roman Church. It's quite admirable, of course, but don't you think a little dangerous as well? It seems to me those people are taking over the country fast enough without our help. Why with the exception of my major-domo and Mr Wainwright's man, I don't think we have a servant who isn't pledged to Rome. That's all the agencies send anymore.'

'That's exactly why I help, Mrs Wainwright. The only thing those foreigners respect and fear is their Church. Even the Irish ball boys at the Casino. We don't keep them in line. Their parish priest does that. Those boys are hired only on the priest's recommendation. Now I ask you, if we weaken the Church, if we try to remove it, what will be their social view, their political action, their moral status? Without their Church, they are a rabble. With it, they are a controllable work force.'

'I hadn't thought of it that way,' Mrs Wainwright said. 'Still, all that Romanism makes me quite nervous. It seems so . . . mysterious, so fervent.'

'The masses are fervent, Mrs Wainwright. It is up to us to see that their fervency is channeled in the right direction. If we don't, we'll have people like the Colonel leading them off in quest of all sorts of outrageous things.'

'Mr Wainwright says he's quite in favor of Colonel Roosevelt these days. He says the Colonel isn't nearly so dangerous as Mr Taft. He says, in fact, the Colonel has become quite sensible.'

Selby looked across the table at Anna Wainwright as if she were half-witted. 'Because he maintains that big business organizations should be prosecuted only when they've committed a crime and that size is not a crime? Don't be misled, my dear Mrs Wainwright. A leopard doesn't change his spots so easily. The Colonel needs our support against President Taft, and he'll say whatever is necessary to gain it. I for one, however, have no intention of giving it.'

'The Colonel always did cause a stir,' Harry said, waving a gold fish fork in the air to illustrate his point. He wasn't in the least interested in politics, but he did love contention – as long as he was not at the center of it. 'The only people as bad as those who love Roosevelt, are those who love to hate him. Tell me, Van Nest, are you still a wide-eyed admirer, or has all this furor about his campaign funds tarnished his image? How do you feel about your hero these days?'

Selby's head swiveled toward Sam and his eyes glinted like steel in the dim light. 'Is the Colonel your hero, Mr Van Nest?'

Sam took a sip of wine. 'I served under him.'

'Now don't be modest,' Harry protested. 'Van Nest was one of the Roughriders, Mr Selby. One of the most heroic, I'm sure.' The pale eyes slid to Amelia. 'Don't you agree, Amelia?'

Trust Harry to remember. 'I seem to recall that we gave him a hero's welcome when he returned home.' As soon as the words were out she regretted them. She still remembered his return. He'd come to see her almost immediately, and she'd been pleased and flattered but a little intimidated too, because he'd seemed suddenly older and more worldly. He'd looked wonderful too, lean with a new hardness, and very tan. The memory was like an ache, and she drained her wine glass suddenly. The footman appeared at her elbow immediately. She felt Sam watching as he refilled it, and as if in defiance she took another sip.

She's drinking too much too quickly, Sam thought, then caught himself. The duchess can take care of herself. Still, he had to admit she didn't look quite so hard now, quite so aloof as she had when he'd first seen her on the receiving line. She still held her head stiffly, as if she were looking down her nose at him, but that could be the dog collar. A three-inch-width of diamonds and rubies was likely to make anyone stiff necked. His eyes were drawn from the collar to the curve of her shoulders. They looked as smooth and white as the calla lilies that were banked between them on the table. She had beautiful shoulders, and he liked the way they moved when she turned to talk to Niebold or Selby. There was something almost seductive about the way her shoulders moved. Damn it, of course there was something seductive. She wasn't a shy girl pretending to be worldly anymore. She was worldly. Ten years of marriage, a marriage of convenience, would have seen to that. She would have learned a good deal more about being seductive than how to hold her shoulders. She would have learned how to attract and hold the men who would make such a marriage bearable. Sam was sure of that. He'd misjudged Amelia in a lot of ways, but he didn't think he'd misjudged her in that way.

He forced himself to look at Selby. It was Selby he had to worry about now. 'We lost most of our horses in Florida and ended up fighting on foot in Cuba. There wasn't anything heroic about it. Still, I can't help thinking the newspapers are giving the Colonel a harder time these days about Standard Oil and the campaign contributions than the Spanish ever gave him. That's Hearst's doing, of course. He tried the same thing in the last campaign with the same results. It won't matter in the long run.'

'Are you suggesting,' Selby asked, 'that the fact that the President accepted a bribe will not matter in the long run?'

'The charge hasn't been proven, Mr Selby. In any event, the Colonel is a politician, and politicians have a habit of caring more about the ends they achieve than the means they use to achieve them. I'm suggesting that in the long run history will acclaim the Colonel a hero. I doubt future biographers will even mention some minor scandal about Standard Oil bribes.'

'There is no such thing as a minor scandal, Mr Van Nest. Wrong is wrong.'

'Undoubtedly, Mr Selby, but as I said, the Colonel is a politician. And, for that matter, I doubt most of us would fare much better under the close scrutiny Roosevelt has been subjected to.'

Harry was delighted with the turn the conversation was taking. 'Are you suggesting, my dear boy, that we all have skeletons in our closets?'

'Of one sort or another,' Sam said keeping his eyes on Selby.

Selby did not even flinch. 'I'm sorry to hear you say that, Mr Van Nest. I'm sorry to hear that a young man like you is so cynical about life. I can only say that I don't agree. I don't believe every man has his sinful secret. Speaking personally, I can assure you my life is an open book. I have nothing to hide.'

'In that case,' Sam said, smiling across the table at the old man, 'you are not only an extraordinary man, Mr Selby, but a very fortunate one.'

'It has,' Selby snapped, the fine white hairs in his nose quivering, 'nothing to do with being fortunate. It has to do with living according to the laws of God and man.'

The laws of God and man, the pompous old devil

191

said. Sam had planned to start with Wainwright, but Selby was asking for trouble. He thought of the piece of paper he'd taken from the files Morgan had given him. It was in his pocket now. 'And if I may return to the subject of your good deeds, Mr Selby, your philanthropies, I wonder if you could tell me more about that orphanage you were speaking of before. The Baptist one.'

'There's little enough to tell, Van Nest. As you know, I'm from the South. I've always felt an obligation toward our less fortunate black brethren.'

'And so you built this orphanage on Willett Street.'

'The orphanage is on Henry Street,' Selby said so sharply that Sam knew he'd struck a chord.

'That's peculiar,' Sam said. 'I could have sworn it was on Willett Street. Right under the bridge. You see, I was asked for a contribution – I imagine the trustees would like to see more of us follow your good example, Mr Selby – and I seem to remember their mentioning the location. They said it was an old row house, still in good condition but in need of some improvements. Children can do a good deal of damage. People think it's only boys, but as I understand it, the girls can get rambunctious too.' The footman had just placed the roast and *jardinière* before Selby, but he did not even notice. His eyes were riveted on Sam as if he were the only one in the room.

Selby knew the house Van Nest meant. The only thing he didn't know was how Van Nest had found out about it. He went there infrequently and then

only during the day when it was closed to
everyone else. He certainly paid enough to have
it closed. Had that damn woman who ran it
talked? Had one of the girls? Selby ran through the
roster in his mind. Perhaps that sullen one with
the long scar. It ran halfway across the smooth
brown belly. He'd asked how she'd got the scar,
but she hadn't answered. No, she hadn't been the
one to talk. She was too quiet for that. It would
be one of the noisier ones, one of those who cried
or screamed. He remembered the girl with the
small pointed breasts. Many of them hadn't begun
to develop breasts yet, but this one had, and after
he'd made her undress she'd held her hands over
them. When he'd taken her hands away, she'd
begun to whimper. The whimpering had turned
to sobs when he'd begun to caress her. He could
still remember the way the small purple-pink
nipples had grown rigid. He'd enjoyed that one,
despite the protests, and she had protested, crying
and pleading as he explored the slender childish
body, pushing him away when he'd pulled her to
him, even pummeling his chest when he'd climbed
on top of her, as if those frail arms could thwart
another child let alone a full-grown man. She'd
still been crying when he'd left the room, but he'd
counted on the woman who ran the house to take
care of that. What else did he pay her for? But
Morgan must have paid more, to the woman and
to one of the girls, and Selby knew why. Morgan
had asked him as a friend, as a gentleman, not to
go in with Walsh. So this was the kind of friend
Morgan was, the kind of gentleman. And his

henchman Van Nest. Mustn't forget Van Nest who was sitting across the table from him now smiling that damn smile as smooth as the claret the footman had just poured in his glass. Selby looked down at the slab of beef on his plate and felt a burning sensation in his chest. He picked up his knife and fork slowly. If he could have driven them through Van Nest's heart, he would have done so with pleasure.

'Well, wherever it is,' Sam said, 'it seems like a fine place. I was quite impressed by the whole operation, Selby. The trustees brought pictures of the children. Even told little stories about them. I imagine they intend to soften up the heart first, then the pocketbook.' Sam noticed that Selby's face had turned from ashen gray to dead white, the same white as his stiff shirt front. Sam almost felt sorry for him. Then he remembered the paper in his pocket, the one with the girl's testimony. That was a story to soften the heart all right – and turn the stomach.

'Yes,' Sam said, 'the stories were quite touching. There was one of a little girl named Vera.' Selby had abandoned any pretense of eating now. Sam looked at the large hands that were gripping the silver knife and fork tightly. They were dotted with liver spots. *He touched me*, the girl had said. *He kept touching me. I started to cry.* Sam felt a wave of nausea and looked away from Selby's hands. 'I'm sure you can imagine the story, Mr Selby. And you'll be happy to know I've decided to make a contribution to your orphanage.' He let his voice linger a little on the word *your*. 'Mr

Morgan has too. After all, we have to stick together in these things.'

Selby said nothing.

'Don't you agree,' Sam pressed. 'That we have to stick together?'

'I agree,' Selby said finally. His voice was almost a whisper, but Sam could hear the anger that choked it. It was an anger Selby wouldn't forget. Well, to hell with Selby, Sam thought. To hell with Selby and his filthy perversions. He didn't mind being hated by a man like Selby. It was, when you stopped to think about it, almost a badge of honor.

As the footmen served the terrapin and poured the champagne, Sam turned to Mrs Corcoran again, but out of the corner of his eye he was watching Amelia. A tall gold candelabrum stood on the table between them, and in the light from the candles her skin and hair seemed to be shimmering with a pale light as if the flame were burning within her. She was leaning a little toward Niebold, listening to something he was saying, and as she raised the glass to her mouth her nose turned up almost imperceptibly in reaction to the effervescence. The reflex unnerved him and he forced himself to look directly at Mrs Corcoran.

'It's none of my business,' Sky was saying in an undertone, 'but then I've told you things tonight – about leaving Carrie, I mean – that I shouldn't have. Just between us, Amelia, is that' – his eyes darted sideways to Sam – 'one of the reasons you won't go back to Duringham?'

Her mouth felt dry and she took another sip of champagne. Was she really so transparent? 'Don't be ridiculous, Sky. We're barely on speaking terms, as you may have noticed.'

'I did notice. That's my point. There's something between you two. I'm not sure what it is, but there have been times tonight when I felt as if I could reach out and touch it.'

'If you do, you may get bitten. Whatever you imagine you see between us is a very hostile animal.'

'All right, we'll change the subject. We'll discuss the weather or the terrapin.'

'Awfully good terrapin,' she said.

'Whatever the reason, Amelia, stick to your guns. Don't go back to Duringham. It isn't just a case of my wanting everyone else in the mess I'm in . . .'

'I know that, Sky. You've never been one to enjoy other people's miseries.' She was thinking but didn't say that Caroline was the one to do that.

'You deserve better than Duringham.'

'Blasphemy.' Amelia smiled into her wine glass, but it wasn't a very happy smile. 'What could be better than a duke?'

'I didn't like the way he treated you. That summer in London, he was so . . . arrogant.' But arrogance was too weak a word, Sky thought, for the emotion he'd seen in Duringham. Sky had sensed a hatred in the duke, a hatred for Amelia that seemed as hard and pure as the love Sky had once felt for Caroline, and like that love, it seemed to go to the very core of the man. 'Don't go back to him, Amelia,' he repeated. The words sounded inadequate in his ears, but she must have heard

196

the emotion behind them because for a moment
her hand rested on his and she looked directly into
his eyes.

'I won't. And thank you.'

'For what?' he asked because he was still feeling
the futility of everything he'd said.

'For understanding. Not many people do.'

'I know.' Without meaning to, he glanced down
the table to where Caroline sat.

The footmen had removed the terrapin and
were serving the partridges. Caroline turned back
to the young man on her left. When she'd turned
away from him after the roast course, he'd been
threatening to go West and never return. Caroline
timed her flirtations, or rather her admirer's
flirtations, as perfectly as Hatfield did the serving
of dinner, and they moved at the same pace. Only
when she'd been sure that she would have to turn
away in a moment had she allowed Marion
Biderwell to mention the burning passion which
was going to send him away forever.

'Now you mustn't talk nonsense,' she began, but
she turned toward him as she said it and saw his
eyes move to the deep décolletage of her dress.

'It's not nonsense.' His voice held all the urgency
of his twenty-two years. 'I mean it, Carrie. I can't
go on this way.'

He could, of course. They always did. He
wouldn't go West, not even for a vacation. He'd
stay here and keep calling on her and writing her,
and gradually the calls and the letters would stop,
and in a year or so she'd hear he was engaged.
Soon after that she'd receive an invitation to the

wedding. Caroline always enjoyed attending the weddings of the young men who'd been in love with her, and she always took special care selecting the gifts for them. She always sent something distinctive, something that would continue to remind the husbands of her long after they had ceased to be grooms.

'You ought to leave him,' Marion Biderwell said and his voice was a hoarse angry whisper. 'You don't care for him. Anybody can see that you don't care for him.'

Caroline looked up at him from under the thick fringe of lashes and her eyes were very sad. She forbid him to say those things, but she didn't say they weren't true. He drained his glass suddenly and put it back on the table with an abrupt movement. 'You have a streak of cruelty, Carrie,' he said and there was a new edge to his anger, one she'd never heard in him before. 'Sometimes I think you just like to play with us; all of us.'

She hadn't expected that from him, from Sky perhaps, from less docile young men, but not from Marion Biderwell. She turned away from him without a word though the courses had not changed. From now on she'd return his letters unopened and tell Hatfield to say she wasn't in when he called.

Edith was discussing their mutual friend the Kaiser with the baron who sat on her right, but now and then she glanced down the long table to where Elizabeth sat between Sydney and the lieutenant. She and Atherton were turned toward each other and their profiles stood out against the softly lighted background of the room like matching pieces of a puzzle. Edith couldn't escape the feeling that the pieces seemed to be moving closer together as they talked. The baron was saying something about an afternoon on the Kaiser's yacht in the Baltic and Edith was making the proper comments at the proper intervals, but she was wondering what the lieutenant was saying that made Elizabeth smile at him that way.

What the lieutenant was saying was not in the least romantic. He was telling Lizzy a story that had to do with his days at Annapolis.

'It was the end of plebe year,' he was saying. 'At the beginning of June Week the plebes boost someone in the class to the top of Herndon Monument. To celebrate the fact that they're not plebes anymore. Legend has it that the man who gets to the top and hangs his cap on it will be the first admiral of his class. Well, I don't know how it happened because I certainly wasn't the lightest fellow in the class, but all of a sudden there I was on top of the monument and everyone was cheering like crazy.'

'But is the legend reliable, Lieutenant?' She was smiling up at him, but she wasn't laughing at him.

'As a matter of fact, I looked into that. The story is that it's worked six times. That means it hasn't worked something like thirty or forty times. I'm not sure how far back the tradition goes.'

'Well, Lieutenant, I guess I'm just going to have to follow your career to see if it works this time.' She was still smiling at him, an intimate smile that seemed to shut out everyone else in the room. Atherton had the feeling that the scent of flowers from the table and from Lizzy when she leaned toward him was growing stronger just as the soft music seemed to be swelling and they seemed to be drawing closer. Then an arm in maroon and gold livery came between them. Elizabeth leaned back in her chair and Atherton snapped to attention as if an order had been given.

The problem now, Sam thought as the ladies left for the drawing room was getting Wainwright alone. Sam caught up with him as he reached one of the two sets of carved double doors leading from the dining room. 'I wonder if we could have a word alone?' he asked.

Wainwright turned to face him. The left eyelid was drooping markedly, and it made him look more petulant than angry. It was, Sam suspected, partly the result of the wine, and he imagined that Wainwright was eager to get on to the library and his brandy. 'It will only take a moment,' Sam lied.

He remembered a small sitting room halfway down the corridor between the dining room and the library. It was fortunate, Sam had to admit, that he had once known Belle Isle well. Morgan was no fool about details like that.

As they were about to turn into the room, Maxwell Fingerhut caught up with them. The timing was terrible. Sam didn't want to lose Wainwright, but could not afford to offend Fingerhut to whom he hadn't spoken at all.

'Van Nest' – Fingerhut stopped him in the

doorway — 'it's been a long time.' He had a girlish, high-pitched voice and as he spoke the fleshy lower lip pulled down in a tremulous tic. Of all the men, Sam supposed he disliked dealing with Fingerhut the most, though he could not say he disliked Fingerhut himself the most. It was simply that the man had a kind of nervous instability. His movements were quick and awkward, and his eyes darted rapidly while he spoke. Sometimes when Sam ran into him at a club or a dinner, he was overly friendly; other times cool. Sam never knew what to expect except that an inadvertent word or gesture might upset Fingerhut's delicate balance and, he suspected, drive him to fury. Sam had never seen Fingerhut in a rage, but he knew one lurked beneath the surface waiting to erupt at the slightest provocation. A minor snub now would make an implacable enemy of Fingerhut, at least for the rest of the evening, but if Fingerhut joined them in the sitting room, Wainwright would escape to the library and his much needed brandy.

'It's good to see you, Max.' Sam shook his hand warmly. 'As a matter of fact, the Commodore and I were talking about you only this morning.'

'You were?' Fingerhut tried to sound urbane, but the pleasure in his voice was as naked as a small boy who has just been complimented by an older one, despite the fact that he was fifteen years Sam's senior.

Sam felt Wainwright shift his weight beside him. 'I want to tell you all about it, Max,' Sam went on, 'but I know that Elias Leighton is looking for you. Said he had a first edition of' — Sam hesitated for only a moment – 'Dryden's *Virgil* he wanted your opinion on. Why don't you go on ahead, and I'll catch up with you later.'

As Sam stood aside to let Wainwright enter the room before him, he felt the man look at him curiously. 'I didn't know Fingerhut knew anything about rare books.'

Sam looked across the room at Wainwright. He was leaning against a window, his weight half supported by the ledge, his hands thrust into the pockets of his trousers. Wainwright was stupid about business and foolhardy about his own interests, but Sam didn't think he was that stupid or foolhardy about people. 'He doesn't, but, as I said, I wanted a word alone with you.'

'You did or Morgan did?'

'I'm a partner in Morgan and Company. Their interest is my interest.'

'What loyalty, Van Nest. It's a shame you aren't working for me.'

Sam took a minute to let the images work through his mind. He saw himself crossing the room to Wainwright, saw his fist moving swiftly until it connected with the arrogant face, saw Wainwright falling and himself turning and leaving the room. He took a deep breath and went straight to the point. As he ticked off one argument after the other against Walsh's scheme, Sam saw a small superior smile begin to play around Wainwright's mouth. 'So, the old man is scared.'

'Concerned,' Sam said. 'With good reason. Another panic isn't going to help anyone.'

Wainwright straightened. 'I don't know about that, Van Nest, but this banking trust is going to help me a great deal.' He started for the door. 'I'm going to come out of this with enough to make what my father left look like a pittance.'

'From what I understand,' Sam said as Wainwright reached for the oversized brass doorknob, 'that's what it's become. Or should I say what you've reduced it to. A pittance.'

Wainwright turned back to him quickly. He didn't look smug now. 'What do you mean by that?'

Sam shrugged. 'You know how word gets around.'

'By word I assume you mean gossip. I sustain a loss here or there, and suddenly it's all over the Street that I'm going bust.'

'No one said anything about going bust, though you must have taken quite a bath on that Central American ferry and steamship thing. It's a funny thing about money. Sometimes it's as hard to hold on to it in the second generation as it is to make it in the first. Take that Central American boat deal. It's exactly the sort of thing your father, as I understand it, made millions on. But times are changing, and what worked yesterday doesn't necessarily work today.'

'That, Van Nest, is exactly why I plan to go into this Walsh deal. He's the coming man. He thinks big. Morgan's strictly nineteenth century. Walsh is twentieth.'

'Morgan practically invented combinations with the Steel Trust back in the nineties.'

203

'A man doesn't have to invent something to know how to use it. Walsh's financial combination is going to make the Steel Trust look like small potatoes.'

'If the government doesn't do it first,' Sam said. 'They're after the Steel Trust right now. And they're bound to go after Walsh's banking trust as soon as he gets it set up.'

'By that time, Van Nest, I'll be holding banking stocks worth three times the shares I trade for them. Even if they break up the trust, I'll come out ahead.'

'If there's a general panic, you won't come out ahead.'

'You know what the trouble with all of you over at Twenty-three Wall is? You can't forget the Panic of '07. Morgan's panic. Morgan's finest moment. Well, I've forgot it, and what's more, I'm willing to take my chances that there won't be another. I'm telling you and you can pass it on to the Commodore if he's interested. I don't believe there's going to be another panic, and I don't believe the government will break up the trust, and I'm going in on this thing with Walsh.' Wainwright started for the door again.

'You've been issuing a lot of new stock in the Southwest Railroads lately, haven't you?' Sam asked.

'I don't see what that has to do with anything.'

'We've been buying a lot of Southwest Railroad stock lately, Wainwright. I won't beat around the bush. If you try to trade that railroad stock for Walsh's shares, you'll find you no longer have controlling interest. And Walsh wants controlling interest.' Sam took a gold cigarette case from his breast pocket and held it out to Wainwright, but Wainwright seemed not to notice it. 'You really ought to stay on top of these things, John. Of course, I know that Central American fiasco has had you worried lately, but it never helps to let other things slide.' Sam remembered the way Wainwright had patronized him only a few minutes ago. 'Perhaps you do need some loyal men working for you. Though I wouldn't recommend expanding at this time. Take that Pacific Steamship deal you've been working on. I don't think there's going to be much of a market for the stock issue. It seems the climate of opinion isn't quite right for that sort of thing now. I imagine that has to do with the Central American failure.'

'You can't stop that stock issue.'

'Of course we can't stop you from offering it, but I think you'll be disappointed in the public response. And as for those shares in Central Beef that you're trying to unload – I believe your order was to sell when they reached seventeen again – I'm afraid you're stuck with those. I doubt if they'll reach seventeen, but if they do, your "sell-mine-first" order with Willows and Selfridge has been preempted.'

Wainwright had stopped halfway to the door, and now he stood staring at Sam. The lid was still drooping but less than it had been, and his complexion, beneath the tan, looked unnaturally pale. 'You've got it all figured out, haven't you? Well there's one thing you and Morgan overlooked. After your handiwork, I'll need Walsh more than ever.'

Sam crushed out the cigarette he'd just lit. 'But will Walsh need you? Oh, you've still got a few canal boat and steamship lines, a railroad here and there, enough to keep you occupied certainly, but scarcely enough to interest a man who thinks on the scale of Jason Walsh. The real point though is that you don't need Walsh at all. We're perfectly happy to let you continue to run the Southwest Railroads, though personally I have a few suggestions for getting them back in the black. And I think you'll find that once it's known the House of Morgan is behind the Pacific Steamship combination, there'll be a considerable market for its issue. As for that Central Beef thing, I'd suggest you sell now and take the loss. In fact, if you like we can see that your "sell-mine-first" order is reinstated. It won't be that great a loss – it was a minor investment to begin with – and once the rest of your interests are in order, you'll be able to sustain it easily. Probably have enough left over for a stallion to service those fillies of yours in Kentucky.'

'You bastard!'

'I'm sorry you feel that way, Wainwright. I think we're behaving quite decently.'

'Because you're not ruining me outright.'

'Because we're bailing you out.'

'The deal with Walsh would have done that. And a damn sight more profitably.'

'I'm afraid we can't allow that.'

'I won't forget this, Van Nest.'

It was, Sam thought, what Morgan had known from the beginning. None of the men would forget it – or him.

'And I warn you, someday you'll be sorry. Damn sorry.' He took a step toward Sam. 'Someday . . .'

'You've made your point, Wainwright. Now if you'll excuse me, I think I'll join the other gentlemen. I'd like a brandy.'

'I bet you would. Tell me one thing, Van Nest, how does it feel to be the great Jupiter Morgan's slimy little messenger boy? How does it feel to do the work he won't stoop . . .'

Sam closed the door behind him. He could imagine the rest. And the answer was it didn't feel very good.

Sam had said he wanted a brandy, but once away from Wainwright he found he wanted a drink less than he wanted solitude. He was not quite ready to face the other men. The lower piazza was deserted except for a marmalade cat that must have strayed up from the beach or the gardener's cottage.

'Mrs Leighton's lowering her standards,' Sam said as he dropped into one of the high-backed wicker chairs facing the sea. 'First me, now you.' The cat circled his leg a few times, sniffing cautiously at his trousers, then disappeared down the stone steps into the shrubbery. 'Don't blame you, fella. I'm not very good company tonight.'

The windows to the house were open and behind him he could hear the sounds of Mrs Leighton's party in progress. It was like a symphony orchestra, he thought, with the women's voices coming from one side and the lower male ones from the other end of the house, but he was not enjoying the music and he wished the night were over.

You're too old for this sort of thing, Sam told himself. You're too old to measure everything you do in terms of your father, in terms of his approval or disapproval. What in hell had he done wrong anyway? He'd merely tried to head off the federal suit that would produce a panic. Selby was degenerate, and there was no need to pity Wainwright either. The pompous fool. If the roles were reversed, Wainwright wouldn't have hesitated to ruin him. Sam supposed that was the difference between them. Wainwright would have enjoyed doing it.

He told himself it was time to go back inside, but didn't move. Another minute, he promised himself, two at the most.

He heard the sound of footsteps on the mosaic tiled floor of the piazza. She walked past him to the low wall and stood leaning against it looking out to sea. He noticed she was carrying a brandy glass, and that her shoulders looked pale in the moonlight. He'd been sitting in one of those high-backed wicker throne chairs and she'd obviously walked by him without realizing he was there. She reached up and rubbed her neck beneath the jeweled dog collar with an index finger.

'Like the head that wears a crown.'

She turned suddenly as if someone had stolen up on her, and he supposed he had.

'Uneasy lies the neck that wears a diamond dog collar.'

She wanted to tear it off and hurl it at him. Damn him. Damn Charles. Damn the collar. Then she remembered Wickert. She'd be free of all of them soon enough. She took a sip of her brandy. 'I didn't know you were out here.'

'Obviously. Would you like me to leave?'

'That's not necessary. I only came out for a breath of air.'

She even talked like her mother now. *Who is Amelia?* 'Ah yes, a breath of air – and a nip of brandy.'

She put the glass down on the wall guiltily, then picked it up again and took another swallow. It was a very defiant swallow.

He laughed. 'You don't have to prove anything to me, Amelia.' That slipped out. He hadn't meant to call her Amelia.

'Well, I must say that's an improvement over Your Grace.'

So that was it. The great lady was going to be flirtatious. He hadn't bothered to stand when he'd first spoken, but he stood now and moved to her side. 'I thought you liked being Lady Amelia.'

There was no reply she could make, especially when he was standing only inches from her looking down at her that way. She wished she hadn't drunk so much wine and then the brandy. It mixed everything up in her head. No, that wasn't true. It didn't mix things up at all. It cleared them. Took away all the politesse and the playacting and made everything simple as black

209

and white, love and hate, male and female. He was still looking down at her, and she wanted to reach up and touch his face. She wondered what it would be like to touch Sam again.

'Ah, Her Grace isn't answering.' Don't go on he told himself. What does it matter to you whether she likes being Lady Amelia or not?

'I think I'd better go in.'

'Allow me, Your Grace,' he said and held his arm out to her. There was nothing she could do but take it.

She told herself he was unnecessarily cruel and she had no feeling for him, but that only made it worse. If she didn't care for him any longer, why did she feel this way merely taking his arm. It was Michael all over again. She hadn't loved Michael but she'd been aroused by him, and she felt the same thing with Sam now. She'd said she had to go in, but she didn't want to go in. She wanted to stay out here alone with Sam, to touch him and be touched by him, to discover what it was like to be made love to by Samuel Van Nest. She imagined her hand undoing the pearl studs, sliding inside the stiff shirt, moving over smooth skin, feeling the warmth and power of his body. The old images flashed through her mind, but now it was Sam she was in bed with rather than Michael and she could picture him above her, the strong slender body disappearing into her own. The thought of it made her dizzy, and she turned her face away quickly so he could not see her expression, but she was sure he could feel her hand trembling on his arm. There was no doubt about it. She was not a nice woman.

VI

When they were young, the Leighton girls joked that their mother had eyes in the back of her head. What she actually had was a keen sense of her daughters' behavior. As she stood in the foyer now seeing people out, Edith seemed to be concerned only with her guests, but she knew where all three girls were and where they had been for the last hour. The knowledge, however, was not especially reassuring.

Edith had placed Lizzy next to Lieutenant Atherton because there'd been no place else to put him, and the girl had only been polite when she turned during the clams or the partridges to talk to him. But it had occurred to Edith that she'd enjoyed the conversation too much, more, in fact, than her conversation with Sydney. And now as Edith appeared to be listening to the baroness, she was aware of Elizabeth standing at the door inviting the lieutenant to join her and Sydney in Sydney's automobile. Edith had no intention of allowing Elizabeth to drive to the ball with Lieutenant Atherton. If Sydney had any sense, he'd put a stop to it, but though Sydney had a great many attributes in Edith's eyes, sense was not one of them.

The baroness had moved on and Douglas Kimball was standing before her telling her how much he'd enjoyed dinner. 'Do you have a lift to the ball, Mr Kimball? I'm sure Mr Hallenbeck would be happy to take you,' Edith went on before Kimball could answer. 'Sydney,' she summoned the boy, 'Mr Kimball will go with you and Elizabeth. Now let's see, Lieutenant you can go with Mr and Mrs Niebold.' The young man could do no damage with Caroline and Schuyler, and Elizabeth would be safe with Kimball.

As they waited on the portico for the automobiles to be brought up, Kimball looked at Sydney Hallenbeck in the light from the electric lanterns overhead. He struck him as very young, younger even than Lizzy. He was round-faced and rosy-cheeked, cherubic almost when he smiled. It was not a look Kimball admired except in an occasional religious painting, but he knew women often found it attractive. He wondered if Elizabeth Leighton did. She stood next to Hallenbeck now, her hand on his arm. Her profile, thrown into relief against the dark cloth of Sydney's evening clothes, was almost painful to him. She'd told him she wasn't going to marry Hallenbeck, but everyone else seemed to assume she was. Tonight he'd overheard two women speaking of the engagement as if it were certain. Hallenbeck, for his part, treated her with a proprietary affection.

Lizzy must have felt him staring at her because she turned and smiled. It was, Kimball thought for perhaps the hundredth time, a very nice smile. It was hard to believe that a girl that smiled that way had a problem in the world. Then Kimball felt Sydney watching him staring at Lizzy. 'You know, Hallenbeck,' he said, hitting a false note of camaraderie that he hated, 'I keep begging Elizabeth to sit for me and she keeps refusing.' He wondered if Hallenbeck had noticed the use of her Christian name.

'You mean Mrs Leighton wants you to do her portrait and Lizzy refuses?'

'No, I want to do her portrait and Lizzy refuses.'

'You want to paint her for nothing? As if she were a model.'

'Well, actually, Hallenbeck, we pay models. Do you think if I offered to pay Lizzy, she'd sit for me? What about it, Lizzy? I'll give you the top rate.'

Sydney was not amused. 'If Miss Leighton' — so he had noticed — 'wants her portrait painted I'll commission it. I'd planned to in a year or two anyway. For the new house.'

Elizabeth turned to Sydney quickly. Kimball couldn't tell if she were still smiling, but she didn't sound as if she were. 'What new house is that, Sydney?'

Hallenbeck said nothing, but he no longer looked cherubic. There was something sullen and stubborn about his mouth now, like a small boy who recognizes the justice of his reprimand but resents it all the same. When Elizabeth turned back to Kimball she was still smiling, but it was a formal smile, Douglas thought, a social mask. Anything might be behind it, or nothing.

The three of them kept up a desultory conversation on the way to Rosecliff, but unlike Sydney's automobile, Kimball's mind kept going not forward to the ball but back to an afternoon the previous spring. It had been an overcast day late in May, the kind that threatens showers continuously but never delivers them, and he'd lost the light in his studio a little before three. As a result he'd gone out for a walk despite the threatening weather. When he saw Elizabeth Leighton coming out of a shop on Fifth Avenue just above Fourteenth Street, he'd stopped regretting the loss of light. She was with another girl, and there was an automobile waiting for them at the curb. The chauffeur was holding the door open, and Lizzy saw him just as she was about to step in. Kimball knew he had to work quickly. The other girl showed no inclination to linger, and he managed to get to the offer of tea before either of them could enter the automobile. The girl declined as quickly as he'd offered, but Lizzy stood there on the sidewalk looking at him curiously from under a silk toque. It wasn't the first hat that he'd seen her in, and he decided that her mother must choose them, because a girl who looked that good couldn't possibly have such bad taste. It was as if someone had attached a heavy formal equipage to a colt.

'Come on, Lizzy.' The other girl's voice was impatient, and Kimball, who considered himself a gentleman, contemplated with equanimity the idea of pushing her into the back seat and slamming the door.

'You go ahead,' Elizabeth said. Afterward Kimball wondered what Lizzy had told her mother about that afternoon, but he wasn't worrying about that then.

They hadn't gone for tea, at least not until later. Elizabeth said it was too soon after lunch, and tea was the last thing she wanted. They walked for a long time, and he kept asking her if she didn't want to do something, and she kept saying this was quite enough. She'd never, she said, walked Fifth Avenue, or any other avenue for that matter, alone with a man, and because that had started a train of thought she'd told him some other things she'd never done. She'd never ridden in a public railroad car or made a purchase, even so minor a purchase as a newspaper, with money or walked into a tearoom alone simply because she'd wanted a cup of tea. In fact, a good many things she hadn't done had to do with being alone.

'Does that mean you'd rather be alone now?' He laughed because he was fairly sure of the answer.

'Oh, no, this is the same as being alone.' He laughed again. 'I mean, this is better. As long as Mama or some chaperone isn't along.' She stopped walking then and looked at him, and her expression was suddenly serious. 'I guess you think I'm wild.'

He took her arm and started walking again. It was, he told himself, a perfectly good excuse for taking her arm. 'Only that you might like to be.'

She went back to the things she'd never done. It seemed she'd been a great many places and seen a great deal, but only at a distance. 'I might as well

215

have stayed home and looked at photographs or lantern slides. For example, Mr Kimball you've lived in Paris. And Italy too.' Kimball admitted he had. 'Well, I've been there, but you've lived there. Do you see the difference?' Kimball did and he was glad she did too.

By the time they'd reached the park it still hadn't begun to rain, but the wind had turned raw and they took a carriage. She didn't say if riding in a hired carriage alone with a man she barely knew were another first, but she looked pleased as he helped her in. When they passed the Metropolitan Museum she said she wanted to stop. 'I've never been to a museum with a real live artist.' In the wake of his experience the previous April the words struck him as particularly apt.

They'd spent less than half an hour inside the museum, despite the fact that she was a good student. She had a quick and intelligent eye and a mercifully silent tongue. He'd never been able to endure people who stood in front of pictures talking about them rather than looking at them. She wasn't one of those, but he'd grown impatient anyway. They'd been standing in front of one of those perfect classical statues when he'd taken her arm and hurried her out of the museum.

Outside they stopped on the stairs in front of the building and when she looked up at him, he could see she was hurt. 'Did I say something terribly stupid?'

'Not in the least.'

'Then why did we leave so abruptly? Don't you like the museum? I admit the collection can't

compare with the Louvre . . .' She sounded like
a copy book and he cut her off.

'I love the museum. I think it's wonderful. But
I think you're more wonderful.'

She looked at him, then away, and her timing
was perfect. He could tell that she was
accustomed to hearing things like that, but not so
accustomed that she didn't want to believe them.

'I mean it, Elizabeth. The museum was full of
dead things.' Was he really saying this, he who'd
always sworn that art lived forever. 'And you're
so alive.' He saw the startled look on her face and
stopped. It was lucky that he had because he'd
been about to say more and more would have been
too much. He warned himself then that he had to
go slowly. At his age he might not have much time,
but she had all the time in the world.

Sky stood at the bottom of the marble staircase
of Belle Isle watching the last guests leave and
waiting for his wife. She'd said she'd gone to look
at the children, but he knew she'd gone to look
at herself. Caroline never doubted her beauty, but
she felt the need to reassess it at regular intervals.
She was probably in her dressing room having her
maid redo her hair while he paced the foyer. And
the fact that Carrie knew he was eager to get to
Rosecliff only made it worse. She'd never minded
keeping him waiting, but now that she knew he
was impatient to see Vanessa, she absolutely
enjoyed it. Well, she wouldn't be able to go on
enjoying it. He'd told Amelia he was leaving her
sister, and he'd meant it. He had Tom Sturgis and

the Walsh deal to thank for that. With the money from this trust, money he'd make himself rather than inherit, he'd be able to turn all the family holdings over to Carrie and the children and still have plenty for himself and Vanessa.

He'd told Vanessa as much this afternoon, but he could tell by her smile that she hadn't believed him. No, that wasn't fair. She believed him, she just didn't feel she ought to encourage him. As she'd told him ever since the beginning, she might want him to leave Caroline and the children for her, but she'd never ask him to. It was a matter of honor to her, just as the money was to him. Vanessa had her scruples there too. Over the years he'd tried to buy her expensive gifts, and once or twice when some speculation had paid off handsomely, he'd wanted to buy her a house. Nothing ostentatious, just a small place, in the east Forties perhaps, where he could see her as often as they liked, but she'd always refused. 'I'll be your mistress, Sky, but I won't be a kept woman. At least not by you. We'll let the old dowagers who need my companionship see to that.'

He was going to keep her now though, and not as a mistress, but as a wife. Sky shifted his weight from one foot to the other. What in hell was Caroline doing up there. Torturing you, my boy, answered a small voice in the back of his head. It wasn't a kind voice, but that didn't mean it was a false one.

Sky saw Vanessa before he entered Rosecliff. He'd deposited Caroline at the door – she was bound to spend another quarter of an hour in the

218

ladies' dressing room – and was lingering in the front garden bounded on three sides by the white terra-cotta facade of the mansion, when he saw Vanessa pull up in his cousin Lydia's carriage. Sky watched as one of the footmen handed her down. She wasn't as beautiful as Carrie and she wasn't nearly as well dressed in old opera cloak that had belonged to Lydia and a plain dress that he, and probably half the other guests, recognized, but she stirred something in him that went beyond beauty or even desire. Perhaps it was the way her eyes found his in the crowd immediately, as if she'd sensed his presence before she'd seen him. He thought of Carrie's entrances. She never saw anyone, she merely soaked up admiration, like a huge thirsty sponge.

He saw Vanessa bend to say something to Lydia, then the old woman went on alone, and Vanessa joined him. When he took her arm and started around the house to the rose garden, she looked about nervously. 'This isn't the most private meeting place,' she said, but she let him lead her away from the other guests.

It was peculiar being in the rose garden at night. The blossoms were barely visible but their fragrance was overwhelming, almost aphrodisiacal Sky thought. 'You look lovely,' he said and his voice was strange, almost hoarse.

Vanessa had been walking in front of him along the narrow path and she turned now and raised her hand to his cheek. 'You always say the right thing, darling.' Before he could answer she came close and lifted her face to his. Her mouth was warm and very soft. 'I don't look any different than I did a few hours ago,' she murmured against his mouth. 'Or at least I don't feel any different.' She took his hand and drew it beneath her cape to the deeply cut neckline of her dress. He moved his fingers beneath the fabric and felt the softness of her breast, and the sensations of a few hours ago flooded back. He was touching her again, not just his hand against her breast, but touching her as he had that afternoon in Lydia's guesthouse, his body molded to hers, sharing the warmth of her skin and the dampness between her breasts where little beads of moisture had gathered. He remembered the salty taste of her skin and felt the heat of her thighs locked around him. The guesthouse had smelled of roses too, but mustily, mingling with the smell of the old furniture and the cretonne throws that protected it and the brackish salt air, mingling too with the scent of her skin and hair, and then the heavier scent of the two of them together. She'd been wild, the way he'd once thought no woman could ever be, and it had aroused a wildness in him, an abandon he'd once dreamed of and now knew, had known for some time because of her, existed.

Her hand trailed down to his trousers and she dropped her head back and looked up at him, smiling. 'You're thinking of this afternoon.'

'You always know what I'm thinking.'

She took a step back, holding both his hands in hers. 'It's lucky I do, darling. If I'd waited for you to read my mind, I'd still be an old maid. In fact as well as name.'

She knew he didn't believe her and never had, but it was true. Because he was married, because of his experience beyond marriage and her lack of it, Sky was convinced he'd seduced her, but Vanessa knew if anyone had been seduced, it had been Sky. She'd known he would be on the boat from Bar Harbor to Boston that night. It was seven years ago, but she could still remember it vividly. It wasn't the sort of thing she was likely to forget.

The attraction had been growing ever since Sky had come to Bar Harbor in mid-July of that summer so many years ago. On her side, the attraction went back farther than that to her debutante days, but she'd known then she had no chance. It wasn't merely that he was such a spectacular catch – rich, well bred, handsome in a robust, very American way – and she was a poor girl without parents or the good name they might have left her had they been more discreet. It wasn't merely that she was no beauty. Her looks were too dramatic for her position in life, and she'd learned early to counteract the dark vivid eyes and the broad cheekbones with a quiet, self-effacing manner. The contradiction between appearance and conduct was not successful. Still, it wasn't any of these things that had made Sky unattainable. It was simply that he'd always been too much in love with Caroline Leighton to notice anyone else. But by that summer in Bar Harbor, he'd been married for five years and had apparently overcome his obsession.

From the moment Sky had mentioned he was taking the night boat to Boston, she'd known what

221

she was going to do, known it as surely as the fact that it was not what she was supposed to do. Vanessa had grown up only a decade behind Edith Wharton, and she occasionally fancied herself an Edith Wharton heroine, materially inferior and spiritually superior to those on whom she depended. But that summer she discovered she was not an Edith Wharton heroine for that fictional woman would have opted for honor – her own, Schuyler's even Caroline's. In that respect Vanessa knew she was more like her parents than she liked to admit. She'd rather risk a brief plunge into the waters of life, even if it meant drowning in disgrace, than stand safely by the side of the pond testing the temperatures with a hesitant toe for the rest of her life.

To be sure, she'd had some hesitation about pursuing Sky. Standing on the deck of the old side-wheeler, the *J. T. Morse*, as it pulled out of Bar Harbor, she wondered how Schuyler would react to finding her on board. Would he think her forward? Worse still, would he think her foolish for having taken his politeness of the last weeks so seriously? As it turned out, he hadn't found her foolish or forward, hadn't even realized that her presence on the Boston boat that night was not accidental. She'd told him as much the next morning when she'd awakened and found him sitting in a chair in the narrow stateroom watching her. He was very polite that morning and, she suspected, a little nervous. She was neither a governess nor an actress. She was from his world, if a slightly shabby corner of it, and worst of all, unmarried. What had happened could mean difficulties for both of them, though at that moment he was probably thinking more of the difficulties she might make for him. That was when she'd told him she'd been on board purposely. She'd gone on telling him that for the next seven years, though he didn't seem to believe it any more now than he had that morning. Perhaps it was his upbringing. He just couldn't believe that she, a nice woman, had taken the initiative. Perhaps his pride would not let him believe that.

'I'm going to tell her tonight,' Sky said. The statement had nothing do with her memory of that night so many years ago, or his of the afternoon, but they both knew what he meant.

Vanessa dropped his hands and turned toward the ocean. He could not see her face. 'During the midnight supper? Or perhaps the cotillion?'

'I'm serious, Vanessa.'

She turned back to him. 'I'm sure you are, darling, but I'd rather not talk about it. If you tell her . . .' She saw the look that crossed his face. 'When you tell her, I'll do whatever you want and go wherever you want, but until you do, I'd rather not discuss it.'

'Most women would want to discuss nothing else.'

She'd already started back toward the house and now she stopped just out of view of the other guests and kissed him quickly. 'That's another thing I don't want to talk about Sky. Most women. Now tell me you love me, not most women, and

223

then wait at least three minutes to follow me inside. Not that it will fool anyone.'

He told her he loved her, which was true, and stood watching her disappear around the corner of the house. She was trying to smooth her hair and doing an inefficient job of it. He thought of Caroline who would never allow a single strand out of place.

Schuyler heard footsteps behind him on the path, and turned quickly. It was Harry Lehr. 'Ah, Niebold, I thought you were someone else. I was looking for . . . But I mustn't tell you. It's to be the great surprise of the evening. Our entertainer, that is.'

Schuyler was barely listening to the words. He was too busy wondering where Lehr had come from and how long he'd been there. Then he reminded himself it didn't matter what Lehr had seen. After tonight nothing like that would matter again.

In the men's dressing room of Belle Isle Sam found Sturgis lingering with a few men who were not especially eager to get on to the ball. All were past the age of dancing. Sturgis was standing beside Selby, and when Sam approached, the old philanthropist turned away so abruptly that he knocked over the stand holding the *boutonnière*. The water from the crystal vials made dark stains on the Samarkand rug, but two footmen moved swiftly and silently to mop it up.

Sturgis was holding his hat, gloves, and walking stick in one hand, and Sam realized his timing was off. While he'd been on the terrace wrestling with disconcerting memories and unsettled scores, Sturgis had almost slipped away. The evening was half over, but Sam still had more than half the job ahead of him. He fell in step beside Sturgis and when they reached the portico, the older man dismissed his automobile. 'I need the exercise,' he explained to Sam. 'Walk off Edith's dinner before we get to Tessie's midnight supper.'

Something about the way he pronounced the name Edith reminded Sam of the story Morgan had told him. Sam had always thought of Edith Leighton as a hard woman, and the name, in his mind, had a crisp, unpleasant sound, but Sturgis had managed to soften it.

'I think I'll join you,' Sam said, 'if you have no objection.'

'Glad of the company,' Sturgis said and started off at a brisk clip. He was a short man who'd gone beyond portliness to become rotund, but his movements were lively and coordinated. He swung his hands as he walked, like many short men who want to appear forceful.

The automobiles and carriages were noisy on the brick drive and the two men did not speak until they had passed through the gates of Belle Isle onto Bellevue Avenue. They had to walk along the side of the road because there were no sidewalks. Why put sidewalks on Bellevue Avenue when no one walked there, no one except the servants, that is.

'Well, Van Nest,' Sturgis said finally, 'how is my old friend the Commodore? I saw *Corsaire* in the

225

harbor this afternoon, and I thought of going out to pay a call, but never got around to it.'

'The Commodore's fine. Sends his regards to you.'

'Fine, you say. Then all that talk about . . .' Sturgis gave Sam a quick sideways look '. . . about his condition is unfounded. They say it has something to do with his stomach.'

'Completely unfounded,' Sam lied. 'He's older, of course, but he's still in good health.' Another sideways look from Sturgis. Sam knew he didn't believe him, just as he knew Sturgis was glad – not glad that Morgan was failing, but glad that he was younger than Morgan and in better health. He could expect to outlive the great J. P. Morgan.

'You know,' Sturgis said, and his voice was warm now, 'I'm ashamed of myself for not finding the time to get out to see the Commodore today. We shared some good times up here. I remember one weekend at his fishing box . . . but I doubt a young man would be interested in some long past party.'

Sam wasn't sure whether Sturgis was worried about boring him or about telling him too much. Had the story concerned Edith Leighton, or, more to the point, her rejection of the young Sturgis? That was silly, of course. He had to stop thinking about Sturgis' infatuation with Edith Leighton. It had nothing to do with tonight.

'Well, anyway,' Sturgis went on, 'there are a lot of old memories between us. And not just pleasant outings. The Commodore and I did a lot of business together.'

It was clear that Sturgis no longer thought of

himself as Morgan's protégé, and Sam was wondering how to remind him of the former relationship without antagonizing him. Aging millionaires might like to remember their origins, but that didn't mean they liked to be reminded of them. 'So the Commodore told me. We were reminiscing about the old days only this afternoon. Or rather he was.'

This time the head turned toward Sam rather than just the eyes. 'Did he tell you he helped me make my first million?' Finally, as if the joke were on all of them, Sturgis laughed. 'The first one's always the hardest one, you know, Sam.'

'He mentioned it. The first and a few since then. He still thinks of you as one of his . . .' Sam was groping for the right word. *Men* sounded patronizing, as if Sturgis worked for Morgan. '. . . allies.'

'Allies. That sounds as if the Commodore has enemies.'

'Not enemies, but perhaps some opposition. We're not happy about Walsh's new scheme.'

Sturgis did not even glance toward Sam now, but there was a change in his voice, almost like a slight chill in the night air. 'What do you know about Jason Walsh's plans?'

Sam outlined the trust briefly but completely.

'I can see the Commodore's still on top of things.' Sturgis sounded a little surprised by the fact. 'But I can't see why he'd be unhappy about the plan.' Out of the corner of his eye Sam saw Sturgis smile. 'Unless it's because he didn't think of it himself.'

'I think his reasons are a little more valid than that.'

'Take it from me, Sam, there are few things in the world more valid than a man's vanity. Especially a big man like Morgan.'

'Or like yourself?'

The eyes darted sideways to Sam again. 'Or like myself, but I'm not in this Walsh thing for vanity. I'm in it for profit. And, fortunately, I'm not in the position of having to oppose it for vanity.'

'What if I could show you other reasons for opposition? Reasons that would make it unprofitable in the long run.'

'I don't believe there are any.'

Sam ran through the litany again. When he finished, Sturgis seemed unimpressed. 'I guess the Commodore is getting old. I've never known him to be afraid before. Certainly not of the government.'

'The government has changed, because the people have made it change.'

'Don't you believe it, my boy. Politicians will always be politicians. Out for their own interests – money and reelection. And because of that we'll always be able to buy them.'

'The country's getting bigger. And more unwieldy. You'll have to buy the people too.'

'Simple enough. The only people who count are the ones with money, and we know how to take care of them. Set up this financial trust, then issue stock on it. Lots of stock. The Steel Trust created a new capital of one point four billion. We're shooting for two point seven. That will give a lot of small investors a small profit and a few big investors a big one. So much for the people, Sam.'

'And what about the possibility of a panic?'

'The country has lived through panics before. I've lived through several myself. I have no doubt you'll live through several more. That's the way the economy works. It needs a good shaking down every now and then. I admit the last one was more than a good shaking down, but we came through. That time Morgan rose to the occasion. Next time it will be someone else.'

Sam could see the lights of Rosecliff in the distance. From here on the road only a few were visible, shimmering through the dense wall of trees. There was a magical quality to those lights. They were disconnected and disembodied, glowing one moment, hidden by foliage the next. Sam found himself drawn to them as if they represented something elusive and desirable in the quiet summer night. Then he remembered they represented only Rosecliff, and he remembered too that they'd be at the ball in minutes and he'd achieved nothing.

'Do you know Henry Ford?' he asked Sturgis. He was using an argument he had not even suggested to Morgan because he knew it was one Morgan would hate.

'An eccentric,' Sturgis pronounced. 'A fanatic. Smart but unreliable. Cars for poor people and all this business about an assembly line.'

'But smart. You admit that.'

'I don't see what he has to do with the financial trust.'

'I've heard from men who know about these things, incidentally, that Ford is planning to increase wages. Every man in his plants, even the lowest paid sweeper, will earn a minimum of four dollars a day.'

Sturgis stopped walking, then started again quickly. 'Just as I said. The man's a crank.'

'Either that or smarter than any of us. His theory is that the more he pays his workers, the more they'll be able to buy.'

'Maybe. Maybe not. I know one thing for sure. They won't be able to buy stocks and bonds. And that's what we're talking about with this trust.'

'Maybe they'll be able to buy politicians – or at least hold them to account, and make it more difficult for people like us to buy them. We're on the edge of a new age, and it's going to be a more democratic one. People, even people without money, are going to have a say in things.'

Sturgis stopped walking again and turned to Sam. 'You know, Van Nest, I think you're a bit of an idealist.' He said it kindly as if he knew it was a mild insult and didn't want to offend him.

'Is that better or worse than a fanatic and an eccentric?'

Sturgis laughed and turned into the long curving drive that led up to Rosecliff. 'The point is, Sam, Ford isn't big enough to make a difference. Suppose he pays a few thousand men a ridiculous wage. A few thousand men with a few extra dollars in their pockets aren't enough to stop this thing. And the Commodore knows it. Suppose the government does make noise. That's all it will be.

Noise. There's going to be so much power behind this trust, they won't be able to do a thing.'

They were drawing closer to the house now and Sam could see the light dancing off the fountain in the front courtyard. The falling water made a gentle accompaniment to the voices of the guests who were pressing toward the entrance. He felt Sturgis take his arm in a friendly gesture.

'I'll tell you something the Commodore used to say to me, Sam. A man always has two reasons for the things he does – a good one and the real one. In this case, the real one is that an old man doesn't like being outdone. It's that simple. Morgan's convinced you this scheme with Walsh is dangerous. Hell, he's probably convinced himself. From what I hear his mind isn't as sharp as it used to be. But the truth is it isn't any more dangerous than the Steel Trust was, and it's just as profitable. If I were you, Sam, I'd try to get in on it. In fact, if you'd like me to, I'll speak to Walsh for you. I know you don't have anything to offer in the way of controlling interests, but a thing like this can always use another smart young man.'

'I'm a partner in Morgan and Company,' Sam said.

'Hell, Van Nest, you're not a company man. I don't know you well, but I know you well enough to know that. Besides, you have to think of yourself. With the Commodore on the way out and young Jack about to step into his shoes, where does that leave you?'

'With a partnership in Morgan and Company.'

Sturgis dropped his arm. 'Have it your own way,

Van Nest, but don't say I didn't warn you.' He must have realized he'd sounded more annoyed than he meant to. 'And give my regards to the Commodore.' Sturgis moved off quickly, and Sam saw him join Schuyler Niebold in the crowd that was passing slowly into the vestibule of Rosecliff.

The lights shining from the arched french doors thrown open to the ballroom and the second floor windows were no longer magical or elusive. They were blinding now, illuminating the white facade with its elaborate carving and flooding the garden courtyard, the *cour d'amour* as it was called. Funny, Sam thought, how Newport could steal so much from Europe and remain so intrinsically American. The stone planters glinted white, and the water lilies floating in the reflecting pools were little rafts of light in the dark water. 'Splendid,' Sam heard a woman say, and he supposed it was. At least Rosecliff wasn't a hybrid monstrosity like some of the houses. It was large, but not ungainly, and the lines were good. The Ionic pilasters and carved floral swags enhanced the facade without cluttering or overpowering it, and the balustrade that hid the third floor gave it a neat, finished look like the border on a square cake. It was a handsome building, Sam admitted, a splendid building. Tonight, illuminated by electricity and gas, candlelight and moonlight, Rosecliff was Newport at its most splendid.

Sam joined the crowd moving through the outer foyer into the great stair hall. Footmen in powdered wigs and satin knee breeches stood around the perimeter of the rooms and at intervals along the wide heart-shaped staircase. Rosecliff had been modeled on the Grand Trianon, and the servants looked as if they had stepped out of the Sun King's court. So did the guests, Sam thought. The costumes were more modern but no less elaborate, or at least the women's weren't. The men held pretty much to a proper penguinlike mold, a somber black-and-white backdrop for the dresses and jewels of the women. Louis had built the Grand Trianon as a hunting lodge where he and his intimates could escape the rigors of court life, and the Newport matrons had constructed their summer 'cottages' as a quiet respite from city life. The end results were ironic, Sam thought, only if you believed that Louis and the ladies of Newport really wanted a rest from society.

At the foot of the sweetheart staircase Sam found Corcoran and his wife standing with a girl beside them. The girl was a younger, slender version of Mrs Corcoran with flaming red hair and milky white skin dotted with freckles that had been insufficiently camouflaged by dusting powder. The skin should have made her appear fragile, but the freckles made her look robust and high spirited. Sam thought without interest that he'd been right. Mrs Corcoran must have been a very pretty girl.

'Ah, Van Nest,' Corcoran said as if they hadn't met in years. 'Good to see you. Bet you haven't met our little girl, our little Agnes here.' Agnes looked a little embarrassed, but not much. She put a strong gloved hand in his and said she knew his sister, Mrs Endicott. That seemed to establish them all as old friends, and though it was Mr Corcoran Sam wanted to speak to, he found himself signing his name on Agnes Corcoran's dance card.

'Only one dance?' Corcoran said. He said it in a hearty tone and Sam felt a little like a country boy being sold the rights to the Brooklyn Bridge as he put his name down for a waltz.

'I didn't dare ask for any more than that,' Sam said. 'It doesn't seem fair for us old men to monopolize all the pretty young girls.'

He'd been speaking as much to Corcoran as his daughter, but it was Agnes who answered. 'Not old, Mr Van Nest, mature. And every girl knows a mature man is more interesting than a callow boy.' The senior Corcorans smiled with pride. Agnes certainly could turn a phrase. Then a young man appeared at Agnes' side and claimed his dance. He may have been a callow boy, but Agnes smiled up at him eagerly, as eagerly as she smiled at Sam as she excused herself and moved off to the ballroom.

The timing was perfect, Sam thought. He'd get Corcoran off for a quiet moment right now, but he lost his train of thought because over Mrs Corcoran's shoulder he saw Amelia descending the wide heart-shaped staircase. She wasn't moving the way he remembered her moving when they were younger, with that easy swinging gait, or even like a duchess. She moved like a queen, a goddamn queen deigning to join her subjects for a few moments. When she saw Sam she stopped and reached a long white-gloved arm out to steady herself against the scrolled railing. Sam remembered the brandy on the terrace and wondered if Lady Amelia were a little tipsy. He knew that something had thrown her off balance, and he wasn't vain enough to think it was he.

He watched as she took the last few stairs, moving regally again over the red carpet, and joined her sister Caroline at the bottom. They were both wearing dark evening dresses with deep décolletages that set off their pale shoulders and long necks beneath the upswept hair. At dinner Amelia's skin had glowed in the candlelight. Now it looked like ice.

He turned to Corcoran. 'I wonder if we could talk for a moment.'

Corcoran didn't look in the least surprised. 'Good idea, Van Nest.' He hesitated for a moment while the polite applause died and the orchestra started up in a waltz. 'But not right now. This is your dance with Agnes, and I wouldn't keep you from that for the world.'

Agnes wasn't the most direct route to James Corcoran, but Sam wasn't foolish enough to doubt that she was a route. He bowed to Mrs Corcoran and started toward the ballroom.

'My dear Elias,' Lehr said, coming up behind Leighton in the men's dressing room. 'I simply must have a word with you.' He took Leighton's arm and steered him past the footman holding the silver tray heaped with dance cards. 'I'm sure you don't want one of those, and I already have mine.' Lehr waved a fat wrist in the air jiggling a dance program in front of Elias' face. It wasn't the first time Leighton wondered how his wife could stand the man.

'Now tell me,' Harry went on in a whisper, 'strictly *entre nous*, of course, what are you up to? The James Corcorans for dinner. I swear, Elias, your wife has the patience of a saint. And Van Nest. He hasn't been in the house since that disastrous business with Amelia. Well, fortunately we took care of that. But now he's back. And you're up to something. Harry knows.'

'Save your imagination for the ladies, Lehr. They appreciate it.'

'Now don't be that way, my dear fellow. I'm not just gossiping. I'm interested for a reason. As I was telling Edith this afternoon, I'd like to make some investments. For Bessie, of course. You wouldn't have any objection to letting an old friend in on the ground floor, as the saying goes.'

Elias shook off his hand. 'Ground floor of what?'

'Why, whatever it is you and Van Nest and Corcoran are up to.'

'I've barely talked to either of them all evening.'

'You haven't talked to them, but Van Nest's been talking to everyone. Huddling with Wainwright. Walking over here with Sturgis. I saw them set out together from Belle Isle. He's up to something. I can tell.'

'Why ask me about it? Ask Van Nest.'

'Van Nest despises me,' Harry said as if he were greatly amused by the fact.

Elias wondered what made Lehr think he didn't.

'Well, Harry, I have no idea what he's up to – if he's up to anything.'

'You know, Elias, you really ought to tell me. Much better to let me in on things than to have me babbling about them. And as it happens, tonight I'll have a particularly good medium through which to speak.'

'I've never known you to need more than your mouth, Harry.'

Lehr gave one of his maniacal laughs. As he'd told Amelia, he could not be insulted. 'You'll be sorry, Elias. Don't say I didn't warn you.' He laughed again and went off, humming to himself and straightening his white tie.

Elias debated warning Van Nest but decided against it. He'd set things up for Sam, but that was as far as he was willing to go. Besides, what harm could Harry's gossip do? No one paid any attention to him except the ladies, and this was not a matter that concerned the ladies.

The terrace was deserted this early in the evening and Elizabeth moved to a shadowy corner of it gratefully. It was the first time she'd escaped from Sydney since the men had rejoined the ladies after brandy. He'd been rude to Kimball on the drive over and even worse to Lieutenant Atherton once they'd arrived. The lieutenant had only been asking for an extra dance, and Sydney had practically torn her card from his hands. Impossible was not a word she usually connected with Sydney, but he was being impossible tonight. A harbinger of Sydney as a husband, she thought.

237

She told herself that was unfair, but didn't really believe it.

Elizabeth moved to the edge of the terrace. The sea beyond the long carpet of lawn was dotted with the white sails of half a dozen ships. They weren't real, she knew. The water here was too shallow and rocky to accommodate anything larger than a small day-sailer, but Mrs Oelrichs, ever resourceful, had commissioned a fleet of cardboard sailing ships. Lizzy had to admit they looked romantic bobbing gently in the swell, their paper sails reflecting the moonlight onto the black sea. She thought of sailing away, from Newport, from her mother, from Sydney. How much easier not to explain or apologize but merely to disappear.

At the end of the lawn a lighthouse, a real one constructed expressly for the ball, blinked its warnings to the toy ships, while in the ballroom behind her the orchestra struck up a twostep and voices swelled with the mounting fervor of the ball. She ought to go in – she was missing the dancing and the excitement, the fun and the flirtations – but if she returned to the pleasures of the ball she'd be returning to Sydney as well, and she was not quite ready for that.

'Lizzy, I couldn't imagine where you'd gone.' She turned and saw Sydney standing in one of the french doors. Silly to think she could escape him merely by coming out to the terrace. His evening clothes were perfectly cut, but they could not camouflage a certain awkwardness. He looked like a boy who's grown too fast or a man who hasn't grown enough. Then Atherton appeared at his side, tall, slender, and very correct in his dress uniform. He took a step past Sydney toward her and she noticed that he moved well.

'I believe this is our dance, Miss Leighton.'

It was his dance, inscribed neatly and properly on her dance card, and there was nothing Sydney could do about it.

Standing with his back to the french doors on the garden side of the ballroom, Douglas Kimball saw Elizabeth enter on the arm of that naval lieutenant. Don't kid yourself, he told himself. His name is Atherton. Lieutenant Timothy Atherton. No one else remembered the name because no one else thought the lieutenant counted, but he'd heard the name when Lizzy had introduced them and hadn't forgotten it.

They made a nice couple, he thought, Lizzy and Lieutenant Atherton. Both young, handsome, and obviously enjoying themselves. He forced himself to imagine how he would paint the scene. It would be difficult to capture the light without making it look garish. The reflection of the candles in the chandeliers danced off the gilded bronze and crystal and created rainbows on the white of Lizzy's dress while the gold braid of the lieutenant's uniform shone like the real thing. But the look on Atherton's face, Kimball knew he could paint that perfectly. It was an intense expression, single-minded and selective, the expression of a man who sees only a single face in a crowded room. Kimball had seen it a hundred times on a hundred different young men in his life, but he didn't think it was trite, merely universal.

The faces are unimportant, Kimball told himself. It's the whole effect you'd be after. He forced himself to look from Lizzy and the lieutenant to the carved rococo ceiling. When the chandeliers were lighted as they were now, heating the small vials of perfume that scented the whole room, the center mural had a *trompe l'oeil* effect, and the clouds seemed to be floating across a clear blue sky. That's what you'd be after, he told himself, the openness of the room, the feeling of movement. He looked to the twin doors at the far end that opened, one on the billiard room, the other on the fountain. The doors were paneled with mirrors and reflected dozens of fountains. Kimball decided he could spend weeks painting the room before he even got to the figures in it.

'Do you approve, Mr Kimball?'

He looked from the doors at the far end of the room to Edith Leighton standing at his side. 'You were contemplating the room with such interest, I was wondering what your opinion was.'

Kimball made a noncommital sound.

'Actually,' Edith went on in a confidential tone, 'I was wondering if you'd do me a favor, Mr Kimball. I wonder if you'd dance with Elizabeth. I believe the young people call it cutting in.'

The only surprising thing about the request was that Mrs Leighton had turned to him instead of Hallenbeck, but perhaps she didn't want to be obvious. Kimball bowed to her and moved off toward Elizabeth. Atherton relinquished her with as much grace as could be expected under the circumstances. Then Lizzy looked up at him and smiled, and he forgot about the canvas he'd been painting in his mind.

'Did Mama send you to cut in on me?'

'Surely you don't think I'd undertake such an unpleasant task on my own.'

'Do you think she suspects anything?'

'Let's just say I think she's worried. I think Lieutenant Atherton has her very worried.'

'You're making fun of me again.'

'I never make fun of you, Elizabeth. Sometimes of myself, but never of you. And you have to admit you've put me in a laughable position.'

She looked up at him and her face was earnest, too earnest for a ballroom, he thought. 'I haven't put you in any position. At least I never meant to.'

'I'm sure you never meant to. Still, you managed to do it – to the three of us – Hallenbeck, Atherton, and me. And I'm in the worst position of all. Or at least the most ridiculous. I'm old enough to be your father.'

'Old enough, perhaps, but an unlikely candidate.' The earnestness was gone now, and she was smiling what he'd come to call her provocative smile. He hadn't seen it until a few weeks ago and he was vain enough to think it hadn't existed till then. 'You're not stuffy enough or rich enough for Mama.' The smile disappeared as the words died. 'Douglas, what am I going to do about Sydney?'

Over Elizabeth's shoulder he saw Edith

watching them. 'I thought you'd already made up your mind about that.'

'I have made up my mind. I told you that. I just don't know how to go about it.'

Now it was Atherton he saw beyond Elizabeth's shoulder. The lieutenant was dancing with a young girl in silver, but he was watching Lizzy. 'Well, it seems to me you'd better find a way soon. And make no mistake about it, Lizzy, you're the one who has to find a way.'

'You mean you won't help at all,' she said as the music came to an end, but before he could answer she took his arm and started moving toward the terrace. 'Quickly,' she whispered, 'before Sydney finds me.'

'And to think,' she went on when they were standing against the marble railing of the terrace, 'that I used to think you'd be just the opposite. I used to think you'd be overbearing. Like Mama.'

'That's because of my age,' he said and smoothed his short beard.

Elizabeth saw the gesture and knew what it meant. 'It has nothing to do with age. It has to do with the way you thought of me. Or at least the way I thought you thought of me. I was convinced you saw me as a blank canvas. One you could cover with your own vision. And your signature.'

'You were wrong. You know that now, don't you?'

'I think I do.'

'In fact, if I saw you as a canvas, it was one that had been painted on too often. What I wanted wasn't to paint another picture on top of all the others, but to chip away at them and discover the original work beneath.'

'And now you've done it.' She smiled at him again, not the closed-mouthed provocative smile but a broad, proud one. It made her look very young.

'Not quite. There are still a few traces left.' He'd turned his back to the low wall of the terrace as he spoke, and saw Sydney Hallenbeck coming through the french doors. 'Perhaps the lieutenant will have better luck,' Kimball said, and disliked himself even as he said it. He was too old for that sort of thing.

Kimball remained on the terrace after Elizabeth and Hallenbeck had returned to the ballroom, and when Lieutenant Atherton emerged from it a few minutes later, Kimball motioned him over. 'Even the navy is entitled to a break, Lieutenant.' Hypocrite, he added to himself. Pretending to befriend the kid when all you're interested in is casing the competition.

The lieutenant took a cigarette case from the inside pocket of his uniform and held it out to Kimball. It's probably the only case here that isn't gold, including my own, Kimball thought as he took a cigarette. He felt a certain kinship with Atherton, but realized with a start, he was viewing things from the vantage point of memory. From where the lieutenant stood, Kimball was simply one more member of a world to which the lieutenant didn't belong. Atherton had no idea that they were both outsiders, and who could blame him? Everything about Kimball seemed to mark him as a member; everything except the important things.

'Not that I'm complaining . . .' the lieutenant said.

'It's just that sometimes the duty's a little hard, is that it? All those young ladies to be attended. I know. I've had the same problem at times. With some of them it's a pleasure and with others . . . well, as I said, the duty can be hard.'

The lieutenant smiled at that, but as Elizabeth and Sydney danced past the doors to the terrace, his expression turned serious. 'And sometimes it's the worst with the ones that ought to be the best.'

Kimball inhaled on the cigarette and looked at Atherton out of the corner of his eye. 'You mean the ones who are within reach, you don't want, and the ones you want are unattainable.'

'At least for a second lieutenant.'

'You won't always be a second lieutenant.'

'Around here anyone less than an admiral might as well be a second lieutenant. Sometimes I feel like one of the footmen. Except my uniform's duller.'

'Oh, I don't know. From where I stand it seems that quite a few young ladies were taken with that uniform – and the lieutenant who wears it.'

'Then you know more than I do, Kimball. They dance with me because they have to dance with someone, but most of the time they're just looking over my shoulder at someone *eligible*. The joke back at the base is that these girls are the same as the girls back home only they have money. You know,' the lieutenant dropped his voice a little, 'the colonel's lady, only with us it's the admiral's lady, and Judy O'Grady.'

'They're both alike under the skin,' Kimball finished for him.

'Only it isn't true. Maybe it's just the money that makes them different, but they are different.'

'That's the first half of the lesson.'

'What's the second?'

'They're not all the same either. The rich, that is. They're different from us, but they're different from each other too. Did you ever notice how most painters make them look alike? Just as most writers make them seem alike. But they're not. When you get beyond that wall of money, you begin to see the differences.'

'*If* you get beyond that wall of money.'

'I admit that it doesn't happen easily or quickly, but I've spent a good part of my life among them – not as one of them, you understand, but among them – and after a while they let you past. That's when you begin to sort them out. Some of them have nothing but their money. Those are the ones who will never accept you unless you have as much as they do. Some of them are frightened you want them only for their money. Those are the sad ones. But the best ones are the ones who know the value of money. They know what it can buy and what it can't. And if they're really good, they want to know about the things it can't buy. That's where people like you and me come into it. In one way or another we represent the outside world to them.'

'That's what she said,' Atherton murmured almost to himself.

Kimball ground out his cigarette with the sole of his evening slipper. 'That's what who said?' he asked, but he knew the answer. Lizzy was one of the good ones, the best one.

He'd joked with her before, comparing her to a painting or a canvas with too many paintings, but the analogy was too lifeless. In Kimball's mind Elizabeth had nothing to do with art or ideas. Lizzy was life. He'd known that the first time he'd seen her. She represented the life he'd almost lost as well as the life he'd never lived because he'd been too busy painting. Lizzy with her curiosity and zest for life was his last chance at life.

The problem, however, was not what Lizzy was for him, but what he might be for her. He was an interesting man, a worldly man, a different sort of man, but an old man, unlike Hallenbeck who shared her youth, and Atherton, who didn't dare admit it, but wanted to share her future. You're an old fool, he told himself, like the pathetic old men he remembered from his student days in Paris, the ones who used to hang around the models and dancers. You'd see them on the boulevards and in the cafes with their well-cut clothes and their expensive jewelry. Their skin was always pink from too much wine and too many massages and the ordeal of trying to stay too young, and the worst ones had pink skulls too, glistening through the few wisps of hair they combed carefully over it. Kimball ran his palm over his hair as if to smooth it. They'd laughed at those men then, and some of his friends had even lived off them. He remembered how the Russian had shown up one day wearing a gold and sapphire earring one of the old men had given his girl. Until then they'd called him the mad Russian, but after that he'd been known as the gypsy. Kimball had never gone so far as to live off any of them, but he'd shared a girl with one of them once. She was a beautiful girl with bold features and a lush figure that always seemed too confined by her clothes. She was better without her clothes, but she was not a good model. She fidgeted constantly and talked incessantly. She'd talked about her old man a great deal. *Mon protecteur*, she'd called him. Kimball had been merely her *amant*. Kimball hadn't minded sharing her, because he hadn't really cared for her. Oh, no, he'd had to wait until he was an old man himself to care for someone. He was just like those old fools he'd laughed at. He'd tried to pretend he wasn't, tried to dignify his undignified passion for a girl half his age with rationalizations about that night last April. He'd come so close to death. Lizzy was so full of life. A true story, undoubtedly, but not an original one. It was what every one of those old men, those *protecteurs*, had thought. They could feel death lapping at their feet just as he'd felt the water surging up the deck that night, and they'd groped after the young bodies as a talisman against death just as he was groping after Lizzy. Kimball remembered a sketch he'd made years ago of one of those old men and a girl in a cafe. The man had his arm around the girl and her flesh was so young and firm it seemed to be fighting back against the fat fingers that squeezed it.

Kimball looked down at his own hands. They were not fat. They were strong and supple and had many years of good work left in them. He was not one of those foolish old men. Many women, he knew, still regarded him as attractive. He remembered Edith Leighton on the beach that morning, but Edith was Lizzy's mother, just as he was, as he'd told her, old enough to be her father. *Climb upon my knee, little girl* . . . The situation, he told himself again, was impossible.

'It's impossible,' the lieutenant said and Kimball started. He'd almost forgotten Atherton and the similarity of their positions. 'An impossible post.'

'Have you had others?' Kimball asked. The lieutenant admitted he hadn't. This was his first assignment. For once Kimball was not amused by the irony of the statement or by the lieutenant's youth.

From where he stood in the hallway between the ballroom and the billiard room Sam could see into both areas. He took a glass of champagne from a passing waiter and turned his back on the ballroom to watch Max Fingerhut setting up for a shot. Max rubbed the end of his cue with the chalk, squinted at the balls on the table, walked to another corner, and rubbed the cue again. His mouth twitched. Sam doubted he'd make the shot successfully, but whether he did or not, the game would be over in a few minutes. He knew it was time to take on Fingerhut, but didn't have the heart for it. Not that he was concerned about Fingerhut, only fed up with Morgan's game, as fed up as Fingerhut looked as one ball glanced off another without moving it. Fingerhut had lost and it was time to move in, but for once Sam decided to indulge himself. He drained the glass of champagne, turned his back on the billiard room, and took a few steps across the ballroom to Amelia. As soon as he saw the startled look on her face, he wondered why he'd bothered.

'This is quite an honor. I didn't think you danced anymore. In fact, I'd heard you didn't come to Newport anymore.'

'I'm touched, Amelia. I didn't think you took that much interest in my comings and goings.'

'Harry was just telling me. He said you hadn't been here since' — the brittle voice flagged a little — 'since your wife died,' she finished lamely. 'I'm sorry.'

She sounded sorry. Watch yourself, he warned. She's a good actress. Hadn't she put on one hell of a show until the day the duke offered the title and she told Hatfield she wasn't in for commoners. 'And where is the duke?' he asked. 'Will he be joining you this summer?'

She looked up at him and the eyes were the way he remembered them, only now the green lights were going off in anger rather than excitement. 'The duke will not be joining me this summer or ever.'

He missed a beat and wondered if she'd noticed. 'I'm sorry,' he murmured, but he didn't sound sorry. He'd been right after all. The duke and his duchess had not lived happily ever after. He told himself she'd only got what she deserved, but for some reason he didn't feel much like gloating. She was no longer looking at him, but he was aware of the closeness of her body and as she turned her head her hair brushed his cheek. That was a shock because her hair smelled exactly as he remembered it, fresh but somehow heady and wild like a summer forest. Above the scent emanating from the chandeliers and the perfume of all the other women he could smell Amelia's hair, and it took him back to too many times too long ago. He remembered the first time she'd put her hair up. There'd been something disquieting about seeing her that way, as if the fact that she'd put her hair up meant she was old enough to have it taken down. And he could remember too the first time he'd taken it down. It was a summer day in the country and the thick coils had started to come undone, and before she could stop him he'd taken out all the pins. He could still remember the way her hair had fallen around her shoulders, the aroma of it, and the way it framed her face. It had felt soft and sun-warmed in his hands.

'What are you thinking of?' She was looking up at him from under those damn thick lashes of hers, and he felt as if he'd been caught off balance. It was a question she used to ask all the time, but like the afternoon he was remembering, that was a long time ago.

'Raleigh.'

'Raleigh?'

'An afternoon there. Your father had just

restocked the stream and we went fishing.'

'You mean the time I caught at least half a dozen trout and you couldn't get a thing.'

'But I was working at a disadvantage. I'd just broken my arm.'

'Sprained it, if I remember correctly.' He wondered how much she did remember and how correctly, but he wasn't going to ask, and then the music came to an end and Harry Lehr joined them. He knew perfectly well that neither of them wanted to see him, but Harry often found that the places he most wanted to be were those he was least welcome. 'It's time, pets. It's time for Tessie's surprise. I'm not free to say who it is, but I can tell you what it is. We're going to have an exhibition of telepathy. Isn't that delicious?' Harry looked from Amelia to Sam and gave a wicked smile that made his eyes almost disappear into the folds of flesh around them. 'And wouldn't I just love to be able to read your minds, children. Why it makes one blush just to think of it.'

'You really are despicable,' Amelia said when Sam had excused himself and left them to get a drink.

'Now, pet, you mustn't get upset about a little good-natured teasing. After all, it was meant in your interest. Uncle Harry was trying to do you a favor. It's going to be a long season, Amelia, a long dry season without your dear duke. I don't delude myself that you take these things as lightly as Carrie. Would it be so terrible if you were to find solace — temporary solace, of course — with a poor lonely widower like Van Nest. Really, my pet, you and I are worldly enough to understand these things, though I doubt even your dear mother, practical soul that she is, would object to a dalliance with Van Nest if it served to keep you and the duke together.'

'Nothing's going to keep us together, Harry. And you're talking a lot of rubbish. As usual.'

'Come now, pet, you can put on your grande dame airs with others, but not with Harry. I remember the way things were, even if no one else does. Oh, how you both carried on. I can tell you, pet, it practically broke my cynical old heart when things didn't work out for you two.'

'I seem to remember your cynical old heart taking a somewhat different position at the time, Harry.' But Lehr had already turned away from her.

'Shhh, pet,' he whispered over his shoulder. 'Tessie's going to announce the entertainment.' And now Harry like everyone else seemed to have forgotten her and Sam and whatever had or had not happened between them as he pressed through the guests to get closer to the platform the footmen had brought in. On it Tessie Oelrichs stood with a man of medium height and powerful build. He had dark curly hair and a rather handsome face. Many of the guests had already recognized him, but Tessie would not relinquish her moment center stage. After entirely too many words of praise she mentioned the name Houdini and murmurs of excitement fluttered over the room as if someone had released a flock of small polite birds.

Sam stood in one of the doors to the ballroom

watching. Interesting, he thought, what could make a dent in the veneer of boredom that covered the very rich. They'd pretend they were above the exploits of the great 'escapologist' – 'too vulgar,' they'd say; 'for the masses,' they'd agree – but there was a definite air of titillation in the room.

'It is well known,' Mrs Oelrichs was saying, 'that Mr Houdini no longer gives exhibitions of telepathy. He has agreed, however, to make an exception tonight.' She hesitated for a moment to let the import of her words sink in. Even the great Houdini, she seemed to be saying, bowed to her wishes. 'For the first time in more than ten years Mr Houdini will display his extraordinary gift of mind-reading.' Sam heard another titter of excitement run through the crowd, and Mrs Oelrichs adjusted the huge canary diamond on her bosom as if to remind the audience that this was Mrs Hermann Oelrichs' ball, not a sideshow carnival. 'There will be no stirring of the souls beyond,' she said severely, her one blind eye veering a little. 'Mr Houdini assures me that he will confine himself to reading the thoughts as well as the pasts and futures of those in this room and not in the beyond. And now, may I present, Mr Harry Houdini.'

When the short stocky man stepped center stage, the murmuring in the audience died, but he waited a few beats before he began to speak. His voice was strong, but smooth as he explained the powers of the mind, not only of his mind, though he thanked Mrs Oelrichs for her kind words, but of any mind that had been trained to receptivity. It was all quite simple, he explained in a way that made it seem anything but, and to demonstrate as much, he would perform a few simple exercises.

'After I have been doubly blindfolded,' he said, 'first with this.' He produced a black eye mask. 'Then with this.' He brandished a white silk scarf. 'I will ask an aide, a volunteer from the audience, to pass among you. He will ask you at random for an object – any simple object off your person,' he added, though he knew few of the guests wore or carried anything simple, 'which he will hold above his head so that all of you may identify it. Then, blindfolded and with my back to the audience, I will identify the object. When I have identified it correctly, I will deduce from the object matters of its owner's past and future.

'Now, ladies and gentlemen, would one of you do me the honor of stepping forward to offer his services as my assistant.' Lehr sprang forward as if to beat the competition, though no one else had raised a hand. 'May I ask your name, sir?' Houdini said. Lehr identified himself and Houdini asked him to place first the mask, then the scarf over his eyes. Lehr did it all with a great flourish, and Houdini turned his back to the audience. 'Now, Mr Lehr, if you would pass among the audience . . .'

Lehr began moving slowly through the crowd that stood around the ballroom. Sam was still standing in one of the doorways beside Elias Leighton. 'Harry Lehr doesn't want to be upstaged by Harry Houdini,' Elias said in an undertone. 'Look at the old nance. Bouncing around like an elephant in heat.'

Lehr stopped beside Lydia Schuyler. 'Lydia, my pet, you must give me something so that we can test the great Houdini's skill.' She handed him her fan and he held it high over his head. 'We're ready to begin, Mr Houdini,' he said in a high piping voice. 'Free your mind of other thoughts Mr Houdini. Nothing else must enter your mind.'

'I sense something useful,' Houdini began slowly. 'And yet delicate. A lady's object. I see . . . I see a fan.' The audience responded with polite exclamations.

'That is correct, Mr Houdini. I am holding a lady's fan.'

'I see the lady . . .' Houdini went on. 'A great lady . . . a great lady with . . . with taste and discernment. A great lady with an interest in the arts. She has only today commissioned a great painting.'

Lydia Schuyler was growing redder by the minute, and from here and there around the ballroom came snickers. Between Lehr and Mrs Corcoran the story of Lydia's attempt to alter the immodest painting had traveled rapidly.

'Am I correct, madam?' Houdini repeated.

Mrs Schuyler gave a curt nod. 'The lady says that you are correct, Mr Houdini,' Lehr said and moved on to Schuyler Niebold. 'Well, Niebold, what will you contribute to the entertainment?' Sky handed him his cigarette case, but he didn't look happy about it, and Harry held the flat gold object up for the audience to see. 'Clear your mind, please, Mr Houdini. Give me your full attention. Ready yourself for the spirit of intelligence. Wait! Clear your mind again. Send all other thoughts away.'

'Listen to the old nancy,' Elias whispered. 'Mumbo-jumboing like some witch doctor.' Sam agreed that it was quite a performance.

'I see an object . . .' Houdini began again slowly. It was almost a chant. 'A bright object. I see a bright shining object. It is . . . it is small. But it is not a jewel. I see it opening and closing. I see a cigarette case. A gold cigarette case. Am I correct, Mr Lehr?'

'You are correct, Mr Houdini.'

'I see the man to whom the case belongs . . . a dark moustache . . . Wait! I feel a force. There is a bond between the lady of the fan and this gentleman. They are husband and . . . no! The bond is not that close. They are somehow related. Mr Lehr, will you ask the gentleman if he is a nephew of the lady with the fan.'

Sky laughed and said that he was.

'I have a sense . . .' Houdini went on. 'Almost an aroma. I believe the gentleman has been gardening recently. No, wait. He has been strolling in the garden.'

'I can pronounce you correct there, Mr Houdini,' Lehr said. 'I met this gentleman in Mrs Oelrichs' rose garden not two hours ago.' Sky was no longer laughing. He took the gold cigarette case from Lehr, but Houdini went on.

'I see a journey in his future. A dangerous journey. A safari . . . no, not a safari . . . I see a

more civilized journey, but still a great danger . . .
I see a dark force . . . a spirit almost . . . a
feminine spirit, dark and haunting.' The current
of laughter that ran through the ballroom was not
especially kind. 'That is the gentleman's future,'
Houdini said, and Lehr moved on to another guest.
Houdini succeeded in identifying a woman's
handkerchief and amusing the audience with
oblique references to the fact that she practically
starved her servants and scrimped on their wages.
After that he named a gentleman's pocketwatch
and suggested to the guests that unlike the
previous lady he was so generous to his servants
he'd been known to bestow quite decent
settlements on at least two maids his wife had
dismissed.

Next Lehr approached Elizabeth. 'Now what
will you offer, Lizzy, my pet?' She gave him one
of Sydney's orchids.

'Open your mind, Mr Houdini. Ready? Can you
feel the power, Mr Houdini? Hold on to the power.
Do not lose it.'

'I sense . . . again, I sense a blossom . . . a
blossom of vivid colors. You are holding a flower,
Mr Lehr. An orchid. An orchid,' he went on
quickly lest the audience grow bored with a feat
they were beginning to take for granted, 'that you
have taken from the dress of a most beautiful
young woman. I see . . . I see a young man . . .
an enamored young man. He has sent the orchid.'

Lehr gave a loud stage laugh. 'That is not mind
reading, Mr Houdini. Who but a beautiful young
woman would wear an orchid. And who but a

smitten young man would send it to her. You must tell us more.'

'Will you hold the orchid higher, please, Mr Lehr. I feel its power . . . its fragrance . . . the orchid is a pledge . . .' Lizzy was blushing furiously, and Sydney, standing just behind her was looking embarrassed but proud. 'But wait! I see something else . . . I see the orchid wither and die . . . and in its place . . . something bright . . . no, not bright . . . something white . . . the white is taking shape now. I see a uniform, an officer's uniform and another young man.'

A current of laughter ran through the room as Lieutenant Atherton took a step away from Lizzy. He looked self-conscious. 'Mr Houdini, you have just detached an officer in the United States Navy from the young lady's side,' Lehr said, and crossed the ballroom amid a great deal of laughter. He stopped in front of Sam. 'Well, Van Nest, what will you give me to test the great Houdini?' Sam fished in his pocket and handed Lehr a coin.

'Clear your mind, Mr Houdini,' Lehr began again. 'Negate all other thoughts.'

'You are holding a coin, Mr Lehr. A coin you have taken from a gentleman. I can see the gentleman . . . he is approaching me slowly . . . from a great distance . . . the gentleman has arrived in Newport only today . . . he has arrived here after a long absence.' Murmurs of wonder again.

'You are correct, Mr Houdini,' Lehr said.

'I see the coin again . . . now I see many coins . . . the gentleman has come here in pursuit of

many coins . . . of a great fortune . . . I see a man,
a heavy-set man of great personal magnetism . . .
I see him standing between this gentleman and his
coins. I regret to say, Mr Lehr, that this gentleman
will not be successful in his quest.' Lehr flashed
a smile at Sam, then at Elias, and moved off into
the crowd.

He approached Amelia. She was standing at the
far end of the room near the doors to the stair hall.
It was as distant from Houdini and his
performance as she could get, but Lehr was not
so easily escaped.

'And what will you contribute, pet? Something
more impressive than your friend Van Nest's coin,
I hope.' He was smiling down at her, and in the
paneled mirrors of the door dozens of thick pink
mouths mocked her.

Amelia reached up and unclasped her choker.
'Ah, I knew you'd rise to the occasion,' Harry said
and held the collar over his head. Now it was the
jewels that were reflected over and over in the
mirrored door. 'Concentrate, Mr Houdini. Help us
both to concentrate for I am very far away from
you. Keep concentrating, Mr Houdini. Renounce
all other thoughts.'

'I see . . . I see a brilliant object . . . a glittering
object . . . I see a jewel . . . no, many jewels . . .
I see a jeweled necklace. No, wait! I see a jeweled
choker.'

'You are correct, Mr Houdini.'

'I see the woman who wears the choker. She too
is coming to me from a great distance . . . even
greater than the gentleman with the coin. She is

coming from across the sea. Has the lady with the choker recently joined us from abroad, Mr Lehr?'

'She has, Mr Houdini.'

'I see her on a ship. Wait! The image is changing. I see an automobile . . . I see her here in Newport in an automobile . . . a Dusenberg . . . I see her in a Dusenberg with a gentleman. Will you ask the lady, Mr Lehr, if she went for a drive with a gentleman this afternoon?'

Something like surprise flickered across Lehr's face, but he regained his composure immediately. 'I don't think, Mr Houdini, that I ought to ask that.' Amelia tried to laugh with the others.

'I see the jeweled choker again . . . and the man . . . the man in the automobile . . . he is somehow connected with the choker . . . with many jewels . . . he will mean many jewels. No, wait! I fear he will mean the loss of jewels.' Houdini was silent for a moment, but there was no sound of impatience from the audience. 'I am sorry, madam, I can see no more. The image has faded.'

Amelia told herself to smile. If ever there was a time to appear amused, it was now. 'I appreciate your warning, Mr Houdini,' she said in a clear tone that carried across the ballroom. 'And I will be very careful of my jewels and strange men in automobiles.'

Everyone laughed, and even Edith looked relieved that Amelia had carried things off as well as could be expected. Then Houdini was removing the scarf and mask and thanking Lehr, and the guests were applauding.

'Really, Harry,' Edith said coming up to Lehr.

Her face was composed but her voice was an angry whisper. 'How could you? It's one thing if you choose to make a spectacle of yourself, but it was unforgivable of you to single out the girls. I'm very displeased with Tessie too. The whole exhibition was in questionable taste.'

'But, Edith, sweet pet, Newport is in questionable taste. That's what makes it so delicious. And I thought Mr Houdini was brilliant.'

'I'm not interested in Mr Houdini. I'm interested in what you told him. Whom was Amelia driving with this afternoon?'

'Now how would I know that, sweet pet?'

'I'm warning you, Harry. You can toy with the others, but not with me.'

He looked into her eyes and knew she meant it. The delicate lines around them that were usually hints of age to come rather than age achieved had gathered into dark creases. Harry had been nibbling one of the hands that fed him. It was a game he loved to play, but it was a game that could be carried too far. 'I swear to you, pet, I don't know whom Amelia went driving with this afternoon. I helped Mr Houdini, of course. Who is better qualified to? But that was one piece of information he unearthed himself. To tell the truth, I'm rather curious myself. Though I can guess. Amelia and Van Nest remind me of Louis XVIII, and you know what they said about him, pet? That he'd learned nothing and forgotten nothing.'

'This is no time for discussions of the Revolution or the Restoration, Harry. I want to know whom

Amelia was with, and I expect you to find out.'

Harry had planned to do just that. He prided himself on being the first to know everything in Newport, but in this case he'd have to settle for second place.

The dancing had started again, and Sam found Fingerhut standing at the side of the ballroom smiling to himself and humming along with the music. He'd obviously enjoyed the entertainment and it showed on his face. Sam couldn't help thinking there was something almost winning about the man's simplicity. The thought encouraged and depressed him at the same time.

'Quite a show,' Sam said. Fingerhut agreed that it had been.

'I wonder if we could have a word, Max. A quiet word and a glass of brandy. There's a room upstairs.'

'If it's about Leighton's book,' Fingerhut said following Sam up the staircase. 'I've already spoken to him. You were wrong. It wasn't Dryden's *Virgil*. It was Smolett.'

'Authentic or fake?'

'Authentic, but not worth what the dealer's asking.' The tic pulled down nervously. 'I told Elias that. Have to watch out for these dealers, you know. They think we're made of money.'

Sam stepped aside to let Fingerhut enter the room before him, then walked to the sideboard where he poured a brandy for each of them.

'Well, what can I do for you, Sam?' Fingerhut took one of the chairs before the fireplace. It was a comfortable-looking chair but he didn't look comfortable in it. He sat with his legs apart and his back straight, as if to show that he was alert. 'It wouldn't have anything to do with that business you're supposed to be up to, at least according to the great Houdini?' Fingerhut laughed, and it was meant to be a deprecating laugh, but the tic at the side of his mouth pulled down again. Sam knew he'd been fascinated by the show, but was unwilling to admit it. Grown men, at least grown men in positions of importance, weren't supposed to be fascinated by magic shows.

He handed Fingerhut a drink and took the chair across from his. 'The man puts on quite an act, doesn't he?'

'Of course, it *is* an act,' Fingerhut agreed. 'I don't believe in any of this mind-reading stuff, but I'd love to know how he pulls it off.'

It was, Sam thought the perfect beginning. If he could make Fingerhut trust him about this, he could make him trust him about the rest. 'With Lehr's help, for one thing.'

'Of course. With Lehr's help,' Max repeated as if he'd been thinking the same thing, though Sam felt fairly sure he hadn't. 'That explains all the inside information. But what about the objects? How did he guess the objects. I was close to the stage, and I'm sure he couldn't see.'

'Did you listen to Lehr?'

'All that mumbo jumbo, you mean? He really did make a fool of himself.' The thought that Lehr had and he hadn't seemed to reassure Fingerhut.

'It was all part of the act, Max. I don't remember exactly what he said, but he was giving Houdini clues. With me, for example, he told him to clear his mind. Then he told him to negate all other thoughts. Now think of it, Max, is *negate* a word you'd be likely to use at a time like that? The first sentence began with a C. The second with an N. I gave Lehr a coin. C . . . N without the vowels. When he got to Amelia . . . the duchess, I mean, he told Houdini to concentrate. I don't remember all the instructions, but they were longer than those he gave with me, and choker has more consonants than coin.'

Fingerhut was looking surprised, but not entirely convinced. 'Seems pretty chancy.'

'I imagine there's some guesswork, but not as much as we're supposed to think. Obviously, Lehr had volunteered his services before this evening, and it wasn't likely anyone would upstage him when the time came. Now suppose Lehr had told Houdini whom he was going to approach and in what order. Lehr, of course, knows everything about everybody in Newport. Gossip's his profession as well as his passion. First he spells out the object to Houdini – and knowing you were dealing with men and women in evening dress it wouldn't be hard to supply the vowels that spelled glove or flower – then he goes into the gossip Lehr supplied. Take Niebold, for example. Everyone knows that he's having an affair with . . . well we both know with whom. And Lehr even said he'd seen Niebold in the garden earlier in the evening. And so on with the rest of us. All Houdini had to do was gain our confidence with that object trick, and then we'd think he'd guessed everything else the same way, when really all he'd done was listen to Lehr's gossip.'

The tic around Fingerhut's mouth pulled down again, but he seemed excited rather than nervous now. 'Just as I thought. The surprising thing is that more people didn't catch on. It was so obvious.'

'Not everyone sees things as clearly as you and I do, Max. Not everyone can ignore the show and go straight to the heart of the matter. And that's what I want to talk to you about.'

'You mean that great fortune Houdini said you're after?'

'I'm here on business, Max, that much is true, but I'm not here to make money. I'm here to keep you from losing it, among other things.'

Fingerhut sat up straighter and the lower lip pulled down tremulously. 'I'm not losing money.'

'Of course, you're not. And you want to keep it that way. That's why I wanted to talk to you about the Walsh deal.'

Fingerhut's hand with the brandy glass stopped halfway to his mouth. 'How did you know about that?'

'Well, I'm not a mind reader like our friend Mr Houdini. It's pretty common knowledge these days. At least by people who know about these things. Like you and me,' he added, and Fingerhut smiled, but it was a very small smile.

'Actually,' Sam said leaning forward with his arms on his knees, 'over at Morgan and Company we're a little concerned about the plan.'

Fingerhut had forgot Houdini and his brandy and was listening closely. Morgan was right. He wasn't entirely stupid. He had a pretty good idea of what he didn't know and was willing to learn. 'You think there won't be enough of a market for the stock issue?'

'Well, that could be a problem, but I think it's more than that.' Sam ran through the familiar arguments about government opposition and a potential panic. He couldn't help thinking that his presentation was getting better with each run through. Maybe he'd take the show on the road after tonight. Like Houdini. If he weren't more successful with Sturgis the second time around, he'd have to find something to do. He could see it all now, Samuel Van Nest and his traveling magic show. Prestidigitation, conjuration, hocus pocus for every business deal.

'Well, I don't know,' Fingerhut said when he'd finished. 'What you say makes some sense, Sam, but then my men have been over the thing pretty thoroughly, and they're not worried.' The lower lip twitched again and Fingerhut took a swallow of his brandy. 'It's so hard to know which side to believe.'

Sam crossed to the sideboard, refilled both glasses, handed one to Fingerhut, and sat again. 'Look, Max, I won't beat around the bush. I came to you for a reason. Because you're the only man in this thing capable of seeing the big picture. Sure, we can talk about how much capital Walsh's plan is going to create and how big a slice of the pie you're going to get – and knowing you, I'm willing to wager you've worked a good deal – but you and I know, Max, that anyone can make a quick killing in a deal like this. Unfortunately, not everyone can see beyond the quick killing to reap the real profit.' Sam took a swallow of his brandy. 'And I don't mean only in dollars.'

'You mean foreign investments. Are you talking about pounds? Or gold?'

'I'm talking about something more valuable than gold, Max. Respect. Esteem. I'm talking about the kind of regard no amount of money can buy.' Fingerhut's tongue darted out of his mouth and ran over his lips, and Sam had to drop his eyes.

He stood and walked to the window. The reflection of the room behind him was superimposed on the lights from the tower and the fake ships. 'Who would you say is the most respected man in the country today, Max? I don't mean heroes like the Colonel or sports figures like Jim Thorpe. I mean men of substance, businessmen.'

'That's easy. The Commodore.'

'I'm inclined to agree with you. The Commodore is the most respected man in America today, and do you know why? Because he saved the country. The Colonel may wave the flag and carry the big stick and Thorpe may bring home a handful of gold medals from Stockholm, but five years ago Morgan bailed the country out of the worst panic it's ever seen. Until now. We agree that the panic this Walsh deal is going to set off will break that record.' Fingerhut had agreed to no such thing, but Sam could see that he was beginning to. 'And naturally the man who heads off this panic is going to outshine even the Commodore.' Sam walked back to the chair and sat again. 'You're that man, Max. You're the only man who can head off Walsh and the panic he's going to set off.'

The lower lip twitched in excitement. 'I wouldn't say I'm the only man, Sam. There are others involved in this thing.'

'Other men with your vision? Your sense of public duty? I don't think so, Max.' Sam leaned back in his chair.

'But how will people know?' Fingerhut said finally. 'Morgan stopped the panic after it started. I'll be heading one off.'

'I'll know. The Commodore will know. Your colleagues, the men who matter, will know. And with something like this, it's only a matter of time before the newspapers find out. And then the whole country. I'm sorry, Max. I know what I'm asking of you isn't easy. When I think of what's going to happen to your private life. Everything you do and say will make news. Your wife will find she's living not with a man but a public figure. And your children' – Sam tried to remember what he'd read that morning about Fingerhut's family – 'your oldest boy is at St Paul's now, isn't he? Just the age when a boy begins to evaluate his father as a man. Well, I'm afraid it won't be an easy job for him. He won't be able to remain impartial when all the other boys, to say nothing of the masters, see you as a hero. It will be up to you, Max, to show the boy you're human.'

Fingerhut agreed it would not be an easy task,

but it was one he felt certain he could carry off. He also agreed to wire Walsh that night. There was, he told Sam, no time to waste.

As soon as Sam returned to the ballroom, Sturgis joined him. 'That Houdini business was a damn fool thing to do, Van Nest. And ungrateful too, after my offer.' The old man spoke quietly, but Sam could hear the anger in his voice. 'I don't care which side you're on, but for God's sake don't go talking it around.'

'You mean if word of this gets out before Walsh is ready, it will ruin everything?'

Sturgis looked up at him and his eyes were like coals, flat and hard, in the round florid face. Suddenly Sam knew that he'd been underestimating Sturgis. In speaking of him as an old friend, Morgan had made him sound pliable, easy-going, a hail-fellow-well-met, and to be sure that was the pose Sturgis often assumed, but he was none of those things. Sturgis was smarter than Fingerhut and Wainwright, and free of Selby's weaknesses, and that combination of intelligence and strength made him a more formidable opponent. Sam hadn't liked the idea of blackmailing Wainwright and Selby, but for a moment he wished he had something on Sturgis. Then he thought of his father again and hated himself and this whole business a little more.

'I won't be threatened, Van Nest.'

'I wasn't trying to threaten you. I had nothing to do with that magic farce.'

It was clear from Sturgis' face that he didn't

believe him. 'If I needed anything to strengthen my resolve to stick with Walsh, it was that indiscretion of yours.'

He wasn't beaten yet, Sam told himself as he watched Sturgis make his way toward the billiard room. He'd give the old man a little time to cool off, then he'd try again. Sturgis couldn't be blackmailed or bribed, but surely he could be made to see reason, Sam told himself, yet he couldn't help remembering the story Morgan had told him that afternoon. Was there anything reasonable about a man who'd fall in love with a woman like Edith Leighton?

VII

Schuyler Niebold rarely agreed with his mother-in-law, but he agreed with her now. Houdini's exhibition had been in poor taste. That business about finding him in the rose garden was bad enough but the reference to a dark feminine spirit was unforgivable. Well, what did it matter? After tonight he'd be away from here, and soon Vanessa would be too and there'd be no need to worry about what anyone said or thought. Certainly he wouldn't have to worry about Caroline anymore. He watched her now circling the floor in Harry Lehr's arms. Harry loved to dance, and he loved to dance with Carrie who was almost as beautiful in movement as she was in repose. What a perfect couple they made, Sky thought. Both of them caring nothing for the substance and everything for the surface. Some people enjoyed the act of dancing, both its art and its intimacy. Vanessa was one of them. Carrie and Lehr cared only for the picture they made in others' eyes. If the ballroom were suddenly emptied of guests but the music continued, they'd stop dancing.

Still she did look beautiful with her chiseled profile turned at the proper angle from Harry to give it maximum exposure to onlookers and her full figure arched backward. The fact that now, after twelve years of marriage he knew how hard she worked to achieve her effects, didn't make them less successful. Sky wondered if he'd ever be entirely free of her. Probably not. And probably Vanessa knew it. Vanessa was clever that way. She did not have a hard cleverness like his mother-in-law, but she saw things for what they were and accepted them. Certainly she'd always been realistic about their affair. 'The thing about being the mistress of a married man,' she'd said to him once when he'd had to beg off a weekend they'd planned to steal, 'is that you learn not to waste the time you have together worrying about the time you don't.'

Vanessa was a realist, he thought, not like his sister-in-law Amelia, who'd just waltzed by with that naval lieutenant. She was intelligent, but she wasn't clever like her mother or clear-sighted like Vanessa. She'd spent most of her life fighting battles she couldn't possibly win, and she'd probably spend the rest of it butting her head against the stone wall of the prison her mother and husband had constructed for her.

And what about you? he asked himself. You've never even tried to fight the battle. Until now. You've spent twelve years drifting between injury and indecision. In the beginning, before Vanessa, the injury had been only to Caroline, and he'd thought of it less as hurting her than saving himself. It had started at the end of their wedding trip. They were returning from a year abroad on the *Oceanic*, and Sky, his confidence shaken by a year of Caroline's indifference — he'd been sure she'd change after their marriage, but he'd been wrong — his desire sharpened to an edge of desperation by a year of making love to a statue, had been hungry for a little feminine understanding. The Contessa, married to a very elderly Count, had understood Sky perfectly. After the Contessa, infidelity had become a way of life. Occasionally Sky remembered a tutor he'd had as a young man, a very serious tutor, who took the forming of character as seriously as he did the imparting of information. 'A sin,' he used to tell Sky, 'is a sin only the first time. After that it becomes a habit.' And it had for Sky, a casual habit with women of his own class and those below it — until Vanessa. No, that wasn't true. In the beginning Vanessa had been no different to him from the others. It had been more than a year before he came to care for her seriously, more than six before he decided to leave his wife and children for her, before he realized that Vanessa was everything he'd once thought Caroline could be. And the worst part of it, Sky thought as he watched his wife and Lehr approaching him, was that sometimes he still fiercely regretted what Carrie hadn't been.

'Quite an exhibition, don't you think' Lehr said. 'Mr Houdini, I mean.'

'And we mustn't forget your part in it, Harry,' Sky said. 'I think exhibition is the correct word there. Do you want to tell us how it was done?'

'My dear fellow, how would I know?'

'I don't suppose you care,' Carrie said after Lehr had left them, 'that everyone has noticed that you haven't danced with your wife once tonight.'

'Why, Carrie, I'm sorry. I thought your card was filled. May I have the honor.'

'And there's no need to be sarcastic about it, Sky,' she said as they moved off in time to the music. 'I don't care whether you dance with me or not, but I do care what people say.'

'They say you dance beautifully, my dear. And I agree.'

'But not as beautifully as Miss Hunter. You agree with that too.'

'Don't, Caroline. I'll dance with you, but I won't argue with you. Not here.'

'Oh, not here, but anywhere else. Where would you like to argue, Sky. In the rose garden? Or is that only for your mistress?'

'I told you I won't argue, Carrie.'

'You should have thought of that before you went into the garden with that woman. You should have thought of it before you and that magician made a fool of me in front of everyone.'

'Blame your friend Lehr for that. He made fools of both of us.'

'And Vanessa. Don't forget your dark and haunting spirit. Your mistress. Your tramp.'

He tightened his hand around hers. 'Stop it, Caroline. I'm warning you.'

'Warning me of what? What more can you possibly do to me? You've humiliated me in front of everyone, carried on with that tramp . . .'

'If you use that word once more . . .'

274

'Tramp.' The beautiful lips formed the word as if they could taste it. 'No better than any of the others. No better than that trashy little maid I had to fire. But you can tell your tramp one thing. I won't give you up. I don't care about you, Sky, but I do care about your name. That belongs to me and the children. Your tramp can have the rest.'

He'd stopped dancing as she'd spoken, but she kept moving and forced him to go on. 'That's just fine,' he said though his voice sounded anything but fine. 'I hadn't planned to tell you this way, Carrie, but I guess now is as good a time as any. I'm leaving you. Tonight. This has dragged on for long . . .'

Now it was she who stopped dancing and he felt her weight against him. Strange that at a time like this he should notice the pressure of her breasts. Then her eyes closed and her body went slack. 'Stop it,' he said in a harsh whisper. 'For God's sake, Caroline, this is no time for one of your acts.' The long pale eyelashes fluttered, but she remained limp in his arms. 'I know you're acting,' he whispered again, but it was too late. People around them had noticed.

'The heat,' someone said.

'She needs air,' someone else cried, though the french doors on both sides of the ballroom had been opened to allow the ball to spill out onto the terraces.

Then Edith and Tessie Oelrichs had pushed through the crowd and dispersed it, and Sky found himself carrying his wife upstairs. He couldn't help thinking that she was no heavier than when they'd first married.

'What happened?' Edith asked after Sky had deposited Caroline on a chaise in one of the bedrooms.

'I don't know,' he lied. He might have to have things out with Caroline, but not with his mother-in-law. 'Perhaps it was the heat. Or too much dancing.' For one terrible moment Sky remembered when Carrie had been pregnant with Leighton. She'd been a great one for fainting then. But that was impossible, or almost so, he thought and tried to remember how long ago they'd gone to that houseparty on Long Island. Then out of the corner of his eye he saw Caroline, her eyes still closed, reach down to smooth the skirt of her gown and knew he'd been right. She had been faking.

Edith walked to one of the windows and opened it. Even now, even doing something useful in a crisis, she swished the long satin train of her gown behind her like a queen turning from her subjects. 'Then I'll let her rest for a while. I'm sure' – she stopped at the door and looked at Sky for a moment – 'that you'll want to stay with her.' It would not do, Edith thought as she closed the door behind her, to have Sky dancing the evening away with Vanessa Hunter while his wife lay upstairs ill.

'It won't work, Carrie,' Sky said when his mother-in-law was gone. He saw the eyelashes flutter again, and she let out a soft moan. 'You can't go on fainting every time I say I'm leaving. Or rather, you can, but I won't be here to see it.

276

Because I am leaving,' he repeated. 'Tonight. And nothing you can say or do will stop me.'

Her eyes were open wide now, and she looked angry. 'What do you expect me to do when my husband says he's leaving. After twelve years of marriage.'

'Twelve years perhaps, but not a very good marriage.'

'And whose fault is that?' She was sitting up straight now and her voice was a loud childish whine. Her weakness seemed to have passed, Sky thought, but he was not amused.

'Both our faults, I suppose.'

'It was your fault, entirely your fault. You and your other women.'

'I don't think there's any point in going through this Carrie.'

'Well, I do. All these years I've been silent. All these years I've pretended I didn't know. Did you think I was blind, Sky? Did you think I was half-witted? Because I would have had to be not to know what was going on. Do you think because that maid was the only one I caught you with, I believed she was the only one? Oh, no, Sky. My eyes have been open all along. Even before I saw the two of you thrashing around on that bed. If you only knew how foolish you looked. And how disgusting. Like animals. Her with her skirts pulled up that way and all that white flesh.' She stopped suddenly as if shocked at what she'd said.

'Why, Carrie, you make it sound almost erotic. Is it possible there's a side to you I don't know? Is it possible' – his voice took on a mock theatrical

277

edge – 'beneath that icy exterior burn the fires of lust?'

'Don't be disgusting.'

'I, disgusting, my dear? You were the one talking about skirts pulled up over white flesh.'

'This is no time for your sarcasm, Sky.'

'No, you're right. It isn't.' He'd got in the habit of ridiculing her, to himself and to her face, because it was the only way he could deal with his desire for her and his disappointment, but the tricks he'd used were no longer necessary. 'I'm sorry, Carrie, about a great deal. But I'm still leaving. I hope you'll divorce me, but if you won't, I'll divorce you.'

'You can't! Mama said you couldn't.'

He laughed in spite of himself. 'Still listening to Mama. I suppose that's why you're not a woman with a woman's desires, Carrie. Because you've never stopped being a little girl. With all a little girl's interests. You like to dress up. And you like to play house. But only to play, mind you. Well, don't worry. You'll be able to go on doing all that. Mama will go on taking care of you. And you'll go on dressing up and going to parties and giving them. And there'll be plenty of money for that. I promise you. That's why I've waited this long. To make sure that you'll have everything you need and that all the family money will pass to the children. We . . . I won't need any of it. Not with this thing Tom Sturgis has helped me into. So you see, Carrie, you won't even miss me.'

'But it's not gentlemanly.'

Sky was standing over the chaise and as he looked down at her now his face was very serious. 'I'm flattered that you still think I'm a gentleman, Carrie. I think I am too. That's why I have to divorce you if you won't divorce me. Because for too many years now I've been living without honor. I've been behaving badly toward you. Toward myself. Toward . . . someone else. I'm not going to do that any longer.'

When he reached the door, he turned back to her. 'I don't think we have any more to say, Carrie. I'll take you home now if you like. I know how important appearances are to you. But I won't stay. Nothing can make me stay,' he added though even as he did, he wondered if that were entirely true. Couldn't Caroline, if she set her mind to it, still find a way to make him stay?

On his way downstairs Sky passed his mother-in-law. 'How is she?' Edith asked.

'I'm taking her home,' Sky said, as if the fact were an answer. He told the footman to have his automobile brought around and then pushed through the guests to the salon. Vanessa was standing near the door. 'I'll come to the guesthouse,' he said quietly. 'As soon as I can get away.'

Her smile was perfect. No one could have guessed he was saying any more than good night. Of course, no one had to guess. Everyone knew.

Edith entered the bedroom without knocking and didn't bother to ask how her daughter felt. Caroline's physical well-being was not what

279

interested her at the moment. 'Sky said he's taking you home.'

'And then leaving. Did he tell you that?' The words were broken by sniffles and sounded petulant.

'What else did he say? Stop crying, Caroline, and tell me what he said before he comes back.'

'He said terrible things to me. About being a woman without' – she made a sound that was more hiccup than sob – 'a woman's desires . . .'

'For heaven's sake, Caroline, I'm not interested in any of that. What did he say about leaving you?'

'He said he wanted me to divorce him, but if I didn't, he'd divorce me. I told him you said he couldn't.' Edith gave her daughter a look that fell somewhere between incredulous and disapproving. 'But he said he'd find a way.'

'Did he say how?' Edith asked, though she knew the answer.

'No, only that he would and I'd never even miss him. He said I'd get all the Niebold money. Or rather the children would. Something about not needing it anymore because of Mr Sturgis.'

'What does Tom Sturgis have to do with it?'

'How should I know, Mama? I'm only repeating what Sky said.' She started to sniffle again as if her inability to answer her mother's question only reminded her of other failures. 'Oh, Mama, what am I going to do?'

'Go home,' Edith said, and started for the door. 'Go home with Sky and don't do anything.'

*   *   *

'This is our dance, I believe,' Harry said. He moved his head forward rather than his body when he bowed and the chins on the round face multiplied.

The strange thing, Amelia thought as they moved out onto the dance floor, was how lightly he moved for a heavy man. Standing or sitting Harry looked like a stuffed animal, but in movement he was fluid and almost graceful. She would have enjoyed dancing with him, if it were a matter of only dancing. Unfortunately, whatever Harry did, he did to his own verbal accompaniment. He talked while he danced, ate, played cards, and listened to music. If he'd ever made love to poor Bessie, he'd probably kept up a running commentary'

'Wasn't Mr Houdini delicious, pet?'

'Mr Houdini and his helper.'

'I? Why I was nothing but a conduit. For example, I merely held your choker so that he could feel its presence. I had no idea what was on your mind. I didn't even know you'd gone driving this afternoon.' He felt her stiffen in his arms. 'But now that I know you did, I can guess with whom. I'm still not sure about the jewels though. I mean about the connection between the man and jewels.'

'Are there any sultans in town, Harry?'

'Would you settle for a sultan of business? Van Nest is no longer the poor boy he used to be, pet. And I hear he's very generous.' There was a salacious edge to his voice, and the small piglike eyes were watching her carefully.

281

'I wasn't driving with Sam this afternoon, Harry. I promise you that.'

But Harry was not so easily discouraged. He moved a little closer and dropped his voice to a confidential whisper, as if to reassure her there was no need to lie to him. 'I'm delighted for you, pet. You're a lucky woman. To have the title and true love. And I do think first loves are always the truest. Though in my case first love, *c'est moi*. Ah, but you and Van Nest that's something else.'

'That's nothing, Harry.'

'Come now, pet, it's Harry you're talking to. King Lehr. I didn't get the title by not knowing what's going on. I may not have seen you two driving this afternoon, but I watched you at dinner and then later when you danced. Why it took me back ten years. Though just for the record, 'Melia, my pet, you look a good deal better than you did ten years ago. I don't know what the duke did for you – or was it the duke? Well, anyway, it was just like the old days watching you and Van Nest tonight. And how you two did carry on in the old days. The secret meetings and those long, calf-like looks no one was supposed to notice and no one could help but notice. And those letters. "Sam, you must help me," ' Harry trilled in a falsetto that somehow didn't sound false on him.

'How did you know about that?'

'You must know by now, pet, that your dear mother keeps nothing from me, absolutely nothing.'

Lehr did not miss the change in her face. The pale skin pulled over the fine bones went a shade paler and she looked like a mask that had been left out in the sun for too long.

'You can't possibly be surprised, Amelia. Not even you are that naive. Or were that naive. Of course, your mother knew about the letters. And had them stopped. And of course she kept Van Nest from the house. What did you expect, pet? That she'd lock you in your room, then let Sam pay you visits? Or did you think Sam had just lost interest? Like that.' The music had ended and Harry snapped a pudgy thumb and forefinger in the air.

'Do you mean Sam did try to see me?'

The heavy lids drooped a little as if he were bored. 'Good Lord, Amelia, do I have to spell it out for you. After all the hints I've given you over the years. And they say Carrie's the stupid one. Yes, pet, the heartsick Mr Van Nest wrote and called and did everything short of taking the traditional draft of poison. As I understand the story, he settled for whiskey. So you see, I'm not in the least surprised that you two have rediscovered each other. I trust you passed a pleasant afternoon, pet.'

Harry smiled as he handed her over to her next partner but he wasn't as pleased as he looked. There was no reason to believe she hadn't been with Van Nest, but in view of her surprise at the things he'd told her, there was no reason to believe she had been either.

The major-domo told him that Mr Houdini was upstairs in the small drawing room that Mrs Oelrichs used as an office. Tessie was coming out

283

of the room as he entered it, and beyond her Lehr saw Houdini stuffing something into the pocket of his trousers. In the old days both Tessie and Houdini would have offered him part of the money, but since he'd married Bessie, everyone assumed he was taken care of. He supposed he was, but he regretted the change. He could have used a little extra pocket money. Bessie was not exactly mean, but she lacked generosity as so many people without style did.

'You were superb,' Mrs Oelrichs said as she swept past him. 'Both my Harrys were superb.'

'I agree,' Houdini said as Harry entered the room and closed the door behind him. 'You're a pro, Mr Lehr.'

'Thank you. I do think I was rather good. Didn't throw you the clues too fast, did I?'

'Your timing was impeccable, and timing is the essence of it all.'

'That and the right information. There's one thing that surprised me,' Lehr said.

'The duchess.'

'You didn't use the information I gave you about her.'

'I found the mysterious man who gives and takes jewels more interesting. Especially in view of the choker.'

'But who was the mysterious man, and how did you know about him?'

Houdini laughed. 'You mean you don't believe in mind reading?'

'I believe in your talents as a showman.'

'That business about the duchess is what

284

telepathists call doing a Brodie. It means putting a few random facts together and taking a long shot. Only in this case it wasn't such a long shot. We'd agreed this afternoon that you would approach certain people in a certain order. One of them was the Duchess of Duringham. Well, I've never met the duchess, but like everyone else I've seen her photograph often. I've even seen a portrait of her. In London. I have an excellent memory, Lehr. Especially for a face that lovely. In any event, I recognized her when I saw her driving this afternoon. She was with a man from Tiffany. Wickert's the name, I believe. He sold me some emerald earbobs for Mrs Houdini's last birthday. As for what the duchess was doing with Wickert, that's where the educated guess came in. It might be anything, but I'm willing to bet she was selling jewels, because if she were buying, her husband would be dealing with Wickert. Tell me, does the duchess play whist or bridge for high stakes? Anything like that?'

'No, it isn't a gambling debt,' Harry said. He was impressed by Houdini, but he was more excited about his secret. 'More like a debt of honor.'

Elizabeth had lived with Carrie long enough to be somewhat wary of her fainting spells. Occasionally she accused herself of a lack of sympathy, but when she did she accused Carrie too. Caroline cried wolf entirely too often. As the guests in the ballroom converged to witness Caroline Niebold's swoon, Lizzy took Kimball's arm and started off the terrace.

'Don't you want to go in?' he'd asked.

'Carrie never faints when she's ill.' Lizzy knew but didn't add that when she was ill, Caroline took to her bed and barred all visitors so that no one would see her looking blotchy and haggard. 'She only faints in a crisis. I've seen that before. But I haven't seen Mrs Oelrichs' lighthouse.'

They were walking arm in arm and she felt rather than saw Douglas laugh. What she'd said about Carrie had amused him, and she liked amusing him.

'Then we'd better take a look at the lighthouse,' Kimball said.

'It's going to be decommissioned tomorrow morning. A hazard to navigation, according to Lieutenant Atherton.' She felt him stiffen at the mention of Atherton, but he said nothing and they kept walking. When they reached the lighthouse, Kimball tried the door at the base of it. It was unlocked. 'We're in luck,' she said stepping inside.

The lighthouse had been built for the party, but after tonight, when the signal was removed in keeping with the admiral's request, it would make a comfortable guesthouse. On the ground floor were a sitting room and a small pantry. A winding iron staircase rose two flights above them. Tessie Oelrichs had obviously spared no expense in creating an authentic nautical atmosphere. Anchors served as doorstops, lanyards held back the draperies, the tables had fiddles to prevent objects from sliding off in heavy seas, and an old binnacle, or rather a new binnacle made to look old, had been transformed into an electric light.

There was even a hammock slung across one corner. 'Newport at its best,' Kimball said.

'Or worst. You taught me that. A year ago I would have thought it was adorable.'

'It's nice to know I've performed some service.'

'Now you're being coy. I also think you're playing hard to get. You have been all evening. Are you having second thoughts?'

'Are you?' he said, holding her eyes with his own.

She turned away from him and without realizing what she was doing, picked up a small compass that had been fashioned into a paperweight and began turning it in her hands. 'Of course not. I've told you that again and again.'

'That's true. Every day since I've been in Newport. Every day you've told me you don't love Hallenbeck and you do love me; that you aren't going to marry Hallenbeck and you are going to marry me. But you haven't bothered to tell anyone else, and now Sydney and everyone else think you're going to marry him.'

She turned back to him and the blue eyes had grown inky. 'I couldn't very well tell him at dinner, could I?'

'Not with Atherton on your other side. And, of course, a ballroom is not the proper setting for farewells. Or the terrace.'

'I was on the terrace with you.'

He brushed the point aside. 'It's never the proper time or place, is it, Lizzy?' He crossed the room to her and his hands were forceful on her arms. She heard the dull thud the compass made

287

as it hit the rug. His strength shocked her as it always did. He was shorter than Sydney and didn't look as powerful, but he didn't have Sydney's fears. Sydney held her as if he were afraid of breaking her. Douglas seemed to know she was not so fragile.

'For God's sake, Lizzy,' his voice was almost a whisper, but she could hear the urgency in it, 'if you've changed your mind, say so, but don't keep putting me off this way. I'm too old for this sort of thing.' He pulled her to him and she could feel his breath against her hair. 'I need you too much.'

'And I need you. More than anyone or anything in the world. I promise I'll tell . . .' she began, but he turned his face until his lips found hers and for the moment at least there was no need for words.

His mouth was soft on hers, not tentative but searching. She felt the soft moustache and tasted the champagne on his tongue and felt a warmth rising within her as sure and strong as if she were a sapling and he were sunshine and earth and water.

His arms were around her, folding her to him and she could feel the wiry power of his body pressed against hers. It was exhilarating and a little frightening and she clung to him in the exhilaration and the fear, her mouth on his, as hungry as his. 'Lizzy,' he said and she tasted rather than heard the word. 'Lizzy,' he repeated because suddenly her name meant more than any other words.

'Yes,' she murmured against his mouth, as if it were a pledge. His lips traced a line down her neck, murmuring words of love against her skin, and she felt his mouth warm against her, moving against her, following the line of her dress where it dipped low in front. She caught her breath and he must have heard the change in her breathing, but he didn't stop. He always had before, but he didn't now, and his hands began to work at the buttons that ran down her back.

Her mind was a kaleidoscope of disjointed thoughts and desires. No, yes, can't, shouldn't, must. She told herself to pull away and only clung to him more desperately. She told herself she was crazy and felt mad with the touch of his hand against her skin. Her hand moved to his chest as if to push him away but through the thin material of his shirt she felt the hard body tense with wanting her. Beneath the shirt his skin was smooth and warm and miraculously different from her own.

He was sliding the dress from her shoulders and his hands moved swiftly at her corset and petticoats. For an instant she found herself thinking how skilled he was at all this, how smoothly his fingers worked at the hooks and eyes and buttons, but then she felt his hands on her breasts, freed from all restraint now, warm and caressing against her, tender at first, but gradually more urgent, and all thought and doubt receded before a rush of desire.

She was clinging to him, her arms around his neck, her body, suddenly naked, pressed against his, but he took her arms from his neck and held her a little away, and in the half light his eyes were like hands on her. She felt a flash of embarrassment, but then she looked into his eyes – they had never been so dark and deep – and there was no longer any embarrassment, only an astonishing pride and pleasure.

She moved into his arms again, her mouth against his again, and began working at his clothes, but she was no good at it and he had to help her. His hands moved like lightning, and she heard something tear but paid no attention, and then she felt the warmth of his skin against her own. There was nothing between them now, no fabric or restraint or even reason. She was no longer thinking but only feeling his hands moving slowly, searchingly over her body, and his mouth in its wake. The pleasure and the desire made her dizzy and she clung to him as if she had no strength left to stand. He led her to the sofa, his arm about her waist, his other hand still exploring, caressing, adoring. 'I love you, Lizzy,' he said again, and repeated the words to her eyes, her mouth, her breasts. 'I love you,' he kept saying, and his voice was gentle like his hands, but behind the tenderness she could feel the strength of his body pressed against hers, excitingly different from the softness of hers. And gently, almost hesitantly he took her hand in his and guided it over his body, and the shock of that, of the pleasure of touching him as well as being touched by him, made her cry out. She never knew what she'd said or if she'd said anything, but he was above her and in the half light from the single lamp she could see his eyes, still dark and wide, and the muscles of his face tense as she had never seen them before, and his hand felt like fire now on her thighs. For a moment she was frightened again, and for a moment she felt something like a flash of pain, but only for a moment and then the fear was gone and the pain and there was only wave after wave of pleasure, wave after wave of Douglas, of loving him, of wanting him, of having him.

Kimball was suddenly aware of his own weight as he always was afterward, and moved until he was beside her on the sofa. She murmured something and turned her head until her cheek lay against his shoulder, but she kept her eyes closed. His mind was working clearly and rapidly, as it always did afterward, and he was a little shocked at himself. He wouldn't have been if she'd been older or more experienced, but she was twenty and a virgin – had been a virgin, he corrected himself – and there was something decidedly dishonorable about his actions. Forget the fact that he loved her. Forget the fact that he wanted to marry her. Somehow in middle age he had become a seducer of young girls. He remembered a doctor he'd met at a dinner party several weeks before. The doctor had just returned from Vienna. *And what effect do you think the experience of the* Titanic *has had upon you, Mr Kimball?* I've become a seducer of young girls.

He felt Lizzy's hand tracing the outline of his moustache. 'I know what you're thinking,' she said. He looked down at her and saw that her eyes were open wide now. Her face was flushed and so was her body, flushed and smooth all over. A small smile played around her mouth. It was a surprisingly self-confident smile. 'You're thinking this shouldn't have happened.'

'I shouldn't have let it.'

'But now that you have, you'll have to make an honest woman out of me.'

'I've wanted to do that ever since I first saw you.'

'I don't believe that. I think it took at least a month for a confirmed old bachelor like you to begin to think of marriage.' She saw him wince at the old. 'You know, Douglas, there's something very flattering about having snared you. When I think of all the women you've avoided, when I think of all the times I've heard people say, "oh, *he*'ll never marry," it's positively shameful how smug I feel.' Her hand had moved from his face to his chest.

'Lizzy,' he said holding her hand against him, 'we have to do something. Right away. It's too late for the last ferry, but . . .'

'But you were the one who said no sneaking away. You were the one who said I had to tell Sydney and Mama.'

'I did, but that was because I didn't want to carry you off in some damn fool elopement and then have you have second thoughts. I wanted you to think about what you were doing and to want it enough to be able to stand up to your mother and Sydney and everything else you were brought up to.'

'You know, Douglas, there are times when you

talk more like a banker than an artist. I thought artists were supposed to be passionate and impulsive.' She smiled again, the new self-confident smile. 'Well, I guess you just were. And I'm glad you were.'

She was still smiling up at him and her hand was tracing its lazy pattern on his chest again. He had never seen her looked so pleased, so sure of herself, but when she spoke again he realized his face must have looked very different. 'I'll tell them, Douglas. Tonight. I promise. I'll tell Sydney as soon as I can get him alone. And then I'll tell Mama.'

He knew she meant it. He only hoped she'd go on meaning it, but a small light of reason that pierced the haze of pleasure still enveloping them told him she'd said the same thing before and meant it then too.

The terrace facing the sea was dotted with couples and Sam threaded his way between them and out onto the lawn. Three down, and what did it matter? Without Sturgis none of it mattered. Sturgis, with a banking empire at home and an even larger one abroad, was too powerful to be ignored. Like Walsh he was one of the few men who could give Morgan a run for his money. In league with Walsh, he could outstrip Morgan. *Should have thought of that*, Sam pictured himself saying to Morgan, *before you made him his first million. Should have been more careful, sir, about whom you gave a leg up. Should have made sure he was a man who understood the meaning of loyalty*. Maybe it was the fact that the million had come too late, as Morgan had said, to win the girl. The girl! It was damn near impossible to think of Edith Leighton as a girl.

Sam wondered if Sturgis were still sentimental about Mrs Leighton. Or had he learned? The way we all have to learn. He didn't think the old man could be that blind, but when it came to women, blindness was a funny thing. Sam knew all about blindness when it came to women. *I'm sorry*, Amelia had said. She'd mentioned Georgina's death and said she was sorry. Oh, they'd all been so sorry for him that night of the accident and for days and nights after that, but would they have been sorry if they'd seen him that afternoon? He supposed they would have been, but in a different way, in a superior, snickering way.

Sam continued down the path toward the water, but the noises of the gravel underfoot couldn't drown out the sound of Georgina's voice anymore than the sight of the sea dotted with its fake white sails could obliterate the picture of Georgina that afternoon. He sat on a low stone wall facing the ocean and tried not to think of that afternoon. The wind had died at sunset as it usually did, and it hadn't come up again. The water looked flat and glassy. It wouldn't be much of a night for sailing. He tried to think about the sea and the wind and race week that was just around the corner, but he knew he was only trying not to think of something else.

It had been a Friday afternoon and he hadn't been due in Newport until the following morning.

That was the arrangement they'd worked out for the summer because Georgina had wanted to take the house and enjoy her first Newport season as Mrs Samuel Tyler Van Nest, and he'd had to spend most of the time in New York because the things Georgina wanted meant someone had to spend his time working. Daddy had already taken care of that, Georgina pointed out more than once, but Sam had wanted to be able to give her those things himself. He'd liked the idea of giving Georgina things, until he'd realized the only thing she wanted from him was his name.

She hadn't expected him until Saturday, though she should have known he'd come up early after the news she'd given him that week. She would have known that if she'd known him at all, but of course she hadn't known him, any more than he'd known her.

He'd decided to surprise her that Friday afternoon, and he'd surprised her, all right, her and her cousin Franklin. Franklin who she'd told Sam was more like a brother than a cousin. Franklin with whom she'd grown up and shared everything. Franklin who had been an usher at their wedding and their first house guest that summer. It would be wonderful, Georgina had said, to have Franklin for company while Sam was away. If it had been anyone but Franklin, her cousin, Sam wouldn't have stood for it. Georgina was too beautiful. Franklin was too charming. And Sam was no fool, or at least he hadn't thought he was until that afternoon.

Georgina and Franklin had been in the garden,

and when Sam had come out of the house, his first thought had been that the lengthening shadows and brisk breeze made it too cool for Georgina to be without a shawl. She and Franklin were sitting with their backs to the house and her thin shoulders looked fragile beneath the silk dress. He'd started toward her as if an arm around her shoulders could protect her from the chill and everything else, but as he'd taken the first step, she'd reached across the inches that separated the two chairs and laid a hand on Franklin's arm.

'Now don't be angry, darling,' she'd said, and Sam had a peculiar feeling that she was speaking to him. It wasn't only the word darling, but the tone of voice, intimate and pleading, but in control too. 'You must admit that the child will have a much better time of it as a Van Nest than as a Lury.'

Funny how Sam could still remember seeing Franklin Lury's broad shoulders square against the wrought-iron back of the chair at that. Funny, he supposed, what you noticed at times like that and what you remembered.

'I still don't like the idea,' Franklin said. 'It's bad enough sharing you, but I won't share my child.' The handsome profile turned toward Georgina, and Sam took a step backward into the shadows of the house. 'If, in fact, it is my child.'

Georgina's hand moved from Franklin's arm to the back of his neck. The long slender fingers caressed it slowly. 'Of course, it's your child, darling. A woman knows about these things.'

Despite the cool breeze Sam was perspiring

heavily, and he felt the lunch he'd eaten on the train up lurch in his stomach.

'It will be your child, darling, with the Van Nest name and advantages. What more could you want for him, or her for that matter?'

Franklin seemed to be debating the answer, but Georgina was not one to drop the advantage even for a moment. Her hand was still on the back of Franklin's neck and she stood and moved to the arm of his chair. As she did something must have caught her attention because she turned suddenly. Sam could tell by the way her expression changed as he took a step toward her that she hadn't known it was he. She'd looked annoyed at first, as if she were about to lecture a servant, but then as he moved from the shadows into the sunlit garden, her face had frozen in fear.

Sam didn't think the rest of it had taken more than three minutes. Georgina had begun talking very quickly and Franklin had stood and started to say something, but Georgina had told him to be quiet, and then Sam had told them both to be quiet. It was only then that he realized he had nothing to say. He'd stood there for a moment still feeling sick and somehow ashamed as if he'd been the one who'd done something wrong. Searching for the right words, he'd suddenly realized there were no words, right or wrong, and he'd turned and left the garden and the house he'd never wanted and Newport. It wasn't until the next morning when he was back in New York that word reached him about Georgina.

He'd had to go to Newport again to bring back

the body and it had been lucky he had because otherwise he might have gone on thinking it was some kind of tragic suicide pact. He should have known Georgina better, but of course, he hadn't known Georgina at all.

According to the servants, Mrs Van Nest and Mr Lury had been on their way to a ball that evening. They had dressed, shared a bottle of champagne, the butler had reported to Sam a little shame-faced as if his bringing the bottle up from the cellar had caused Mr Lury to drive the Packard off the road, and left for the evening. Mrs Van Nest had been careful to say she'd be at Beachbound, the butler told him. 'In case you telephoned, sir.'

He hadn't telephoned, and Franklin had driven off the road, and Georgina and the child she was carrying that might have been his or might have been Lury's, despite Georgina's profession of omniscience, was dead. There was no point going over it again and again.

Nina said he was hard. His mother said he was cynical. Well, who wouldn't be? He remembered the way Georgina's hand had looked on the back of Lury's neck and the sound of her voice, so intimate it embarrassed him because he associated that tone with other words and other times. Who the hell, he thought, wouldn't be?

He turned at the sound of footsteps on the gravel path and saw Amelia standing a few feet from him. His mother was right. She did look like Georgina. Or Georgina had looked like her. He guessed that was more to the point.

'Escaping from the party?' she asked.

'Like the great Houdini. I only wish he'd stuck to one of his escape acts tonight and stayed away from the mind-reading hoax.'

'Did he do much harm? To that business he mentioned, I mean.'

He started to say he wasn't here on business, but he was tired of the masquerade. He was tired of all the masquerades he'd played tonight. 'A little,' he admitted.

'I'm sorry.'

Again. She was sorry about his failure tonight and had been sorry about Georgina. Was she sorry about that summer too? *Sorry I left you standing at the gate, Sam*, she'd say in a minute. Well, at least it hadn't been the church.

He shrugged as if it made no difference. 'Can't be helped. The damage is done. Past history.' He hadn't stood when she approached and he looked up at her now. She was silhouetted against the sea and the dark dress blended into the blackness of the ocean so that the white shoulders and face seemed to be floating above him in the night like a disembodied spirit. He looked away from her out to sea.

'Past history,' he repeated, 'like everything else here. All night I've been talking about how times are changing, but not here, not in Newport. On Bellevue Avenue people change clothes and mates, but never their minds.'

She took a step so that she was in his line of vision again. 'That's not true of everyone. Some people change.'

'Are you saying you've changed, Amelia?'

'I might surprise you.'

He did not want to tell her that she'd already done that. He did not want to go into any of that. 'I'm sure you're a source of surprise to us all. "The surprising duchess" or was it "the unpredictable duchess"? I seem to remember a caption like that in one of the New York Sunday supplements a few years ago. What was it you were doing? Something about a maypole and a revival of some medieval rites?'

'It wasn't a maypole, it was a fence. I was chained to it.'

'Yes, that was it. With several other high-born suffragists, though I don't believe any of the others was a duchess. I don't imagine the duke appreciated that.'

She didn't know how the conversation had taken this turn, except perhaps that it was the turn Sam wanted it to take. Harry's explanation might have changed things for her, but not for him. Ten years and two marriages weren't so easily obliterated. 'Why are you always so rude to me?'

'Why? Surely you can figure that out, Amelia.' He wished he hadn't said that. It was tantamount to a confession of how much she'd hurt him, how much he'd cared.

The admission must have made her confident because she'd taken the few steps that separated them and was standing only inches from him. He was still sitting on the low wall and her face was only a little above his and very near. She moved her hand to his shoulder. 'What if I could explain everything, Sam?'

The fingers on his shoulder were without weight or force, but he was intensely aware of them and of her face hovering above him in the soft night like a pale incandescent flower. He wanted to brush his lips against it, to feel and taste the smooth skin. He wanted it so much he could feel himself trembling with the desire and the fear of it.

With an abrupt movement he stood but her hand didn't fall from his shoulder. 'There's nothing to explain, Amelia. I told you, times have changed. Everywhere but Newport. And I'm leaving Newport in the morning.' Her hand fell from his shoulder then, and she turned away quickly.

VIII

By the time Lizzy and Kimball returned to the ballroom the last of the guests were emerging from the dining room, and the midnight supper was almost over. Only a few of the older people remained at the small tables that had been set up sending footmen back for second and third portions of the lobster in aspic or the fresh strawberries in cream.

'Lizzy, my pet, where have you been?'

Elizabeth could tell from the film of perspiration on Harry's upper lip and the distracted look on his face that the question was rhetorical. Now that he'd found her, he didn't care where she'd been, and she simply smiled and said nothing.

'Now that Carrie's gone, you'll have to lead the cotillion with me. I've already squared it with Sydney. I know you'd promised the cotillion to him – naturally – but this is an emergency. I must have you to start off.' Half a dozen footmen were entering the ballroom now, each carrying a model of a Chinese junk laden with favors for the cotillion. 'Now no complaints about Sydney or the cotillion,' Harry said, though Lizzy had made none. 'You know,' Harry went on to Kimball who was standing beside them, 'all the young people want to do away with the cotillion. They'd rather waltz and two-step. I won't even mention all those bear and bunny and turkey dances to ragtime. More of an opportunity for romance, I imagine, or rather they imagine. But that's where they're wrong. What could be more romantic than a cotillion? Think of it, after each figure you get to favor a new partner. Why, Lizzy, you can even favor the lieutenant' – Harry shot Kimball a conspiratorial look – 'and no one can possibly object. Not during the cotillion.'

Harry straightened the gold whistle that hung on a chain around his neck. Most cotillion leaders used a whistle to signal the end of the various figures, but only Harry kept his own gold whistle as a badge of office. 'Now come along, pet.' He held his arm out to Elizabeth. 'You're going to lead off with King Lehr, so try to look as regal as possible.'

Elizabeth took Harry's arm, but before she did, she touched Kimball's hand lightly. He smiled at her for that, and she knew it was meant to be a reassuring smile, but there was something constrained about it. She wanted to say something, to be as reassuring as he'd tried to, but Harry was impatient beside her, and the other nine couples were already on the floor for the 'grand chain.' As one of the leaders, she couldn't keep them waiting, not even for Douglas.

The orchestra started up and Harry swung into action. He was in his element. He loved dancing and he loved arranging things. After only a few

minutes he blew his whistle. It did not do to let
the first figure go on for too long. There were too
few dancers at that point and too many spectators,
and boredom could easily set in.

Lizzy moved with the other girls to the three
footmen who held the men's favors. They were
small which meant it wasn't a sporting cotillion.
No polo sticks or tennis rackets this time. Cigarette
lighters or money clips for the men, and she was
willing to bet she'd have another jeweled and
enameled pin or charm before the night was over.
As she took the favor and turned back to the
ballroom she saw Sydney standing in a corner with
several other young men. Harry had said he'd
squared things with him, but Sydney didn't look
as if everything were squared. He was trying to
smile, but the soft full mouth was pulled down in
a sullen expression. It was the least she could do,
she thought, and crossed the ballroom quickly.
When she held the favor out to him his expression
changed, and as soon as it did Lizzy cursed herself.
She was only encouraging him. As they moved
onto the dance floor for the second figure, she saw
Douglas watching her from the sidelines. There
was no expression at all on his face.

Lehr had chosen Amelia for his second partner,
and even his duties as cotillion leader did not keep
him from talking. 'The little man from Tiffany,
pet. I couldn't have been more surprised.
Whatever are you up to?'

Out in the garden with Sam she'd forgot about
Wickert, but now the more immediate problem
came back to her. She couldn't have Harry ruining

things before she'd even got them under way. There was only one way to get Harry off a scent. Put him on a better one. 'I should have known I couldn't keep anything from you, Harry. I was buying a gift. And trying to do it as discreetly as possible.' She dropped her eyes for a moment as if she were embarrassed. 'It's a gift for a man, Harry.' When she raised her eyes to his, she saw he was trying to decide whether to believe her or not. 'And now that you've wormed my secret out of me, you'd better blow your whistle. Besides,' she added, feeling suddenly and dangerously inspired, 'there's someone I'd like to favor.'

She didn't like the idea of favoring Sam, not after what had happened in the garden, but she liked the idea of having her mother find out what she was up to with Wickert less. Sam looked surprised when she approached him, not pleased, she thought, just surprised. She held the favor out to him stiffly. For a moment they stood that way with her holding the gift out and him staring down at it as if it were some dangerous object. Then he recovered himself, took the favor, and led her out on the floor.

She turned to him and placed her hand on his shoulder, but she would not look at him. He had the feeling she was angry and he supposed she had a right to be after the way he'd behaved in the garden, but if she were angry, why had she favored him?

'I'm not very good at cotillions,' he said.

'You'll do.'

'You're killing me with flattery, Amelia.'

306

She heard the way he said Amelia. Why couldn't he make up his mind? 'What I mean is you'll serve the purpose.'

'What purpose is that?'

She looked up at him, and her eyes were defiant now. 'To have Harry Lehr think I'm interested in you. Again,' she added as she heard the sound of the whistle above the music and moved off to the favors. She saw Harry watching her, and behind him she saw Sam select a favor and cross the ballroom to the Corcoran girl whom Lehr and her mother and everyone else disapproved of so thoroughly. It was just like Sam to single her out. Well, Sam could dance with whomever he wanted. So long as Lehr was convinced that she wanted to dance with Sam.

Edith sat with several others watching the cotillion. 'Elizabeth dances so well,' Beatrice Hallenbeck said when Lizzy favored Sydney. 'She carries herself so well,' she'd added when Lizzy had gone on to choose Kimball, but when she'd favored Lieutenant Atherton, Mrs Hallenbeck had simply shifted her weight in her chair. Edith could hear the other woman's breathing. She sounded asthmatic.

'Sydney's orchids were lovely,' Edith said. 'Elizabeth loves orchids.'

Beatrice Hallenbeck said nothing, and they continued to watch the cotillion in silence. It never stops, Edith thought. Not only Elizabeth but all three of them. You marry them off, marry them off far better than they could on their own, and you think you're finished, but you're not finished, not when one daughter can't seem to manage anything more complicated than her coiffure and the other is hellbent on her own martyrdom. People were always telling Edith that life had been good to her, but life hadn't been good to her at all. It had given her a recalcitrant husband and three impossible daughters. One's a fool, the second's a renegade, and the third shows every sign of becoming a camp follower. Life hadn't been good to her in the least, but she'd fought it every step of the way and she'd go on fighting it.

As the orchestra brought the cotillion to a close, she motioned Amelia over. 'Come upstairs with me, Amelia. I want to talk to you. I want to know,' Edith said when she'd closed the door to the same room where she'd questioned Caroline, 'what you were doing driving with that man from Tiffany this afternoon.'

So Harry had got to her mother before the cotillion and she'd favored Sam for nothing. 'I'm a married woman, Mother. I can drive with whomever I want.'

'Don't be a fool Amelia. I didn't think you were driving with him socially. Even you must have some sense of relative position. What were you doing with him?'

Amelia walked to the fireplace. Slowly, as if she were playing for time, she touched the floral arrangement with her toe. 'Didn't Harry tell you what I was doing?'

'Harry told me whom you were with. I can guess the rest, but I want you to tell me.'

'I was buying a gift,' she said, moving the irises gently with her evening slipper.

'Don't lie to me, Amelia. You'd been to your father to ask him for the money Duringham wants to let you divorce him. Fortunately, he had the good sense to refuse you.'

Amelia whirled on her mother. 'He told you that?'

'Your father only thinks he can keep secrets from me, Amelia. You asked for five million. He refused. I doubt very much you'd go shopping after that, but if you did, I doubt you'd do it secretly in an automobile. One doesn't buy gifts from Wickert in an automobile. I can guess what you were doing, and I'm sure Wickert will confirm my suspicions tomorrow morning. You were trying to sell your jewels. You were trying to raise the money to buy Charles off.'

'You're wrong, Mother. I'd already tried that in London. I couldn't raise enough.'

'No, I shouldn't think so. Not even with the Marie Antoinette collar.' Edith saw her daughter's hand move to her throat. 'Yes, Amelia, you pretend to hate that collar, but I suspect you're quite fond of it. And who wouldn't be. It's a handsome piece. That's why you aren't going to sell it or any of your other jewels. You won't be able to raise five million on them. And Charles won't take a penny less. In fact, he won't even take five million anymore.'

Amelia was still standing before the fireplace, and now Edith walked to it and examined her reflection in the mirror above the mantel, as if the conversation were closed. She saw her daughter's reflection beside her own. The profile was razor sharp against the softly lighted room.

'What do you mean he won't take five million anymore?'

Edith heard the hoarseness in Amelia's voice, almost a hushed fear, and knew she'd won. 'I didn't want to mention it until everything was settled, Amelia, but after what I've heard tonight, I realize I can't wait any longer. I've had a letter from Charles. In answer to my own.'

'You wrote to Charles?' The voice was louder now and angry, but Edith wasn't worried. Like most people, Amelia didn't know how to use her anger. It made her less rather than more effective.

'I see nothing unusual about my communicating with my son-in-law. After all, I am concerned about Anthony.'

Amelia stared at her mother who'd begun fixing her hair. She's enjoying this, Amelia thought. 'You don't give a damn about Anthony. Any more than you do about any of us.'

Edith turned from her own reflection to her daughter, and her face was a mask of disapproval. 'I won't have you swearing at me, Amelia. And as for Anthony, I scarcely think you're in a position to accuse others of not caring for him. You're the one who abandoned him.'

Her mother might as well have slapped her. She would have preferred being slapped. 'You know, Mother,' Amelia began, and her voice was more controlled than Edith had expected, 'for a great lady you're a very good street fighter.'

Edith looked at her for what felt like a long time before she answered. 'If I hadn't been one, I never would have become the other. That's something you've never understood.'

It was, Amelia thought, the most honest thing her mother had ever said to her. She crossed the room and dropped into a chair facing her mother, but her eyes were on the floor. 'How is Tony?'

'Very well, I'm happy to say. He and Charles are just back from the lodge in Scotland. Charles said the fishing was very good. They hated to leave, but they couldn't stay any longer. Not' – she hesitated, pretending to examine a bronze cupid on the mantel – 'if he plans to join you before the end of the season. I believe he's going to book passage on the *Mauritania*.'

Amelia's expression did not change. Her eyes were still focused on the rug and her hands lay lifeless on the arms of the chair. She was so still that for a moment Edith thought she might not have heard. 'On the *Mauritania*,' Amelia repeated as if it were the single important fact in everything her mother had said. 'Of course, Charles always preferred the Cunard over the White Star.'

'He said he'd wire as soon as he knew when he'd be arriving. He's very eager to see you.'

'What if I'm not eager to see him? What if I'm not here when he arrives?' Amelia asked, but her voice was flat, like a bad actress reciting lines she'd memorized but didn't really believe.

'Where else would you possibly be? You have no one to go to. You have no money except what

311

I dole out to you. Or what Charles gives you.'

'What Charles gives me from my own money.'

'I beg your pardon, Amelia. I said you have no money. And as long as you don't, there's no way you can leave here. I hope you're not still counting on that ridiculous scheme to sell your jewels. I plan to telephone Tiffany first thing in the morning. And of course we'll go on keeping them in the safe in my room.'

'At least it's easier locking up jewels than locking up a daughter.'

Edith did not bother to answer. She'd won her point, as she'd known she would, and there was no need for further discussion.

'Did he say,' Amelia began, 'did Charles say whether he was bringing Tony with him?'

Edith stopped with her hand on the doorknob and looked at her daughter. 'Yes, he did say. He doesn't feel he can bring Tony. Not this time. I'm sorry about that. I'd like to see my grandson. The marquess. But I guess that will have to wait until I go abroad next June. I think I'll spend the season with you in London. With you and the duke.'

Edith pronounced the word with a clipped finality, and the sound of the door closing behind her reinforced it. So much for divorce. *Click*. So much for Wickert and freedom. *Click*. So much for the fact that Sam really had cared so many years ago. *Click*.

Charles would be here in less than a month, and she'd be going back to the old life. Well, not quite. This time there'd be no Michael. There could, of course, be others if she chose. She remembered an afternoon a year or two after she'd married. She was having tea at Lady Millicent Townsen's. Millicent was esteemed in court circles. 'The king,' she'd said referring to the late king, not the present one, 'is very fond of you, my dear.'

'I'm flattered,' Amelia had answered.

Millicent had sipped her tea and looked at Amelia thoughtfully. 'I don't think you understand,' she'd said finally, and gone on to explain. Millicent had made things very clear and Amelia had understood. Just as she understood now what she was going back to. There wouldn't be the king, of course, because the new king wasn't like that, and there wouldn't be Michael, because she wouldn't go back to him – *you don't love me, Amelia, you love making love* – but there could be others, as Millicent had pointed out. Amelia pictured herself following in Lady Townsen's footsteps, working her way through Burke's Peerage. 'Of course, one has to be careful,' Millicent had warned. 'You did hear what happened to poor dear Linda. She was dreadfully ill. Lost her hair and her looks. One can pick up that sort of thing from one's husband too – I have an aunt who did – but I've always thought it less likely. So one must be careful, my dear . . .'

No. She might be going back to Charles, but she wouldn't go back to that life. She saw herself growing old and trying to stay young, coloring her hair in secret and sneaking off to the Continent for miracle treatments, envying younger women and fighting desperately to hold on to younger and younger men. To the world she'd be the Duchess

313

of Duringham, but to those who knew her she'd be a joke, a pathetic joke like the one Millicent had become in the ten years Amelia had known her. I won't, she told herself. 'I swear I won't,' she repeated aloud, but somewhere behind the conscious thoughts she felt a terrible dull fear. She'd sworn she wouldn't go back to Charles too.

There was a knock at the door. 'Mama said she'd left you up here,' Elizabeth said. 'You've got to help me.' Amelia was looking up at her, but Lizzy had the feeling she wasn't quite seeing her. 'Amelia, are you listening to me?'

'I'm sorry. Yes, I'm listening.'

'You've got to come with us. To the Middletons. Everyone's going on to Seaview to dance.'

'Everyone under twenty-one is going on to Seaview, and I don't qualify.'

'Please, Amelia. I need you.'

'Need me? I should think Sydney would be enough. Sydney and the lieutenant.'

'I need you for moral support and for Douglas. He says he's too old too, but he has to be there.'

'Douglas?'

'Douglas Kimball of course.'

'Why does he have to be there?'

'Try to pay attention, Amelia. I can't put it off any longer. I have to tell Sydney tonight, and I certainly don't want to wait till he takes me home from the Middletons. I don't even want him to take me home.'

Amelia was paying attention now. 'I take it what you intend to tell Sydney is that you won't marry him.'

'I can't marry him.'

'I imagine Sydney will think it's more a matter of *won't*, but I won't quibble with you. And what about the lieutenant? Have you told him you can marry him? Has he had the nerve to ask?'

'I wish everyone would stop talking to me about the lieutenant. Just because I came up with his name for Mama.'

'You might as well stop pretending, Lizzy. Once you tell Sydney and Mother, everyone will guess about you and Lieutenant Atherton.'

'If you'd just listen, Amelia. I've been trying to explain all that. I'm going to marry Douglas.'

'Douglas Kimball?'

'What other Douglas?'

'Douglas Kimball?'

'Stop saying his name that way.'

'I'm sorry, Lizzy, it's just that I'm surprised. I thought you were in love with Lieutenant Atherton.'

'Well, I'm not. I'm in love with Douglas, and I'm going to marry him as soon as possible.'

'Have you told Mother? No, that's a stupid question. If you'd told her, I'd have heard the noise.'

'I've been trying to get up the courage to tell her, and Sydney, all summer. Douglas has been angry about it, and I know he's right, but every time I started, I lost my nerve. I always felt so sorry for Sydney, and so guilty for not wanting to marry him, and of course Mama never listens. I've been putting it off for weeks, but now I have to tell them both.'

315

'Why now?'

Elizabeth walked to the mantel and looked at her reflection in the mirror. Strange she didn't look any different. She'd always been sure she would. Another girlish misconception laid to rest, Douglas would say. She turned back to Amelia. 'Because Mrs Hallenbeck has finally given her approval, and she and Sydney have started making plans. A house adjoining hers, and we'll live with her until it's ready.'

Amelia groaned.

'I know. That's why I have to tell Sydney tonight. And Mama.'

'When you do, tell Mother I mean, Douglas better be waiting outside. With the engine running. But Douglas Kimball,' Amelia added almost to herself. 'Who would have thought it.' She was looking at her sister with a strange expression.

'You would have preferred Lieutenant Atherton, wouldn't you? For me, I mean.'

'He would have been the logical one.'

'Only Carrie was lucky enough to fall in love with the logical one,' Elizabeth said, but she dropped her eyes, and Amelia turned away. They both knew that Carrie had not fallen in love with Sky and had never, in fact, loved anyone except herself, but it was a betrayal to admit it, even to each other. Whatever else Caroline was, she was still their sister.

'It's more than just logic,' Amelia said. 'There's something about the lieutenant . . . I don't know . . . like a fresh wind. Do you know the ball scene

316

in *Madame Bovary* when she feels faint from
waltzing – we all know Carrie does – anyway,
do you remember when the count sends footmen
around breaking all the windows? That was what
I remembered when I thought you were going to
marry the lieutenant. I thought you were breaking
all Mother's windows and letting in a fresh wind.'

'I am, only Douglas is the wind. Don't look like
that, Amelia, he is.'

'How old is he, Lizzy?'

'Forty . . .' Elizabeth dragged out the word and
Amelia wasn't sure if she were going on. '. . .
five,' she added finally.

'For God's sake, Lizzy, don't lie about his age.
A few years won't make a difference to Mother
or anyone else, and it will only make him feel
terrible. Forty-five, well that's a nice round
number, but not exactly one I associate with fresh
winds.'

'That's because you don't know Douglas. He's
different from anyone I've ever known. He sees
things differently. He's more alive. You know,
Amelia,' she dropped her voice as if she didn't
want to be overheard, though there was no one
else in the room, 'sometimes I think that's because
he came so close to dying. When I first met him,
he was still in terrible shape from the sinking. I
didn't know that at the time of course.'

'But he's better now.'

Elizabeth smiled. 'Entirely. He says I'm his
treatment. His cure.'

Amelia stood. 'Well, never let it be said I stood
in the way of modern medicine. All the same,

when you speak to Mother, don't tell her that part about the treatment and the cure.' She was silent for a moment. 'Not that it's going to make any difference what you tell her. Just remember what I said. Have Douglas keep the engine running. And whatever you do, don't give her a chance to get between the two of you.'

'If you ask me, Amelia, he still cares for you.'

'Who?' she asked though she knew very well whom Lizzy meant.

'Sam. I can tell the way he looks at you.'

'He looks at me, Lizzy, with disdain, but that's beside the point.' And it was, of course, now that Charles was coming for her. Charles was to the point, and for the moment so were Lizzy and Kimball. She still couldn't get used to the idea, though she was happy for Lizzy, happy and concerned. That must be what the other feeling was, concern for what lay ahead. It couldn't possibly be envy, not after all these years, not for her own sister.

'I'm furious with you, Sam.' His sister Nina came up to him in the entrance hall. She was wearing her evening cape and behind her he saw Endicott standing in the doorway. 'You didn't dance with me once tonight. On the other hand, I'm very pleased with you. I saw you favor Agnes Corcoran during the cotillion. Pretty little thing, isn't she?' Sam agreed that she was. 'And I saw Amelia Leighton favor you.'

'Amelia, Lady Pugh,' he corrected.

318

'She's more than pretty. I haven't seen her in years. She looks beautiful.'

'If you say so, Nina.'

'I hear there are rumors of divorce.'

'If you say so, Nina.'

'The same old Sam. For a moment when I saw you here tonight I thought you might be turning over a new leaf, but I see I was wrong.'

Over Nina's head he saw Amelia and her sister moving down the staircase, and, Hallenbeck and Douglas Kimball meet them at the bottom. Amid the snatches of laughter – they all seemed to be trying hard to have a good time – he heard them mention the party at Seaview. Amelia was a little old for that, wasn't she? But then so was Kimball. Well, it was none of his business if the two of them wanted to act like kids.

'If I did turn over a new leaf, Nina, what would you do? You'd have no one left to reform.'

She moved closer and put a hand on his arm. 'Maybe I'd just like to repay you, Sam.'

'By throwing me together with Agnes Corcoran?'

'We were talking about Amelia Leighton.'

It wasn't Leighton anymore, but he didn't bother to correct her this time. 'You were talking about her, Nina.'

'Aren't you ever going to forgive her?'

He didn't exactly shake off her hand, only moved his arm a little. 'There's nothing to forgive.'

'You must have heard the stories. How Mrs Leighton wore her down until she agreed to marry Duringham.'

'It's funny those stories didn't start until after she married him. At the time I seem to recall that everyone said it was a marriage made in heaven. Or some similarly blissful place. And she certainly seemed happy about it. She looked happy, damn near radiant at the wedding.'

'But you weren't at the . . .' Nina caught herself.

Sam could still remember the crush outside the church. He'd hung back at the edge of the crowd because he hadn't wanted anyone to recognize him, as if anyone would be looking for him. There'd been two girls beside him who kept jumping in the air trying to get a glimpse of the happy couple. 'Ohh,' one of them had crooned as she'd come down heavily on Sam's foot. 'He's beautiful.'

'You're a cynic,' Nina said, as she always did, but this time her voice held more pity than accusation.

Nina's timing was perfect. She left Sam standing alone in the entrance hall just as Corcoran entered it. When Sam said he'd still like to speak to him, Corcoran replied he'd like a good long conversation rather than a few words.

'We were just leaving,' Corcoran said. 'Mrs C. and I are going to drop Agnes at Seaview. I understand the young people go on till dawn. Then you and I can settle down to something quieter, Van Nest. Like to show you my library. I don't know a damn thing about books, rare or any other kind, but people tell me I got a good collection.

Bought it all at once from some fellow in Boston. You know the kind of thing. The old man made the fortune, the son began collecting books and pictures, the grandsons concentrated on horses and women, and by the time they were gone there was nothing left.' If there were anything personal behind Corcoran's words, nothing in his face showed it. 'Still,' he went on, 'I paid an arm and a leg for the library. You can tell me if you think it was worth it.'

There were four of them in the back of the Peerless and it was all very friendly, or at least all three Corcorans seemed to regard Sam as an old friend. Still he was surprised when they turned into the driveway of Seaview and Agnes said perhaps she wouldn't stay at the party at all but go on home with them.

'Now you go along with the young people,' Corcoran said. His voice was not stern, but it was different from the way it had been as they'd talked on the way over, and Agnes said good night to Sam and went off to the party.

'Whiskey or brandy?' Corcoran said when they were alone in the library. 'I'm still a whiskey man myself. Can't seem to develop a taste for brandy. Maybe it's just too rich for my blood.'

Sam said he'd have whiskey too and Corcoran took a decanter from the sideboard and filled two glasses halfway. 'I don't like to wake the servants at this hour,' he explained.

'Well, what do you think of it?' Corcoran handed Sam one of the glasses and looked around the room. It was large and rectangular with shelf after shelf of beautifully bound books. There must have been miles of books, Sam thought. 'That's my classical corner. All Greek and Latin. The real thing I mean, no translations. And that's my French wall.' Corcoran made a sound that was somewhere between a grunt and a chuckle. 'I can't read a word of it. Not a single word. But Agnes is learning French. You ought to hear her. Sounds like a real frog.'

Sam put his drink down on one of the steps of the circular ladder standing beside the shelves and took down a volume of Montaigne. The tooled leather binding was in excellent condition and the pages had never been cut.

'Pristine,' Corcoran said. Sam agreed that it was. 'You know the damnedest thing though, Van Nest. Well, here let me show you.' Corcoran handed him back his drink and pushed the ladder to the far end of the room. The wheels made no sound on the Chinese carpet. Corcoran was a tall man and had to climb only halfway up to reach the top shelves. He took down an oversized volume, obviously a collection of paintings, and handed it to Sam.

Sam looked at the title. *Great Art of the Eastern World*. 'I'm afraid the title doesn't tell the whole story,' Corcoran said. 'Go ahead, take a look at it.'

Sam put his drink down again and began to leaf through the book. It was an expensive edition and the colors of the reproductions, all done in a stylized oriental manner, were good. He stopped at one of the full-page pictures. At first it was hard to tell how many figures there were, but gradually he sorted out appendages and then players. There were three women and an obese man. The women were all naked, but the man wore a kimono that hung open. His exposed skin looked wet and shiny. The women, two of them voluptuous, the third slender and almost boyish, were demonstrating their ability as contortionists. 'They seem to be giving each other and the fat gentleman a good deal of pleasure,' Sam said, but his mind was racing, trying to figure out if the book were somehow the key to Corcoran. Did he have a taste for pornography, oriental women, or expensive and unusual practices? Sam didn't think any of these, but then he hadn't thought Kirkland Selby was a man given to raping underaged virgins either.

'What surprised me,' Corcoran said taking the book from Sam and climbing the ladder again to put it back in place – the lesson, whatever it was, was obviously over – 'wasn't the picture. I've seen worse than that. Hell, I've done worse than that. What surprised me was that a Boston gentleman should have a book like that – several books like that – in his library. Just shows how much I knew. That's one thing you'll discover about me, Sam. I'm not afraid to admit it when I don't know something. And I'm not afraid to learn either.'

Corcoran put a hand on Sam's elbow and steered him across the room to two leather club chairs in front of the hearth. The fireplace of carved walnut was inlaid with tiles illustrating scenes from classical mythology. 'But you didn't come here to

323

listen to me talk about myself or to look at my collection of pornography, did you?' Corcoran said, lowering himself into one of the chairs and carefully adjusting his trouser legs as he did. He had, Sam could tell, the self-made man's respect for meticulousness of dress.

'Actually I did come here to talk about you, or at least some of your interests. The ones that are involved with Walsh.'

Corcoran laughed. 'Yes, I guessed as much. With Mr Houdini's help, of course. Well, what exactly is it you're after?'

Sam ran the litany again. He wondered if he sounded as bored as he felt. Corcoran's face showed nothing.

'You make it sound pretty dangerous,' Corcoran said, when Sam had finished.

'It is dangerous, Corcoran.'

'Call me Jim.' He gave a short, self-deprecatory laugh. 'I won't say everyone does, but I wish you would. Yes, I suppose there is some risk involved, but you don't make millions without risking something, do you, Sam? I take it you know how much we stand to make with this thing. I'm willing to risk quite a bit for my share of more than four billion.'

Sam started to say something, but Corcoran held up his hand. 'On the other hand, I'm willing to sacrifice the same amount for something I really want. I'll make a lot of money with Walsh, but then I make a lot of money no matter what I do. No, it isn't money-making schemes I need, Sam.' Corcoran took a sip of his drink.

'What is it you need then . . . Jim?'

Corcoran crossed his legs and adjusted his trousers again. 'There's no single answer to that. Or at least no single simple answer. That book I showed you a few minutes ago . . .'

'So he did have peculiar tastes. Sam told himself to look on the light side. Picture the new sign on 23 Wall. *Morgan & Co. Investors and Procurers.* Or had the sign been there all along, as his father had always said, and he'd been the only one too naive to notice.

'As I told you, I was surprised to find it and several like it in this collection I bought. As I also told you, there are a lot of things I don't know about society, Sam. Mrs C.'s the same way, though just between the two of us, she isn't as quick to admit it. Now, Agnes is a different story. She picks things up fast. I tell you, I heard her chattering away in those shops on the *Rue de la Paix*, and I would have sworn she was a native. She can sing and play the piano as good as any of them too. And she draws. Sketches, she calls it. I wanted to hang some of the stuff she did, but she wouldn't let me. Said they weren't good enough, and anyway, it just wasn't done. That's what she's always saying. "It just isn't done, Daddy." I told you, she picks things up real quick. Unfortunately' – Corcoran stood – 'Can I get you another drink, Sam? I'm going to have one. Unfortunately,' Corcoran went on. He was standing at the sideboard with his back to Sam as he spoke. 'Being quick isn't enough.' He turned back to Sam. 'Not all her quickness or her looks, and you've got to admit she's pretty' – Sam admitted it — 'or all my money is enough. Here, this will keep the morning chill away.' He handed Sam a glass filled with whiskey and sat across from him again. 'Because it can't buy Agnes the kind of marriage she wants.' Corcoran's face was impassive, but he was watching Sam closely. 'You know what kind of marriage I mean, Sam.'

Sam knew perfectly what kind of marriage he meant. He was wishing they were back with pornography. Procurer, yes. Sacrificial lamb, no. 'I'm afraid I don't see the connection between Miss Corcoran's . . .'

'Agnes, Sam. There's no need for formality between us,' Corcoran said, though his voice did not sound quite as hearty as it had.

'. . . between her marriage and Walsh's scheme,' Sam went on, though he saw the connection as perfectly as he saw the kind of marriage.

'Don't you, Sam?'

Sam looked from Corcoran to the fireplace. The tile at the top righthand side portrayed Zeus intervening on behalf of his daughter Athena in her battle against Pallas. Pallas was dying what appeared to be an agonizing death.

'Miss Corcoran . . . Agnes is a delightful girl . . . child,' Sam corrected himself. He was striving for the avuncular tone, but he knew it was no good. He'd never get out of this by pretending to be too old for Agnes. Not even his sister thought he was too old for her. 'And I'm sure she'll make a fine wife.' Damn it. He was beginning to sound like a character in a Victorian novel. 'Of course, I don't know her very well.'

Suddenly Corcoran's face changed. At first Sam thought he was angry, but then he heard the bark of laughter. 'Good God, Sam. I don't want you to marry her. Hell, with all due respect, boy, I wouldn't let you marry her.'

Sam struggled to keep his smile within the bounds of propriety. 'I'd like to know why not.' He didn't have to struggle for the hearty tone. He felt like a condemned man who'd just been reprieved.

'Because Agnes needs a man who's part of this world, not one who's running away from it. Because, and this may sound strange to you, you don't love her and I want someone who cares about Agnes enough to want to make her happy. And most of all, because I don't want anyone who'll rock the boat, Agnes' or mine, and you like rocking boats, Sam. I want someone like . . . what's his name . . . Hallenbeck, Sydney Hallenbeck.'

'I'm afraid I can't help you there.'

'That's where you're wrong, Sam. You, or at least your family, can help me with Hallenbeck and a great many others like him. This is our second season in Newport, and as you may have gathered tonight, Mrs C. and Agnes aren't exactly making great strides. We were invited to Belle Isle only because Elias Leighton wanted something from me. Now I know what it is. As for the ball, well, we've been to two or three of those, but it never goes any further. To tell you the truth, Mrs C. and Agnes are pretty lonely up here. Sometimes I think Mrs C. misses the old days on Central Park

West when we were just coming up in the world. We lived in a hotel and thought it was pretty fine. Until Agnes found out what fine really was.' Corcoran took a long swallow of his drink. 'I seem to be rambling. What I want, Sam, and I'm not asking it as a favor. I'm willing to pay for it with the Walsh deal. I want the women in your family to take up the women in mine.' Corcoran's sharp chin jutted forward in a canny smile. It was, Sam imagined, the way he looked when he'd just bought another city council. 'Simple enough.'

'Not quite so simple. For one thing my mother rarely goes out anymore.'

'I know that, Sam, which means that when she does go out to someone's house or when she entertains for someone at her own, it's a real event. The Van Nest name is still worth a lot. It's something not even all my money can buy, as you just proved. And if Mrs Van Nest chooses to dine at the Corcorans' or to give a party for Miss Corcoran, you can be sure others will follow. Of course, we wouldn't expect too much of your mother. I understand she's getting on in years. There are your sisters. Agnes has already met one of them, Mrs Endicott.'

Maybe I'd just like to repay you, Nina had said. She'd get the chance, all right. And he knew his mother would go along with the plan too. She'd always felt she and her daughters had taken too much from him and given too little in return. Who knows, she might even enjoy it. His mother always did have an unpredictable sense of humor. She might just enjoy turning down the reigning matriarchs' invitations and showing up at Mrs Corcoran's.

'Of course, I don't expect you or Mrs Van Nest to worry about the expense. I'll see to all that.'

Sam drained his drink and put the empty glass on the table beside him. 'Out of the question,' he said and saw the startled look on Corcoran's face. 'The money, I mean. Mother would be terribly offended if you tried to pay for a dinner she gave. Even one in honor of your daughter.'

The breeze had come up again, and Sam felt it welcome against his face. He was hoping it would clear his head. Corcoran was as generous with his whiskey as he appeared to be with his money. He took out his pocket watch, and held it up to the electric lantern that illuminated the end of Corcoran's driveway. Three-forty. No wonder he was tired.

Sam started down Bellevue Avenue. Corcoran had offered him his automobile, but Sam had refused. He could walk back to Rosecliff almost as quickly, and he was counting on the walk to revive him. He'd need everything he had against Sturgis now. Sturgis had said he wouldn't be threatened. He'd said he'd never change his mind now, not after that Houdini business, but Sam had to try. Hell he'd blackmailed two men tonight, lied to a third or at least misled him, and sold his own mother to a fourth. Don't stop now, boy. Might as well go all the way.

The windows of Rosecliff glittered in the darkness like the jewels on a Newport dowager's gown, but inside the house had that worn and tattered after-the-ball appearance. The roses and orchids looked as wilted as the remaining guests. The ballroom floor, so immaculate a few hours ago, was littered. It was a very polite litter – the gold cord from a dance card, a piece of broken crystal, spilled champagne, and crumbled petits fours – but not a very attractive one. The orchestra sounded listless, as if they didn't care that no one was dancing. The young people had gone off to their Bunny Hugs and Grizzly Bears and the older guests stood or sat around the room making desultory conversation. It was a discouraging sight and for once this evening, Sam thought, his surroundings matched his mood. Then he saw Sturgis standing at the bottom of the stairs. Sturgis looked as if the evening were just beginning. His hands were in the pockets of his trousers and he was rolling his weight back and forth from heel to toe in time to the music. His face didn't change as Sam approached him. At first Sam was encouraged, then he realized Sturgis didn't really see him. He was looking at him, but he wasn't thinking of him. Sam was about to speak when Sturgis turned away from him. She was standing on the landing of the staircase and she hadn't said a word, but Sturgis had turned to her as if he'd felt her presence.

'I'm ready,' Edith Leighton said coming down the stairs. As she reached the bottom a white-gloved arm emerged from the gold metallic cloth of her cape and found its way to Sturgis' arm. 'I do appreciate this, Tom. It's kind of you to see me home.'

'Nonsense, Edith, and you know it. It's kind of you to let me see you home.'

For a moment Sam had the distinct impression he was an undergraduate again doing his duty at a debutante dance.

Sydney was at the wheel of the automobile with Elizabeth beside him and Amelia and Kimball in the back seat. No one said much, but then no one ever could say much bouncing along that way in an open car. You either shouted or sang or were silent, and since no one in the group felt like singing or shouting – at least not in high spirits – they remained silent.

At least they hadn't taken that damn lieutenant with them, Sydney was thinking as they turned up the drive to Seaview. Then the familiar white uniform sprang out at him from the sea of black coats milling about the front veranda.

Sydney pulled the automobile up behind several others parked in the driveway, and Atherton was at Lizzy's door immediately. There was something about the way he helped Lizzy down that Sydney didn't like. The lieutenant seemed to be more in command now, of himself, of the situation, even of Lizzy.

Inside the party was already underway. There was no ballroom at Seaview, but the doors between the front and rear drawing rooms had been opened, the furniture pushed back, and the rugs rolled up. The music was so loud it was hard to believe it came from a single box that stood against the wall of the back room.

See that ragtime couple over there,
Watch them throw their shoulders in the air,
Snap their fingers, honey I declare,

Sydney and the lieutenant claimed Lizzy for a dance immediately, but she turned to Kimball. 'I promised Douglas I'd teach him the Grizzly Bear, though there isn't much to teach. All you do is put your arms around each other and walk.'

Douglas did not look as if he wanted to learn the Grizzly Bear, Amelia thought, but he moved onto the dance floor with Lizzy, and Atherton turned to Amelia. She hadn't come to dance and started to say as much, but realized it would sound foolish. Besides, she liked to dance. She was supposed to be too old to, of course, especially ragtime where it was a matter of moving the feet less and the body more but she didn't feel too old to. She told the lieutenant she'd love to dance and they went off leaving Sydney standing on the sidelines staring morosely after Lizzy and Kimball. 'I want to talk to you Lizzy,' he said in an undertone when they returned at the end of the dance.

'I want to talk to you too, Sydney,' she said and took his arm. The solarium was at the far end of the house, away from the music and the other guests. It was warmer there and the air felt thick and damp. There were small trees and blossoming plants all around. 'It's like being in a jungle,' Elizabeth said, but for the first time in his life Sydney had no time for pleasantries.

'Why have you been avoiding me all night, Lizzy?'

332

'I haven't been . . .' She saw the look on his face. 'Well, I haven't meant to avoid you.'

'It's just that you had so many obligations to the lieutenant.'

'I wish everyone would leave me alone about Lieutenant Atherton.'

'I wish Atherton would leave you alone.'

'He will.'

Sydney had been leaning on the back of a wicker chair staring at the floor as he spoke, but she saw his head snap up at her last words. 'Do you mean . . .'

Lizzy held up her hand as if to stop him as well as his words. 'Wait, Sydney. Let me explain.' There was a silence then. She could hear her own breathing and Sydney's, short and sharp. She could hear the music drifting across from the far end of the house, a lively beat and more jumbled, meaningless words. She realized in horror that her fingers, hidden in the folds of her dress, were keeping time against her leg. 'I can't marry you. I'm sorry, Sydney, but I just can't.' It had all come out in a single desperate breath.

He didn't look angry, only confused. 'But I assumed . . . everyone expected . . .' He pulled himself up. 'I thought it was agreed.'

'I'm sorry, Sydney. I know you did, and it's my fault. I should have told you before. But you never really said anything. Not until tonight.' She knew it wasn't a very good excuse and her voice gave her away.

'I didn't think I had to. In view of . . . in view of everything.' The anger was coming now, and it made Lizzy feel better. 'You knew I was just waiting for Mother to agree.'

Elizabeth said nothing, but that only seemed to make him more angry.

'It's that damn lieutenant, isn't it?'

'It has nothing to do with him.'

'The hell it doesn't, but you can't marry him, Lizzy. He's no one. And he's poor. Your mother will never let you marry him.'

'I told you, it has nothing to do with Lieutenant Atherton.'

The timing could not have been worse. Suddenly Atherton appeared between the two orange trees that framed the door. 'Did I hear someone mention my name?' He executed a mock half-bow toward Lizzy. There was a glass in his hand, she noticed, but it was empty.

'Get out of here,' Sydney said.

Atherton kept his eyes on Lizzy and flashed a delighted smile. 'But I distinctly heard the lady mention my name.'

It still might have been all right if Atherton hadn't held out his hand, the one without the empty glass, and taken a step toward Elizabeth. Unfortunately Sydney was standing equidistant from both of them, like the physical incarnation of the emotional triangle he thought they represented, and he reached Atherton before the lieutenant reached Lizzy. Atherton must not have been as drunk as he'd looked because his reflexes were quick, too quick, in fact. He turned as he saw Sydney coming at him and was just in time to allow his chin to connect with Sydney's fist. The noise of the empty glass shattering on the marble floor almost drowned out the sound of a hand hitting a jaw.

'Stop it,' Lizzy screamed, but by now neither of them was paying attention to her. Atherton had been pushed backward by the impact of Sydney's punch, but he hadn't fallen, and he wasn't even off balance. The two men were about the same height, but Sydney was heavier, and much slower. He was still standing there looking surprised at what he'd done when Atherton came back at him. The lieutenant had some grievances against the world he found himself in that summer, and he took them out on Sydney. Not that Sydney didn't fight back. He had his own grievances that night, and he gave them all he had. In fact, once when Lizzy tried to separate them, he came close to hitting her by mistake. He was not only slower than Atherton, he was less accurate.

By that time Kimball and Amelia had arrived in the solarium, as well as several other guests who'd heard Lizzy's screams and then the sound of a rubber tree crashing through the hundreds of tiny glass squares of one wall. It took several men to separate Sydney and Atherton. In the half hour of confusion that followed, only Douglas seemed to retain any sense of reason. After making sure that neither of them felt anything was broken, he sent each man to a different room to wash off the blood and make themselves look as good as they insisted they felt. Then he got someone to start up the Victrola again and managed to herd the dancers back to the drawing rooms. When he returned to the solarium he found Amelia sitting with her arm around Lizzy's shoulders. They both looked more startled than anything else.

'I gather you started to tell him, but didn't get to finish,' Douglas said, taking a wicker chair opposite them.

'I started to, but Lieutenant Atherton showed up before I could finish.'

'I think,' Amelia said standing, 'that I'd better go see how the lieutenant is. He's not as badly hurt as Sydney, but then he doesn't have as many friends here.'

She found Atherton in a guest room at the top of the stairs. He was sitting on the end of a chaise holding a towel against his mouth. He must have taken off his tunic to wash and he reached for it self-consciously as she entered. Amelia wondered again at Elizabeth's tastes. There was no denying that Kimball had a certain magnetism, but Atherton half-dressed and disheveled, was a very attractive man.

'How are you?' she asked as he shrugged into the tunic.

'How's Hallenbeck?'

Amelia couldn't tell if he was speaking from concern or bravado.

'A little worse than you I suspect. But he doesn't have to worry about the repercussions. You're going to have a hard time explaining that mouth to whomever you have to explain things like that.'

It was one of the things he'd been thinking, but only one. 'It'll be worth it.' He started to smile but as he moved his mouth it turned into a wince.

Amelia had a feeling she knew what was coming and was sorry she'd come up now.

'I knew he was angry, but I didn't know he was that angry.' He took the towel from his face and looked at it before he spoke again. The bloodstains seemed to give him courage. 'What I mean is, if he hates me that much, maybe Elizabeth gave him some reason to hate me.'

Amelia sat on the end of the bed and looked directly into his eyes. They were pale blue and very honest. She remembered Tony when he was only five or six and she'd had to explain that his favorite dog, an Irish setter that had been born just around the time he had, had been shot accidentally by a poacher. Charles had left the explaining to her.

'She gave him a reason to be angry, Lieutenant, but it wasn't you. I don't blame you for thinking it was. I thought the same thing until a few hours ago.' Amelia saw the handsome features move a little, as if he'd been trained to hide emotion but could not help showing it now, and went on quickly. 'She's in love with Douglas Kimball. She's going to marry him.' The features moved again, but they did not collapse. He was too well trained for that.

Atherton said nothing, and she could imagine the thoughts going through his mind. To lose her to someone like Sydney, someone with money and position and all the things he'd never have, was one thing. To lose her to an old man, and she knew that was the way he thought of Kimball, was somehow doubly unfair.

Amelia stood. 'I know it isn't fair.' He looked up at her in surprise. 'But not much in life is, Lieutenant.'

She saw the look he gave her then. She was the enemy again. What, he must be thinking, could she possibly know about life's injustices.

Sydney had thought the whole thing through. Standing over the sink in Linus Middleton's bath with his head thrown back to stop the bleeding from his nose, he'd gone over the whole thing in his mind. He wasn't sorry about the fight, though he did wish he'd come out a little better in it. It was the rest of it that he was trying to sort out. Lizzy was infatuated with that damn officer. Sydney didn't like the idea but he liked the idea better than the one that she might be in love with him. She couldn't be, of course. Girls like Lizzy didn't go around falling in love with people like Atherton. She'd realize that in a few weeks if she didn't now. She'd realize it and be contrite, and he'd forgive her because he could forgive Lizzy a great deal. Still, he'd have to be more careful in the future, have to see that she didn't meet people who might give her strange ideas. It wasn't a problem that seriously worried him. Once they were married, once they were installed in the house adjoining his mother's and Elizabeth had children to worry about, children and him, Sydney thought and was pleased to see that the bleeding in his nose had stopped, he wouldn't have to worry about Lizzy's getting peculiar ideas.

In any event, he'd say no more about it tonight.

There'd been enough of a fuss already. Lizzy had said earlier that she needed time, and he was willing to give her time. Several days, at least. In the meantime, he'd be correct and a little aloof. A little removed, a little dignity, he reasoned as he entered the solarium and found Lizzy sitting with Kimball, were exactly what the situation called for.

'Are you all right, Sydney?' she asked, but she didn't move from the swing where she was sitting beside Kimball.

'Of course, I'm all right,' Sydney said, but in fact his nose throbbed when he talked and his head felt peculiar. He started to straighten his tailcoat, but noticed again that the right sleeve had been pulled out. There was a good deal of blood on his shirt too. He'd have to get rid of the shirt before his mother saw it. 'I'll take you home now, Lizzy.'

'Sit down, Sydney.' He didn't move. 'Please,' she added. He sat in the chair across from the swing.

'There's something I want to tell you,' Lizzy began again.

'I've already heard more than I want to.'

Kimball started to say something, but Elizabeth put a hand on his arm. 'Maybe you have, Sydney, and I'm sorry, but you haven't heard all of it, and I'd like you to. I told you before that I can't marry you, but you didn't give me a chance to tell you why. I can't marry you because I'm going to marry Douglas.'

'Douglas,' he repeated as if the name had no meaning for him.

'Me,' Kimball said.

Sydney looked from Lizzy to Kimball and back to Lizzy again. 'You're going to marry Kimball?'

Douglas saw Sydney's right hand moving slowly upward and stiffened for the attack, but it kept moving until it reached his forehead. Kimball was glad. It wasn't that he was afraid of Hallenbeck or even of being hurt, though he didn't relish the idea. It was only that he didn't think a fight, another fight, would make things any clearer. Sydney rubbed his fingers back and forth across his skin as if the whole thing were too much for him. 'You can't marry Kimball. He's old enough to be your father.'

She saw Douglas wince. 'That's true,' he said, 'but I'm not her father. And I'm going to be her husband.'

Sydney looked from one to the other again. There was anger in his face, but it was anger without an edge. Clearly he'd had enough. 'Just tell me one thing, Lizzy.' His voice was superior and there was something ugly about that superiority. 'How long have you two been carrying on behind my back?'

'Sydney,' Lizzy began, but this time it was Kimball who cut her off.

He came to his feet quickly and although he was not a big man he looked impressive standing there over Sydney. 'No one's been carrying on behind your back. You and Elizabeth weren't engaged, despite what a lot of people thought. In fact, as I understand, you didn't even ask her to marry you until tonight. So I'm afraid I was ahead of you there.'

Elizabeth stood and put her hand in Douglas'. 'That's true, Sydney. I'm sorry but . . .'

'No one has to be sorry for me,' Hallenbeck snapped. 'It's you two . . .' he began but didn't go on.

'There's one more thing,' Kimball said, looking down at Sydney who was no longer looking up at them. 'Atherton.'

'What about Atherton.' The head came up again as if he were suddenly interested. 'Is he hurt?'

'He will be if this gets around,' Douglas said. 'If Mrs Middleton or anyone else complains to the Admiral that Atherton was brawling here, it will be the end of his career. So for the record, Hallenbeck, you and I were fighting tonight. Since Lizzy and I are leaving, it will make more sense anyway.'

'That explains the window and my appearance, but what about his?'

Kimball did not want to say that there was a good deal less to explain about Atherton's appearance. 'We'll say he was trying to separate us. And as for the window, I'll take care of that.'

'I'll take care of the window. After all, it was my fight, not yours, no matter what official story we put out. Besides,' he added, 'I can afford it more easily than you can.'

Kimball shrugged. Hallenbeck's wealth, and his comparative lack of it were not things that bothered him.

After Lizzy left with Kimball, Sydney sat alone in the solarium trying to figure things out again. He'd thought he'd put it all together, but apparently he'd put it together the wrong way. The most painful thing was not what had happened, but when it had happened. How long had she been pretending to care for him while she really cared for that damned artist? As he thought of all the things he'd said and she'd never said, he clenched and unclenched his big fist. It still hurt from the fight, but the motion was an attempt to alleviate another pain. He was still sitting that way, holding one hand in the other and opening and closing it slowly when Agnes Corcoran found him. Agnes had seen part of the fight and heard the talk, and Agnes was not a stupid girl.

'Are you all right, Mr Hallenbeck?'

Sydney's manners rarely failed him, but they did at that moment. He sat there looking up at her blankly.

'Can I get you something? Coffee. Or perhaps some champagne. I think champagne's a better idea.' She looked at the hand that was still opening and closing in the other like a newborn animal that was just getting its legs. 'If you don't want to drink it, you can always soak your hand in it. At least you don't need a steak for your eye. I suspect the lieutenant will.' She saw she'd caught his interest with that. 'You wait right here. I'll be back with a bottle of champagne in a minute.' It took her three, and this time he stood when she entered, and filled the two glasses she'd brought with the bottle. When he'd finished pouring, she took his hand in both of hers and looked at the knuckles.

'Poor little hand.'

No one had ever called his hand little, unless you counted his mother, and he'd been very little himself then.

'It's nothing,' he said.

She handed him one of the glasses from the table and took the other herself. 'I knew you'd say that. You're what they call the strong silent type, Mr Hallenbeck.'

She sat on the swing and Sydney sat next to her. When she turned to face him he noticed the way her hair curved forward over her cheeks before it was caught behind her neck and swept upward on her head. He'd never known a girl with red hair before, except that parlor maid his mother had fired years ago when he'd mentioned the fact.

'What are you staring at?'

'Your hair, Miss Corcoran.'

'Agnes. Has it come undone?'

'No, I was thinking how pretty it is.' He'd actually been thinking that he'd like to touch it, but he wasn't going to tell her that.

She smiled and sipped her champagne and said nothing. Agnes may not have been the conversationalist she and her parents believed she was, but there was one thing you could say for her. She knew when to keep quiet.

It wasn't just the hair, Sydney was thinking and noticed that her leg, limb his mother would have corrected him, was moving in time to the music. She was a pretty girl, a very pretty girl, though he knew his mother wouldn't think so. Well, his mother didn't like the music Agnes was keeping time to either, but he did. He liked the music that his mother insisted was vulgar and primitive — and he knew what she meant by primitive — and he liked Agnes Corcoran, though his mother would probably use the same words to describe her. But his mother wasn't here now and Agnes was, and he decided he'd like to dance with her, a vulgar, primitive ragtime dance, and he could tell from the way she was leaning toward him, smiling up at him, that she'd like that too. It made him feel good, no matter what his mother might say.

There was no reason to stay now that Lizzy and Kimball were gone, Amelia told herself, but then there was no place else she particularly wanted to go. Couples were still dancing in the drawing rooms and from the butler's pantry she smelled bacon and eggs. She didn't want bacon and eggs, but she did want a drink.

In the pantry she found Dudley Davenport shouting down the dumbwaiter to someone below. 'If you don't hurry with those eggs, I will wake the cook.'

'We're coming, Dudley,' came a feminine voice from below.

How many early-morning parties like this had Amelia gone to during her own days in Newport? She couldn't count them, but she could remember that they were always the best part of the evening. All the formality was gone and all the chaperones. The dancing would continue until sunrise and under the guise of not bothering the servants people would disappear to make breakfast or find more champagne, and they'd make a terrible mess and an awful lot of noise before it all ended. She remembered one party, she couldn't recall the house, but she remembered the steep stairs that led from the pantry to the kitchen. Sam had said he was going to make perfect fried eggs. 'Not a broken yolk in the bunch,' he'd said as he'd slid them onto the plate.

'Where did you learn to do that?' she'd asked in amazement.

'Never forget, Amelia, that I'm an officer as well as a gentleman.'

She kept trying to remember the house but all she could remember was the narrow winding staircase. Going back down a second time she'd slipped and he'd caught her before she'd fallen. It had been dark on the stairway and she could barely see his face as it came closer to hers, but she had felt the rough beard against her skin and the mouth tracing the curve of her cheek until it found her lips. 'Where did you learn to do that?' Her mouth had teased at his as she'd asked the question. He'd laughed very softly but he hadn't bothered to answer this time, and they'd stayed on those stairs for a long time, longer than they should have, she'd known at the time, and only the sound of voices calling for them had forced them back to the party.

Davenport was working hard at the ropes of the dumbwaiter now, and he managed to bring a tray with several bottles of champagne and brandy level with the opening. 'It's not eggs but it will have to do,' Davenport said, and began handing the bottles out. Someone else was pouring, and a third young man was handing out glasses, and Amelia took one from him and left the pantry by the back door.

Seaview was on the bay side of the island within view of the yacht basin. The house was built on the highest point of the property and the smooth green lawn sloped down to the beach that formed a neat white boundary now between the darkness of the grass and the water. Toward town she could see the light at the end of the yacht club dock and around that steady beacon the fainter lights of the anchored boats bobbing gently, casting long shimmering reflections on the water.

Amelia started down the hill to the beach. Even at this distance she could hear snatches of music from the Victrola. She felt the breeze off the water and shivered. It was funny about ragtime. The lyrics were always less romantic than waltzes, but the music was just the opposite. No, not more romantic, more sensual. Ragtime made her think of things that a waltz never did. She looked toward the yacht basin again. There were several large boats, but she knew the largest one was *Corsaire*. Sam would be back on it by now. *Nereids* was moored a little beyond it. Her father would be aboard by now too. And tomorrow they'd all be off, Sam and her father and all the other men, sailing wherever they pleased. It was hell to be a woman, she thought. Oh, certainly there were a few who'd fought their way out. There were those women she'd known in London, the ones she'd chained herself to that fence with, as Sam had said. Some of them had freed themselves, but they'd done it by saying no to everything else in life. Men could have it all, but women had to choose between freedom and everything else, and by everything else she knew she didn't mean only marriage and children. She reached up to rub her neck where the collar chafed and thought of her mother. There were a dozen women like her mother in Newport, probably more, women who had everything they wanted. Amelia wondered why she wasn't one of those women. Because she was no good at manipulation, that was why. Men got what they wanted directly. Women had to maneuver their way around men. And Amelia was no good at maneuvering. 'You're lacking in the feminine graces,' Charles had said to her that afternoon in the main library at Thynnleigh. 'Isn't she, Simon?' Charles had continued, but Simon had gone on paging through some pound and paddock magazine and said nothing. 'Take that incident a few years ago with the king. His Majesty was very taken with my wife, Simon. Don't look surprised, Amelia. Millicent told me all about it. But my wife' – Charles moved to the arm of Simon's club chair and put an arm around his shoulders – 'Her Grace would have none of it. Now I don't mind her throwing away the benefits that would have accrued to her as a royal favorite, but think of the advantages we would have gained.'

Simon looked up from the magazine and laughed. 'It wasn't very considerate of you, Amelia. After all, Edward was an old man by then. He couldn't have been very demanding.'

'It's as I said, Simon. My wife is entirely lacking in the feminine graces.'

Amelia had left the room without answering them. By then she'd learned it never paid to answer them at times like that.

Perhaps she had been foolish as Charles and Simon had said. Perhaps she should have been kinder to the king in his declining years instead of waiting for a penniless younger son to come along. Perhaps a little less passion and a little more practicality would have paid off. She pictured herself going to the present king. *I beg you to put aside your prejudices against divorce, Sir. For me. For the memory of your father. In appreciation of the happiness I gave him in his declining years.*

Not likely, Amelia thought. 'Not bloody likely,' she repeated aloud to the night.

Sam left Rosecliff quickly. With Sturgis gone there was no reason to stay. Out on Bellevue Avenue the air was cool against his face, but the breeze that had felt bracing before was only chilly now. Still, he was walking aimlessly in no rush to get back to *Corsaire* or Morgan.

An automobile passed leaving a gust of warmer air in its wake. He wondered idly if it were Sturgis'. Outsmarted by Edith Leighton. Again.

Four-fifths successful, but four-fifths wasn't successful enough. Maybe with luck they'd still stop Walsh, but he doubted it. Even if they did, he wouldn't get the thirty-five million. He'd get a neat little promotion at Morgan and Company.

He remembered the argument he'd had with Morgan a few months ago. Now that he'd lost Sturgis, now that he'd lost the thirty-five million and the power and freedom it would have bought, that argument would become the recurrent theme of his life.

'Airplanes aren't an industry,' Morgan had said. 'They're a toy.'

'That's what they used to say about automobiles. First they were toys, then they were rich men's toys. Until Ford proved they were something else.'

'That's different, Sam.'

'It's always different, until someone proves it's the same.'

'And you want to be the man to prove it about airplanes.'

He wasn't going to answer that one. 'There's a war coming in Europe. Maybe not this year, maybe not next, but it's coming. You only have to look at the new German naval budget to know that.'

'That's right, Sam. The naval budget. The Germans are beefing up their navy. What does that have to do with airplanes? You're not trying to tell me they're going to use airplanes to fight a war.'

'That's exactly what I'm trying to tell you.'

Morgan had given him a strange look then, as if he were trying to figure out something about him. 'I can't agree with you, Sam,' he'd said finally. 'And I don't think it's a sound investment. Buy yourself an airplane to play with, and from now on try to keep Morgan business and your own pleasure separate.'

Like tonight, Sam thought. Tonight had been strictly Morgan business even if it went under the guise of pleasure. *Even the dance with Amelia?* a cold voice in the back of his consciousness asked. That was curiosity, he answered. *And what did you find out?* Only that she hasn't changed. *Neither have you,* the voice came back. *You were trembling so much you could barely dance. And what about later in the garden. She comes close and puts a hand on your shoulder and you go to pieces like some kid.* But I kept her away. *You kept her away because you're afraid of her. After all these years and all these women, even after Georgina, you're still afraid of her. Because you still want her. Where are you going now? Back to town? Like hell. You're going to Seaview. But how do you know she's still there? Maybe she went off somewhere with Kimball.*

He told himself he just wanted to walk along the beach for a while, just look at the water and get tonight out of his mind. Of course he wasn't going to the party. If nothing else, and it seemed to him there was a great deal else, he was too old for that party, though he could, of course, get a glimpse of it from the beach.

He saw her standing there before she saw him. She had taken off her shoes, and probably her stockings, he thought irrelevantly but he knew there was nothing irrelevant about that thought, and was standing at the water's edge holding her skirt above her ankles. The wind off the water molded her dress to her, blowing it out in billows behind her, and leaning a little forward that way with her face held up to the sky, she looked like the figurehead of a ship. Then she reached up to brush a strand of hair out of her eyes and she didn't look like a figurehead at all. She looked like a woman, and he wanted her very much. He wasn't sure he liked her and he knew he didn't trust her, but he wanted her.

'Amelia.' She turned and must have been startled to see him because she dropped the folds of skirt she'd been holding. 'You'll get your dress wet,' he said and took her hand to pull her back from the water's edge before the next wave broke.

'Thank you,' she said. Her voice was cool and her hand felt colder before she pulled it away.

'What are you doing out here?'

His voice was soft. She wished he'd stop. No, she didn't wish that, but she wished he'd make up his mind. 'Getting away from the kiddies.' She gestured toward the house.

'What about Kimball?' His voice wasn't quite so soft now, but it wasn't the way it had been in the garden of Rosecliff.

'He's gone off with Lizzy. She's going to marry him.'

Sam let out a breath of air that was almost like a long low whistle. 'Does your mother know?'

'I imagine she will before the night's out. They just told Sydney and they were going home to tell her.'

351

They were silent for a moment. 'I wish them luck,' Sam said finally. He did not mean it the way people usually do when they talk about a forthcoming marriage, and they both knew it. 'Do you feel like walking for a while?' he said after another silence.

She looked up at him and there was more confusion in her face than anger. 'I'm sorry,' he said. 'I'm sorry if I was rude in the garden. I've had a lot on my mind tonight.' It wasn't a lie even if it wasn't the truth about what had happened earlier.

'So Houdini said.'

They'd started walking now, slowly as people do along the beach when they have no destination. The marks left in the damp sand by her bare feet looked very small beside the larger prints from his shoes. 'Did you fix everything?'

'Not exactly everything.'

She knew from the way he said it that he hadn't managed to fix things at all. 'Is it very bad?'

'Not very bad. Just not as good as I'd hoped it might be. I was supposed to get something done, and I didn't get it done. If I had, I could have gone on to do anything I wanted. I would have had complete freedom. To say nothing of a whole bunch of airplanes.'

'You mean,' she was remembering his old passion for horses and boats, 'you were going to chuck it all and do what you wanted.'

He laughed. 'Hell, no. I wasn't going to chuck it all. Not now. Or not then, I should say. Not when I'd finally hit the top. I used to think I would. After

352

my father died and I went into Morgan and Company that was the plan. Make a certain amount and then quit. To live as a gentleman.' His voice was self-deprecating now.

'I remember.'

He'd been looking down at the sand as they walked, but now he turned to her. 'Do you?' he said very softly, as if he weren't asking a question at all, and when she didn't answer he went on. 'I thought that then, but I don't anymore. At any rate, it doesn't matter. I wouldn't have chucked it all if I'd won, and I certainly won't now that I've lost.'

They'd come to a private dock that reached out onto the black water like a long white finger pointing away from the island and Sam stopped. 'Would you like a drink?' he asked. 'Or to put it another way, I would. Will you keep me company? Out there.' He nodded toward the end of the dock where a small yacht was tied.

'Is that yours?'

'Only by marriage. It's Endicott's. My sister's husband. That's their place up there.' He pointed to the half-timbered house that sat like an ungainly animal on the crest of the property. It was entirely dark.

It took her a long time to answer, so long that he was sure she was going to say no. 'If there's food as well as whiskey, I'll even make you breakfast. Perfect eggs, if you remember.'

'You never did tell me where you learned to do that.'

'It's not exactly a great trick. Most people know

how unless they have two hundred servants to do it for them. I think that was the number one of the papers quoted in a piece about your castle. Thynnleigh, isn't it?'

'Maybe we'd better forget the drink.'

'Sorry,' he said. He said it quickly but not automatically. He really hadn't meant to start that again. 'No more comments about castles or . . . or anything else. Besides you don't want to let me drink alone. Dangerous habit, you know.'

'You used to pride yourself on having a good many.' She'd begun walking again, and when they reached the boat, he had to tug at the lines to bring it close enough for her to climb aboard. She managed very well considering the long narrow skirt and lack of shoes, but then Amelia had always managed things like that well.

'It's getting cool. Do you want to go below?'

'I'd rather stay here.' She sat in a corner of the cockpit.

'Then take this.' He took off his tailcoat and handed it to her.

'I'm all right,' she said, but he insisted, and she took it and put it over her shoulders. He disappeared down the hatch then and came back in a few minutes with two glasses of brandy. There were eggs as well, but she said she wasn't hungry. He handed her one of the glasses and sat in the opposite corner, his back propped against the bulkhead. She was sitting in the stern end of the cockpit facing him, but not looking at him, sitting very straight, as she'd been taught to, her hands holding the brandy glass in her lap carefully as if it were a small bouquet. His eye followed the long line of leg evident beneath the folds of her dress and there was something ludicrous about her bare feet beneath all that pearl-encrusted lace. No, not ludicrous, but strangely sensual like the statues he'd seen in Egypt of queens sitting erect and stylized and somehow seductive.

'What are you smiling at?'

He hadn't realized he was smiling. 'You. That's quite a costume. Your gown and that diamond collar, and my coat and your bare feet.'

'If the collar bothers you that much, I'll take it off.'

He started to say that it didn't bother him, but in fact it did. It bothered him a great deal.

She reached behind her neck with both hands and unfastened it. It took her a few moments and he thought he heard her murmur something. Finally she got it free and held it in the palm of one hand. It was a small mountain of diamonds and rubies that she seemed to be weighing, as if she didn't know what to do with it.

With a sudden movement of her hand she tossed it to him. Her aim wasn't very good, but with a movement that was quick and sure as a reflex, he reached out and caught it. It probably would have hit the deck beyond his head, but it might have gone into the water.

He held the necklace up between them, and the stones glittered in the moonlight, but she wasn't looking at them. She was smiling at him, a very self-satisfied smile.

'I frightened you, didn't I?'

He shrugged. 'It's your necklace. You can be as reckless with it as you want.' But she could tell he was impressed.

'I wasn't reckless, Sam. I have faith in you. I knew you'd catch it.'

He looked at the stones again. 'That's a lot of faith. About a half million's worth, I'd guess.'

'Two hundred thousand. That was all I got, though you're right. It's probably worth at least twice that. But you're as bad as everyone else in Newport. Tell you something's beautiful . . .'

'I never said it was beautiful.'

'Well then tell you something's valuable, and you believe it. Look again, Sam. Carefully. No one has bothered to all night. It's fake. Glass and paste. The rubies and diamonds are back in England.'

'In the family vault?'

'In a jeweler's vault. I sold it. That's how I know how much it's worth. Or rather how much it's worth when you have to sell quickly. And secretly. So you see,' she went on and her voice sounded more embarrassed than angry now, as if she knew she'd said too much, 'I didn't have so much faith in you after all. I'm sorry.'

'Do you need money, Amelia?' He hadn't thought about saying that. It had come out almost as another reflex.

'As a matter of fact I do. Five million to be exact.'

If the sum startled him, he didn't show it. He merely looked down into his glass for what seemed like a long time, then took a swallow.

'I was only joking, Sam. I wasn't asking you for five million.'

'I don't have five million,' he said, and his voice sounded strange.

'Pity,' she said and took a long swallow of her brandy. There was something in the gesture more reckless than tossing her necklace. 'My husband won't settle for a penny less. Twelve million to marry but only five million to divorce. I'm sure there's some logic there, but I'd rather not think about it.'

'You sound bitter.'

'Realistic,' she said.

'No, bitter.' But who wouldn't be, he thought, as he had about himself when Nina had called him cynical. 'What about your father?'

'Throwing good money after bad. I think that's the way he'd put it. Look, Sam, if you don't mind I'd rather not talk about it. I know I brought it up, but I wouldn't have if you hadn't started in on the choker and two hundred servants and all the rest.' She drained the glass and smiled at him, but it was no longer a self-satisfied smile. 'As a matter of fact, there were only a hundred and eighty-three.' She held the empty glass out to him.

He went below, and when he came back she was sitting with her back against the other bulkhead. Her legs were drawn up on the seat and she was hugging her knees to her chest. She took the glass from him without looking at him. Her face was turned up to the stars and he could see her features clearly in the moonlight. Her skin looked smooth and white. In the bright lights of Rosecliff he'd thought of the skin as cold, like marble, but now it looked warm again as it had at dinner, warm as if lighted from within. He wanted to touch her, to see if it were warm, but suddenly she looked up at him standing above her. 'Still, it was kind of you. To ask if I needed money, I mean.'

He sat against the other bulkhead again. 'Kind but futile.'

She didn't answer and they sat in silence for some time. The only sound was the noise of the water slapping against the hull and a sort of quiet groaning as the lines that held the boat to the dock stretched and tightened. A few wisps of cloud floated over the stars that would begin to fade soon, but the clouds were not thick enough to darken the moon.

'You have my cigarettes,' he said.

'What?'

'In the breast pocket of my coat.'

She reached into the pocket — there was something strangely intimate about doing that — took the gold case, and handed it to him. Out of the corner of her eye she watched as he took a cigarette, then a lighter from his trouser pocket. He cupped one hand over the flame to shield it from the wind. The long, slender fingers were exactly as she remembered them. He leaned back against the bulkhead again and the smoke made a small ascending cloud as he exhaled. They were silent again for what seemed like a long while. Finally she saw an ember describe an arc through the air as he tossed the cigarette into the water.

'Amelia,' he said and his voice sounded strange in the darkness, 'those stories . . .' He let the words drift off.

'Which stories?'

'Those stories about your mother locking you in your room and all that. Were they true?' Not that I'll believe the answer, he added to himself, but he knew he would believe her.

She took another sip of her drink, and thought of Charles. 'I don't think I ought to answer that. Now that I'm not getting a divorce. Indelicate,' she added and laughed. It was a terrible rasping sound.

'The hell with delicacy.'

His voice startled her, and she turned her head until she was facing him. 'Yes, Sam, the stories were true. And yes, I wrote you, but Mother stopped the letter. Just as she stopped yours. At least that's what Harry Lehr told me tonight. And yes she gave the orders that I was seeing no one. Yes to all of it.'

He was watching her closely as she spoke. The moon was behind him and she couldn't see the expression on his face but the outline of his jaw was silhouetted against the night. It looked tense and angry, and she wanted to reach out to stroke his face, to soften the expression. Instead she looked out to sea again. 'According to Harry we were both terribly naive not to know as much.' But we aren't naive anymore, she added to herself. She was remembering Michael, but she wasn't thinking of Michael. She was thinking of Sam, how his face had looked in shadows a moment ago. He reached out to put the glass down on the deck and out of the corner of her eye she saw the way his shirt pulled against his shoulder. She imagined what it would be like to touch him, to feel the strength of that shoulder and the smoothness of the skin beneath the shirt. She imagined it all and felt a current of heat run through her though the breeze was still cool.

It was funny the way girls were brought up, she thought. They told you to be wary of men. They told you what to do about men's wanting you, but they never told you what to do about wanting them. They never told you what to do when you felt your muscles tense and your stomach contract with wanting them.

'I heard the stories about your mother forcing you to marry him,' he said, 'but I didn't believe them. Probably because I wanted to believe them so much. I'm sorry.'

'We both are.' She struggled to make her voice sound impersonal because she wasn't going to make the same mistake she had in the garden. 'But it was all a long time ago. And things worked out for you. At least for a while,' she added because she didn't want to sound cruel, but she hated his wife or at least the idea of his wife.

He didn't say anything to that but turned so he was facing her and leaned over the space that separated them. His hand was gentle at the back of her neck, drawing her to him, and then his mouth was soft and almost tentative against her own. She reached up and touched his face. His skin was warm. She felt his mouth growing more urgent on hers as if it too had a memory and then his hands were in her hair. She felt him taking the pins out and her hair falling around her shoulders and his fingers tangled in it. His tongue was sharp with the taste of brandy and she supposed her own was too. She'd been wrong to think she could imagine it, any of it, because the reality was more overpowering than wish or memory, and her mouth found his again and again, forced it back to hers when he kissed her eyes or her neck, because she wanted to taste him. Her hands moved from his face to his shoulders and she could feel the strength of him and the desire too because she could feel the muscles tense at her touch.

He lifted his face from hers and she was close enough, even in this faint moonlight, to see his eyes. They were like velvet. 'Come below.' His voice sounded strange and almost hoarse.

She let him lead her below, through the main saloon to the captain's cabin. It was dark and he stopped to light a small kerosene lamp in a corner. He had to strike the match twice before it flared, and his face in the flame of the lamp looked tense again but no longer angry. When he turned back to her, he saw she was watching him. He took a step toward her and put his arms around her. 'I want to be able to see you. I've made love to you thousands of times in my mind, but never in real life, and I want to see you.'

It was strange how slowly it all happened. They should have been impatient after all these years, but they were both moving slowly, deliberately, as if they'd waited too long to rush now.

She began to undress, and he began to help her, still not rushing, stopping to kiss her shoulder, to caress her breast. And his hands would move back to her hair again, tangling themselves in its thickness, and move to her neck where it had been rubbed raw by the choker. He kissed her neck and touched it gently as if his mouth and his hands could make the irritation disappear. And finally when she was almost naked she began at his clothing. Her hands fumbled at the studs of his evening shirt. She was shocked and then delighted that he wore nothing beneath it.

'You're no gentleman,' she said, her lips against the warm flesh of his chest.

'That's right,' he said, and he laughed a little, but neither the voice nor the laugh sounded natural. Her clothes lay in a heap at their feet now and she was entirely naked and his hands were moving slowly over her body as she worked at the suspenders and trousers, and all the time she kept moving against him, turning her body back and forth to his touch. Then they were both naked, clinging to each other in the center of the small cabin, and she dropped her head back and looked up at him because she wanted to see him just as he wanted to see her, to make what she had imagined so often real. Her hand moved to his face again, tracing the contour of his cheek, the soft hollow that was so beautiful, and the line of his mouth. Her hand moved over his face as if she were memorizing something.

He reached up and held her fingers against his mouth. 'I love you, Amelia.'

'You don't have to.' Her eyes held his as if she wanted to make sure he knew what she meant. She wanted him whether he loved her or not.

'But I do,' he said, and his mouth found hers again.

The bunk was narrow and made for sleep rather than love, but neither of them noticed. His hands were moving again and his mouth followed. She felt the soft lips and behind them the hard teeth teasing at her breast, and cried out not in pain but in the pleasure he gave her. She watched him moving and saw in the flickering light of the lamp the network of tendon and muscle beneath the smooth skin, and her hands traced the lines of his body, just as his did hers, trailing from her breasts down the long curve of waist and hip and thigh, and his mouth followed as if he had to taste as well as touch her. His tongue was like a flame flickering at her skin, kindling a hundred small fires that were mounting steadily until she was sure she'd be consumed by them. She touched him and felt the strength of his passion, fired by hers, firing hers. Her mouth moved down his body, across the strong chest and hard belly, hungry for him, desperate for him. He murmured something, she couldn't tell if it were her name or merely a moan of pleasure, she wasn't aware of the words or what they meant, only of his hands and mouth, still caressing, still tasting, but more urgent now, and his lips found hers again. 'Sam,' she murmured, and 'please,' and 'Sam' again, though her own words made no more sense to her than his, and as he entered her she felt a surge of pleasure that made her cry out again.

He was above her now and his skin looked damp and smooth in the wavering light from the lamp and she could not help touching him, clinging to him, moving against him. The desire had become something beyond her now, or him, an overwhelming force driving them further and further, beyond thought or reason, love or passion into a dark realm of pure pleasure, and she felt herself racing along with him, one with him, racing faster and faster into that midnight black world that suddenly, shockingly exploded in ecstasy, and then echoed and reechoed through her body, like the reverberations of a bell that had been rung deep within her.

Slowly she felt herself coming back, felt the waves of warmth washing over her body, soothing now, calming after the white-hot excitement, and she could feel the weight of his body on hers, relaxed now too, and hear his uneven breathing mingled with her own just as their bodies still were.

He lifted his head and looked at her. 'My God,' he whispered. He sounded almost surprised, and she was glad he did.

She pushed the hair back from his forehead. It was damp with perspiration.

He shifted his weight so he was lying on his side next to her with his head propped up on one arm and the other still across her body as if he were afraid of letting her go. 'My God,' he said again and this time he sounded euphoric and very young. His hand moved to her face. Her cheeks were flushed and her skin felt very warm. 'Aren't you going to say anything?'

'I love you,' she said and realized it was true. He didn't have to love her, she'd said, but she couldn't help loving him.

'I know. I didn't for a long time, but I do now.'

They lay like that for a while, their bodies still molded together, his head beside hers so that his mouth touched her cheek. Finally he sat up and rummaged through the pile of clothing on the cabin floor for his cigarette case. 'Are you hungry?' he asked. She shook her head. 'Another drink?' She shook her head again. 'Cold?'

'I am now that you're gone.'

He came back to the bunk with a blanket and spread it over both of them. He was on his back now looking up at her propped against the side of the bunk and stroking her hair. 'I keep thinking . . . I know it's stupid. There isn't any point in regretting the past, but I keep thinking of all those wasted years.'

As soon as he said it, she realized she'd been thinking of something for the last few minutes, something she knew it was foolish to think of now, but that she couldn't help thinking of now. 'They weren't entirely wasted. People say you were very happy. Your marriage was, I mean.'

'I think I will get another drink after all.' He got up and walked aft to the galley.

'I'm sorry,' she said when he returned with two glasses. 'I shouldn't have mentioned that now.'

He lay down beside her again. He didn't look

angry, but he no longer looked happy either. 'Don't believe everything people say, Amelia. My marriage was a joke. A very bad joke on me. If she hadn't been killed in that accident, we would have divorced.'

'I'm sorry,' she said, but she didn't feel sorry, and she was a little ashamed of herself.

'Do you want to hear about it?' He was surprised at himself. He'd never talked about it to anyone.

'If you want to talk about it.'

'There isn't much to talk about. An old story and a pretty trite one. There was another man.'

'She must have been mad.'

He'd been staring at the cabin roof and now he turned to her and his hand moved to her hair again. 'That's one of the reasons I love you. But only one, you understand. Anyway, that's the story of my marriage. Or at least what it boils down to. Another man.'

'We have a lot in common.'

His hand had moved from her hair to her shoulder. 'I can only repeat what you said. He must have been crazy. Anyone who would prefer another woman to you would have to be crazy.'

'Not another woman, another man. Or rather a man.'

His hand had stopped moving on her shoulder, and he looked surprised again, but it was not a nice kind of surprise. 'Bastard,' he murmured under his breath. 'I'm sorry.'

'For the word or the fact.'

'How can you joke about it?'

'I don't know. I never have before. I've never

366

told anyone before. I think I was too ashamed. As if it were my fault.'

'It's not.'

'I know now. I guess that's why I could tell you. All these years I've been thinking there was some flaw in me. Even after . . . even after Tony was born I kept thinking that, but I don't anymore.'

He was silent for a moment, thinking of what she'd said and of something else. He could guess what she'd been about to say, and he didn't think it had anything to do with her son. It had to do with someone else. He didn't want to ask her about that now because he didn't want to think about that now, but he knew someday he would ask her. And he knew he'd mind. He had no right to, but he knew he would.

'Well, all that's behind you now,' he said and his hand was stroking her hair again.

The problem had disappeared for a few hours, but it was back now. 'I only wish that were true. Something may have happened to us, Sam, but not to the rest of the world. He still wants five million to divorce me, and I still don't have five million.'

'We can get it.'

'I've been trying to for months now. That's why I sold the choker. When he found out about that he took the two hundred thousand. 'On deposit,' he said, 'toward the five million.' That's why I went to my father. But none of it's any good. I can't get that much, and he won't take any less. In fact, I don't even know if he'll take that anymore. He fought the idea of a divorce for years. Nothing to do with me, only appearances, and he agreed to it only last spring, but now Mother has written to him . . .'

'Your mother is, as usual, inordinately helpful.'

'. . . and she says he's coming over. In a few weeks.'

'You won't be here.'

'Where will I be?'

'Anywhere. Some place where he can't find you.'

'That's what I'd planned originally.' She told him about Wickert. 'But Mother found out about it, thanks to Lehr and Mr Houdini, and she'll see to it that Tiffany doesn't buy anything. By now she's probably locked up everything that I'm not wearing.'

'I have enough money for that. I may not be able to put my hands on five million, but I have enough money to take you away.'

She bent and kissed him. 'I can see the headlines now. ''DUCHESS AND BANKER FOUND IN LOVE NEST.'' '

'Do you care?'

'For me, not at all.' She kissed him again. 'Especially after tonight. But I have a son. I don't suppose I'm a very good mother. I don't suppose he even cares for me very much. But I still love him. And I don't think I could do that to him. I don't expect you to understand that, but it's true.'

But he could understand it, even if he didn't want to.

'Then I'll send you away alone.'

She smiled. 'After tonight, how long do you think we'd stay away from each other? How long do you think I could stay away from you? That's the point, Sam. If I stay married to Charles, if I go back to England' – she saw the look on his face – 'not immediately, but eventually, and keep up appearances, Charles won't care what I do. I'll be able to see you as often as we can manage it, and he won't say a word. But if I run off, if I embarrass him in front of his friends and disgrace him in front of the king, he'll drag me through the mud, and you, and even his own son. Maybe what I'm suggesting isn't very honorable, but I'm old enough to know that I can't have everything, and I want you, Sam, and some shred of affection or respect or whatever you call it from my son more than I want an easy conscience.'

'I can't share you,' he said, and she felt the arm that was holding her to him tighten.

'You won't have to. If I go back, Charles will leave me alone. I'm sure of that.'

He started to say something, but she bent her head to his until her mouth was on his again. 'It's the only way, Sam,' she murmured. 'Please.'

His arms were still holding her to him tensely, but as her mouth moved on his, she felt them relax, and his hands began the familiar journey again, slowly again, as if he would never tire of touching her, as if they had all the time in the world.

'Don't forget your jewels.' Sam held the choker out to her and laughed at what had finally become a joke, but he no longer felt like laughing. They were standing on opposite sides of the cabin. It was a small cabin, and they couldn't have been more than a few feet from each other, but it felt like more than that. She'd dressed and put up her hair again and even in bare feet she looked proper and distant from him. It never occurred to him that he looked exactly the same to her. She took the necklace from him, but didn't put it on.

He climbed into the cockpit first and helped her up. There was a faint line of white over the island. Soon the white would take on a reddish cast and false dawn would turn real. And everything else with it, Sam supposed. As they started down the dock he saw her shiver and put his coat around her shoulders again.

'Thank you,' Amelia said. It was cool, cooler than it had been before they'd gone below, but she hadn't shivered from the chill. It was one thing to lie there beside him in the half-darkened privacy of someone's boat and talk about how they'd work things out. It had all seemed so simple and sensible and possible then, but now on her way back to Belle Isle and eventually Charles it no longer looked simple or sensible or even possible. How much time could she spend in America? How often could he get abroad? And would Charles really be as accommodating as she'd told Sam? He wouldn't have minded handing her over to the king: That was practically his patriotic duty. He wouldn't have minded his brother or one of his own set, but an outsider? Someone who might give her happiness? Ten years had taught her a great deal about Charles' noble nature. It was never enough for him to have something. Others had to be lacking that same thing. The arrangement reinforced his sense of superiority, though Amelia had often found it strange that it needed reinforcing.

They were retracing their steps along the beach. The incoming tide had covered their footprints, but her evening slippers and the brandy glass lay on the sand where she'd left them. Sam bent and picked up her shoes. When he straightened to hand them to her and looked into her eyes, he saw there were no green lights going off.

'It will be all right,' he said, though he didn't see how it could be, with an ocean between them and a husband beside her. He wasn't young enough to think that love conquered all, or even counted for all. Not when it was up against thirty-five hundred miles.

IX

Sky had told her to watch for the light in the guesthouse, and Vanessa had sat in her room staring out the window at the dark little cottage and listening to the clock on the end table. She'd never realized how loudly it ticked. Finally she'd seen a light and run from the house, quietly, of course, because she didn't want to wake Lydia or Kirkland Selby. When she'd reached the guest-house she'd realized the light was the night watch-man's lantern. Vanessa hated that watchman. He'd taken Sky's money and kept his mouth shut, at least to Lydia, but his eyes were something else. Whenever she arrived home late with Lydia and he opened the gate for them, he let his eyes linger on her, not long enough for Lydia to notice, but longer than anyone in his position should. Once when she'd been alone in the garden early one morning, he'd come up to her with a lace handkerchief. 'I found this in the guesthouse, miss. It wouldn't be yours, would it?' As a matter of fact it was hers but he had found it in the tulip beds rather than the guesthouse. Vanessa had seen him pick it up, but she was not going to argue with him. She told him it was not hers.

'Are you sure, miss?' He raised the handkerchief to his nose and sniffed, but his eyes never left hers. 'It has such a nice scent, I was sure it was yours and not the madam's.'

She told him again that it was not hers. He heard the shrillness in her voice and smiled. He was a young man, probably a few years younger than she was, and his teeth were large and even. 'In that case, miss, I'll just hold on to it until I find who it does belong to.' And then, still smiling down at her as she sat there in the garden chair, he'd undone one button of his shirt and slipped the handkerchief inside it.

She closed the door to the guest cottage behind her, but did not turn on the light. There'd be no more snickering servants or knowing looks from men and icy ones from women now. As Mrs Schuyler Niebold, even the second Mrs Schuyler Niebold, she'd be beyond that. For years now she'd been telling herself she didn't care about the title or the respectability or the sneers that came with the lack of them. She didn't care about anything but Sam, and that was true. She'd go on this way as long as he wanted to. She would also have run away with him years ago leaving the name and the money to Caroline, but then she was accustomed to being poor, and Sky had the rich man's fear of poverty. In the beginning he'd never talked of divorce from Caroline and marriage to her, then when he'd begun to speak of it, there'd been the single condition that had seemed foolish to her and crucial to him. He had to leave all the Schuyler and Niebold money to Carrie in trust for the children, despite the fact that there was more than enough Leighton money for all three of them. Vanessa hadn't argued with him. She supposed that was the only honor she had left, that and never letting Sky keep her. She'd known what she was walking into the night they'd gone to her cabin on the old side-wheeler that made the night run from Bar Harbor to Boston.

She wished there were a clock in the guesthouse. She felt as if she'd been waiting for hours, but there was no way of telling. Her judgment at times like this, she knew, was not to be trusted.

How strange it would be to be finished with all the waiting. She would be if what Sky had said tonight were true, and it must be because Sky was scrupulous about that sort of thing. He'd never made a promise he hadn't kept. She didn't suppose it was much of a code of honor, any more than hers was about not accepting his money or trying to get him to leave Caroline, but it was their honor, and they'd both stuck to it. If Sky had said he was going to divorce Caroline and marry her, he would do it. She was sure of that.

Caroline sat at the dressing table brushing her hair. She had not closed the door to the small sitting room between her bedroom and Sky's and could hear him opening and closing armoires and drawers. The middle of the night was a foolish time to leave, she'd pointed out, but he'd refused to wait until morning. 'I'll have the rest of my things sent for later,' he'd said. 'But I'm getting out now.' She'd seen something in his face then, something she'd been too miserable to notice before. Sky was afraid, afraid of her and the fact that she might keep him here.

She put down her brush and walked to the closet. They all thought she was stupid. Mama, Sky, Amelia, even Lizzy. You're such a great beauty, they always told her. But so dumb, they all seemed to be thinking. But she wasn't dumb, not when it came to Sky. She took off the Chinese robe, removed the corset and underclothes she'd been wearing beneath, and put the robe on again. It would be distasteful, she thought, but it was necessary.

She crossed the sitting room and stopped in the door to Sky's bedroom. He was sitting at his desk writing and did not look up. 'You're making a mistake, Sky. You know that.' Her voice was very soft, not pleading exactly, but coaxing, and when he heard the change from the threats and whines that were still running through his head, he looked up sharply.

'I don't think so.' He folded the paper he'd been writing on and put it in an envelope. There was another just like it on the desk. 'I'm leaving these for the children. I wanted to explain things to them in my own way.'

She moved to the side of his chair and put a hand on his shoulder. It tensed under her touch. 'You could do that tomorrow morning. At least stay the night Sky. You know you'll be sorry if you don't see the children before you leave.'

He shook off her hand and stood. 'I'll see them

after things are settled.' He took the silver-backed brush from his dresser and tossed it into the small Gladstone. When he looked back at her he saw that she was smiling. It was a smile he'd never seen before.

'Do you know what I think, Sky?'

'To be perfectly truthful, Carrie, I don't care what you think.'

'I think you're in such a hurry to leave because you're scared. You're afraid that if you don't leave now, you never will. And you won't, Sky. You know that. There's too much holding you here.'

He'd changed from his evening clothes to the trousers of a suit and a shirt, but the jacket still lay on the bed and he had not put his collar on yet. He took a fresh one from a drawer and began fastening it.

'Here,' she said, 'let me help you.'

He pushed her hands away. 'It won't work, Carrie.'

'He looked very foolish with his collar fastened on one side, standing out on the other, and his face unnaturally flushed beneath the deep tan, but this wasn't the time to tell him so. 'You are afraid, aren't you, Sky?' He had begun working at his collar again and she took one of his hands in both of hers and held it against her. He neither spoke nor moved, but she saw his moustache move imperceptibly as if he were clenching his teeth. Slowly with one hand she untied her robe and slid his hand beneath the silk. His fingers felt hot against her skin.

He pulled his hand away as if he were the one

who was afraid of being burned, but didn't move. He was staring down at her, his face still red and his breath coming in short rasps. Then suddenly the expression changed and he began to laugh. It was a strange laugh, loud and uncontrolled. He took a few steps backward and sat on the edge of the bed. 'When I think of all the times I've wanted you to do that, all the times I've dreamed of your doing that. If only I'd known. If only I'd known that all I had to do was threaten to leave.' He stopped laughing as suddenly as he'd started. 'Only it isn't just a threat, Carrie. I'm going. You were right about one thing. I was afraid of you. Until now. When I married you I thought you were the most beautiful woman I'd ever seen or ever would see, and the amazing thing I discovered when we were married was that the beauty was real. I could live with you day in and day out, sleep beside you and wake up beside you and never see your face in an unflattering light or catch you in an awkward pose. God, you were beautiful. Like a statue. That was something else I learned. The beauty was real, but not the woman. It wasn't just sex, Carrie, though I admit that was a big part of it. I never saw the reflection of a genuine emotion on that lovely face of yours. You whimpered when you didn't get your way, and you giggled when someone complimented you, but you never cried or laughed, never thrilled to a painting, or a sunset . . . or me.' He crossed to the Gladstone and began strapping it up. 'As I said, I learned all that about you pretty quickly, and I learned to live with it. But I just learned something else, something that would make me leave if I hadn't already planned to. You have the mind – I won't say heart because I doubt one exists beneath that soft white breast – of a lady of the evening, as they're politely called. A prostitute. To put it as bluntly as possible, my dear, a whore. You've never once given your body out of pleasure or even kindness – I won't mention desire – but tonight, after twelve years, you were willing to sell it.' He had shrugged into his jacket and now he picked up the Gladstone in one hand and a straw hat in the other. 'I'm sorry, Carrie, but I'm not buying.'

The last thing he saw as he closed the door was his wife standing there in the middle of the room, her kimono half open and her face a shocked ghostly white.

'Can I offer you a brandy?' Edith asked when Tom Sturgis' chauffeur had pulled the automobile up under the portico of Belle Isle.

'I was hoping you'd ask, Edith.'

Edith led him into the library. It was the room at Belle Isle men seemed to like most, at least men other than Harry Lehr. The dark wood paneling and rows of oiled bindings made them think of their own clubs, she supposed, and the furniture was a mixture of Renaissance and Jacobean. The fabrics were rough and the colors muted, and there wasn't a piece of French satin or gilt in sight. Thanks to tonight's dinner there was even a lingering aroma of cigar smoke. It was exactly the kind of room Tom Sturgis would feel comfortable in and Edith wanted Tom Sturgis to feel comfortable. Unlike James Corcoran, she did not hesitate to ring for a servant.

It took some time for the footman to return with the brandy for him and crème de menthe for her, but Edith was very good at small talk. They inquired about each other's health. She asked about his kennels and the model farm he'd built on Long Island. He asked about her charities and her children. 'You should have had a family of your own, Tom,' she said when the footman had left them alone again.

'Ah, Edith, you know the answer to that.' It was the reply she'd expected, but it was said in a more perfunctory manner than expected. He was standing at the Renaissance library table behind the sofa where she was sitting, and when she turned to look at him she found that he was examining a Cellini bronze. She hoped this wasn't going to be more difficult than she'd expected.

'You know, Tom, I've never told you this. I've hardly dared to admit it to myself.' Her voice was soft and as halting as a girl's. When he put the bronze down and looked at her, she turned away from him again. 'It isn't something a woman my age, in my position ought to allow herself to think, but sometimes . . . well, sometimes I've thought we made a mistake.'

She'd kept her head turned away as she'd spoken, but out of the corner of her eye, she saw him move and felt his weight beside her on the sofa. She'd been silly to worry. This was going to be as easy as she'd thought.

'Why, Edith . . .' He sounded as young as she'd

been trying to, but the hand that closed around hers did not feel young. It was dry and chafed.

'Not that we can change anything, of course. But it gives me happiness' – she turned to him now. He'd had her profile, the best side though both were good, but the full face with the warm smile would be better – 'just to think sometimes what might have been.'

'I think about it constantly.' It was only a small lie. He used to think about it constantly, and he still thought about it when he saw her.

'Do you remember the first time we met? It was at the opera. I was staying with my cousins, the Benjamin Kimberlys, and you came into their box. It was the first time I ever saw you.'

'It wasn't the first time I saw you. That was why I asked Ezra Kimberly to take me over.'

'Was it Ezra who brought you? I don't remember. I didn't notice anyone but you. Do you know, Tom, I still have the program. They sang *Norma*.'

'You may not remember Ezra, but I don't remember the music. All I could think of was the Kimberlys' beautiful cousin from Bethlehem, Pennsylvania.' It always pleased him to remember Edith as a simple girl from a small town in Pennsylvania, and he didn't even notice the slight change of expression that indicated that it didn't please her as well.

Edith put the small glass of crème de menthe she was holding in her free hand down on the library table behind them. She had to be careful about this particular memory. She had to remind him of the early part of the evening without bringing back its conclusion. 'Do you remember the dance my cousins gave that spring? There was that small music room tucked away in back of the house.'

Tom Sturgis was not the sort of man who could be described as wistful, but he looked wistful at that moment. 'I wouldn't be likely to forget it, Edith.'

It had been pleasant to let Tom Sturgis kiss her in that quiet room. He'd been so pathetically grateful, and she'd been very conscious of her power. She hadn't even minded the fact that he was an inch shorter than she. Edith had a theory about short men, and it had a great deal to do with her admiration for Napoleon. In fact, when she thought about it, though she rarely did, she had to admit that she'd enjoyed letting Tom kiss her more than she'd enjoyed letting Elias Leighton, but Tom was an obscure young man working for a salary at a New York branch of a European banking house, and Elias Leighton was the only son of a man who'd made a fortune in coal and steel and several other of those mysterious materials men made fortunes in. She'd let Tom kiss her that night, but she'd let Elias Leighton propose to her.

'You said something to me that night, Tom.'

He imagined he had, and he'd said a good deal about Leighton afterward, but he didn't want to remember most of it now.

'You said,' Edith went on, 'that if I ever needed you, if you could ever do anything to help me, I should feel free to ask you. I never have, Tom. But

I am now. I'm in trouble, and you're the only one who can help.'

Sturgis couldn't imagine what he could do that Elias Leighton couldn't, but he was eager to find out. 'What about Elias?'

'Elias is useless.' She moved the hand that still lay in his. 'He doesn't understand women. He doesn't understand me, Tom.'

'You know I'll do whatever I can, Edith.'

'It's about Schuyler. He wants to leave Caroline.'

'So I've heard.'

'We can't let him do it. Think of poor Caroline. Think of the babies.'

'I'll talk to him if you like, but I don't think it will do any good.'

'I wish you would, Tom. And one other thing. Apparently Schuyler feels he can leave his family, afford to leave his family, because of something to do with you. He told Caroline you're going to help him make a great deal of money.'

'I let him in on something.'

Her long slender fingers wound more tightly around his shorter ones. 'You must stop it, Tom. Whatever it is, I beg you to stop it.' He let go of her hand and took the brandy glass from the table behind them. 'It's only more money to you, Tom, and everyone knows that's one thing you don't need.'

He laughed. 'No one can have too much money, Edith.'

'You can if it's at the expense of my daughter's happiness. My happiness. Think of it. You can go

383

through with this thing, whatever it is — I wouldn't dream of asking you to tell me — or you can give me the nicest present anyone could possibly give me.' Edith could tell from his face that he was thinking, thinking very hard, and it didn't do to give him too much time to think. 'Anyone can give jewels or yachts or houses. Why just look at all Elias has given me. But he's never given me happiness. Only you can do that. Please say you will.'

Her eyes, she knew, were brimming, but Sturgis was not looking at her eyes. He was looking into his glass and he seemed to go on looking into it for an interminable length of time. Edith was very displeased. A real gentleman would not have hesitated for a moment. Sturgis was clearly not a real gentleman, but Sturgis was all she had. She watched as he put his glass down on the library table again and stood. He walked the length of the room and back, but he was still not looking at her. His hands were in his pockets and his head was pulled down into his shoulders so that his neck had disappeared entirely. Edith had never placed much importance on men's appearances, but suddenly it seemed impossible that she should be begging favors from a toad. He paced the room a second time, and she was furious. Every instinct was telling her to dismiss him. 'If it's that much trouble . . .' she wanted to say. 'If I mean so little to you . . . if money means so much . . .' She knew all the withering statements and exactly how she'd look when she said them. She pictured Sturgis, creeping toadlike out the door. He stopped at the table behind the sofa again and picked up the Cellini again. Good Lord, the man didn't have a shred of sensitivity. She opened her mouth, about to tell him to take the bronze if he found it so fascinating and get out of her house, but he put the statue down suddenly and looked directly into her eyes. Then he smiled. 'Of course, Edith. Of course, I'll take care of this business with Schuyler for you.'

She was relieved and grateful, and to show him as much, she poured him another brandy with her own hands, but as she did, Edith couldn't help wondering how much of his deliberation had been real and how much had been for his own pleasure – and her discomfort.

Schuyler was not in his room or Caroline's as Edith had expected. She found him, instead, in his daughter's room. He was standing beside the bed staring down at her. She noticed the day suit, hat, and Gladstone immediately.

'An extraordinary costume for four-thirty in the morning,' she said when they were out in the hall.

'Carrie will tell you everything.'

'Carrie has already told me more than I want to hear. And I can guess the rest, Schuyler. You can't go through with it, of course.'

'I don't want to discuss it, Belle . . .' He stopped abruptly.

'You always did have beautiful manners, Schuyler. I have no intention of discussing anything with you, but Tom Sturgis is in the library. He wants to speak to you.'

'At this hour?'

'If you can dress for traveling at this hour, I see no reason why Tom can't discuss business at this hour. You were involved in some business undertakings with him, weren't you?'

Sky was no longer listening. He'd taken the stairs two at a time and had already reached the first landing.

Sturgis and Sky were in the library for fewer than ten minutes. There was little enough to say. Sturgis did not mention personal motives, his own or Sky's. He knew very well that Edith hadn't really wanted him to talk to Sky, only to take care of the financial end of things. He simply said there'd been a change in plans, and rapidly ticked off the same arguments Sam Van Nest had presented several hours earlier.

Sky did not argue. He knew there was no point in arguing with Tom Sturgis about this. The first time Sturgis had approached him, he'd realized that despite the Niebold name, he was a very small duchy in the financial empire Walsh was building, and as such he had no vote. He could go along with the others, but he could not set policy.

He was still listening to Sturgis' explanation but his mind was racing ahead. There must be another way, but he knew there was not. What was left of the Niebold money, and it was a good deal by most people's standards if not by Jason Walsh's, was earmarked for his children. Times were changing and they might be able to live with the stigma of their parents' divorce, but times would never change so much that they could live with the stigma of no money.

There was another side to it too. He couldn't go off with Vanessa without money. He knew what it would be like. They'd travel around Europe staying in second-class hotels and seedy pensions. He'd seen men try it, and it never worked. The women grew shabbier, the men more resentful, and both ended up forgetting whatever it was they'd run away for in the first place.

'I'm sorry if this inconveniences you,' Sturgis was saying. He sounded sincere, but Sky noticed that the old man's eyes did not meet his as he spoke.

When Edith heard the front door close she returned to the library to say good night to Sturgis. As she crossed the entrance hall she saw Sky's Gladstone on the long marble table beneath the huge gilt-framed mirror. The bag looked small and inconsequential against the overpowering dimensions of the room.

Cutting across Lydia's property to the guesthouse, Sky passed the night watchman. 'Evening, sir,' he said, but Sky did not even hear him.

He was wondering how to explain things, but he didn't have to explain any of it. He should have known he wouldn't have to. Vanessa knew as soon as she saw his face.

'It's better for the children this way,' she said immediately. 'And Edith Wharton would be proud of me.'

'What does Mrs Wharton have to do with it?'

'Nothing, darling. It's a joke, a private joke.' But he noticed that she turned her face away as she said it, and her voice didn't sound as if she believed it were funny. For a while after that night her voice didn't sound as if she believed anything.

'I've burned all my bridges,' Elizabeth said to Douglas when they left Seaview. He gave her a sideways look. 'Not quite all. Do you want me to go with you?'

'I want you to come back very soon. Or as Amelia says, keep the engine running. But I want to tell Mama on my own. Show you the stuff this blank canvas is made of.' That and one other thing, Elizabeth thought. She knew her mother was going to say some very nasty things, and she didn't want Douglas to hear them. 'Anyway, if we want to make the early boat to New York, you'll have to get your things.' She stopped for a moment, then went on. 'You'll have to buy me everything, you know. I'll take a few things now, but I won't be able to send for anything. Mama will be far too angry for that. I won't have a trousseau. Will you mind?'

'Terribly,' he said and kissed her. She didn't think people did that, kissed each other right out in front of someone's house, but she was glad Douglas had.

Edith said a great many nasty things, some of them even nastier than Elizabeth had expected. Douglas had left her at the gate, because she'd seen all the lights and told him it would be better if he didn't see her in. He swore he'd be back in less than an hour.

She found her mother in the front hall saying good night to Mr Sturgis. 'You're home early, Elizabeth,' Sturgis said. 'I thought young people didn't stop dancing until dawn.'

'Where's Sydney?' Edith asked.

'Sydney didn't bring me home.'

It was just as Edith had thought. A fool, a renegade, and now a camp follower.

'Wait for me in the music room, Elizabeth.' Edith turned to Sturgis, and her voice softened. 'I want to say good night to Mr Sturgis.'

Butter, Lizzy thought irreverently, would not melt in her mouth.

Edith was not long getting back to her daughter or around to the various nasty things Elizabeth had anticipated, although it took her longer than might be expected because it took her some minutes to rid herself of the idea that Lizzy was infatuated with Lieutenant Atherton. When she finally realized Kimball was the culprit, she looked stunned, and for a moment another expression moved across her face, but Lizzy couldn't quite read it.

'He's after your money, of course. He'll change his mind when he sees that you're cut off without a penny.'

'I don't think so, Mama. Both of us realize I'm going to be cut off. Besides, Douglas has plenty of money.'

'You have no idea what plenty of money is,

Elizabeth,' but Edith must have known she was on the wrong track. There was no doubt that Kimball was after Elizabeth, rather than her money, and Edith wasn't sure how to combat that.

'It's disgusting. An old man like that running after a young girl. Degenerate.'

'When Alison Howley married the baron you didn't think it was disgusting or degenerate. He was years older than Douglas and had yellow teeth that smelled just awful.'

'He was a widower with a very old title. A nobleman who wanted companionship in his declining years.'

'What he wanted was young girls. As many as he could get. He tried to touch me once. In an archery contest at the Howley's. He pretended it was my bow, but he knew it was me.'

'Elizabeth!'

'It's true, Mama. And I wasn't the only one. All the girls knew about him. He was nothing but an old lecher.'

'And what do you think Kimball is?'

Elizabeth told herself to be very calm. Her mother was always at an advantage when someone else made a scene. 'What do you think he is, Mama? It seems to me this morning at Bailey's you couldn't have been more cordial. I had the feeling you were planning on annexing him. Like Harry.'

Elizabeth always saw more than anyone thought she did. 'That will be enough, Elizabeth. This morning I was under the misapprehension that Mr Kimball was a gentleman as well as an artist. He'll no longer be welcome here, of course.'

'Then neither will I.'

Edith put a hand on Elizabeth's shoulder and pushed her gently but firmly into a chair. While they'd both been standing, Edith had had to look up to her daughter. Now the perspective was corrected.

'I can tell from the way you speak, Elizabeth, that this has been a great lark for you. I don't approve of your lark and I'll see to it that Mr Kimball is no longer invited where you are, but I will not punish you for it. And I'm sure we can keep Sydney from finding out about it.'

'I've already told Sydney.'

Lizzy watched her mother's face. At least she no longer thought it was a lark. 'You stupid, stupid child.'

'I'm not a child, Mama. I'm a woman, and if I was old enough to marry Sydney, I'm old enough to marry Douglas.'

'Douglas! I don't want to hear that man's name. I wish to God he'd gone down on that ship.'

'Mama!'

'The other gentlemen did. Mr Astor and Mr Hutchins. Even Mr Guggenheim, and he was a Jew. But your Mr Kimball managed to survive. Took the place of some poor woman or child.'

'Douglas didn't get into a lifeboat on the ship, Mama. He jumped and they picked him up later from the sea.'

'That's what he told you.'

'That's the truth,' she screamed.

'If it is, there's no reason to shout about it, Elizabeth. Obviously, you have your own doubts about Mr Kimball's honor.'

'I have no doubts about Douglas.' Her voice was quiet again, but there was a strain of tension beneath it. 'I'm going to marry him, Mama, I'm going do it no matter what you say, so you might as well give in and be a good sport about it.'

'A good sport! Is that an expression you picked up from Kimball?'

'As a matter of fact, that's Sydney's expression.'

Edith was quiet for a moment, but only a moment. She was not so easily thrown off course. 'You are going to marry Sydney as arranged. Don't underestimate me, Elizabeth. I have ways of making you do as I wish.'

'I don't think so, Mama. Not anymore. Times have changed. Marriages aren't arranged anymore. And girls aren't locked in their rooms.' She stood. 'I'm going to change now. Douglas and I are taking the early boat to New York.'

'Elizabeth.' Edith started to put her hand on her daughter's shoulder as if to force her back into her chair, but Lizzy caught her hand and they stood that way for a moment, their faces only inches apart, their hands locked in the air between them like an absurd parody of two Indian wrestlers. Elizabeth's eyes that had always seemed too trusting were hard now, as hard as her mother's, and it was Edith who dropped her hand and turned away.

'I warn you, Elizabeth, if you marry that man, you are no longer my daughter.'

'I'm sorry, Mama, but I'm going to be Douglas' wife. And my own woman. I won't let you do to me what you did to Amelia.'

Edith turned back to her daughter and the smile on her face was cruel. 'Your own woman? Married to a demanding old man?'

'Married to a man who just happens to be older than I am.'

Elizabeth started out of the room, then stopped at the door and turned back to her mother. 'Please wish me good luck, Mama,' she said. The only answer was silence, the deafening silence of marble halls and vast empty rooms.

It wasn't over, Edith told herself. She'd stopped Schuyler and intercepted Amelia, and she'd find a way to defeat Elizabeth. Edith's mind always functioned better when her body was in movement and she paced out to the piazza. There was a chill breeze off the water and the sea was still black, but the sky was beginning to lighten in the east. She was tired, tired and cold, but she wouldn't go in for a shawl any more than she'd give up and go to bed.

She heard footsteps on the mosaic tiles behind her. 'If that's you, Elizabeth I don't want to hear any more unless it's an apology.'

'It's I, Mama,' Caroline said. 'Lizzy's upstairs changing. She says she's leaving with Kimball.'

'So she thinks.'

'Did you see Sky?' Caroline was less interested in her sister's romantic comedy than her own tragedy.

'I saw him, and Mr Sturgis saw him, and

everything has been taken care of. I imagine he's telling Miss Hunter now.'

'I won't take him back. Not after the terrible things he said to me.'

Edith had been looking out to sea, but now her head swiveled to her daughter. 'Listen to me, Caroline. I've had about enough of you tonight. Of all my daughters. I didn't go begging to Tom Sturgis to have you tell me you won't take Schuyler back. You'll take him back, and if you have any sense, you'll give him whatever it is he needs to keep him.'

Caroline was sniffling again. 'Never. Not after the things he said to me. I'll make him pay. I swear I will.'

Edith sighed and turned back to the view of the lawns and the sea. 'You're a very foolish woman, Caroline. But, fortunately, you're a docile one. I expect you to be as nice as you can to Schuyler when he returns. I don't suppose it will make much difference. He won't give up Vanessa Hunter, but then we won't give up Schuyler. He knows that now. Your sister says times have changed, but not for you and Schuyler. You're both part of the old guard, the *ancien regime* as Harry would say.'

The sound of an automobile engine on the front drive was no more than a quiet purr here on the piazza, but Edith picked up the sound as a hound does a scent. Her high-heeled shoes sounded a sharp tattoo on the marble floor as she crossed the entrance hall. Kimball was standing in the small stone vestibule between the outer grille doors and the heavy oak inner ones.

'I'm afraid I'll have to ask you to leave, Mr Kimball.' Her voice was controlled, but her face was taut with hatred.

'I wasn't planning to stay, Mrs Leighton.'

'Immediately, Mr Kimball. Or I'll have the servants remove you forcibly. I assure you that's not an idle threat.'

'I never thought it was, Mrs Leighton.' He was stalling for time and knew it. If he had to scuffle with Hatfield to gain time — and Lizzy — he'd do that too.

Gracefully, like a ballet dancer, Edith lifted one hand toward the heavy velvet bell cord.

'You don't have to ring for Hatfield, Mama.' Elizabeth had spoken from the top of the wide marble staircase and now she came down it quickly with a light step as if she were still the carefree daughter of the house. 'We're leaving.' She crossed the hall to them and slipped her hand in Kimball's. 'Goodbye, Mama,' she said, and there was a slight tremor beneath the determination of her voice.

What Elizabeth did then was a reflex, but she never regretted it. She took a step toward her mother and bent to kiss her cheek. But Edith's reflexes were as ingrained as Elizabeth's. She turned away from her daughter's kiss as if from a scorpion's sting.

It was not yet light but as they retraced their steps again toward Endicott's dock Sam could make out the figure of a man standing at the end of it. When the figure turned, Sam recognized Morgan's secretary, Charles King. King approached them quickly and kept his eyes on Sam. If he wondered who Amelia was or what she was doing walking along the beach with Van Nest at dawn, nothing in his manner indicated as much. He was a very good secretary.

'Mr Morgan sent me, Mr Van Nest.'

'How did you know where to find me?'

'I didn't. I had the launch take me into the yacht club and I tried Rosecliff. Finally, I had the launch bring me over here to Mr Endicott's. I thought you might have stopped at your sister's. Mr Morgan is eager for some word.'

He bet Mr Morgan was eager for some word. Sam told himself it was a reasonable request, but he wasn't feeling particularly reasonable. 'Tell Mr Morgan to go to . . .' He felt Amelia's hand tighten on his arm. 'Tell Mr Morgan to go to breakfast, King. I'll be with him shortly.'

King was not that good a secretary after all. Sam could see the surprise and disapproval on his face.

'You could have gone,' Amelia said, when King had started back toward the launch.

'Not unless you'll come with me. We'll go straight to New York.'

'We've been through this.'

They had, Sam thought, and he had a feeling they'd go through it again and again, until it became a familiar record scratched and damaged from too much use.

He was wondering how he was going to get Amelia back to Belle Isle where she seemed so determined to go when a black Brewster town car drove past. The road ran close to the water here, and they were easily visible from it. The automobile stopped a few yards down the road, then backed up. Tom Sturgis was in the rear, and when he stepped out his face was the same gray as the predawn sky. A few hours ago he'd had the heightened coloring that comes from too much food and drink, but now it had drained away and his chin sagged beneath a pale shadow of beard. Sam rubbed the stubble on his own cheek. It had been a long night.

'I was on my way down to the yacht club, Sam, to have the launch take me out to *Corsaire*. Lucky I found you here.' Sturgis' eyes moved to Amelia. They showed the curiosity King had managed to hide, but he merely said good morning to her. 'I wanted to give you the good news as soon as possible. Timing's important with something like this.'

Suddenly the exhaustion was gone, and Sam felt a surge of energy as if he'd just taken a shot of whiskey. Out of the corner of his eye he saw that King had not got into the launch. He was standing on the dock watching them, and Sam signaled to him to wait. 'Is there good news?' he asked Sturgis.

'I've been thinking about what you said. Been turning it over in my mind all night. You're right, Sam. Times are changing. We can't afford to take the chance. I'm going to tell Walsh that myself.'

A number of celebratory images flashed through Sam's mind. Some were absurd, some involved Amelia and were downright salacious, but he simply patted Sturgis on the shoulder in an affectionate, sportsmanlike way. 'Well, Tom' – he'd never called him Tom before, but he was going to do a lot of things now he'd never done before – 'I'm glad you see things that way. All of us down at Twenty-three Wall are glad.'

Sturgis smiled, but it didn't make him look any less tired. 'I thought you would be.'

'And I wonder, Tom,' Sam said as Sturgis climbed back into the Brewster, 'if you could give us a lift. Back to Belle Isle.' He could tell from the look on Amelia's face that she hadn't understood what had just happened.

'No trouble at all,' Sturgis said and held the door open from the inside for Amelia. 'Only I think I'll have Willis drop me off first – it's on the way – and then take you on to Belle Isle. I'm all in.'

Sam told Sturgis he wanted a word with King first, and a word was all it took. This time the look King gave him before he turned to get into the launch was one of admiration.

'I have a confession to make,' Sturgis said when the automobile had pulled up before his own house. 'You weren't entirely responsible for my change of mind Sam.' Sturgis was about to get out and he patted Amelia's hand. 'Your dear mother helped. She made me see things more clearly.' Sturgis knew it was a foolish thing to say, but Edith had always made him slightly foolish. He wanted to mention her once more tonight, and to whom could he mention her? Certainly not his valet.'

'I'll have to thank Mrs Leighton,' Sam said.

'Yes. Yes, you do that,' Sturgis answered as he got out of the Brewster and turned away from them to his own front door.

'You didn't understand what he was saying, did you?' Sam asked when the driver had started toward Belle Isle.

'I gather it means you did whatever you were supposed to do well after all.'

'It means,' he said reaching an arm around her shoulders, 'thirty-five million dollars among other things. And I have five of them earmarked already.' She started to say something, but he went on quickly. 'We're not going to argue about it.'

'I wasn't going to argue about it, Sam. I was going to ask if it's possible to wire five million dollars.'

He laughed. 'Of course, it is. At least I think it is. I know I'm going to find out as soon as we get back to New York. I'll have to wire Hussey too. He'll want to get started on plans right away.'

'Plans for what?'

'A factory. An airplane factory.'

'You're going to build airplanes?'

'Among other things.'

'Such as?'

He started to explain, then stopped and began laughing again. Suddenly it seemed he couldn't stop laughing. 'You'll find out, Amelia. I promise you that. And one other thing,' Sam said as Sturgis' auto turned into the drive of Belle Isle. 'We'll do something about your son.'

It was exactly what she'd been thinking, only

she didn't feel nearly so optimistic about it as he sounded. 'It won't be easy.'

'Hell, after the last twenty-four hours it'll be child's play.' He sounded euphoric, but suddenly his face turned serious and he took her hand. 'No, you're right. It won't be easy, but we'll work out something.' He smiled again. 'Besides, I hate to sound smug. No, that's not true. I love sounding smug about this. You've got money on your side now. Surely if we can buy your divorce, we can buy your son. Even if it's only for part of each year.'

'Wait here,' Amelia said when they'd reached the vestibule of Belle Isle.

'Not on your life. I made that mistake once, if you remember. Anyway, I want to thank your mother. I promised Sturgis I would.'

They found Edith and Caroline on the piazza. The horizon was pink now rather than white, but the light did not flatter the women. In their elaborate ball gowns stiff with embroidery and beading, they looked like garish painted dolls that had been left out overnight and weathered badly. The emeralds at Edith's throat and ears gave her face a sallow cast, and Caroline's violet eyes were sunk in black smudges. They were sitting straightbacked in two wrought-iron chairs, but somehow they managed to look wilted.

At the sound of footsteps Edith turned from the view of the sea to the french windows that opened onto the piazza. Her ashen face showed no surprise, and when she spoke her voice was cool as if she were past emotion. 'There you are, Amelia.'

'Yes, Mother, here we both are.'

'It was kind of you to bring Her Grace home, Samuel.' The words were a dismissal, but Sam Van Nest would not be so easily dismissed. 'I'm not bringing Amelia home, Mrs Leighton. I'm taking her away. We're going be married.'

'Amelia is already married.'

'Yes, you saw to that. But she's going to get a divorce.'

Edith looked from Sam to her daughter. 'Duringham will never give you a divorce.'

'You know Charles better than that, Mother. He'll give me a divorce – for a price.'

Edith smiled a disdainful smile. 'Exactly. Charles' price is five million. Where would you get five million dollars? From Samuel? I don't think so. Perhaps you think Mr Morgan is going to give it to you.' She started to turn away from them as if the conversation were closed, but Sam's words checked her motion.

'As a matter of fact, Morgan's going to give me a good deal more than that, Mrs Leighton. And I have you to thank. You see, the Commodore is willing to pay me a great deal of money to convince several men not to do something they want to do. I was successful with all of them except one. Then you stepped into the picture. You changed Tom Sturgis' mind for me, Mrs Leighton. I'm extremely grateful. Amelia and I both are.'

'What are you talking about?' she demanded. Her voice was still imperious, but her eyes glinted with the desperation of a trapped animal.

'I'm talking about Amelia's divorce. Thanks to you, I can buy it for her.'

Edith's eyes moved from Sam to Amelia as if she were searching for the weakness in the enemy's lines. 'We don't divorce, Amelia.'

'*We*'re not going to, Mother. *I* am.'

'Never!' The word came out as a shriek.

'As soon as possible,' Amelia said.

'I stopped you once and I'll stop you again.'

'Not this time, Mrs Leighton.' Sam took Amelia's hand.

Edith saw the gesture and crossed the piazza to them. She took Amelia's free hand between her own two and clutched it as if she were praying. 'Think of the title.'

'I never wanted the title.'

'Think of Tony.' Edith was wringing Amelia's hand as if she could milk the concession from her. 'You can't abandon your son. It's heartless.'

The words stung as they were meant to, but the pain wasn't enough nor was the pity Amelia suddenly felt for her mother. 'I'm not going to abandon Tony, Mother, but I'm going to save myself.'

Edith dropped her hand then and took a step back as if to put a distance between them. Her face was once more a mask of disdain, for Amelia's intransigence, for her own lapse. 'The collar,' she said. 'The Marie Antoinette collar is insured in my name. I'll have the police stop you at the ferry.'

Amelia felt a rush of relief. The battle was over. She was finally free.

She'd put the choker on before they'd come into the house, and now she turned her back to Sam so he could undo the clasp. Then she took it from him and handed it to Edith. 'Here, Mother. You keep it. I've never liked it anyway.'

'You can't,' Edith said in disbelief.

'Goodbye, Mother.' And then, though it was no longer a reflex for Amelia as it was for her sister, she bent to kiss her mother's cheek just as Elizabeth had. This time Edith was too stunned to turn away.

The first rays of sunlight had crept across the wide carpet of lawn and up the stairs of the piazza to where Edith Leighton stood, but they did not warm her. Slowly, as if she were in a trance, she turned her back to the house and sat in one of the chairs facing the sea. She would not look at her daughter and this man who'd done so much damage, but she could not shut them out entirely. Behind her she heard the sound of footsteps moving rapidly through the long marble halls of Belle Isle. The noise was loud at first as if it were mocking her, but it grew gradually fainter until it died away completely. There was a moment of silence then broken only by the innocent sound of birds welcoming another perfect Newport morning. Then a sharp clang echoed through the house. It was the prison-like sound of iron clashing against iron as the huge grille doors closed behind Amelia and Sam.

News traveled rapidly in Newport. Harry Lehr had learned of the fight between Sydney Hallenbeck and the lieutenant only a few hours after it happened. Within half an hour of hearing the news he arrived at Belle Isle. He was just in time to see Amelia leaving with Sam Van Nest. It was too delicious for words. He could barely keep from running through the vast high-ceilinged hall, but when he reached the doors leading out to the piazza, he stopped and assumed a funereal expression as easily as he might don a hat.

'My pets,' he said, and Edith and Caroline who had been sitting in silence turned to him. 'You both look absolutely distraught. And no wonder. I saw Amelia and Van Nest on the way out. And I heard about Lizzy and Kimball. Tragic.' He took a chair opposite Edith and leaned forward sympathetically. 'Poor Sydney. Though I don't imagine he'll have much trouble finding someone to console him. Not with the Hallenbeck name and money. And Sydney's such a charming boy. I can't imagine what Lizzy's thinking. As for Amelia, she's always been difficult, but this time she may be going too far. Duringham's bound to hear about her and Sam, and he won't . . .'

'Harry!' Edith's voice was sharp, but she was no longer out of control. 'I do wish you'd stop babbling.'

'I'm just trying to console you, pet.'

'Console me.' Her back was straight now. 'I can't imagine what for.'

'Well, for Lizzy and Kimball for one. I never did trust that man . . .'

'You're speaking of my future son-in-law, Harry. A brilliant artist and a gentleman.' Edith's voice

404

was full of conviction. She'd found her new tack
and was sailing full speed ahead.

'But what about Sydney?'

'What about Sydney? Oh, I admit I thought he
might be a good match for Elizabeth, but Elizabeth
didn't want him, and let's face it Harry, times are
changing. One can't force a girl into marriage
these days. Any more than one can force a girl to
stay married.'

'Mama . . .' Caroline's huge eyes were full of
confusion, but they had nothing on Lehr's.

'I was speaking to Mrs Vanderbilt about it just
the other day. I mean Mrs Belmont. She
understood perfectly, of course, since she
divorced Vanderbilt herself. I advised her on the
matter at the time. Just as I've advised Amelia.
The days when a woman had to put up with
anything from her husband are gone, Harry.'
Carrie started to say something, but Edith went
on quickly. 'Now Caroline and I are fortunate. Mr
Leighton has always treated me beautifully, and
Schuyler is absolutely devoted to Caroline, as you
know.'

Lehr was no longer confused. He was watching
Edith with fascination. Talk about snatching
victory from the jaws of defeat. He'd been sure
she was finished this time, but he realized now
she'd never be finished until the minister said his
eulogy and they all laid flowers on the grave. Not
even then. The legend of Edith Leighton would
live on. When they wrote the histories of Newport
and the four hundred, she'd be right there on top.
Some would say she'd been wonderful and others

terrible, but they'd all say something about her.

The early morning sun had continued its path across the piazza, shortening the shadows imperceptibly, and as it reached Edith's chair, it struck the choker that lay in her lap. The light danced off the stones like a hundred colored swords, and Harry shifted his position so as not to be blinded by them.

'Yes, Harry, it's all changing, and we've got to keep up. And by keeping up I certainly don't mean making a fool of yourself and your friends with some absurd mental telepathy act. I warn you, Harry, I haven't forgotten last night, though fortunately it did no harm, as you can see. You couldn't have been more wrong about Elizabeth and the lieutenant, and I'm sure you'll want to apologize to Schuyler for whatever it was you were trying to insinuate. As I was saying, Harry, times are changing, and I for one have no patience with outdated gossip and foolish innuendo. That's all *passé*. We've got to keep up with more important things. As I was telling Mrs Belmont, time and tide wait for no man, Harry, but if we women keep running we're bound to keep up with it.'

From the August 1, 1912, issue of *Town Topics*:

The height of the Newport season was reached
here last Saturday at a gala ball given by Mrs
Hermann Oelrichs at her villa Rosecliff and at
the many dinner parties that preceded it. Mrs
Elias Leighton, who has on occasion been
accused of a certain conservatism in her
choice of guests, won a reputation for
originality by combining at her dinner at Belle
Isle some of society's most disparate elements.
Over Mrs Leighton's sumptuous dinner one
could observe that noted philanthropist Mr
Kirkland Selby chatting with that well-known
sportsman Mr Samuel Van Nest, and Mr Elias
Leighton, who has been too long absent from
Newport, enjoying the company of that
favorite of society hostesses, Mr Harry Lehr.

The three Leighton girls, who have been
regarded for some time as the undisputed
belles of Newport's *haute monde*, all dined at
Belle Isle and went on to the ball at Rosecliff
where Miss Elizabeth Leighton led off the
cotillion with Mr Lehr. If last night's dancing

is any indication, Miss Leighton will soon announce her engagement to that handsome and popular leader of the younger set Mr Sydney Hallenbeck.

Miss Leighton's older sister, the Duchess of Duringham, could also be seen dancing as gaily as she did during her debutante days. I would be concerned about the behavior of this lovely young matron if Mrs Leighton had not made it known that Her Grace is looking forward to the arrival of her husband the duke later in the season.

Unfortunately the rumors surrounding the eldest Leighton sister, Mrs Schuyler Niebold, and her husband, have not been similarly laid to rest. I can only deplore the stories concerning Mr Niebold for surely no Newport gentleman has been so fortunate in his choice of a wife.

A new face both at Mrs Leighton's dinner and the ball that followed was that of Lieutenant Timothy Atherton. It was obvious to all present that though Atherton is only a second lieutenant, he was a much favored dancing partner. The lieutenant's popularity is obvious proof that birth and breeding will out, since it is well known, though Lieutenant Atherton never mentions the fact, that he is the nephew of Admiral Atherton.

Another new face was that of Miss Agnes Corcoran who attended the ball with her parents Mr and Mrs James Corcoran. One hears talk – chiefly from the Corcorans – that the Corcorans are invited everywhere, but I must admit that this is the first time they have actually appeared at a truly exclusive ball or dinner. I hasten to add that I do not think their appearance at Saturday night's festivities is a harbinger of things to come. Newport's hostesses are not so sensitive to money that they are insensitive to its age, and while many have shortened the late Mrs Astor's three generations required for making a gentleman to two, no one is here yet willing to accept the first.

The speculation about Mrs Oelrichs' entertainment was amply rewarded when that renowned escapologist, Mr Harry Houdini delighted the guests with a display of telepathy in which Mr Lehr assisted. During the exhibition such pillars of the financial community as Mr Thomas Sturgis and Mr John Wainwright could be seen enjoying themselves as freely as children at a party. Mrs Lydia Schuyler pronounced the entertainment superb and her guest, Miss Vanessa Hunter, a welcome if familiar addition to any gathering, concurred.

Unfortunately, Mr J. P. Morgan was unable to attend the ball although *Corsaire* was spotted in the yacht basin over the weekend. Rumors of the Commodore's failing health persist despite denials by close associates.

After the ball the young people went on to Seaview for dancing to ragtime music, and though there are reports of the usual hijinks,

I feel sure the guests were only giving rein to their youthful spirits and no serious damage was done. All in all, the evening was declared a success by hostesses and guests alike and is sure to prove a topic of conversation for the rest of the season and beyond.